CW01020270

"The Red Blot"
and
"The Voodoo Master"

TWO CLASSIC ADVENTURES OF

THE Shadow™

by Walter B. Gibson
writing as Maxwell Grant

Published by Sanctum Productions for
NOSTALGIA VENTURES, INC.
P.O. Box 231183; Encinitas, CA 92023-1183

Copyright © 1933, 1936 by Street & Smith Publications, Inc. Copyright © renewed 1960, 1963 by The Condé Nast Publications, Inc. All rights reserved.

This edition copyright © 2006 by Sanctum Productions/Nostalgia Ventures, Inc.

The Shadow copyright © 2006 Advance Magazine Publishers Inc./The Condé Nast Publications. "The Shadow" and the phrase "Who knows what evil lurks in the hearts of men?" are registered trademarks of Advance Magazine Publishers Inc. d/b/a The Condé Nast Publications. The phrases "The Shadow Knows" and "The weed of crime bears bitter fruit" are trademarks owned by Advance Magazine Publishers Inc. d/b/a The Condé Nast Publications.

"Spotlight on The Shadow" © 2006 by Anthony Tollin.
"Man of Magic and Mystery" © 2006 by Will Murray.

This Nostalgia Ventures edition is an unabridged republication of the text and illustrations of two stories from *The Shadow Magazine,* as originally published by Street & Smith Publications, Inc., N.Y.: *The Red Blot* from the June 1, 1933 issue, and *The Voodoo Master* from the March 1, 1936 issue. Typographical errors have been tacitly corrected in this edition.

International Standard Book Numbers:
ISBN 1-932806-53-9   13 DIGIT 978-1-932806-53-3

Series editor: Anthony Tollin
P.O. Box 761474
San Antonio, TX 78245-1474
sanctumotr@earthlink.net

Consulting editor: Will Murray

Copy editor: Joseph Wrzos

Cover restoration: Michael Piper

Nostalgia Ventures, Inc.
P.O. Box 231183; Encinitas, CA 92023-1183

Visit The Shadow at www.nostalgiatown.com

Volume 3

The entire contents of this book are protected by copyright, and must not be reprinted without the publisher's permission.

CONTENTS

Two Complete Novels From The Shadow's Private Annals As told to Maxwell Grant

Thrilling Tales and Features

Cover art by George Rozen
Interior illustrations by Tom Lovell

THE RED BLOT

Baffling crime grows rampant ~ nothing can stop it.
But the crooks learn the power of The Shadow in this
thrilling epic, taken from The Shadow's private annals

as told to

Maxwell Grant

CHAPTER I
THE SHADOW'S QUEST

A swift, repeated ticking was audible amid a total darkness. But for that sound, intense silence would have pervaded the thickness of absolute gloom. It was not until a sharper noise occurred that any sign of a human presence was revealed.

A click came from a spot above the ticking. A blue light suddenly cast an eerie glow downward upon the surface of a polished table. There, beneath the rays of the strange, shaded lamp, appeared the ticking object.

It was a clock of curious construction. Set at an angle upon the tabletop, this timepiece showed no hands upon its large face. Instead, it had three cir-

cles, the innermost marked with twelve numbers; the outer circles divided with sixty.

From grooves on the outer edge of each circle extended rings, so designed that they surrounded only one number at a time. Just as the light came on, the rings of the outer circles moved. The extreme ring made another jump a second later; but the intermediate one still remained constant, like the one in the center.

A clock that moved with intermittent precision, this odd dial was designed to mark the passing seconds by its outer circle; the minutes by the second one; and the hours by the center circle. Although the mechanism was regular in sound, the indications came at definite intervals, with an unusual psychological result.

To the eyes that watched this clock, a single second seemed like a prolonged space of time, not as an idly moving series of moments. Each minute, formed of sixty such intervals, was episodic. An hour, as shown upon this clock, was a tremendous stretch of time that allowed for limitless accomplishment.

SUCH was the clock that rested in The Shadow's sanctum. The weird blue light that glistened upon the circled dial existed only in that secret room. This was the abode where the master who fought with crime reviewed his plans and formed new strategy.

The appearance of the light marked the presence of The Shadow himself. He, alone, visited this mystic room, located in some unknown section of Manhattan. In the midst of strenuous campaigns, The Shadow could always seek the seclusion of this sanctuary, there to mock his enemies and devise new ways to end the schemes of malefactors.

To gangdom, The Shadow was known only as a powerful being whose unseen hand reached everywhere. There were mobsmen who claimed to have seen him—but only at a distance. Those who had met The Shadow face to face no longer lived to assert their claims.

Dying gangsters—toughened characters of the type who died grimly—had coughed out their lives through trembling lips, gasping the name of The Shadow. Time and again, sneering big shots had been struck down just as they were about to reap the profits of some heinous crime. Here, again, the hand of The Shadow had intervened.

None knew the identity of The Shadow. It was something that the underworld had long sought. All rats of crime were eager to eliminate The Shadow. His power had caused consternation in other cities than New York—both in America and abroad—yet none had ever balked his might.

It was known that The Shadow must be a master of detection, for he had uncovered the most ingenious of crimes. It was known also that he could travel swiftly and unseen, for he had frequently appeared in the heart of an enemy's camp.

As for his indomitable purpose—that was understood. The Shadow showed no mercy to those who did not deserve it.

It was believed that The Shadow was a master of disguise. That, alone, could account for some of the amazing parts that he had played. It was also believed that he sometimes employed the aid of trained and skillful agents, for the magnitude of his activities had shown that capable men had been present when needed.

Yet The Shadow had always managed to keep his temporary identities unknown; and his agents remained within the cover of the shroud of mystery that constantly blanketed The Shadow from the eyes of his foemen.

Despite the efforts of those who sought to thwart him; despite the fact that he never invoked the aid of the police in his own behalf; The Shadow roamed at will in his untiring search for men of evil. None had ever managed to discover the location of his sanctum; in fact, the existence of such a spot was regarded as doubtful by those who discussed its possibility.

Thus The Shadow found complete seclusion in that corner of the black-walled room where blue light shone upon a tabletop and a strangely dialed clock marked each passing second with a long, gripping throb.

THE SHADOW!

As weird as he sounds; as awesome as the mocking laugh that marks his triumph; as mysterious as the black night in which he works—that is The Shadow.

Avenger of crime, stern dispenser of severe justice, the scourge of criminals —he furnishes the most thrilling accounts of battles against crime that you can read to-day. Don't miss this story, and every one following.

THE light and the clock were not the only tokens of The Shadow's presence on this night. Into the circle of illumination crept two objects that seemed like living creatures detached from the body to which they belonged.

The hands of The Shadow!

Long and white, they showed a combination of velvety smoothness and great muscular power. These were the hands that had fought so well against crime; and one of them bore the token, which was the positive symbol of The Shadow.

This mark was a gleaming gem which shone from the third finger of the left hand. It was The Shadow's girasol, a rare fire opal, unmatched in all the world. Its color was a mingling of hues; the glowing depths of the stone changed from brilliant blue to dull crimson, and all the shades between.

From the girasol came splashes of fiery light, like the glimmer of living sparks. A dying ember, ever emitting its final darts of minute flame— such was The Shadow's girasol.

The hands moved in a fashion that portrayed ease of operation. An envelope came into view; from it a thin bundle of papers. The fingers unfolded a sheet; the hidden eyes behind the light made a brief perusal; then that paper was replaced by another.

Despite the ease of the hands, their speed and precision were amazing, when judged by the clock upon the table. An observer would not have believed that those indications on the outer circle of the dial were mere seconds. It seemed as though The Shadow, even when engaged upon the routine procedure of summarizing the reports from his agents, could hold back time in its passage.

The simple scene in the sanctum was an explanation of The Shadow's uncanny ability to come out best in his wars with men of crime. He was a being who dealt in split seconds when he worked!

Another envelope—a third. Papers removed, read, and replaced. Clippings, also; and when The Shadow's summary was complete, a few remainders were left for careful perusal. Report sheets and newspaper items—the white hands spread them upon the tabletop.

Every one of these papers dealt with a single subject. The right hand of The Shadow appeared with a pen. Upon a sheet of blank paper, it inscribed a phrase which summarized it in one title:

THE RED BLOT

The ink which The Shadow used was crimson. It shone in vivid contrast to the light above. Eyes from the dark viewed the words; then the poised hand gave the pen a shake.

A large blob of ink spattered upon the white paper. It spread irregularly until it formed a grotesquely shaped blotch of drying fluid that looked like a huge drop of blood.

No action could have been more significant. The words meant nothing now. There, beneath them, was the very sign which had been mentioned—a crimson mark that illustrated the title.

The Red Blot!

WHILE the ink still dried beneath the light, a low, sinister laugh came from the darkness. That tone—the mocking voice of The Shadow—was the feature of the master's presence that had struck stark terror into many an evil gangster's heart.

The laugh of The Shadow! It came as a challenge to all malefactors.

The pen was laid aside. The fingers lifted the report sheets and the clippings, one by one. Alike, these items told a story of unsolved crime. Here, in New York, subtle evil was in progress.

A bank messenger shot down in open daylight. A chase of elusive assailants, who disappeared after a cordon of police had closed in upon them. A huge blot of crimson upon the sidewalk at the spot where the man had been slain.

The messenger's blood? That had been the theory, until the second crime!

Three masked marauders had entered a club where gambling was in progress. They had extinguished the lights; with flashlights, they had covered the players and threatened them with guns. They had reaped a harvest of cash.

While they were robbing their victims, police had arrived. The crooks had fled and, despite the closeness of the chase, had made an escape so effective that they might have actually melted. Upon the green baize of the central card table in the club was discovered a huge dab of dulled crimson—again the red blot!

A third crime—the theft of a painting valued at many thousands—had been perpetrated at the home of a New York millionaire. Servants had arrived as the criminals were departing with the painting that they had cut from its immense frame. Two servants had been shot; one mortally wounded.

Again, the evil raiders had escaped. Behind them, in the empty frame, they had left their mark—a red blot!

THE RED BLOT!

In the underworld, it was believed that a mastermind of crime had chosen that mark. The Red Blot was a name—not a sign. Some supercrook had assembled a squad of daring gangsters, who would stop at nothing.

The police had advanced the same theory. The newspapers had taken up the cry.

Then had come the fourth crime. A big-time fight promoter—supposed to carry a bankroll of more than a hundred grand upon his person—had been found strangled in his apartment. Upon the starched front of the victim's dress shirt was that same dread sign of spattered crimson—the mark of The Red Blot!

Men of wealth—from legitimate commercial barons to those who dealt in hazardous enterprises—were in trepidation. The newspapers had called upon the police to apprehend this supercriminal. The police had not gathered a single clew.

Underworld and social swim alike—neither revealed the presence of a mastermind to whom these crimes could be attributed. Police, with their stool pigeons at work, had covered all of gangdom's daring workers; the ones who might be logically picked as henchmen of the super-crook. They had not brought in a single suspect.

The Shadow, too, had been seeking traces of The Red Blot. His agents had been at work. Their reports were barren. These crimes which had emanated from the underworld, and had struck in higher places, left no trail.

But The Shadow's way was not to follow crime when it bore the mark of well-linked continuity. He had been seeking the forebodings of crime that he might anticipate the next stroke of The Red Blot.

The clock upon the table was more important than all these clippings and reports of frustrated efforts to line up the cause of past outrages. The Shadow, through his own investigations in the underworld, had been watching for an impending stroke.

Even whispered inklings had been lacking. Until tonight, each crime had given no preliminary sign. Often had The Shadow thwarted crooks by prying into their games before the lid had been raised.

Now, amid the quiet of the underworld, he had caught the words he wanted. Here, he was biding his time until the proper second for his calculated plan.

The ticking of the clock went on. A long second seemed to hover; then the indicators on all three dials moved at once, That final second marked the completion of a minute which, in turn, showed the end of an hour.

Before the second indicator moved again, The Shadow's hand had swept up the scattered bits of paper. A click sounded from the lamp. The room was plunged in darkness. Something swished through the gloom.

Then came a peal of laughter. The Shadow's mirth rang ghoulishly through the blackness. As his invisible form moved toward the secret door of the sanctum, the master of the night sent forth his mocking challenge in chilling tones that foretold disaster to evil brains of crime.

Blackened walls caught up the merriment.

Weird reverberations sounded as cries from goblin throats. Corridors of space seemed to open with whispered answers to The Shadow's taunt.

Those strange, terrifying sounds persisted long. When the last echo had faded into nothingness, only the smooth, quick ticking of the clock was audible.

The Shadow had departed upon his quest.

CHAPTER II
WITHIN THE SAFE

IT was exactly ten o'clock when The Shadow departed from his sanctum. A half hour later, a strange phenomenon occurred at the intersection of two obscure streets on the lower East Side.

A moving patch of blackness passed along the sidewalk beneath the glare of a street lamp. It was one of the many shadows that had crossed that spot during the evening. But in one respect, this moving splotch differed from all others. There was no sign of the person who cast it.

A long streak of darkness, which terminated in a perfect silhouette. This was the only mark that betrayed the presence of The Shadow. Somewhere in the darkness of the brick wall beside the sidewalk, the being whom the underworld so greatly feared, had passed unseen.

Some fifty feet from the corner stood a dilapidated brick building of three-story height. Beside it ran an obscure alleyway. This structure, apparently an old residence that had seen better days, was actually a most important adjunct to the decrepit neighborhood.

Three golden balls glimmered faintly above the dim front door. Blackened windows showed the outlines of heavy bars. This building housed the pawnshop of Timothy Baruch, one of the oddest characters on this section of the East Side.

Old Baruch's place was known throughout the underworld. The man had been a pawnbroker for many years, and it was an adage among thieves and burglars that Baruch's bids on stolen goods could be accepted as reliable.

Baruch was not the usual type of "fence," who disposed of stolen articles. His place was termed a "hockshop," even by those who had dealt with him undercover.

For Timothy Baruch was a canny individual who had ways of assuring police and detectives that his transactions were legitimate; and the great proportion of his business was in keeping with the policies of better-class pawnshops.

The old pawnbroker was unpretentious. He made no great show of worldliness. Nevertheless, it had been noised about that his safe contained pilfered jewels and other rarities of great value.

These rumors had never gotten back to Baruch's ears, hence the old man dwelt in security. He was sure that his pretense of poverty would suffice to keep malefactors from his property. Moreover, he relied upon his connection with the underworld and the security of his safe as positive protection.

Underworld connections might fade; but the fame of Baruch's safe would remain. The huge strongbox was the one thing in which Baruch had invested heavily.

Various gangsters had viewed it; and they held to the opinion that there were but two safecrackers skilled enough to open it. One was "Tweezers" Darley, at present retired from active practice; the other was "Moocher" Gleetz, no longer in Manhattan.

Perhaps Timothy Baruch knew of the inactivity of these two safecrackers; at any rate, his safe remained inviolate, despite the fact that his barred doors and windows were not as formidable as they might have been.

THE SHADOW now stood in front of Baruch's pawnshop. There, within the fringe of darkness cast by the old building, his tall form was invisible. No motion, no sound, betrayed The Shadow's presence as he glided into the entrance of the alleyway.

The invisible visitor did not continue to the rear of the building, the spot where access would have been most likely. Instead, he stopped beside the wall and began a strange upward ascent in the midst of almost total darkness.

A low, squidgy sound was the only token of The Shadow's progress. It continued until the unseen figure reached the second floor.

Here, the windows were barred with gratings only. Working in the darkness, The Shadow easily removed the barrier from one window. His lithe figure entered a room on the second floor.

Silent inspection showed the room was empty. A tiny flashlight gleamed. Its luminous spot, no larger than a silver dollar, performed several functions.

First it glittered about the room to show a closed door that evidently led to a hallway. Then it gleamed upon four peculiar, cup-shaped objects of rubber that lay upon the floor. These disappeared into darkness as The Shadow with a black-gloved hand placed them beneath his cloak.

These were the devices which The Shadow had used to facilitate his precipitous climb—rubber suction cups capable of supporting considerable weight with safety.

Finally, the light twinkled upon the dial of a watch. The time was twenty minutes of eleven. A low whisper crept through the room and stirred up vague, mocking echoes. The Shadow was ahead of schedule.

The light went out. A few moments later, the room was empty. Only the occasional glimmer of the flash revealed The Shadow's progress down a stairway to the ground floor. When the light finally reappeared, it shone upon the blackened front of Timothy Baruch's safe, in a back room on the ground floor.

Seventeen minutes of eleven. Again that whispered laugh. The flashlight, set upon some hidden object, displayed a wider range of illumination as the gloves slipped from the hands of The Shadow.

Long, sensitive fingers began their work upon the dials of the safe. The burning girasol sent forth its amazing sparks while the hands were operating.

The safe was, indeed, formidable. The turning dials seemed to defy The Shadow's probing touch. Slowly, carefully, the fingers worked, while keen ears listened for the sound of falling tumblers. Minutes drifted by; at last, a sound from the blackened door of the safe told that The Shadow's task was successful.

The light glimmered upon the watch. Eight minutes before eleven. The Shadow had accomplished his work in nine minutes. A finger touched the watch significantly.

The numbers that it indicated upon the face showed that The Shadow had planned to begin at ten forty-five and end at ten fifty-five. Starting two minutes ahead of schedule, he had gained another minute!

A hand turned the knob. The door of the safe moved slowly outward. Within The Shadow's grasp lay the contents of this treasure box.

Why had The Shadow come to obtain it?

There could be but one reason. The close adherence to a scheduled routine proved that The Shadow was not here to commit crime himself; his purpose was to forestall the efforts of crooks who were soon due!

SURPRISE would be in store for those who attacked this strongbox. Instead of wealth, they would find only what The Shadow might choose to leave for them. The Shadow had anticipated crime tonight. He was to view the contents of this safe before the others saw it.

The door was open. The Shadow's light glimmered into the interior of the safe. It paused motionless, its glare revealing an amazing situation that brought a momentary period of inaction. Even The Shadow had not expected the surprising sight which his eyes now saw.

No money; no jewels; no articles of value. The interior of the safe was a blank, save for a single object. Yet that one article was more startling than any dazzling array of hoarded gems.

A piece of white paper lay upon the bottom of

the safe. It contained no writing; but in its center was a signature more potent than any inscription could have been. Its crimson hue and its grotesque shape told by whose order it had come there.

The sheet of paper which lay in the rifled safe bore the crimson splotch of crime—the mark of The Red Blot!

CHAPTER III
THE SHADOW SPEAKS

THE flashlight moved again. Its probing ray was swift, yet thorough, as the keen eyes of The Shadow commenced an inspection of the interior of the safe. A hand, now covered with a black glove, lifted the crimson-spotted paper from the floor. The flashlight's gleam moved beyond the sheet so that the paper became transparent.

Every detail, even to texture and watermark, was observed by The Shadow. At last, the hand replaced the paper exactly where it had been found. The door of the safe moved sullenly shut. The flashlight shone upon the front of the strongbox; then along the floor.

Clews were here—for The Shadow—yet there was no evidence of sufficient importance. The previous crimes engineered by The Red Blot had not been covered well; in every instance, the elusiveness of the evildoers had been their chief forte.

The Shadow had come here to anticipate crime. The misdeed had already taken place. Nevertheless, The Shadow remained. His tiny light showed the surface of the watch. Eleven o'clock. The glimmer disappeared. The Shadow still remained.

Why?

The answer came a few seconds after the light was out. A vague, scratching sound began less than a dozen yards from the place where The Shadow stood. The noise was from outside the building. Someone was trying to enter.

A curious paradox! The Shadow had scheduled his work to be finished by eleven o'clock, the time that the crooks were due to arrive. He had found traces of completed crime; yet here was indication that the criminals had not been present until this hour!

Silence reigned before the closed but rifled safe in Timothy Baruch's pawnshop. The outside scratching continued. It changed to a series of muffled thuds. A pause; then boards creaked. The marauders were within the building.

The beam of a powerful flashlight swept across the floor. It kept away from the walls, where its rays might have shown through barred windows. Hence it failed to reveal the tall, motionless figure that stood in a corner. The Shadow had become a shadow.

The torch was focused upon the front of the safe. Two hardened faces came into view. While one grim, square-jawed ruffian held the lantern, the other, sharp-faced and blinking, thrust out a hand and grasped a dial.

THE identity of these men was plain. Any mobster would have recognized the pair, well known in the underworld. One—the man with the lantern—was Hurley Brewster, a dock-walloper, who had abandoned a safe-blowing career to organize gangs of mobsters. The other—the man whose hand was on the safe—was Tweezers Darley, whose skill at opening strongboxes was so widely recognized.

"Take it slow, Tweezers," urged Hurley. "Remember—you ain't been doin' this work for some time. Them tumblers is tricky."

"Leave it to me, Hurley," growled Tweezers. "I hope the bulls think the same as you—that a guy gets slow when he lays off a while. Then they won't ask me any questions."

"They won't be askin' nothin'," snorted Hurley. "When I set the time fuse, this old box will blow flooey after we've cleared out. Keep busy, there, bozo."

"Less noise," retorted Tweezers. "I'll have this thing done inside an hour, if you leave me alone."

That ended the conversation for a while. Minutes dragged by while Tweezers worked on. Half an hour elapsed before the safe manipulator paused.

"Say, Hurley"—Tweezers's voice was irritable—"this sure is a tough baby. I'll bet you Moocher Gleetz couldn't make any better speed. I'm right back at the beginning."

"Maybe we'll have to blow it."

"No. Give me time. You know what they've said. Moocher or me—we're the only ones."

"And Moocher ain't around."

"Yeah?" Tweezers's tone was a snarl. "Maybe if he had been around, you'd have taken him in on the job instead of me?"

"I ain't sayin' that," returned Hurley. "Stick with it, bozo! I'm countin' on you!"

Twelve minutes more of silence while Tweezers worked. Suddenly the sharp-faced man emitted a low cry of satisfaction. He placed his hand upon the knob of the safe.

"Got it, Hurley!" he asserted. "We'll pull open the door and mop up the gravy. I told you it wouldn't take me a full hour. I'd like to see anybody do it in less time than I took! You won't find the guy in New York, I'm telling you!"

Hurley Brewster offered no argument. Tweezers Darley's boast stood. Yet even then, within fifteen feet of the safe openers, stood one who had completed Tweezers's forty-two minute job in nine minutes by the watch.

The door came open. The torch gleamed. A snarl came from Hurley Brewster. The dock-walloper was staring at the paper on the floor of the safe.

"The Red Blot!" Hurley's words were a harsh growl. "He's beat us to this lay. Look at that, Tweezers! Can you beat it? Say—"

The square-jawed man pulled back from the safe. In sudden apprehension, he swung his light toward the side of the room.

At the same instant, a slight click sounded, and the glare of another torch met that which came from Hurley Brewster's hand.

Hurley and Tweezers alike caught the glimpse of a strange, black clad outline—the figure of a being who had advanced from the wall. One black glove held the flashlight; the other gripped a huge automatic.

It was Tweezers, this time, who uttered a startled cry of recognition. Where Hurley had growled in anger at the sight of the red blot, Tweezers gasped in fear when he saw the form that loomed ahead.

"The Shadow!"

BOTH ruffians were armed; but they made no attempt to reach for their weapons. Their hands went up, and Hurley's torch clattered to the floor, then rolled to a stop.

With backs against the opened safe, the crooks faced the glare that betokened The Shadow. The expressions upon their evil countenances showed plainly the effect which the arrival of The Shadow had created.

A low, sinister laugh crept through the room. The Shadow held these men of evil at his mercy. He had captured them in the act of crime, and both knew the reputed methods of The Shadow when he dealt with crooks such as themselves.

"You fear me!" The Shadow's tone was a scornful whisper. "You have cause to fear The Shadow! I came here to thwart you in the act of crime. I found the trace of one beside whom you are mere novices!"

"The Red Blot!" blurted Tweezers Darley.

"The Red Blot," announced The Shadow, in his awesome tone, "has been here before you. That is fortunate—for you. The Red Blot is the one whom I seek."

"I don't know nothin'," gasped Hurley Brewster, "Honest—we ain't workin' with The Red Blot! Ain't that empty safe enough—with all the gravy gone? Before we got here?"

"You planned this crime," The Shadow, invisible, was speaking sternly, "in a dive called Red Mike's. You set the hour at eleven o'clock."

Tweezers threw a scared look at Hurley. Neither man would have believed that their con-

versation could have been overheard. The ears of The Shadow! How had they listened in? Tweezers and Hurley exchanged stupefied looks.

"Therefore," ruled The Shadow. "I have questions which you must answer. Where else did either of you discuss this planned crime? Who could have heard you?"

Blank looks were exchanged between the two ruffians. Both understood the purpose of The Shadow's demand. The safe had obviously been opened earlier in the evening. It was the work of the unknown criminal known as The Red Blot. Through indiscretion on the part of either Hurley Brewster or Tweezers Darley, the master plotter could have learned this game.

It was Tweezers who spoke, staring sidelong at Hurley; then toward the light which The Shadow held. Tweezers's words came like a confession, drawn forth by his fear of the invisible enemy who had questioned him.

"SOMEBODY must have got wise when I called Hurley," said Tweezers in a sulky tone. "You remember, Hurley"—Tweezers was looking furtively toward his companion for corroboration—"the night after we made the deal? I was to call you to make sure the lay was all right—and I may have said too much."

"Where did you call from?" came The Shadow's demand, in a tone that carried no interrogation, a tone that gangsters feared.

Hurley was glowering at Tweezers. The square-jawed ruffian recalled the incident. He was incensed because his companion was squealing to The Shadow.

"I—I—don't know." Tweezers had caught Hurley's look, and was hedging. "Let's see—it was when I—"

"Answer the question!"

The command came in a shuddering tone that made Tweezers Darley cower. Hurley Brewster, defiantly facing the light, chewed his lips, and lost his nerve as he heard the sardonic sound of The Shadow's words.

"At the Black Ship," blurted Tweezers.

"Name those whom you saw there," ordered The Shadow.

"I didn't know any of them," pleaded Tweezers, "none except old Louie, who runs the joint. There was a little, rat-faced guy hanging around, though. Louie couldn't have heard me on the phone, but the little guy might have. Kind of a hunched-up fellow—looked like a hophead—"

Tweezers threw another glance toward Hurley. The square-jawed dock-walloper was staring toward him no longer. Instead, Hurley's eyes were directed toward a point to the left of the glaring light.

As Tweezers faltered in his admission to The

Shadow, he saw a sudden look of determination appear upon Hurley's tough face. Although Hurley made no move, Tweezers knew that something unexpected had occurred—something which Hurley alone had noticed.

Trapped by The Shadow, forced to listen to his companion's blurted words, the hard-faced dockwalloper was looking for a break which would enable him and Tweezers to engineer an escape.

The Red Blot had beaten Hurley and Tweezers to their job; The Shadow had surprised and captured them; now, another factor was about to enter into this curious series of events.

Tense, yet wisely restrained, Hurley saw the break coming. Tweezers caught the situation, also. Had The Shadow been unwary, his position would have been a serious one. But The Shadow worked in split seconds.

His keen eyes were watching Tweezers Darley. They saw the look of sudden interest that appeared upon the safecracker's peaked face. Instantly, The Shadow noted Hurley Brewster's steady gaze—the expression which had caught Tweezers's attention.

Like a flash, The Shadow swung to face the direction in which Hurley was staring. His torch cut a swath as it spread its glare toward the front of the room.

The glow revealed a group of uniformed policemen; the fraction of a second later, the powerful illumination of a bull's-eye lantern filled the entire room.

The Shadow's tall form was only momentarily revealed. The light in the gloved hand went out; the figure in black seemed to fade as it made a whirling glide toward the side of the room.

Revolvers barked as the invaders fired at the spot where they had seen the light. Futile bullets plastered themselves against the wall. The police were firing at blankness. The Shadow was gone—so rapidly that no one had caught more than a fleeting glance of his sable-hued shape.

But amid the echoes of revolver shots came the rippling sound of a vague laugh—a tone of undefinable mirth that seemed to hover at the spot where The Shadow, himself, no longer stood.

CHAPTER IV
THE LAW DECIDES

To Hurley Brewster and Tweezers Darley, the intervention of the police was opportunity. Raiding bluecoats had fired at the light. They had failed to clip The Shadow—had failed, even, to recognize the elusive personage whom they had mistaken for an enemy.

The Shadow had been forced to meet the emergency; his swing toward the wall had carried him straight through the door that led to the stairway. Wisely, The Shadow had posted himself at that strategic spot.

With the raid directed toward the door, Hurley and Tweezers dropped toward the floor in front of the safe, drawing their revolvers as they sought this protection.

A policeman saw them and opened fire. Crouching and sidling hastily toward the door that led to the rear of the building, the crooks returned the shots with gusto.

A policeman fell, wounded. Others dropped behind odd articles of furniture that were in this backroom. A filing cabinet was cover for one; another entrenched himself behind a large chair. Two officers jumped behind the opened door through which The Shadow had gone.

The man with the lantern was crouched by the front door of the room. The police had entered through the pawnshop itself. This fellow kept the light in action; for the odds lay with the police. But Hurley Brewster was a tough customer with the gat.

"Clear a path through the back door," he growled to Tweezers. "I'll take care of these bimbos."

The dockwalloper opened fire as he spoke. He had drawn a second revolver, and his huge smoke wagons sent whizzing bullets toward the barricaded raiders.

He had but one purpose; to keep the officers under cover. He succeeded. Then, with a malicious snarl, Hurley aimed point-blank toward the wounded policeman on the floor.

Tweezers was shouting from the door, crying that the way was clear. Hurley ignored the call for the moment. He was set to deliver death to a helpless victim. The other policemen recognized their comrade's desperate position, but they were too late as they sprang from their places of safety. Hurley's finger was already on the trigger.

Then came a shot from the blackened doorway across the room—the exit through which The Shadow had departed! Unerring aim found its human target. As Hurley Brewster's lips mouthed a curse, the dock-walloper's arm dropped, and his body sagged. Both revolvers dropped from numbed fingers.

The Shadow had winged a leaden messenger straight from the muzzle of his automatic into the crook's black heart!

POLICEMEN were raising their guns. They were firing now—adding bullets to Hurley's toppled body. Each thought that one of his companions had fired the first good shot. Only one man knew what actually had happened.

Tweezers Darley, just beyond the rear door of the room, had seen the blaze of The Shadow's

JOE CARDONA, ace detective of the New York police force, and MERTON HEMBROKE, a younger, newer man on the force who is rapidly stepping into the shoes of the older man because of The Red Blot. Cardona is thwarted at every turn. Hembroke fares better, but not well enough to bring the crimes to an end. What is the mystery which baffles them?

automatic. He knew who had dropped Hurley Brewster; and with eager frenzy, he made a quick effort to gain revenge. Behind the doorway, he thrust out his revolver and aimed straight toward that blackened area where he knew The Shadow must be.

The automatic roared again. This time its target was not a body; it was a hand—the fist of Tweezers Darley. A cry followed The Shadow's second shot. Tweezers's gun fell. Grasping his mutilated fingers, the safecracker staggered away, rendered powerless by The Shadow's skillful stroke.

Bluecoats were surging through the room. Some were helping their wounded comrade. Others were on the trail of Tweezers, firing after the fleeing safecracker. More were piling through the doorway from which The Shadow had fired those telling shots, seeking vainly for one who had vanished in that direction.

A tall, powerful man in plainclothes strode into the room. He came from the front doorway; and he pressed a wall switch which brought lights and made the bulls-eye lantern unnecessary. He was joined by another plainclothes man—the one who had handled the lantern.

At the same time, a stoop-shouldered old fellow came into the room through the door from the stairway. With faltering step, Timothy Baruch hastened to the open safe, and emitted a cry of anguish when he saw that it was empty. He turned to face the big man who appeared to be the leader of the raiding crew.

"Baruch?" questioned the big fellow.

The old man nodded.

"I'm Detective Hembroke," returned the other, "from headquarters. Got a tip-off there was something going on here tonight. Came in through your front door. Don't you ever lock it?"

"The front door?" queried Baruch, in a dazed tone. "Sure, it was locked—on the inside—"

"Not tonight," returned Hembroke shortly. "Unless these birds came in that way, or opened it after they were in here."

Timothy Baruch held his head in his hands. He stared at the dead form of Hurley Brewster.

"You got that fellow?" he queried. "Are there anymore?"

"Two," said Hembroke. "One went out the back way; the other headed upstairs. We'll get them. My men are after them."

The sleuth's assurance was gratifying to Baruch. The old man had heard of Merton Hembroke, the New York detective whose swift and effective action had won high commendation. It was noised about that this new crime trailer was gaining precedence over Detective Joe Cardona, hitherto regarded as the ace of Manhattan sleuths.

Policemen were coming in to report to their leader. One brought the information that the man who had run from the back door had been plugged; that he could not be far away. Officers were scouring the neighborhood for traces of him.

The others, however, had a barren report. They had been upstairs and down cellar; yet had found no trace of the man who had dived through the side door of the room.

WITH men close beside him, Hembroke strode to the rifled safe. He noted the sheet of paper lying upon the floor. He picked it up and held it to the light. A stern expression appeared upon the detective's face.

"The Red Blot!" exclaimed Hembroke. "So that guy's in again, eh? Well"—Hembroke laughed gruffly—"we did better than Cardona's ever done. We nabbed one of The Red Blot's workers. I know that mug!"

Still holding the paper, Hembroke was staring at Hurley Brewster's body. The detective pondered a moment, then laughed again as he gave the dock-walloper's identity.

"Hurley Brewster," stated Hembroke. "But who were the birds with him?"

As if in answer to the sleuth's question, two policemen appeared at the rear door, carrying the inert form of Tweezers Darley. They deposited their burden on the floor. Tweezers, like Hurley, was dead.

"So that's the guy," snorted Hembroke. "Tweezers Darley. I've got the lay now.

"Good work, men—I'm glad you plugged him. Tweezers Darley, the only safecracker in New York who could have opened this box. Working for The Red Blot—he and Hurley Brewster."

Turning, the detective put a savage question to the officers who had searched the house.

"What about the other man?" he demanded. "He's the one that must have grabbed the swag! Where is he?"

"He couldn't have got out of the house," returned a policeman. "But he isn't in here, either."

"That's no answer!" growled Hembroke. "He's either here, or he isn't here. Which is it?"

"He's not in the house," insisted another searcher.

"All right," declared Hembroke gloomily, "then he must have made a getaway. That's tough, men. Sorry, Baruch." The detective turned toward the old man, who was seated pitifully in a large chair. "We did the best we could. The tip-off didn't arrive in time for us to prevent the robbery. Nevertheless, we've landed two of the crooks and maybe we'll get the third."

The old man made no response. Hembroke noted the tired look upon his drawn face. Half clad, in trousers and shirt, Timothy Baruch had evidently arisen hastily after hearing the commotion.

"Help him up to his room," ordered the detective. "He's all in."

Two policemen responded. They conducted the old man up the stairs. When they returned, a few minutes later, they completed the entire raiding squad, for all others had assembled for new orders.

Hembroke was studying the bodies of Hurley Brewster and Tweezers Darley. He made no comment. The others waited for his decision.

During this interim, they heard the front door open and close heavily. Before anyone could make a move, a stoop-shouldered man came wild-eyed into the room. He was clad in hat and overcoat. Hembroke uttered a surprised ejaculation as he recognized the face of Timothy Baruch.

"What has happened here?" the old pawnbroker gasped. "I go away this evening. I think that all is well—"

Baruch spread his hands and uttered a shriek as he saw the rifled safe. Perplexed looks passed among the policemen. Baruch had gone upstairs—now he was in from the outside!

It was Hembroke who supplied the solution. The detective gave it in the form of a shouted order.

"Get upstairs!" he cried. "Grab the old man that's up there! He's the one we want—a fake, playing the part of Baruch!"

TWO policemen galloped to the steps. Hembroke, after a moment's hesitation, followed at their heels.

The officers reached the room where they had left Timothy Baruch. Their flashlights played upon an empty bed; then toward the open window.

That was the new goal. The flashlights flickered from the window to the alleyway beneath. They showed blankness.

In the space of a few minutes, the pretended Timothy Baruch had made a prompt departure. Some amazing master of disguise had not only evaded capture, but had actually been present to hear Morton Hembroke's comments; for this elusive being had played the part of Timothy Baruch prior to the real pawnbroker's arrival.

Nothing in the alleyway; yet to the ears of one policeman came a faint echo that seemed like a weird whisper in the night breeze. It was the strange tone of a mocking laugh—the triumphant cry of The Shadow.

The policeman did not recognize the strain, for it came from a considerable distance. Morton Hembroke, by the bed in the room, did not hear the eerie cry. The detective and his men knew only that they had been cleverly tricked by a stranger who had vanished into the night.

The Shadow!

No longer playing the part of Timothy Baruch, he had again become the creature of darkness. Garbed in the folds of his black cloak, he was wending his silent, unseen way from this locality.

A whispered laugh lingered in a deserted street. The Shadow had played a part tonight. Too late to forestall The Red Blot, who had acted at an early hour, The Shadow had found other men of crime and had stopped them from deeds of murder.

From sullen lips, he had gained an inkling of the scheme behind tonight's odd episode. A bunched-up little fellow, one with the features of a dope addict—Tweezers Darley—before he died, had spoken of such a man. This was the person whom The Shadow now would seek; for that individual was, in all probability, a spy for the mastermind who used the signature of a crimson spot.

Many denizens of the underworld might answer to the description given by Tweezers. The Shadow would eliminate them one by one, until he found the one he wanted. The Red Blot's purpose? The Shadow had divined it.

Some secret spy had informed The Red Blot of the work which Hurley and Tweezers had planned. The Red Blot had ordered his minions to grab the swag. The police tip-off had been given later, so that Hurley and Tweezers would be grabbed at the empty safe, where the sign of The Red Blot already lay.

The Shadow's laugh sounded vaguely in the darkness. When The Red Blot struck again, The Shadow would be there to meet his minions. The

Shadow had trapped Hurley Brewster and Tweezers Darley before the police net had fallen.

He, The Shadow, held the clew he needed. It would not take him long to pick out the secret spy whom The Red Blot had planted in the underworld!

The Shadow knew.

CHAPTER V
PLOTTED CRIME

EARLY the next evening, a man emerged from a subway kiosk on the East Side, and strolled along until he reached a cross street. He turned into that thoroughfare and continued his progress through a neighborhood that became more and more disreputable.

Underneath the massive structure of an elevated line, into an ill-kept street that was scarcely more than an alley, down a narrow space between two crumbling buildings, and into a dirty doorway, he went. These maneuvers brought the man to a flight of tumbledown stairs. At the head of the steps he knocked twice upon a door that needed painting.

The portal opened. The visitor entered a room that was lighted by a single gas jet. Another man drew back and grinned as he recognized the arrival. The visitor sat down upon a battered chair; his host took a seat upon a flimsy cot that had an inverted bucket propped under one corner in lieu of a leg.

There was a marked contrast between the two men who were holding this meeting in the squalid room. The visitor revealed a square, determined face that possessed a decided ugliness. Puffy lips, mean eyes, and coarse, rough-shaven cheeks, betrayed the identity of a man well known in the underworld—"Socks" Mallory, murderer long wanted by the police.

The owner of the room was a little man, in comparison with powerful Socks Mallory. Seated on the cot, he made a bunched-up figure, his pitiful frame rendered more pathetic by the weakness of his face.

Pasty, ratlike in expression, with all the characteristics of a drug addict, this skulking creature was one who furtively roamed the underworld, too unimportant to gain more than contempt from the average mobsman. In the badlands, he was known as "Spider" Carew.

There was a significance about this meeting. Both men were wanted. The police had long been searching for Socks Mallory, one-time racketeer, who was now known to be a murderer. But Socks Mallory had not been found in Manhattan.

Spider Carew, in turn, was wanted, but not by the police. He was wanted by The Shadow. For, within twenty-four hours of eliminating

effort, the master of darkness had come to the firm conclusion that The Red Blot's spy could be only Spider Carew himself, and none other.

BOTH Socks and Spider seemed quite at ease in the obscure hideout where they were now located. In fact, Socks Mallory was gloating in expression, and Spider seemed to reflect the big man's satisfied air.

"How about last night?" questioned Socks, in a gruff voice. "It worked out O.K., didn't it, Spider?"

"Sure thing," grunted the pasty-faced individual. "I gave you the lay, didn't I?"

"Yeah. But that wasn't all of it. When Hembroke and the bulls made the raid, they fixed everything jake, though they didn't know it."

"What was the idea, Socks? You didn't tell me—"

"About the raid? Why should I? I'm working for The Red Blot—not for Spider Carew."

"I know that, Socks—ain't I workin' for The Red Blot, too? But what I mean is—this is different—"

"I get you, Spider," nodded Socks, leaning back in his chair. "It don't pay to be curious, but since you're that way, I'll let you in on the idea."

"You know the setup. You know that I'm working for The Red Blot. You know that I've got a gang of real guys that beat any crowd of gorillas. Every man in my outfit"—Socks swelled proudly—"is wanted by the bulls. Wanted bad, too. Like myself. They think we've all scrammed. But you know where we are—right here in New York—but in a place they'll never find us."

Spider Carew nodded.

"All right," continued Socks. "When we pull a job, it's soft. We pick a lay—bust in—clean up and make a getaway."

"How?" queried Spider Carew eagerly. "Where? That's somethin' I ain't been able to figure out!"

"You'll learn tonight, Spider," interposed Socks. "Just keep quiet while I'm talking.

"As I was saying, we pull the jobs perfect, and we know how to duck out after we're through. Everytime we work, we leave the sign of The Red Blot."

"Why?"

"Because this stuff we've been doing is nothing compared with the big jobs ahead. Nothing! Savvy that? We want to make The Red Blot so important that we'll have people scared right. We've done it, too!"

Socks delivered a smile which showed an ugly-toothed mouth in a grotesque contortion.

"But last night," suggested Spider, "you worked different. You ain't told me why."

"I'm getting there!" growled Socks. "Listen,

and I'll tell you! First of all, old Baruch's hock-shop wasn't in the location we wanted. When you tipped us off that you heard Tweezers Darley talking to Hurley Brewster over the phone, we were all set to do something about it. But we figured a smooth, quiet job was the best. So we pulled it—long before Tweezers and Hurley were due to show up.

"Who do you think worked the main spring? Who do you think we've got in our outfit who would crack that safe in Baruch's joint?"

"Moocher Gleetz," returned Spider.

"Good guess," rejoined Socks, with a broad grin. "Well, where is Moocher supposed to be right now?"

"Out in the sticks somewhere."

"Sure. Well, if the safe had been found cracked, with The Red Blot to blame, the cops would have figured one of two guys—Moocher Gleetz or Tweezers Darley. We wanted them to figure Tweezers—and nobody else.

"So, after we pulled the job—when we knew that Tweezers would still be working on the safe, with Hurley alongside of him—we phoned a neat tip-off to Merton Hembroke. Told him what was up.

"He traveled there with a squad—down to Baruch's. He found the front door open, like we'd left it for him. You know the rest. The bulls got Tweezer and Hurley. The Red Blot got the swag!"

SPIDER CAREW nodded; but his wan face expressed anxiety. Socks Mallory noted it and grunted.

"Getting cold feet, Spider?" he queried. "Turning yellow?"

"Don't say that, Socks!" protested the stoop-shouldered gangster. "I ain't yellow. But I got a right to be worried, ain't I?"

"Well—what's the worry?"

"These lays I've been givin' you. Look at last night. Say—there's plenty of gorillas who'd croak me if they knew I was in on the frame-up that wound up by Tweezers and Hurley takin' the bump!"

"Nobody's going to know. Those mugs are dead. They can't talk."

"They can't," agreed Spider, "but there's other guys that may. If I keep spyin' for you—"

"That's all over," assured Socks. "We're ready for the big works now. I'm using you tonight, Spider, and when the job is finished, you travel along with us. Say—we've been coming out of cover and getting back again, haven't we? Well, after tonight, we're going to stay undercover all the time, and do the jobs, too. What do you think of that?"

"It can't be done!"

"It can't, eh? Well, you'll see it done—and you'll be helping us. You'll know plenty, Spider. You'll know everything!"

Socks Mallory sat back and laughed. He seemed to enjoy his companion's bewilderment.

"The Red Blot is some smart guy," commented Spider, in a wondering tone. "Some mighty smart guy. That's all I've got to say."

"Here's the lay for tonight," declared Socks, in a businesslike tone. "You know where the old East Side Bank is. Well, there's a sort of alley runs alongside of it. Straight across from the alley is an old building that's not worth a nickel. You can get in there and watch from one of the windows—but be close to the door while you watch.

"We're coming up the alley from the opposite direction. We're going to smash into the bank. You'll see us do it. Then we'll come out again—the same way we went in—and that's where you join up. Cut across the street and run with us. Stick with the mob—you'll be O.K."

"Say"—Spider's tone was apprehensive—"you ain't chancin' that, are you, Socks? There'll be an alarm when you bust in—there'll be all kinds of cops down there—"

"Sure," interposed Socks. "We'll be making the getaway when they show up. They'll be all around us—like a net—and that's where we'll fool them like we did before."

"But there won't be enough dough to make it worthwhile!"

"Listen, Spider," interrupted Socks gruffly; "I know what I'm doing. First of all, the East Side Bank is an old crib. Easy to bust into, though we can't dodge the alarms. All right. We've got the system for the getaway.

"Maybe somebody would have tried it before—except that the East Side Bank is a dump that don't do big business. But right now, there's a lot of dough piled in that joint—cash that nobody knows about except The Red Blot. It's a setup. Savvy?"

SPIDER nodded to show that he had a glimmer of understanding. As the secret spy of The Red Blot, he knew that the master crook must be a man of great resourcefulness.

"So you be there," repeated Socks, "just like I told you. Scram when we scram. Then you're one of us. Maybe"—a malicious smile came upon Mallory's sullen lips—"maybe I'll take you along with me tomorrow night when I pull the undercover job. It's going to be sweet."

Rising from his chair, Socks leaned close to Spider's ear and whispered harshly.

"Tomorrow night," he said, "I'm going to bump off Tony Loretti!"

"The big guy that runs all the nightclubs?" gasped Spider. "Say, Socks, he's a big shot! If you go after him, there'll be a mess!"

"Don't I know it?" queried Socks. "Wasn't Loretti's racket my idea? Didn't I run the Club Janeiro until he muscled in and chased me out?

"That was my joint, and I'm going to get it back! The Red Blot wants me to do it—there's a reason why. So Tony Loretti gets his tomorrow night."

With this thrust, Socks laughed hoarsely and arose from his chair. He nudged Spider Carew with a short, friendly punch; then turned toward the door.

"I'm going back," informed Socks. "I'll be getting the mob ready. We'll be at the East Side Bank inside of two hours. You know where to be. That's all."

The door closed upon Socks Mallory's departing form. Spider Carew remained seated upon the cot. The pasty-faced ruffian's countenance went through a series of curious contortions. Through Spider's mind was passing all that Socks had said.

For weeks, Spider had been Socks Mallory's listening post. All that happened in the badlands; comments which concerned the activities of The Red Blot; other forms of useful news—these had been given to Socks by Spider whenever Socks paid his scheduled visits to Spider's hideout.

Secure because of his unimportance, Spider had prowled through the underworld, peering into every hangout, overhearing what was going on. His duties had been amplified; he had been deputed to watch for opportunities that The Red Blot could use.

Thus, Spider Carew had been responsible for The Red Blot gaining the spoils from Timothy Baruch's pawnshop safe. But now, Spider realized that he was no more than a trifling member in The Red Blot's array of criminal talent.

A tip-off to Merton Hembroke! That had been nervy. A raid upon the East Side Bank! That would add to the prestige as well as the gain which The Red Blot had acquired.

Who was The Red Blot? Spider Carew did not know. He realized only that anyone who could govern such powerful mobsters as Socks Mallory and Moocher Gleetz must, indeed, be a supercrook.

Immunity! That was The Red Blot's gift. Capable men of crime, handicapped by the fact that they were wanted, had managed, somehow, to dwell in Manhattan, and to operate in security as long as they followed The Red Blot's bidding.

Spider could feel the lure. He was fearful, now that he had betrayed Hurley Brewster and Tweezers Darley. The deaths of those two men weighed heavily on Spider's mind.

Not that Spider Carew had a conscience. He merely knew the law of gangdom and realized that he had disobeyed it. He, too, wanted immunity. Socks Mallory had promised it, beginning with tonight.

SOMETIME after Socks had gone, Spider Carew stirred. He arose from the cot, donned a shabby coat and cap, then extinguished the gaslight. With skulking progress, the hunched mobster descended the rickety stairway. He reached the alley and shuffled along toward the street where the elevated ran.

Tonight, Spider thought, would be his last in this sector of the underworld. So believing, the shifty gangster headed toward the Black Ship, to look in on whatever might be doing.

Furtively, with eyes frequently looking back over his shoulder, Spider pursued his timorous route. His shadow made a peculiar, huddled blot, as it passed beneath the glare of a street lamp.

Spider Carew still looked back over his shoulder after he had left the illuminated area. If anyone was on his trail—Spider always suspected such—the follower would be apparent now.

No human form appeared within the range of light. Spider grinned sheepishly.

Strangely, with all his caution, Spider was deceived. He had seen no sign of life beneath the street lamp, yet the indication was there. While Spider stared, a long streak of darkness glided across that zone of illumination. It was the elongated silhouette of a living person, yet Spider, looking for a solid body, did not see it.

Spider Carew went along his way. He did not look backward again. His hunched form threw its huddled blotch at every light; shortly afterward, that same long silhouette put in its inevitable appearance.

That patch of moving darkness had a sinister meaning. Silent and unseen, it was the sure indication of the presence which every skulking rat like Spider Carew feared above all others. The Red Blot's spy would have been filled with trepidation had he known who was following him.

The Shadow, master of darkness, had picked up the trail of Spider Carew!

Where Spider went tonight, there would The Shadow be! Plotted crime was due to strike again. This time it was not from Spider's suggestion, but the secret spy would be there to watch it.

Trouble loomed for The Red Blot's minions. Unwittingly, Spider was acting as a guide to the scene of crime!

CHAPTER VI
THE BANK ROBBERY

WHEN Spider Carew left the dive known as the Black Ship, he headed off into a twisting course that eventually brought him in the neighborhood of the East Side Bank. Following the sidewalk just below an elevated structure, Spider made a final turn, and sneaked along a side street until he came to the building opposite the bank.

This was an old house which had been empty for many months. Spider found a space at the side and wiggled through a window. A few minutes later, he was peering through a grimy pane at the front of the house.

Back at the spot where Spider had left the sidewalk, a gloomy patch of blackness showed strangely on the paving. There seemed to be no reason for that splotch of darkness. Motionless, it indicated nothing. Nevertheless, it was the mark of a living presence.

The Shadow, invisible in the semi-darkness, was studying the path which Spider Carew had taken. Keen, burning eyes were looking toward the window which the shuffling gangster had entered.

The Shadow knew that there could be no cause for crime within that dilapidated building. He readily divined that Spider's only purpose could be that of a hidden watcher.

The front of the East Side Bank showed upon the other side of the street. The building was a brick structure that had the appearance of a jail. An antiquated institution, the East Side Bank still continued to do business with large wholesale concerns, which found its location a convenience. At the same time, the directors had not seen fit to modernize the building. Of all the banks in Manhattan, this one was least equipped to withstand a foray of accomplished burglars.

Spider Carew's presence in the building across from the bank was a good indication that the bank itself was intended as a target for crime. The Shadow, moving silently along the street, below the level of Spider's vision, spotted the space between the bank and the adjoining building.

Picking a strategic point, the being of darkness crossed the street so artfully that his passage was indicated only by a flitting splotch upon the asphalt. Gaining a place some distance below the bank building, The Shadow worked his way backward toward the entrance of the alleyway.

SPIDER CAREW did not see The Shadow. Peering from his window, the squeamish little gangster was too engrossed with what he was viewing at the side of the bank.

Dim light glimmered through from the street a block away; and against that glow, Spider saw the outlines of human forms.

Socks Mallory and his men! They were here now. As Spider watched, he saw the raiders turn toward the side of the bank. The surprise attack had begun. No time was being lost. A little door, set in an areaway that opened from the passage, was the spot which had been picked by the attackers.

Spider Carew thought that he, alone, was viewing these operations. He was wrong. The Shadow had reached the entrance of the passage. His keen eyes were viewing the activity. Yet The Shadow, a silent, unseen shape, remained motionless; then glided slowly away in the direction from which he had come, moving rapidly from the beleaguered bank.

Keenly, he had sensed that an attack upon the mob would drive the criminals back along their chosen avenue. In flight, the gangsters would head for that distant street. That was where The Shadow would forestall them.

Spider Carew could hear the muffled sounds of a breaking door. Steel jimmies had done quick work. The henchmen of The Red Blot were breaking through. The dull ringing of a bell came to Spider's ears. The alarm was sounding.

Spider knew the efficiency of bank alarms; and the quickness with which police could respond. Socks Mallory and his marauders had entered. They would be returning shortly. It was nearly time to join them.

The little mobster unlocked the sash of the old window and raised it, ready to drop out into the street. Then, as the report of an automatic reechoed through the space opposite, Spider dropped back to a spot of shelter, and peered over the sill in front of him.

A flash of flame from down the alleyway. Another reechoing shot! Someone had entered from the farther block, to open fire upon the men who were guarding the broken door! Spider could hear a wild cry rising—passed along by those on watch!

Revolver shots burst forth. Spider Carew watched an amazing conflict. A squad of mobsmen were tumbling into the space beside the bank, opening fire upon this unexpected enemy who had entered the path which they had left open for retreat.

THOSE within the bank had heard the surprise. Their work unfinished, they were coming to aid, thinking that the police had already arrived.

Well had The Shadow planned! He had waited until the crooks had broken through, and had started the alarms. Now, by swift attack, he was harassing them while the law was on the way!

Spider Carew saw one mobsman collapse; then another. The rest were clinging close to the edges of the passage, seeking refuge in the space that led into the rear of the bank, firing vainly at an invisible fighter whose very presence seemed elusive.

Blasts from the automatics came at unexpected intervals. When mobsters fired at a spot, The Shadow was no longer there. The strange battle continued; then came the clang of a police car, swinging from the distance.

The mobsters under Socks Mallory could not have heard that noise, but their leader must have sensed that police intervention was imminent. Spider Carew saw half a dozen revolver bursts at once; then another outpour; then a pause.

The answer?

Powerful blasts from the automatics wielded by the hidden fighter at the other end of the passage. The mobsters began a sudden retreat toward the street from which Spider watched. They fired blindly; then broke into a run. One of their number tumbled forward, to be dragged along by two of his companions.

The police car was coming down the street. Spider could see its lights. He saw the mobsters scatter. Socks Mallory was among them, as they ran down the street, firing back at the police car as they fled.

The automobile jammed to a stop directly in front of the bank building. A mobster jumped up from nowhere; leaping upon the hood of the car, he aimed straight through the windshield. Spider saw a flash of flame from the very entrance of the space between the buildings. Simultaneously with the roar of The Shadow's automatic, the gangster on the hood took a long, sprawling dive to the street.

Four officers were out of the car. Two were running for the side of the bank. They passed the very spot where Spider had seen the automatic flash. The other pair of officers were chasing Socks Mallory and his fleeing men.

Then, by a mere chance, Spider saw the sight that chilled his blood. In the midst of the momentary quiet that reigned about the abandoned police car, a tall, mysterious figure came into the fringe of the light which the headlamps cast.

Spider saw that shape and recognized its identity. The Shadow, garbed in black cloak and broad-brimmed slouch hat. He was the being who had delivered that counterstroke to rout Socks Mallory and his crowd of mobsmen!

The Shadow! Spider Carew crouched in fright as his trembling lips formed the name of the dread avenger. Sickening terror gripped the cowering crook who had served as The Red Blot's spy. Spider realized that his own plan was blocked. He could not join Socks Mallory now!

The dread figure of The Shadow disappeared with amazing swiftness. Spider knew where it had gone. The Shadow was doubling back through that passage to the other street, to again deter the mobsmen in their flight!

SPIDER could see four motionless forms; these men had fallen from The Shadow's fire. Others had been wounded, but were keeping on with Socks Mallory. Spider could offer no aid. His own skin was his only thought.

Stumbling through darkness, Spider reached a back window of the old house, He tumbled through and landed heavily on cement. He did not mind the bruising fall. He saw an opening between two houses at the rear, and scurried through. He had only one design—to reach his hideout before The Shadow could take up his trail.

Meanwhile, The Shadow was still in action. The black-clad fighter had doubled back through the passage. Reaching the street behind the bank, his keen vision caught the sight of fleeing gangsters at the next corner. The automatic roared in time to clip one of the running men.

Revolver shots sounded in the street. The Shadow dropped back out of sight. New police were in the game. Had they not arrived, The Shadow could have carried on; now, with the officers taking up the chase, his presence was not needed.

The noise of pursuit died in the distance. Revolver shots echoed from nearby blocks. Socks Mallory and his men were in a jam. Their crime had been frustrated; their escape had been delayed.

Policemen, entering the space by the front of the bank building, stopped as they heard a strange cry which reverberated through the narrow passage. The tones of a triumphant, mocking laugh— a weird burst of mirth that seemed to come from another sphere!

The laugh of The Shadow!

The policemen did not recognize it, but the cry filled them with alarm. Hesitating, they turned strong flashlight beams down the open space. The glare revealed nothing. The only token of a living presence was the persistent throb of sobbing echoes that had not yet died away.

The Shadow was gone. He had met the hordes of The Red Blot, and had routed them in their grim game. They had fled, like rats, for cover, behind their desperate leader, Socks Mallory.

Thwarted crime! That had been The Shadow's accomplishment tonight. A police cordon was closing about the area which surrounded the East Side Bank. It might suffice to trap Socks Mallory and his men; it would never snare The Shadow.

Like a phantom of darkness, the invisible warrior had departed.

CHAPTER VII
OVER THE WIRE

RALPH WESTON, police commissioner, was seated in a small office which was located in his luxurious apartment. Here, twenty-four hours after the battle near the East Side Bank, he was studying the reports of thwarted crime.

Weston was a dynamic sort of man. He had been a success as police commissioner because of his persistent efforts to get at the roots of crime. To him, the menace of The Red Blot had been quite as real and as horrifying as the newspapers had chosen to make it.

Weston was grim this evening. On two successive nights, the police had encountered unusual crime. Weston was apprehensive about tonight. He knew that the law had gained success; yet victory had been barren.

Two nights ago, Detective Merton Hembroke had made an effective raid. With a squad of police, he had entered the pawnshop of Timothy Baruch. Two criminals—Hurley Brewster and Tweezers Darley—had been surprised at an opened safe. Both had been slain.

That was good; the unfortunate part was that Baruch's safe had been rifled, and the crimson splotch upon a sheet of white paper had signified the evil hand of the unknown mastermind called The Red Blot.

Last night, a squad of mobsters had attacked the East Side Bank. Police, responding to the alarm, had driven them off. Five gangsters had fallen; others, wounded, had kept on. Two dead men; three who had died from their wounds—of the latter not one had spoken. Sullenly, they had kept sealed lips regarding The Red Blot.

No crimson splotch had appeared last night; yet Weston was sure that The Red Blot was in back of it. All five of the dead mobsters had been men of crime whom the police had believed were out of New York.

Commissioner Weston picked up an afternoon newspaper. His own picture appeared upon the front page, together with his statement that The Red Blot must be found. Weston, in fact, had issued words which savored of immunity to anyone who would put the police on the direct trail to the master crook.

WESTON began to pace his little office. He had talked with Inspector Timothy Klein not long before, the subject being the proper handling of these new crimes.

Detective Joe Cardona, dubbed the ace of the New York force, was still investigating the first cases in which The Red Blot had appeared. In the meantime, another sleuth had sprung into active prominence. Merton Hembroke, whose surprise raid at Baruch's had marked the first success against The Red Blot, was working on the affair at the East Side Bank.

Commissioner Weston had a marked respect for Joe Cardona's ability. At the same time, he was disappointed at the ace's lack of results. On certain occasions, in the past, Weston had been harsh with Cardona. Every time, Joe had come through in the end.

Tonight, Weston had the same problem, but there was a chance for a new solution. Instead of relying upon Cardona, he could depend on Hembroke. No doubt about it: Hembroke was a comer. Klein had just reported that Hembroke was at headquarters, sticking there, hoping for some break that would lead him closer to The Red Blot.

The ringing of the telephone interrupted Ralph Weston's soliloquy. The police commissioner picked up the instrument and grumbled a short "Hello." A pause; then came a response in a whining tone that Weston did not recognize.

"Hello!" demanded the commissioner. "Who is it?"

"Are you Commissioner Weston?" came the query.

"The commissioner speaking," said Weston.

"Say"—the voice was nervous—"is that straight dope you was givin' tonight in the paper? If there's a guy that's got somethin' on The Red Blot—you'll treat him square if he squawks?"

"Do you know something?" challenged Weston.

"Yeah," said the voice. "But I ain't goin' to talk unless I can see you. I don't trust the bulls. I ain't—"

"Is this a hoax?" demanded Weston.

"I ain't kiddin', Commissioner," persisted the voice, in a new, plaintive tone.

"Say—I'll give you some dope over the phone—right now—if you'll give me a chance to come up to your place. You can have the bulls there. I'll tell you who I am before I come, if only you'll promise to give me the chance."

COMMISSIONER WESTON was a sage individual. He sensed that he had a real informant on the other end of the wire. To alarm the man might end the call; to give him too much assurance might mean a change of mind on the fellow's part. Tactful and practical, Weston decided to learn what he could while the opportunity was here.

"If this is no hoax," he said, in a calm voice, "I am quite ready to talk with you. It does not matter if you have participated in crime which involves this man they call The Red Blot—"

"I ain't done nothin', Commissioner," the voice intervened. "Let me give you the lowdown. Are you listenin'?"

"Yes."

"I've been tippin' off a guy, understand? Talkin' with a fellow who works for The Red Blot. He wanted me to go along with him—get the idea? I was scared.

"The Red Blot's goin' to pull somethin' big, Commissioner. You can't stop him, but there's a guy that's goin' to make trouble for him. The Shadow—that's who, Commissioner! The

Shadow is out to get The Red Blot! I've seen him—The Shadow!"

Commissioner Weston repressed a snort of disdain. He had heard of The Shadow—a strange phantom garbed in black who warred with crime. One of Joe Cardona's pet beliefs—The Shadow.

This awed voice, speaking from somewhere in the underworld, was adding new testimony to prove the existence of The Shadow, a thought which Weston had constantly tried to belittle.

"If The Shadow gets The Red Blot"—the voice seemed more scared than before—"he'll go after the whole works. He'll get me, maybe, because I know about The Red Blot. That's why I'm tippin' you off."

"Tipping me off?" queried Weston testily. "You haven't told me anything yet."

"You've got to believe me," complained the voice. "Listen, Commissioner—put this down and you'll know I'm right. There's a guy named Socks Mallory. He's supposed to be out of New York. He's here—he was in on last night's job. He's out to get a big shot named Tony Loretti—"

"Yes! Yes!" Weston spoke eagerly as the voice broke off.

"I can't tell you no more," pleaded the informant. "I've got to see you. If Socks Mallory knew that I was squealin', he'd get me, sure.

"Listen, Commissioner. I'll come up there if you'll let me. I'll tell you how I'll come—and you can cover me all along the way. Send along some dicks—they'll know me, an' they can stick close to me."

"Go ahead," ordered Weston. "I'll agree to see you."

"An hour from now," said the voice, in a relieved tone. "Say—you're on the level—"

"Absolutely."

"O.K., then. I'll get on the Lexington Avenue sub at Fourteenth Street, an hour from now. Tell the dicks to cover me. Spider Carew—that's me. They'll know Spider Carew. I'm a little guy, wearin' a cap, an' sweater under a coat. I'll get on a local to Thirty-third Street. Off there an' over to your place. Let the dicks trail me—but if they grab me, I won't talk. I've got to see you, Commissioner."

"That's exactly right, Carew," said Weston, in a soothing tone. "Come right along. You will not be molested. That is my promise."

"I'm goin' back to my hideout,'" informed Spider. "Then I'll do a quick sneak over to the sub. I'll play straight, Commissioner!"

The receiver clicked. The call was ended.

COMMISSIONER WESTON lost no time. He called Inspector Klein.

"One hour from now," Weston told the inspector, "a man named Spider Carew will enter the Lexington Avenue subway at Fourteenth Street. He is coming here. I want him trailed, but he is not to be arrested."

Klein's reply of acquiescence came over the wire.

"He is a small man, Klein," explained Weston. "He wears a cap, and a sweater underneath his coat. He will take a local train to Thirty-third Street; from there he will walk here."

Weston hung up the receiver after Klein had promised to make the arrangements promptly. A few minutes later, the bell rang, and the commissioner again heard the inspector's voice.

"I told Detective Sergeant Markham to cover Spider Carew," explained Klein. "He was to leave with three men. In the meantime, Hembroke came into my office."

"Good!" exclaimed Weston. "You put him on the job also?"

"Yes," returned Klein, "He gave me a valuable suggestion. The detectives will leave here separately; each will arrive at Fourteenth Street within thirty minutes. They will post themselves so that they can watch each other. When one spots Spider Carew, all will follow the lead."

"Excellent," decided Weston. "That is better than sending them as a squad."

"Anything else, Commissioner?"

"Yes."

Weston recalled his conversation with Spider. Normally, the commissioner would have mentioned the names of Socks Mallory and Tony Loretti; but another name crowded those from his mind.

"This man Carew"—Weston's tone became a bit ironical—"said that he feared The Shadow. I am telling you that, inspector, but there is no need to mention it to our men. You know my opinion regarding The Shadow. He may be a myth for all I know. That is all, inspector."

The call ended, Commissioner Weston sat at his desk. He now recalled the names of Mallory and Loretti, and jotted them on a pad. These could wait. Spider Carew had committed himself, and would surely come here now. Direct questioning would bring more detailed information about The Red Blot.

As Weston pondered, he found himself thinking of The Shadow. Despite his disbelief in the activities of that mysterious being who fought with crime, the commissioner could not forget the awed tone of Spider's voice.

The Shadow! Weston was doubting his own opinions. Spider Carew had said that he had seen The Shadow. That would be one subject upon which Weston would examine the informant, when Spider Carew arrived for his appointment!

CHAPTER VIII
ON THE SUBWAY

APPROXIMATELY one hour after he had telephoned to Police Commissioner Weston, Spider Carew arrived at the Fourteenth Street station of the East Side subway. The slinking gangster was more furtive than ever. He looked about suspiciously, half expecting someone to accost him.

Detectives were here, Spider was sure. He feared that they might not play the game. Spider was worried about the double cross that he was perpetrating on Socks; yet Spider felt sure that there was nothing to fear from the gang leader who served The Red Blot.

The great menace in Spider's mind was The Shadow. That fear dwarfed all others. Nothing— so Spider was convinced—could stop the wrath of The Shadow. The little mobster feared that the black-garbed avenger might already be on his trail.

Down the steps of the subway, to the platform where both local and express trains stopped on their way uptown, Spider went. Forty or fifty people were here. Spider clung to a little cluster. He tried not to notice anyone.

Men were watching Spider Carew now. Detective Sergeant Markham, Detective Merton Hembroke, and three other sleuths—all five kept up a stern vigil. A local rolled into the station, Spider Carew sidled into the third car. Hembroke, watching, saw three detectives follow. Then Hembroke boarded the train also.

Where was Markham? Hembroke, always keen, looked back to the platform. He saw Markham still waiting. The detective sergeant was moving along the platform.

Hembroke frowned. Working independently, Markham had decided to stay for some special purpose.

The local pulled out. Hembroke shrugged his shoulders. He set an example for the other detectives by keeping away from Spider Carew. The rat-faced little gangster was hanging on to a strap, staring out through an open window.

BACK on the Fourteenth Street platform, Detective Sergeant Markham was staring suspiciously at a man who was resting against a post which bore a chewing-gum machine. As Markham glanced in the fellow's direction, the man turned his back and began to make a pretense of dropping a coin in the slot. Markham was sure that he had seen this man before. Tall, heavy— someone connected with crime—

Markham's thoughts broke off as an express roared into the station. He saw the man start slowly for one car; then, on an impulse, hurry down the platform and board the train at another

spot. The doors were closing. Markham leaped aboard, two cars away from his quarry.

As the train started, the detective sergeant was on his way to the car where the other man had entered. There were four watching Spider Carew; it would be well to watch this fellow also. There might be some connection, Markham decided.

The detective sergeant reached the car where the man was just as the express was passing the Eighteenth Street local station.

Then came the unexpected. Before Markham's eyes, a drama of crime crept into actuality, so subtly that the detective sergeant did not realize what was about to happen until the actual deed occurred.

First, Markham recognized the profile of the man whom he was watching. A pair of bloated lips, a pudgy nose, a bulging forehead; these and roughly shaven cheeks awoke the detective sergeant's recollections.

Socks Mallory! One-time racketeer—owner of the Club Janeiro—a man wanted for murder! That was the fellow whom Markham had followed on a hunch!

The local train had pulled out of Eighteenth Street, and at the very moment when Markham made his discovery of Mallory's identity, the express was overtaking the local. The detective sergeant caught a peculiar gleam in Mallory's eye. He realized that the man was watching for something as he stared from the window.

Markham looked in the same direction. He was near the front of the car; Mallory just beyond the center. Thus, as the express slowly moved past the speed-gaining local, Markham was the first to spy the occupants of the third car in the other train.

Spider Carew was gripping a strap. Hembroke and the three other detectives were all at least ten feet away from him. Markham noted the anxious look on Spider's face.

The express moved slowly by; Markham looked through his own car, and suddenly realized that Socks Mallory was on a direct line with Spider Carew.

The trains were traveling at almost uniform speed. In the local, the detectives who were watching Spider saw a hunted look come on the stoop-shouldered gangster's face. They looked into the express. They, like Markham, saw Socks Mallory!

The hard-faced gang leader yanked a revolver from his pocket. With a sure, determined motion, he leveled the weapon through the open window before him, and covered Spider point-blank.

With the roaring trains side by side, in the midst of terrific noise, Mallory had a perfect shot at a range of no more than six feet!

The flash of the revolver was accompanied by

**With the roaring trains side by side
. . . Mallory had a perfect shot . . .**

a roar that was scarcely heard above the rumbling of the trains. A second report followed immediately afterward, as Socks Mallory made sure.

THE second bullet was not needed. The first found its mark; the next caught Spider Carew as he was toppling away from the strap.

The detectives in the local pulled out their revolvers. Markham, in the express, duplicated the action.

Socks Mallory was too swift. His next deed eliminated all but Markham. With his free hand, the killer reached up and yanked the emergency cord which ran through the car. The air brakes whistled. The cars of the local swept along in rapid succession as the express came to a jolting stop.

Socks Mallory was springing toward the end of the car. No one moved to stop him. Markham could not fire; too many people were in the way. By the time the detective sergeant had reached the end of the car, Socks had opened the door between the cars, and was leaping to the local track.

Markham delivered bullets that flattened themselves against a post between the tracks. He leaped from the train to follow the escaping killer. Somewhere along the tracks, heading back toward the Eighteenth Street station—that was the way which Socks had taken.

Markham kept grimly on. Socks Mallory was well ahead; the detective sergeant could see no trace of him. It took Markham some four minutes to reach the Eighteenth Street station; meanwhile an uptown local and roaring downtown trains had forced him to stick to the uptown express track.

At sight of the lighted station platforms, Markham paused. He realized that Socks could have scurried by this point; but he knew that the killer would have been seen had he clambered up either platform.

Markham waited a full minute, undecided whether to keep on, or to take to a station platform. Suddenly a flashlight glared from the uptown station. Markham heard a voice shouting his name. Cautiously, the detective sergeant went across the local track and raised his arms, to be pulled up to the platform.

It was Merton Hembroke who had called. The detective was explaining how he had arrived back at Eighteenth Street so suddenly.

"Saw the express stop," he said. "Left one man at Twenty-third Street when the local reached there. Another to get on the telephone. Brought one man here with me. He's on the platform opposite. Man on the wire is telling headquarters to cover Fourteenth and Twenty-eighth."

"The emergency exits?" queried Markham. "I passed one on the way here, but I didn't see the man I was after."

"Couple of policemen at Twenty-third," responded Hembroke. "Sent them to cover the emergencies. They're getting others. Headquarters will take care of it. I came here in a taxi—in a hurry. Say, Markham, I saw the guy. I thought I recognized him. Do you know who he was?"

"Socks Mallory," returned Markham. "Wanted for murder."

"That's the bird!" exclaimed Hembroke. "I know him now! Say—I've got to pass that word along quick."

"Go ahead," said Markham. "I'll take charge here and along the line. Leave it to me, Hembroke."

THE detective was momentarily piqued at Markham's assumption of command; then a thought occurred to him. He spoke in the tone of a subordinate, even though his words were a suggestion.

"Suppose I hop up to the commissioner's," he said. "After I've passed along the dope on Socks Mallory. The commissioner was waiting for Spider Carew to show up—and Spider's dead."

"O.K.," agreed Markham.

Detective Hembroke hurried to the street. He encountered two policemen as he reached the top of the steps. He flashed his badge.

"Detective Sergeant Markham is in charge," said Hembroke. "Socks Mallory is the man we're looking for."

As Hembroke paused upon the street corner, a police car sirened up to where he stood. Inspector Timothy Klein alighted. He saw the detective. Hembroke stepped forward and gave the information regarding Socks Mallory; then added that he was on his way to Weston's, at Markham's approval.

"Very good," agreed Klein. "Hurry along, Hembroke."

All along the avenue, police and detectives were coming to the search for the escaped killer. Socks Mallory's daring deed had been quick in its execution. The response of the law had not been lacking.

Detective Hembroke smiled grimly as he boarded a cab and gave Weston's address. Socks Mallory was underground. Every exit of the subway for blocks was covered. Whether or not the killer was captured, nothing but commendation could be made for Detective Hembroke's promptitude.

CHAPTER IX
THE SHADOW'S CLEW

WHILE policemen and detectives were engaged in the swift and thorough search for Spider Carew's murderer, another quest was under way—one which Spider had dreaded, and had taken drastic measures to forestall.

The Shadow, moving through the underworld, had reached the end of a trail. He was at the threshold of the secret hideout which Spider Carew had so recently abandoned.

The turn of last night's events had forced The Shadow to abandon his original course. The Shadow had used Spider as a means of locating the spot where the minions of The Red Blot were to perpetrate their plotted crime. Then, in order to rout the marauders, he had given no further heed to Spider.

After his battle with Socks Mallory's mobsters, The Shadow had again been forced to give up the chase. He had left that to the police; they had failed. The Red Blot's henchmen had made another mysterious disappearance.

Two courses lay before The Shadow. One was to study the vicinity of the East Side Bank; the other was to locate Spider Carew's hideout. The Shadow had chosen the latter. Spider Carew, spy and informant, was a connecting link with The Red Blot's evil hand.

The Shadow, however, was confronted with a most difficult quest. He had picked up Spider's trail outside the hideout. To discover the place itself meant a deductive process beginning with the spot where he had first seen Spider.

The Shadow knew the badlands well. He had waited until afternoon; then, in the guise of an obscure mobsman, he had begun his survey. Gradually, he had eliminated different districts until he had centered upon several blocks. In one of these, The Shadow was sure, Spider Carew must be located.

Fate had played strange tricks that evening. Spider Carew, seeking to avoid The Shadow, had left his hideout while The Shadow, himself, was in the vicinity. By pure accident, Spider had taken a street which The Shadow had just abandoned; had made his phone call, and had doubled back to the hideout.

Leaving again, he had once more prowled a lucky course that had enabled him to escape The Shadow's search. Less than three minutes after Spider had gone from the alley by his hideout, The Shadow, unseen in the garb of black that he had adopted after nightfall, had come to that exact locality.

Spider, to avoid The Shadow, had pleaded by telephone with Commissioner Weston. His interview granted, Spider had given little thought to Socks Mallory. He had felt sure that Socks would never know his game. But in eluding The Shadow, Spider had fallen prey to Socks Mallory's killing hand!

THE SHADOW understood the psychology of Spider Carew's ilk. He knew that the stoop-shouldered skulker would prefer his hideout as the best place of security. That was exactly where The Shadow would have found Spider; but for the freakish idea which had entered the little mobster's mind—the odd thought of communicating with Commissioner Weston.

Thus, with Spider dead, with the hue and cry out for Socks Mallory, The Shadow was still on his set task. Gliding weirdly through the alleyway, this master of darkness paused when he came to the battered door which marked the entrance to Spider's hideout.

This place impressed The Shadow because of its obscurity. Softly, the black-garbed phantom entered the doorway and flickered his tiny flashlight upon the rickety steps. There, he saw signs of use: a boarded hole in one step halfway up the flight. The Shadow ascended.

In total darkness, the invisible investigator tried the door at the top. It opened; The Shadow's light again glittered. It fell upon the gas jet. A match flickered; the room was illuminated. The Shadow, his form grotesque and sinister in the wavering light, viewed Spider Carew's hiding place.

A newspaper lay on the cot. A sheet of paper was resting on the chair. A black-gloved hand plucked up the second object. Keen eyes read a note which Spider Carew had scrawled. It was the little mobster's effort to lull Socks Mallory, should the gang leader come here during the absence of Spider Carew.

The keen eyes read a warning:

> Look out. The Shaddo is wise. I seen him last nite. He meens trouble for you. I am goin to scramm so he cant find me. I dont want him to folow me becuz if he got here he mite get on your trale. Wach out when you go to get Tony. The Shaddo may be thare.

The Shadow studied this laborious letter. On the surface, it appeared to be a genuine bid by Spider to give Socks Mallory a helpful tip. However, The Shadow knew that it lacked sincerity. It would have deceived Socks Mallory, but not The Shadow.

Where would Spider have gone? This obscure hideout was the most logical place for him to have remained. Knowing that The Shadow had spotted him, Spider would not have made a change. He was the type to rely upon the security that he already possessed.

What was in Spider's mind?

The last two sentences were full of meaning to The Shadow. They were unnecessary—these words that mentioned a specific event. There was but one excuse for them. Spider Carew had a reason of his own to expect trouble for Socks Mallory when the latter went to get the person called Tony. A coward, Spider was trying to square himself in advance.

A soft laugh came from The Shadow's hidden lips.

Tony! There was one Tony whom Socks Mallory would like to get. Tony Loretti.

Perhaps Spider had fled to seek Loretti's protection. Keenly, The Shadow divined that Socks had revealed to Spider that he intended to bump off the nightclub racketeer.

Again the laugh. The Shadow had rejected the theory that Spider had gone to warn Loretti. Had he chosen such a course, Spider would not have mentioned the big shot's name. Double-crossing Socks, Spider would have wanted the gang leader to enter a trap unsuspecting.

No; there must be some other destination which Spider Carew had chosen.

The Shadow's gaze fell upon the newspaper. It was folded; and as the gloved hands lifted it, the keen eyes saw the crumpling marks of thumbprints. Spider Carew had gripped this newspaper lightly while he had read words of importance to himself.

THE photograph of Police Commissioner

"SPIDER" CAREW and "SOCKS" MALLORY, who furnish the gun-shooting end of this thrilling story. One is small-fry in the game; the other is the "big shot," but he, too, seems to obey the orders of some one else. Both are working for The Red Blot to terrify a helpless city.

Weston; the statement which the high official had made: these were the factors that had inspired Spider Carew. Again, The Shadow laughed. He had found the answer to Spider Carew's absence.

Spider Carew had squealed to the police commissioner!

Nothing more than a pawn in the game which The Red Blot backed, Spider had realized that the law would welcome his revelations. His part as Socks Mallory's informant—even though it had been spy work for The Red Blot—was not sufficient to put him behind prison bars. Spider Carew had decided to become a stool pigeon.

The warning note was his ruse to keep in right with Socks, should Weston ordain that Spider must return to the underworld to glean new information. By now, Spider would be telling what he knew—provided that nothing had intervened to balk his plan.

The Shadow held the clew to The Red Blot's next stroke. The master plotter was using Socks Mallory as his right arm.

Murder was in the offing. Tony Loretti was to be the victim.

Was it to satisfy Mallory's grudge against the big shot? Or was there a hidden purpose behind the contemplated deed?

Again, The Shadow's soft laugh made strange whispers come in tremors through that little room. The gaslight flickered as though the ghoulish reverberations had swayed the flame. The purpose did not matter. The Shadow's object was to meet The Red Blot's minions.

A black-gloved hand extinguished the gas. Softly, The Shadow departed from Spider's hideout. Newspaper and note lay in darkness, at the exact spots where The Shadow had found them. There was no token remaining of The Shadow's visit.

A silent figure hovered along the darkened street. It crossed a thoroughfare beneath an elevated line. Nearing a more prosperous avenue, the weird form paused beside a parked cab. The door opened so quietly that the sleepy driver did not notice it.

The taxi man's first knowledge that he had a fare came when a solemn voice spoke through the window. The driver stared in startled amazement; then grinned when he heard the uptown address which the speaker gave.

A long ride ahead; a good fare to collect. That satisfied the driver. He nodded as he heard the final instructions from his unexpected passenger, thinking only of the fare.

"There are two entrances," explained the even voice. "One on the avenue; the other on the side street above. Go past the first. Turn the corner. Stop at the second. You will see the words 'Club Janeiro' above the door."

The Club Janeiro! There, tonight, The Shadow would make use of his newest clew. At that pleasure palace, the master of darkness would await the next stroke of The Red Blot!

CHAPTER X
THE CLUB JANEIRO

"YOU say the murderer escaped—with five of you there to seize him?"

The question came from Commissioner Weston. The police official was talking to Detective Merton Hembroke.

"One of us was there to seize him," responded Hembroke laconically. "Four of us were in the local; Markham was the only one in the express."

"Inefficient!" growled Weston. "Very poor judgment on the part of Markham."

"Markham did quite well tonight," rejoined Hembroke. The detective seemed to be completely at ease in his mild correction of the commissioner's statement. "He suspected trouble on the express. That's how he happened to be there. He didn't prevent the murder; but he recognized the man who killed Spider Carew."

"That's good!" exclaimed Weston.

"Moreover," continued Hembroke, calmly seating himself on the opposite side of the commissioner's small desk, "the man who killed Spider was already wanted for murder."

"Ah!" Weston looked up in surprise. From the moment that Detective Hembroke had arrived at the apartment, there had been one startling statement after another. Merton Hembroke was an unusual sleuth. He had the faculty of whetting a listener's interest; and he was unfolding a keen description of the subway shooting, which Weston was accepting with eager ears.

"Wanted for murder," repeated Hembroke. "A former racketeer—supposed to be somewhere other than New York. A crook known as Socks Mallory!"

The name brought a prompt response. Weston was on his feet, pounding his desk. His voice sounded loudly in that little office as he seized a piece of paper and thrust it into Hembroke's hands.

"Socks Mallory!" cried the commissioner. "Look at that, Hembroke! That's the name Spider Carew gave me over the telephone! Socks Mallory—working for The Red Blot!"

"There are two names here," remarked Hembroke.

"Certainly!" exclaimed Weston. "The other is the man whom Mallory is out to get. Carew told me that, also."

"Tony Loretti!" Hembroke whistled. "Say— you know who he is, don't you, Commissioner?"

"He runs a nightclub," returned Weston. "I've been to the place. A shady character, this Loretti— but one who seems to keep clear of crime."

"Yes," agreed Hembroke, "but there's more to it than that. Tony Loretti put Socks Mallory out of the running, so far as the nightclub racket was concerned. No wonder Socks is out to get Loretti!"

"Where could we find Loretti?"

"Up at the Club Janeiro. That's his headquarters. Socks Mallory tried to run that place until Loretti chased him out. But Loretti is safe enough tonight, Commissioner."

"Why?"

"Because we've got Mallory bottled up in the subway. Maybe they've caught him by this time."

Commissioner Weston shook his head as he heard Hembroke's words. It struck him that this time the detective might be far from right.

"Suppose Mallory has made his escape?" suggested Weston. "He doesn't know that Spider Carew told me about Loretti. If Mallory is free, the Club Janeiro will be the place where he will go. That's where we're going, Hembroke. Right now!"

The detective smiled and nodded in response.

"You and I," added the commissioner, "and five men from headquarters."

"Just one thing, Commissioner," objected Hembroke cautiously. "If Socks has made a getaway and is heading for the Club Janeiro, it wouldn't be wise to have too big a crowd laying for him when—"

"Don't worry about that," returned the commissioner grimly, as he picked up the telephone to call headquarters. "I'm taking charge of this expedition, Hembroke. You're my right-hand man tonight. We'll post our watchers properly."

TWENTY minutes later, Commissioner Ralph Weston and Detective Merton Hembroke alighted from a taxicab at the Club Janeiro. They strolled through the front door.

As they entered the huge central room of the gay nightclub, the commissioner's quick eye noted five detectives posted at tables just within the door. Motioning to Hembroke, Weston moved toward another table.

Hardly had the two seated themselves before a headwaiter approached and spoke to Commissioner Weston in a low, careful tone.

"Good evening, Commissioner," said the man. "Mr. Loretti told me to welcome you here. He is in his office, should you care to see him."

Weston glanced sourly at Hembroke. The detective responded with a similar expression. Coming here unannounced, Weston had been discovered immediately.

"What about it?" Weston asked the detective.

"We might as well see Loretti," returned Hembroke. "He knows we're here."

The commissioner nodded to the headwaiter. The man conducted Weston and Hembroke to the rear of the large dining room. The trio passed through an archway. A short passage; then a corridor that led off in both directions.

The waiter kept on, however, until he reached a door at the end. He knocked; a voice responded. The man opened the door and ushered Weston and Hembroke into a fair-sized room that had the appearance of an office.

There were two persons here. One was a middle-sized, dark-faced man with black hair, who showed gold teeth when he grinned. The other was a black-haired woman attired in a gorgeous Spanish costume—clothes which betokened her nationality.

The smiling man arose and bowed. He extended his hand to Ralph Weston, and nodded to Merton Hembroke.

"It pleases me to welcome you here, Commissioner," he said. "I am Tony Loretti. This lady is Senorita Juanita Pasquales. She has full charge of the Club Janeiro."

"How did you know I was coming here?" demanded Weston.

"Very simply," responded Loretti. "About five minutes ago, my headwaiter reported that two detectives had come into the Club Janeiro. He heard them say something about watching for the commissioner. So I instructed my man to await your arrival and to invite you here."

Weston was forced to smile. He studied Tony Loretti carefully.

The man's career was known to the police. Tony Loretti had muscled into the nightclub business—the old racket of offering protection against criminal activities.

Loretti had been successful in his enterprise, and had managed to make it appear quite legitimate. Where other racketeers had picked established business upon which to prey, Tony had wisely chosen a form of business which really needed some sort of protection.

Nightclubs had been overrun by trouble-making mobsters until Tony Loretti had taken hold. Since then, these gay spots had known a period of real prosperity, with Tony Loretti assuming the proportions of an overlord.

Juanita Pasquales owned and operated the Club Janeiro. Other persons handled different nightclubs. Tony Loretti, having chosen the Club Janeiro merely as a headquarters, let his subordinates make the rounds and take a percentage of the profits.

"I PRESUME," purred Loretti, while Weston still watched him, "that you are intending some sort of an investigation? If that is the case, Mr. Commissioner, I shall be pleased to aid you."

Weston shook his head solemnly. He decided that Loretti must be in ignorance of the real reason for the police visit; therefore, the best plan would be to give him the correct information, and note his response.

"We have come here to protect you, Loretti," announced the commissioner. "A certain murderer is at large. We intend to capture him. We have learned that you are intended as his next victim."

A raucous laugh came from Tony Loretti. He turned to Juanita Pasquales, who responded to his mirth with a quiet smile.

"Someone out to get me?" queried Loretti, in an incredulous tone. "That is impossible! Tell me—do you know the name of this man who wants to make trouble for himself?"

"Yes," stated Weston. "The man is known as Socks Mallory."

"Mallory!" Loretti's brows narrowed. "Is he here in New York?"

"He killed a man tonight," returned Weston. "Murdered his victim in the Lexington Avenue subway."

"Socks Mallory!" Tony Loretti pronounced the name with a sneer. "He is a tough customer. He threatened me once before, but lacked nerve to take a shot at me. Let me thank you, Commissioner, for this information. I shall assure you that if Mallory comes here tonight, he will do me no harm. I need no police protection."

"Perhaps not," said Weston dryly. "Nevertheless, you'll take it, Loretti. Is this office your headquarters?"

"Yes," admitted Loretti sullenly.

"These other rooms?" Weston pointed to the doors.

"My private office to the right," returned Loretti. "Senorita Pasquales has the office on the left. This is sort of a reception room."

"Come on, Hembroke," ordered the commissioner.

The two investigators entered each office in turn. The rooms were small ones. The one used by Loretti had a mahogany desk and several chairs. The office which belonged to Juanita Pasquales was furnished with table, chairs, filing cabinet, and a broad, shelved cabinet with glass doors. The shelves showed only stacks of newspapers and scattered magazines.

"All right," announced Weston, when he returned to the central office, "we're going to watch this place, Loretti."

"Suit yourself, Mr. Commissioner," was the reply. "Let me warn you, though, that it can only make trouble. I know how to look out for myself. I need no police protection. If Mallory is coming here, you'll only scare him away."

"There's logic in that, Commissioner," declared Hembroke.

"I know it," agreed Weston. "That's why I wanted to make sure that no one else was in these rooms. There's just one entrance to this suite. You will be here, Loretti. Stay here."

"I always do," returned Loretti suavely.

"And you, Miss Pasquales?" questioned Weston. "Where do you intend to be this evening?"

"On the floor," returned the woman. "The show goes on in about fifteen minutes. It will last one hour."

"Good," approved Weston. "You will come out with us, Miss Pasquales. Loretti, I'm going to post men in those two side corridors just beyond the door of this suite. There will be others—including myself—in the big room of the nightclub. If Socks Mallory comes here tonight we'll trap him."

A gleaming smile appeared upon Tony Loretti's lips. The nightclub governor approved this plan.

"All right, Commissioner," he said. "Those side passages go to the dressing rooms, and they serve as exits, also. If your men lay low, it will work out, maybe."

"Hembroke," said Weston to the detective, "I'm putting you in charge of those corridors. Take three men. Make sure that all the entertainers have gone out to the floor. You and one man take a corridor; the other two men stay opposite. I'll keep the extra man with me. Get busy!"

HEMBROKE nodded and left the office. It was several minutes before he returned to announce that all was ready.

The commissioner nodded to Juanita Pasquales. The senorita left the office, and Weston watched through the half-opened door as he saw her conduct a troop of entertainers out through the archway to the main room.

Hembroke had disappeared; now, while Weston still waited, the detective came from the corridor on the left to announce that the dressing rooms were clear.

"My men are posted," he added. "Wait about two minutes, until I get set. Then you can go out to the main room, Commissioner. Look down the corridors as you go by. You'll see that we're well out of sight. Weems—he's the extra man of the squad—is at a table just past the archway."

Commissioner Weston waited the required period. He glanced at Tony Loretti, and the man smiled confidently. Weston left the office, and closed the door behind him. At the crossing of the passages, he looked first to the right; then to the left.

The side corridors were gloomy. No one was in sight. The detectives must be hiding at the ends, beyond the dressing rooms. Weston smiled in satisfaction. He went through the archway.

A screen hid the main room of the nightclub. Weston sidled past the edge and looked about for Weems. He saw the detective at a nearby table. The man was watching the screen that concealed the archway.

The commissioner strolled past the table and paused to speak in a low tone.

"Keep watching, Weems," he ordered. "I'm going to take a table of my own, where I can watch, too. If there's any trouble, jump past the screen."

Weems nodded.

Looking for a vacant table, Weston found himself in a quandary. He felt that more men should have come; but it would be unwise to summon them now. Weems was the only sleuth covering that archway. Weston realized that he, the police commissioner, might have to do service if trouble occurred.

The thought made Weston smile; nevertheless, he was still a trifle worried. Hembroke and the other detectives were posted. It was too late to make new arrangements. Ralph Weston glanced around, and in that moment observed a tall man entering through a side entrance of the Club Janeiro.

INSTANTLY, Weston recognized the newcomer. That hawklike countenance, stern and impassive; those keen eyes, and thin, determined lips! Here was a man whom Weston had met before; a unique character among the wealthy residents of Manhattan.

Lamont Cranston, millionaire adventurer, globe-trotter, whose travels had carried him to the wilds of Tibet; a man to whom big-game hunting in the African jungle was a mere pastime!

The headwaiter of the Club Janeiro was not far from where Weston stood. The commissioner moved over and spoke to him.

"Do you see the man who has just entered?" questioned Weston. "His name is Lamont Cranston. Go quickly. Bring him to my table."

"Yes, sir," returned the headwaiter.

Weston took a seat at a vacant table and waited. A few minutes later, he saw Cranston approaching. The millionaire betrayed no expression of surprise. He merely came to Weston's table, drew back a chair, and sat down, as though he had been expected.

"Good evening, Cranston," said the commissioner.

"Good evening," responded the calm-faced millionaire.

Cranston was immaculate in evening clothes. He picked up a menu, gave an order to a waiter, and looked quizzically at Weston.

The police commissioner smiled and picked up a card himself. He gave an order, also. He looked around, saw that no one was close by, and spoke in an admiring tone.

"You're a cool one, Cranston," declared the commissioner. "How did you know that I didn't want you to show a lot of enthusiasm over meeting me here?"

"I seldom express enthusiasm," responded Cranston quietly. "Moreover, I knew that the police commissioner would not care to appear conspicuous at the Club Janeiro. What has brought you here, Weston?"

"Cranston," returned the commissioner, in a low whisper, "we are looking for a murderer tonight. A man called Socks Mallory. He is scheduled to make an attempt upon Tony Loretti, the big shot of the nightclubs."

"Interesting," commented Cranston. "Where is Loretti at present?"

"In his office," answered Weston, "past that screen. I have four men posted in side corridors. That man four tables away from us is another detective. He and I are watching this end. There may be trouble. I could use another man."

"Meaning—"

"Yourself."

A faint smile appeared upon Cranston's lips. The millionaire bowed his head in acknowledgment of the compliment.

"I have two automatics with me," whispered the commissioner. "If you care to assist, one is ready for you. Under the table—"

"Pass it," said Cranston calmly.

The automatic changed hands. Commissioner Weston sat back in his chair with a satisfied smile. The waiter came with the order. Weston and Cranston began to eat, conversing quietly while they watched the screen.

New confidence held the commissioner. He felt that he could rely upon Lamont Cranston. There was something about Cranston's manner that made Ralph Weston realize that he had chosen an intrepid aide.

THERE was cause for the impression. Had Commissioner Ralph Weston known the identity of this person who had agreed to aid him, he would have been amazed beyond recall. Had he known Lamont Cranston's purpose here tonight, he would have been doubly astonished.

This calm-faced personage had come to the Club Janeiro for the same purpose as Commissioner Weston and his band of sleuths. He was here to encounter Socks Mallory. The features of Lamont Cranston were a guise that he had adopted to serve him for the occasion.

Beneath that full-dress coat were two automatics, compared to which Weston's guns were puny weapons. The police commissioner was dining with The Shadow!

Again, the mysterious warrior had been forced to change his plans. Alone, he could have watched Tony Loretti, unseen. But with police on hand, with Commissioner Weston calling upon him for aid, The Shadow found it necessary to bide his time.

In the guise of Lamont Cranston, he waited. He, The Shadow, was the aide of Commissioner Ralph Weston—the police official who believed The Shadow to be a myth!

CHAPTER XI
AGAIN THE BLOT

IN the center office of his suite, Tony Loretti was serene. A quarter of an hour had passed since Police Commissioner Weston had left. The strains of music were coming in muffled tones from beyond the door. The floor show was on.

Strolling into his own private office, Loretti opened a desk drawer and pulled out a revolver. He handled the shining weapon with a smile, then replaced it, but left the drawer open.

Tony Loretti recalled that he was under police protection tonight. Officers of the law might question his possession of a revolver, should they enter unexpectedly.

Commissioner Weston's statement that Socks Mallory was in Manhattan was not a cause of great alarm to Tony Loretti. Some months ago, Mallory had started the nightclub protective racket, beginning with the Club Janeiro as his

headquarters. Loretti had appropriated the idea; his power had driven Mallory out of the game.

Attempting retaliation, Socks had encountered gangsters secretly employed by Loretti. After a short fight, Socks had fled in a taxi. He had killed the driver at the end of the ride; and was now wanted for murder while Tony Loretti dwelt in security.

Loretti had henchmen in the Club Janeiro tonight. He could have summoned them to stay on watch for Socks Mallory. But, since the police commissioner had chosen to interfere, it would be discreet to rely upon the law. Afterward, Socks might still be a menace. He could be dealt with then.

Tony Loretti laughed. He was positive that Socks Mallory would make no attempt tonight. Socks was shrewd enough to spot the presence of the police commissioner and five headquarters detectives.

Nevertheless, Tony Loretti was a rascal who played safe. The revolver in the opened drawer gave him a feeling of complete assurance.

Consulting a large sheet of paper, Tony read over the figures that told of the present week's receipts. Nightclubs were doing well. Those under Loretti's wing were managing best of all.

Tony's cut was a moderate one, considering the power that this racketeer possessed. That was the part of wisdom. It kept the nightclub proprietors from becoming antagonistic. They were getting off cheap.

Engrossed in his study of the figures, Tony Loretti did not hear the creeping sound that came from the central office. When he looked up, in sudden startlement, he acted too late. Loretti's hand stopped on its way to the desk drawer. Just within the door were three men!

HARDENED ruffians they were; and the leader, a few paces in front of the others, was grinning as he covered Loretti with a large revolver. A gasp of recognition came from the big shot's lips.

"Socks Mallory!"

"Glad to see me, eh, Tony?" snarled Socks. "Get up out of that chair! Back to the wall. Come on—move!"

Loretti complied. Socks grumbled orders to his men. With pale face, Loretti was standing across the room, his hands up beside his head, his eyes staring beadily as Socks Mallory advanced.

"Thought I couldn't get you, eh?" grinned Socks. "Well, I'm here. I've got you. Let's see you take it!"

Fiendishly, Socks pressed the trigger. The revolver boomed quick, successive shots.

With the first discharge, Tony Loretti tumbled. Socks Mallory, driving the muzzle downward after each recoil, pumped lead into the big shot's body.

Six bullets—each delivered with equal venom. They were not directed with careful aim. Socks Mallory knew well enough that Tony Loretti would not survive this cannonade. As the final report echoed through the little office, Socks Mallory's men switched out the lights.

Total darkness persisted through the suite, until one man opened the door that led to the corridor, and fired wild shots like a paean of triumph. This was by Socks Mallory's design. He wanted the world to know that he had given Tony Loretti the works.

Music ended in the nightclub. Screams of women sounded from the big dining room. Then came shouts in the darkened corridors. Answering gun shots, delivered by detectives, came in response to the challenge which Socks Mallory had ordered.

Beyond the screen, Police Commissioner Weston had heard the first echoes of the cannonade. The official leaped to his feet and watched as he drew his automatic.

Weems, at the other table, also pulled a revolver and stood in readiness. Lamont Cranston, however, was the one who acted with most promptitude.

Rising with easy swiftness, the millionaire swept toward the screen and hovered there; holding the gun which Weston had given him. His keen eyes peered down the corridor, where the new series of shots were now in progress. With a motion of his hand, Cranston beckoned the police commissioner forward. With Weems at his heels, Weston hurried to the spot.

Detectives were in the corridor. The door of the suite was open; Merton Hembroke was standing in the central office. The detective had turned on the light. Looking back, he spied Weston and called to the commissioner.

"It started in here!" was Hembroke's cry. "They must have gotten Loretti! Come on!"

Detectives flocked to Hembroke's aid. Commissioner Weston, with Lamont Cranston beside him, entered the central office to find that the detectives had spread into the other rooms of the suite. Another call came from Loretti's office. Weston headed in that direction.

WITH Cranston still beside him, Weston found Hembroke leaning over the prone body of Tony Loretti. The big shot was still alive. His lips were moving.

"Who got you?" demanded Hembroke.

"Socks—Socks Mallory," came Loretti's gasping words, "He—he and—some others. They—they—"

Choking, his dark face twisted, the big shot coughed out his life. His body shook with a final tremor.

Tony Loretti was dead.

"There's nobody in here," came a voice at the door. It was Weems. "Where did they go, Hembroke?"

"Search everywhere!" ordered Weston. "The corridors—the dressing rooms. Spread, men!"

Detectives hurried to do the commissioner's bidding. Weston snatched up the telephone from Loretti's desk. He put in a call for headquarters. Within two minutes, he was talking to Inspector Klein.

"A squad of men up to the Club Janeiro," ordered Weston. "Just a moment, Klein—what resulted in the subway? The search there... Yes... No results, eh? Well, the answer is here... Yes, here at the Club Janeiro... Socks Mallory came here after his getaway... He's murdered Tony Loretti... Get the men up here! I have Hembroke in charge!"

Hembroke had left the death room during the commissioner's call to Klein. The detective returned to discover Weston still beside the telephone.

Loretti's body lay unwatched upon the floor. Lamont Cranston, calmly smoking a cigarette, was standing in a corner of the office.

"It beats me, Commissioner," admitted Hembroke. "Socks and whoever was with him have made a clean getaway. I thought we had them sure!"

"What happened in the corridors?" inquired Weston.

"We were posted at the ends," explained Hembroke. "Two of us one way; two the other, so we could keep tabs on the outside. We heard the shots. We headed down together; had everything covered right.

"I was the first one on the job; I saw someone at the point where the corridors cross. I fired; but I had to be careful not to hit my men coming from the other direction."

Commissioner Weston nodded.

"I figured," continued Hembroke, "that the killers were heading out into the nightclub. I ordered the others to go that way, while I came in here. Then I saw you and Weems—and this gentleman who was with you."

"We came in from the nightclub," explained Weston. "No one got away in that direction."

"It beats me," repeated Hembroke. "Socks Mallory got out of these offices. We covered every way out. He may have headed for the nightclub; then doubled back and taken one of the side passages. That's the only explanation."

"But how did he get in?" questioned the commissioner. "We searched this place; you looked through the dressing rooms before you posted your men."

"I know it," admitted Hembroke.

"At the same time," went on Weston, "this is no more startling than the subway mystery. Mallory was trapped there this evening; yet he came here and killed Loretti!"

SILENCE followed. Cranston puffed his cigarette while Weston and Hembroke stood in puzzlement. The other detectives were still searching outside and trying to restore order in the nightclub. This room where death had struck was like an oasis in a desert of confusion.

Weems came in to announce that the entertainers wanted to get back to the dressing rooms. Senorita Pasquales was anxious to learn what had happened, Weems said.

"Let them into the dressing rooms," ordered Weston. "You take charge outside, Hembroke. Keep the senorita out for a while. Wait for Klein and his men; they will be here any minute now."

Hembroke and Weems departed. Commissioner Weston turned to Lamont Cranston.

"This is amazing!" exclaimed Weston.

In reply, Cranston passed the extra automatic to the commissioner.

"I shall not require this any longer," remarked the millionaire.

"An amazing mystery," repeated Weston, as he took the automatic from Cranston's hand. "Socks Mallory wanted revenge. He had a grudge against Tony Loretti. I wonder, though, if there could be a further motive—"

"Perhaps," interposed Cranston, "it would be wise to examine that sheet of paper which is lying beneath your left foot. You brushed it from the table when you seized the telephone."

Commissioner Weston looked in the direction indicated. He picked up what appeared to be a blank piece of paper. When he turned it over, he saw that it was a page of figured tabulations. But the cash receipts of Tony Loretti's racketeering were not the cause of the startled cry which came from Weston.

In the center of the sheet, the commissioner saw an inky, crimson blotch. It was the signature of new crime plotted by a supercrook.

"The Red Blot!"

Weston uttered the name with a gasp. The hand of the hidden fiend was in back of this new murder.

Grimly, the commissioner recalled Spider Carew's words across the wire. Socks Mallory was working for The Red Blot! Here was the proof of the dead informant's statement!

"Cranston," declared Weston solemnly, as he turned the paper so the millionaire could see it, "I

advise you to stick to big-game hunting. Things like this are severe blows to those connected with the law. This is the sign of a master crook, an unknown criminal who has been called The Red Blot.

"We must investigate this. It will mean long, hopeless work. You have probably read in the newspapers how The Red Blot has been working. He has reached his zenith, tonight."

"Interesting," was Cranston's quiet comment. "Of course, Weston, I would not dispute with one who knows crime as well as you. But if you asked for my opinion—"

"It would be?"

"—that any crook clever enough to have perpetrated tonight's crime is merely at the beginning of his schemes. Keep that paper, Weston. See if I am right."

Lamont Cranston extended his hand as a friendly token of departure. During that final grasp, he repeated his cold opinion.

"The Red Blot," remarked the millionaire, "will strike again—soon—and his next stroke will he more formidable than this or any that has preceded tonight's murder!"

COMMISSIONER WESTON found himself nodding as Cranston departed. There was a firm conviction in the quiet tone to which Weston had listened. The words of Lamont Cranston awoke vague dread in the commissioner's mind.

When Inspector Timothy Klein strode into the room a few minutes later, he found Commissioner Ralph Weston still holding the ledger sheet which bore the mark of The Red Blot.

"Inspector," ordered Weston, "post men here, and keep them on duty. Quiz every waiter; everyone who might know anything. That includes the orchestra and the entertainers."

"Socks Mallory is the murderer—so Loretti said when he was dying—but The Red Blot is in back of this crime!"

Outside the Club Janeiro, Lamont Cranston, in evening clothes, was strolling along the side street. In leisurely fashion, the millionaire flicked his cigarette over the curb; then stopped at a waiting taxicab. The driver grinned and opened the door.

"Keep the ten dollars that I gave you," remarked Cranston quietly. "It will cover the ride uptown and the time that you have been waiting."

"But there's more than five dollars comin' back to you—" The cab driver, hesitating, realized that mention of the money might cause him to lose the handsome tip.

"Never mind the change," smiled Cranston. "Drive me to Forty-ninth and Broadway; then turn west, and continue to Ninth Avenue. The ten-spot will be yours."

The driver nodded. Cranston entered the cab.

While the vehicle rolled down Broadway, the passenger undertook a surprising transformation. Lifting the rear seat of the cab, he drew out black folds of cloth and the crushed shape of a slouch hat. The cloth became a cloak as it slipped over Cranston's shoulders. The hat, implanted upon the millionaire's head, completely concealed the rider's features.

Black gloves completed thc mctamorphosis. Lamont Cranston had become The Shadow. The tall form rested in darkness; the cab appeared to be empty. It was empty, shortly after the driver swerved west on Forty-ninth Street.

As the cab slowed for traffic, the door on the right opened softly. A fleeting figure moved through darkness and dropped free of the cab as an invisible hand closed the door.

A coupe was parked on the side street. With three long strides, The Shadow gained it unseen; a few moments later, he was behind the wheel of the automobile.

WHEN the cab driver stopped at Ninth Avenue and Forty-ninth Street, he was amazed to discover that his passenger was gone. Meanwhile, a trim coupe was wending its way southward down Eighth Avenue.

A whispered laugh came from the unseen lips of the personage who drove that car. An echo of the past, The Shadow's mirth carried a strange foreboding. It might have been a warning for those who dealt in crime.

The Shadow knew what Commissioner Weston did not know; that the crimes of The Red Blot must be dependent upon some plan of action that was unknown in the annals of New York police experience.

There was purpose behind each crime; this mysterious killing of Tony Loretti was more than a mere feud. How was Socks Mallory evading the police so successfully? Where was Moocher Gleetz? The Shadow wanted the answers to these questions.

Working in darkness, The Shadow had ignored The Red Blot in order to search for Spider Carew's hiding place. He had found that spot too late. Once again, The Shadow would take up the trail of one who would lead him to the source.

Socks Mallory! He was The Shadow's quarry now. His trail had ended at the Club Janeiro; from that spot, The Shadow would take it up once the police surveillance had lifted.

New crimes might occur in the meantime, but The Shadow would not abandon this definite quest.

Again The Red Blot! That supercrook had become a colossus of the underworld. His identi-

ty was unknown, even to The Shadow; but his hand could be detected.

The Shadow, past master in the war against crime, was ready to deliver a counterthrust!

CHAPTER XII
THE RED BLOT SPREADS

THE menace of The Red Blot had become a hideous reality. The next day's newspapers were filled with accounts of the slaying in the subway and the murder of Tony Loretti.

The two crimes had been linked; and the appearance of The Red Blot's crimson symbol at the Club Janeiro was sufficient proof that the master crook had ordained the death of Spider Carew. For in each instance the police knew the identity of the killer—Socks Mallory.

Public opinion seemed to grasp the very thought that Lamont Cranston had expressed to Police Commissioner Ralph Weston. The crimes of The Red Blot had merely passed the preliminary stage. Some great outrage was due to occur soon.

The methods of The Red Blot were modern. Established as the most insidious criminal that New York had ever known, he had spread a pall of terror throughout Manhattan. His crimes had been swift and varied; none knew where he might strike next.

Speculation was rife. Men of important affairs felt unsafe. Some great crime was brewing, and the versatility of The Red Blot was a pressing threat. Wherever people discussed current events, mention of The Red Blot was made.

"Read about de Red Blot! Tony Loretti moidered by de Red Blot! Police still hunting for de killer!"

A newsboy's cry came to the ears of two men who were riding up Broadway in a taxicab. One of the hearers—an elderly, gray-haired gentleman, turned to his young companion and asked a question:

"What is The Red Blot, Crozer? That is the second newsboy who has been shouting about it."

"The Red Blot is a criminal, sir," responded Crozer. "The New York newspapers have been filled with accounts of his activities. I was reading the latest news while we were coming in on the Limited this afternoon."

"I have not looked at today's newspapers," remarked the elderly gentleman. "But I do not recall any mention of The Red Blot in the Chicago journals that I read yesterday."

"That is readily explainable, Mr. Woodstock," rejoined the young man. "There were two bold murders committed last night by a man believed to be in The Red Blot's service. It is sensational news today, sir."

The elderly man nodded; then his thoughts drifted to more important matters. Yet he could not help but draw a contrast between what the newspapers accepted as news, and the factors which they ignored.

While an unknown criminal—The Red Blot—was receiving tremendous headlines, Selfridge Woodstock, leading financier of the Middle West, had arrived unannounced in Manhattan, accompanied by his secretary, to arrange a series of building operations that would involve one hundred million dollars.

Selfridge Woodstock smiled. Long after The Red Blot had been forgotten, the people of Manhattan would stare in admiration at the tremendous structures created through the financial genius of this builder from the Middle West.

IT was evening on Broadway. Early lights were blazing at Times Square when the taxicab turned right and rolled toward a massive building which occupied an entire block. Crozer, the secretary, spoke to his employer.

"This is the Hotel Gigantic, Mr. Woodstock," remarked the young man. "It is the latest building erected by the Amalgamated Builders."

"An excellent place to hold our meeting," smiled Woodstock, as he alighted from the cab.

Within the gorgeous lobby of the Gigantic, Crozer made an inquiry at the desk; then announced to Woodstock that the meeting was being held on the twenty-fourth floor. The two men entered an elevator and rode swiftly upward.

On the twenty-fourth floor, they turned along a corridor and followed it until Crozer stopped at a door near the end. A knock; the door opened; and the visitors walked in to receive a welcome.

A tall, gray-haired man in a gray suit gave Selfridge Woodstock a friendly smile and handclasp. Woodstock had met this chap before. Dobson Pringle, the virile president of the Amalgamated Builders' Association. Pringle introduced Woodstock to a group of directors.

There was only one who impressed the Chicago man. That was Felix Cushman, chairman of the directors. Cushman was a stocky, black-haired man with quick eyes and a protruding lower lip.

There was a large table in the center of the room. Pringle and Cushman together ushered Selfridge Woodstock to the principal chair, and the rest of the group seated themselves.

Pringle, glancing about, noted a quiet, white-haired man who had been standing at the side of the room. He beckoned and introduced this individual to Woodstock.

"Mr. Carlton Carmody," announced Pringle.

"Our chief architect. A very capable man, Mr. Woodstock. Very capable."

"I am pleased to meet you, Mr. Carmody," said Woodstock, in a friendly tone. "Any man responsible for the plans of so excellent a building as this great hotel is indeed worthy of commendation."

"I did not design the Hotel Gigantic," remarked Carmody, with a smile. "It was the work of Hubert Craft."

"Indeed, yes!" exclaimed Woodstock, turning to Pringle. "I remember now. A wonderful architect, Craft. Interesting chap, too, though eccentric. I understood he died a few months ago."

"He did," informed Pringle. "Overturned in a pleasure boat on Long Island Sound. Poor old Craft—he was our chief architect for more than seven years. Long experience before that. He was connected with the city for many years."

Felix Cushman was tapping lightly on the table. His dark eyes were directed toward Pringle. The president of the association nodded.

"This is a directors' meeting," declared Cushman bluntly. "Our time is very valuable tonight. You will excuse me if I seem brusque, Mr. Woodstock. I believe in efficiency. You have our prospectus there, Pringle? Will you read it, please?"

Dobson Pringle brought out a large document from his portfolio. He began to read aloud. Selfridge Woodstock listened thoughtfully, his chin resting in his hand. Felix Cushman, firm in gaze, watched the old financier intently.

THE document concerned the reorganization of the Amalgamated Builders' Association, dependent entirely upon the cooperation of interests controlled by Selfridge Woodstock of Chicago. With the support of the Western financier it would be possible to institute a building campaign on a vaster scale than any previously attempted.

When Pringle had finished his reading, Selfridge Woodstock turned to his secretary. He asked for notes which Crozer had been making. Referring to these, Woodstock put forward questions.

It was Felix Cushman who gave answer. One by one, the chairman of directors defined the clauses, while Crozer made new notations. When this discussion had been completed, Selfridge Woodstock eyed the black-haired man squarely and put an important question.

"What," he asked, "are the available funds of the Amalgamated Builders' Association?"

"The list," said Cushman to Pringle. The president produced it. Woodstock studied the figures.

"Fifty million dollars," declared Woodstock. "These are ready funds—at least negotiable securities which can be promptly liquidated?"

"Positively," announced Cushman.

MONEY—THE GOAL
SELFRIDGE WOODSTOCK and DOBSON PRINGLE, associates in Amalgamated Builders, aim of The Red Blot in his bold stroke to grasp a fortune in a kidnaping plot which is to serve as a basis for further crime. Big business meets a master crook—what is the result?

"That is all I care to know, gentlemen," decided Woodstock. "Crozer, how much time do we have to catch the Bar Harbor Express?"

"Thirty minutes, sir."

Then Selfridge Woodstock arose and smiled. He noted the anxious look on the faces watching him. His smile broadened.

"I am going to my Maine lodge tonight, gentlemen," he said. "This appointment was planned as a little stopover on the way.

"Perhaps you may be surprised to know that I do business in such short time; but that happens to be the way of my choice. Your proposition suits me. I shall be glad to invest the fifty million dollars which you require to proceed with the new enterprise."

A gasp passed around the group.

These men had expected a refusal from the financier, so quickly had his decision been made. Instead, Selfridge Woodstock had accepted their terms without question!

Words of appreciation were coming from all sides. Selfridge Woodstock, donning coat and hat with Crozer's aid, was still smiling at the sensation which he had created. He shook hands around the group; then added a few words.

"My word is my bond, gentlemen," declared Woodstock. "I shall be in Maine one week; then to Chicago by way of Canada. Send the papers to my office there; send your representative. I shall go through with the deal exactly as you have proposed it."

Nodding his good-bye, Selfridge Woodstock left the room, accompanied by Crozer. The financier's last glimpse was one of beaming faces, among which those of Dobson Pringle and Felix Cushman predominated.

SELFRIDGE WOODSTOCK chuckled as he walked along the silent corridor with his secretary. When they reached the elevators, Crozer pushed the button, and smiled at his employer's good humor. Selfridge Woodstock loved the element of surprise, and he utilized it even in the most important transactions.

"They didn't know," said the financier, "that I was sold on their proposition before I came here.

Fifty million dollars! No wonder it took their breath, Crozer. They have that amount themselves, but it represents the investment of several moneyed men."

A man had stepped from another corridor while Selfridge Woodstock was speaking. His hat was pulled low over his features. His hands were in his pockets.

The metal door of the elevator shaft slid open. Woodstock and Crozer boarded the car; the stranger followed them. The door slid shut. The stranger brought his hand from his coat pocket. Something glimmered as he delivered a ferocious blow to the back of the operator's head.

As the attendant fell, the ruffian turned and covered Woodstock and Crozer with the weapon he had used. It was a large revolver.

Instinctively, the financier and his secretary raised their hands. They saw a fierce, unshaven face confronting them—features which marked this man as the daring criminal whom the New York police now sought—Socks Mallory, right arm of The Red Blot.

With his left hand, Socks managed the elevator control. The car shot down the shaft, floor after floor. The swift descent decreased in speed. Socks Mallory brought the car to a stop and opened the door.

Woodstock and his secretary found themselves staring into the muzzles of three more revolvers. They realized, from the darkness outside the car, that they were at the very bottom of the shaft.

"Get out," growled Socks Mallory, thrusting his gun forward. "Make it fast!"

The two men walked from the car, stepping down to a cement floor. A small opening yawned ahead of them. With mobsters jostling them with guns, the prisoners were thrust into a narrow, descending passageway.

They could hear Socks Mallory talking to another man behind them. The gang leader was giving instructions. There was a grunted response; a few seconds later, the elevator door shut.

Flashlights glimmered, to show a passageway through solid rock.

With Socks Mallory prodding from in back, the prisoners were hurried forward.

The Red Blot had spread tonight. The minions of that mighty crook had spirited away the richest financier of the Middle West, from the midst of the Hotel Gigantic!

CHAPTER XIII
THE ULTIMATUM

THE departure of Selfridge Woodstock and his secretary had left the directors of the Amalgamated Builders' Association in high fettle. Felix Cushman, the sharp-visaged chairman of the board, was prompt to state the importance of what had occurred.

"Gentlemen," he said, "this means absolute success to our projects. By acquiring the cooperation of Selfridge Woodstock, by gaining his consent to duplicate the amount of our resources, we have assured ourselves against unexpected competition. Our president, Mr. Pringle, can tell you that."

Pringle was nodding solemnly.

"Yes," he asserted, "there is every reason to believe that Woodstock intended to put his money into building operations, here in New York. I have dealt with Woodstock before; I knew him to be a man of quick and definite decisions. We have gained Woodstock's support; moreover, we will not lose him, now that he has decided to go with us."

"We have made millions here tonight," added Cushman. "Pringle says that he will not lose Woodstock. I tell you that we cannot afford to lose him. We have large resources, but they would not be large enough to offset any combination that might be formed to compete with us. Woodstock, however, has settled everything in our favor.

"I tell you again, gentlemen, those few minutes that he was here were worth millions to all of you who have large holdings in Amalgamated Builders!"

The directors, men of many millions, responded warmly to these statements. Cushman, the wealthiest of all, came in for strong approval. Pringle, too, was given his share of commendation. Although a comparatively small holder of Amalgamated securities, Pringle's position as president made him important.

Pringle had for years been connected with New York building promoters. He had, in a way, been inherited by Amalgamated Builders when a smaller concern had been absorbed by the large association.

Next to Pringle, Amalgamated had possessed Hubert Craft, the celebrated architect who had designed the most modern of the buildings which Amalgamated had promoted.

Pringle, now, made reference to the dead architect, in a thoughtful tone.

"This would have been glorious for Craft," remarked the president. "Gentlemen, our new projects will include some of the finest structures that will appear upon Manhattan's skyline!"

"We can count on Carmody," mentioned one of the directors.

This was the first reference to the architect who now served as successor to Hubert Craft. Still standing by the wall, Carmody acknowledged the compliment with a short bow.

A retiring, noncommittal sort of man, Carmody had plodded on to his present position of importance. Nevertheless, his ability in building design had gained him merited recognition.

A TELEPHONE began to ring. Noting that the directors were again engaged in conversation, Carmody answered it. Talk ceased while the others listened to the architect's words.

"Mr. Pringle?" queried Carmody. "He's here... Yes... I understand... Wait a moment—you say it has been waiting for him, and should be delivered now... At the desk... One moment, please..."

Carmody covered the mouthpiece and turned to the men at the large table.

"An odd message for you, Mr. Pringle," the architect announced. "Someone says that he left a message for you at the desk, in the lobby; but it was not to be delivered until you call for it."

"Who is on the wire?" questioned Pringle.

"I don't know," returned Carmody. "A voice that I never heard before. Insisting that you get the message at the desk."

Pringle arose and came over to the telephone. He took the instrument from Carmody, and began to speak. He heard a voice cut off at the other end.

"This is Mr. Pringle," the president stated. "Who are you?"

No reply.

Pringle looked puzzled. He jiggled the hook. The hotel operator responded. Pringle began to complain that his call had been cut off; then changed to tell the operator to give him the desk.

"Hello," he said. "This is Dobson Pringle. You have a message there for me?... Very good... I was to call for it, eh?... Send it up to the twenty-fourth floor... Yes, where the Amalgamated Builders' Association is holding its directors' meeting."

PRINGLE put down the telephone and went back to the table. He resumed his conversation with the directors. Between three and four minutes later, there was a knock at the door. Carmody answered it, and received a square envelope. He tipped the attendant, dismissed him, and brought the message to Pringle.

The building president uttered an ejaculation of surprise, as he showed the envelope to Felix Cushman. Although it bore the name of Dobson Pringle on the wrapper, it was also

**They saw a fierce, unshaven face confronting them . . .
Socks Mallory, right arm of The Red Blot!**

marked in the corner, with underscored words:

For the Directors.

Both Pringle's name and this notation were inscribed in red ink. The president opened the envelope and spread a sheet of paper on the table. He stared at red-inked lines.

With Felix Cushman looking over his shoulder, Pringle slowly read these words, in an astounded voice:

To Dobson Pringle and those concerned with the management of the Amalgamated Builders' Association:

You have just completed a fifty-million-dollar agreement with Selfridge Woodstock of Chicago. You hold the agreement; but I hold Woodstock.

He will not be released until you have made the arrangements which I require. My agent will call at your conference room in the Amalgamated Building tomorrow night at half past nine.

At that time, you will deliver to him the sum

of five million dollars, in cash or negotiable securities of which no record has been kept. In return for this payment, Selfridge Woodstock will be released.

The presence of police officials in the conference room, or any attempt to violate the terms provided above, will mean an immediate ending of negotiations.

Dobson Pringle stared aghast as he completed the reading of the message. The others were on their feet, asking excited questions.

"What is the signature?" came one query.

Neither Dobson Pringle nor Felix Cushman answered. As though in reply, Pringle let the paper flutter from his fingers. It became a target for anxious eyes as it rested upon the table. Astonished gasps followed.

Beneath the red-inked lines was no signature; yet the paper contained a sign of identity that every witness recognized. Splattered there was the crimson blotch of which all had heard—the sign of The Red Blot!

MEN looked at one another in bewilderment. This amazing message, coming so soon after the departure of Selfridge Woodstock, was a veritable bombshell. It was Dobson Pringle, the voluble, gray-haired president of the association, who first broke the tension with a statement that expressed the feeling of most of the men.

"This must be a hoax!" he asserted, with a weak attempt at a belittling laugh. "Selfridge Woodstock was here with us only a few minutes ago—"

"Hoax or no hoax," interjected Felix Cushman sternly, "it is both a threat and a demand. It may mean danger for Woodstock. He should be informed about this at once!"

With mingled anger and apprehension upon his sharp-featured face, Cushman strode to the telephone and called the desk. The others listened to his words.

"Felix Cushman calling," the man said. "Chairman of the Amalgamated Building directors, meeting on the twenty-fourth floor... Yes, this is Mr. Cushman himself... A gentleman has just left our meeting... Yes, going down in the elevator. His name is Selfridge Woodstock, of Chicago... Accompanied by his secretary. He may be in the lobby now... Tell him he must return at once. Page him immediately!"

Still maintaining his anxious expression, Felix Cushman faced the other men while he stood with the telephone in his grasp. Long minutes moved by; there was no further response across the wire. It was obvious that the paging of Selfridge Woodstock was bringing no result—the man was gone!

The feeling of uneasiness was becoming an expression of alarm. Worried looks passed among the assembled group. These men realized that some unseen enemy might be at work; that on the eve of success in their fifty-million-dollar negotiation, they faced utter ruin of all their plans.

Instinctively, eyes were lowered toward the table. There, with its insidious inscription, lay the message that had caused this consternation.

A hoax?

None believed it now. With the increased tension of the dragging minutes, every man realized that the crimson-penned note was an ultimatum from The Red Blot!

CHAPTER XIV
THE CRIME UNSOLVED

"PAGING Mr. Selfridge Woodstock!"

The bellboy's repeated cry was passing through the huge lobby of the Hotel Gigantic. It was echoed, now, by other callers; for the urgency of Cushman's request had caused the clerk to use every possible effort in finding the Chicago financier.

The paging was unnoticed by a short, solemn-looking man who was standing in a corner of the lobby. Although it was this individual's duty to watch for unusual events in the hotel lobby, he saw nothing out of the way in a bellboy's call. The solemn-looking man was Belville, senior house detective of the Hotel Gigantic.

"Hello, Belville."

This quiet greeting was more important to the house detective than the loud paging of Selfridge Woodstock. Turning, Belville recognized the keen, firm-chiseled countenance of Detective Merton Hembroke.

"Hello, Hembroke," returned Belville. "How come you're here tonight?"

"Still looking for Socks Mallory," confided Hembroke.

"The killer that's working for The Red Blot?" queried Belville, in an awed tone.

"That's the guy," answered Hembroke. "I've got a hunch, Belville, that he's living high. Joe Cardona's after him, too; but he's got stools working in the East Side. That's not my idea. I figure that Socks Mallory is playing ritzy."

Belville nodded. He held a great respect for Merton Hembroke, coming ace of the New York City detective force.

"This isn't the first swanky hotel lobby I've been in tonight," added Hembroke. "You can believe it or not, Belville; I'm going to cross Socks Mallory's path one of these nights."

Belville grinned approvingly.

"Paging Mr. Selfridge Woodstock—Mr. Selfridge Woodstock—"

Hembroke noted the cry and turned to Belville with a questioning air.

"What's going on?" he asked. "They were paging that fellow Woodstock when I came into the lobby. Rather unusual—all this racket—isn't it?"

As if in answer, a bellboy approached and spoke to the house detective. Belville was wanted at the desk. Hembroke followed as the houseman went in that direction.

"Something's happened," the clerk told Belville. "We just got a call from the twenty-fourth floor to get hold of a man named Selfridge Woodstock. Now there's a report that Elevator No. 9 is stopped on the eighth—"

Belville nodded and started toward the elevators. Hembroke kept with him. Another house detective joined them in an empty elevator. Belville ordered the operator to make for the eighth floor in a hurry.

WHEN the trio stepped from the car, they found four hotel guests clustered in front of the open door of Elevator No. 9. They were holding the limp form of a uniformed operator.

"What's happened?" demanded Belville.

"Saw the boy lying here," responded one of the guests. "Knocked out. Look at him."

"Take care of this, Belville," ordered Hembroke, "I'm going up to the twenty-fourth to find out about this man Woodstock. Get in touch with me right away."

The detective entered the waiting elevator and was whisked upward. One minute later, he strode into the room where the directors of the Amalgamated Builders' Association were still gathered. He spied Felix Cushman at the telephone.

"You're calling about a man named Woodstock?" queried Hembroke.

"Yes," returned Cushman anxiously. "Have you traced him?"

"No. There was trouble on an elevator. I'm Detective Hembroke from headquarters. What's the trouble?"

Dobson Pringle, stepping forward, handed The Red Blot's note to Hembroke.

The detective's eyebrows furrowed. "The Red Blot!" he exclaimed. "How long ago did Selfridge Woodstock leave here?"

"Not much over ten minutes," informed Pringle.

"Where was he going?" quizzed Hembroke.

"To the Grand Central Station," declared Pringle. "To take the Bar Harbor Express."

Hembroke seized the telephone. He jiggled the hook, gained the operator's attention, and put in a call for detective headquarters.

"Abduction suspected at Hotel Gigantic," said Hembroke tersely. "Selfridge Woodstock, of Chicago, on way to Grand Central to get the Bar Harbor Express. Cover there at once..."

He paused to gain a quick description of Woodstock from Cushman; also to learn that the financier was accompanied by his secretary.

"... Elderly man," added Hembroke, over the telephone. "Gray hair... Accompanied by young man... Secretary... Send squad to Gigantic Hotel... Elevator operator found unconscious."

HEMBROKE'S call was the beginning of a swift investigation. One hour later, the directors of the Amalgamated Builders' Association still sat in session; but a new man was at their head. Police Commissioner Ralph Weston had taken this room as his temporary headquarters.

Three other representatives of the law were present. Inspector Timothy Klein, full-faced and solemn, was seated beside the commissioner. Detective Merton Hembroke, alert as ever, was standing near the table. A new figure had appeared: that of a stocky, swarthy man whose visage was firm set and determined.

This was Detective Joe Cardona, whose reputation as a go-getter was fading in favor of Merton Hembroke.

The door of the room was closed. Police Commissioner Weston spoke freely as he fingered the red-inked message which had come as an ultimatum from The Red Blot.

"There is no doubt about it, gentlemen," asserted Weston frankly. "Selfridge Woodstock has been abducted by The Red Blot. The elevator operator has given us full proof of that. He was struck down when Woodstock and his secretary entered the car on the twenty-fourth floor. He was unconscious when he was removed from the stopped car at the eighth.

"We have searched every floor of the hotel, from basement to roof garden. The search is still on, but we have gained no trace of Selfridge Woodstock. In spite of Detective Hembroke's fortunate presence in this very hotel, and the promptness with which this case was handled, we are forced to admit that The Red Blot has baffled us.

"This, gentlemen, is a terrible climax to a series of bold crimes. Nevertheless, its very magnitude has given us an opportunity to treat with the supercriminal who is known as The Red Blot. The abduction of Selfridge Woodstock is but his first step. According to this message, he plans another—the collecting of five million dollars from your association."

The commissioner paused to read over the terms of the ultimatum. Then, in a serious tone, he set forth a definite proposition.

"Gentlemen," he said, "The Red Blot demands that you hold a meeting in your conference room tomorrow evening at nine thirty, there to deliver the required sum to his agent. That meeting is as important to the law as it is to you. Before I decide upon my action, let me ask what you would intend to do about it."

Weston looked from one director to another. He singled out Felix Cushman and Dobson Pringle as the ones who would naturally act as spokesmen. Cushman was the first to respond.

"Five million dollars is a large sum, Commissioner," he said. "Nevertheless, it is but ten percent of the amount which Selfridge Woodstock intends to supply to us."

"With Woodstock, we gain fifty million; without him, we lose that amount. Somehow, The Red Blot knows our situation. If we could guarantee Selfridge Woodstock's release, I would say that the accomplishment would be worth the payment of five millions."

Audible gasps followed Cushman's statement; nevertheless, the directors were forced to give their nods of approval.

"Cushman is right," declared Dobson Pringle. "He is right, so far as monetary consideration is concerned. But how are we to assure ourselves that this is not a hoax; that Woodstock will actually be released?"

COMMISSIONER WESTON drummed the table thoughtfully. At last, he spoke in a decided tone.

"This case," he announced, "involves the most amazing method of demanding ransom that I have ever known. Usually, people are told to put money in some outlandish spot. But here is a criminal who announces his intention of sending his representative to a scheduled business meeting.

"Obviously, The Red Blot's agent will walk into a trap. I would suggest that you assemble to meet him, as required. We, the police, can take care of the rest."

"An excellent suggestion," observed Dobson Pringle. "You mean that you will have men stationed close by."

"Exactly," affirmed Weston. "We shall make no attempt to scare away The Red Blot's agent. Your association will fulfill the terms required."

"Regarding the money?" questioned Pringle.

"Hardly," smiled Weston.

"One moment," objected Felix Cushman. "Please read that last paragraph, Commissioner. Remember what I have said; that we must assure

the release of Selfridge Woodstock. If we assemble without the money, we will not be fulfilling the required terms. That—according to The Red Blot's statement—will mean the end of negotiations."

"You are prepared to have five million dollars?" questioned Weston, in astonishment. "You would place that sum in jeopardy—"

"I would not care to do so," interposed Cushman. "Nevertheless, I adhere to my original statement. The release of Selfridge Woodstock would be worth that sum to our association."

"Gentlemen"—Cushman spoke to the directors—"we all know that Selfridge Woodstock is a man of immense wealth. His release would not only assure the success of our enterprises; it would also gain us the heartfelt thanks of the man himself. To Selfridge Woodstock, five million dollars is not an immense sum."

"At the same time"—Cushman was back to Weston—"it would be folly to deliberately sacrifice five million dollars by placing it into the hands of The Red Blot."

The situation seemed to be reaching the stage of a dilemma. Commissioner Weston tried to offer new assurance.

"Your meeting tomorrow night," he declared, "will be well protected. I have already advised that you meet The Red Blot's agent. I do not approve of the delivery of ransom money. Still, I would like to have these negotiations bring results—not only the arrest of The Red Blot's agent, but the capture of the criminal himself. If he should appear—the agent, I mean—and you could treat with him—"

"He might demand to see the money," interposed Cushman.

"Exactly," decided Weston. "Therein lies the difficulty. On the contrary, if you could demand to see Selfridge Woodstock—"

"Why not?" exclaimed Dobson Pringle, leaping ahead of the commissioner's suggestion. "Let us have the money for the agent. Cash—or securities—to the extent of five million. Perhaps the agent will be prepared to produce Selfridge Woodstock then. At least, we could sound him out."

"The money will be in jeopardy!" warned Weston.

"What about your police?" questioned Cushman angrily. "A few minutes ago, you told us they would be prepared to seize The Red Blot's agent. Would they be paralyzed if the man tried to run away with our money?"

"They would not!" retorted the commissioner, rising to his feet. Then, in a quiet tone, he added, "There is nothing to be lost by the action which you suggest. I have advised the meeting tomorrow night, under the conditions which are proposed in this demand from The Red Blot. I did not expect that you would have the required amount available; if you are willing to take chances with five million dollars, I have no objection."

"It is a drastic step," remarked one of the directors.

"Drastic, yes," agreed Cushman. "But I favor it. Our conference room is an isolated spot. I can readily see how some emissary—unknown to us— can come there. We could not possibly recognize him as The Red Blot's agent until he demands the money. That moment, I believe, will be the vital one to our hopes. We can arrange to have the funds on hand—but if you disapprove, gentlemen, I am willing to forgo the plan."

While the directors sat in consideration of the proposal, Dobson Pringle interjected a severe note of dissatisfaction.

"I am the president of this association," he asserted. "It seems to me that you are taking too much upon your own shoulders, Cushman. Suggestions in this matter should come from me, not from you!"

This outburst of personal objection had an electric effect upon Felix Cushman. The dark-haired man faced Pringle with blazing eyes.

"So far as we are concerned," he retorted, "you are nothing but a figurehead, Pringle! The appropriation of funds lies in the hands of the directors—not the president. Your duties concern actual building operations. Objections from you are not likely to be sustained. I trust that the directors will remember that fact."

Cushman turned to the directors as he finished speaking. Commissioner Weston saw immediately that this man held the whip hand over the others. Pringle's interjection had awakened what appeared to be a feud over the ownership of power.

THE result was an immediate reaction on the part of the directors. One by one, each voiced his approval of Cushman's plan. When the vote had been taken, Dobson Pringle arose and spoke with a subdued spirit.

"I accept your decision, gentlemen," he declared. "It was merely my desire to offer sound advice. I stand rebuked; therefore, I shall cooperate in full. Nevertheless, I still feel that we are running too great a risk, now that I have given the subject careful consideration."

"Your apology is accepted, Pringle," returned Cushman testily. "As chairman of directors, I shall arrange the appropriation of five million dollars to have on hand tomorrow night. I shall confer with you, Commissioner Weston, so that we may have the funds brought to our conference room under police guard."

"If we search the premises before the money is brought in; if we have every outlet guarded so that no one can leave the place, I can see no risk involved. The primary objective is to effect the release of Selfridge Woodstock."

"Nothing must be said about this arrangement," warned Commissioner Weston. "I shall attend to the details. I shall come to your offices in the Amalgamated Building tomorrow morning, and make the necessary strategic arrangements."

Thus came the final arrangements for the next night. With five million dollars as the bait, Commissioner Weston was ready to lay the snare that would enmesh The Red Blot's emissary!

CHAPTER XV
IN THE LAIR

A MAN was seated in a curious, stone-walled office. The room was windowless; a single light hung from the ceiling between the door and a desk on the opposite side. The man's back was toward the door; he was reading a newspaper spread upon the desk.

A buzzer sounded. The man at the desk folded the newspaper. He arose and turned toward the light. The action revealed his face. It was the hard-featured, unshaven countenance of Socks Mallory.

Opening the door, Mallory stepped into a narrow, stone-walled passage. This corridor, like the little office, had but a single light. It terminated in steel doors—one at either end. Mallory went to the door at the right end, pulled a lever, and opened the barrier.

A lanky and side-jawed individual stepped through the opening. His greeting to Mallory was a twisted grin.

The newcomer's face was one well known in the underworld of New York, although it had not been seen there for a long time. The visitor was Moocher Gleetz, the cracksman.

Socks Mallory closed the steel door and conducted Moocher into the little office. The visitor spied the newspaper and emitted an eager grunt.

"Say," he exclaimed, "where'd you get this? The gang has all been wanting to lamp a paper— ever since last night—"

"Let them wait a while," growled Socks. "Look it over, Moocher. It's got good news."

"How'd you get it?" inquired Moocher, as he picked up the sheet. "You been talking with The Blot?"

"What do you think I'm doing in here?" queried Socks, with a rough laugh. "Playing solitaire? Sure, I've seen The Blot. Tell the gang that everything is O.K."

Moocher read the headlines and began to devour the story beneath them. He chuckled as he perused the details of the unsolved mystery at the Hotel Gigantic.

"Five million bucks!" he exclaimed. "The news hounds got that part of it, didn't they? But look here, Socks; there's nothing here about the delivery of the dough. You told me that was fixed—"

"The police managed to keep that part out," grinned Socks. "Weston thinks he's going to pull a fast one on us. Don't worry. I'll pick up that dough, in person—tonight! I just need a couple of the gang to help me, that's all."

"O.K., Socks. That's all I want to know."

"Five million tonight, Moocher. The other big job comes tomorrow night. After that, we can blow."

"How's the big boy from Chicago?"

"Resting nice, up at the other end of the hall. But he's not going home, just yet. He knows too much of the game, now."

A TICKING clock on the desk showed eleven. This was indication that it was the morning following the episode at the Hotel Gigantic. Moocher Gleetz finished his study of the newspaper, and turned to Socks Mallory.

"Say," he questioned, "am I going with you tonight? Maybe it wouldn't hurt to have me along."

"Not you, Moocher," interrupted Socks. "I want you to watch the Club Janeiro."

"The bulls have left there," objected Moocher. "They didn't find anything."

"I know that. They moved out this morning. But I got a note from Juanita—and if she's got the right dope, we'd better keep watching that place."

"You mean the bulls may be wise?"

"No. They're dumb. But there was a guy in the place last night who may be smart. You know that the police commissioner was there two nights ago, when I knocked off Tony Loretti. Well"—a sneer appeared upon Mallory's ugly face—"he had a friend with him—a high-hat guy named Cranston. He's the bird we're watching. He was at the Club Janeiro last night."

"I get you. One of those smart babies that thinks he's an amateur dick, eh? Going to wise up to something that fooled the commissioner."

"Right. That's the way we figure him. Just the sort of bird who might fall into something. Well, we're not taking any chances, Moocher. The place is clear now; and if he snoops around tonight, we'll get him sure."

"I'm to watch for the signal?"

"From the inside. "Dynamite" Hoskins is coming through tonight. We'll need him for the big job. He's got three gorillas with him, and they're going to join up—but they'll follow him. They'll hold back; and if this bird Cranston snoops, you'll get the signal from Juanita."

"Which will put the smart Aleck in between."

"You guessed it."

Moocher Gleetz strolled toward the door; then paused to light a cigarette.

"Say, Socks," he remarked, "maybe you pulled a boner knocking off Tony Loretti."

"Yeah?" queried Socks. "That's my business, Moocher. What would you have done?"

"Let him ride for a while."

"That shows just how much you don't know. Loretti was a wise guy, Moocher. He had Juanita worried. She was afraid he'd find out the lay. That's why The Blot said I could bump him. I wanted to get him, anyway."

"O.K.; but it brought the bulls to the Club Janeiro, didn't it?"

"What of it? They've gone away, haven't they? They're thinking about the Hotel Gigantic instead. Don't be dumb, Moocher. When I started this racket with The Blot, the Club Janeiro was our best bet. It was the joint where we could get the gang to make the dive undercover when we needed them.

"Along comes Loretti. Muscles in on my night-club racket—I was going easy on it, too, because it was only a blind—and he grabs off the Club Janeiro. Then I got into trouble.

"Here, tonight, we're waiting for Dynamite Hoskins. He had the date all set, long ago. He's been out of New York. His orders were to come to the Club Janeiro and get the instructions there. I can't give them to him—but Juanita can. Suppose Tony Loretti was there tonight? How would we tip off Dynamite?"

"I get you now, Socks."

"It's time you did. I handled things right when I gave Loretti the works. Slide along, Moocher. Tell the mob I'll be out there soon. We've got them in a good humor. Let's keep them that way."

"No trouble about that, Socks. There's nowhere for them to go. Say—this is a great racket. Wouldn't Joe Cardona and Mert Hembroke go goofy if they knew our lay?"

"Slide along, Moocher. I'll be seeing you."

AFTER Moocher had departed, Socks Mallory went to the left end of the corridor and opened the steel door that was located there. The gap revealed a passage that led to the right; also, a steep flight of steps that led downward until they disappeared in blackness. Socks followed the steps. He returned several minutes later, closed the corridor door, and went into the stone-walled office.

From a drawer in the desk, Socks produced a

folded sheet of paper. He spread it out before him. It was a large map of Manhattan; upon it were traced lines in inks of different colors. Socks gave a satisfied grunt as he surveyed this chart. Finally, he replaced the map in the drawer, a satisfied look on his features.

A buzzer sounded; its note was different from the one which had announced Moocher Gleetz. Socks picked up a telephone from beside the desk. He was eager as he placed the receiver to his ear.

"Hello," he said. "Yes... Sure, I was just talking to Moocher... Yeah—he'll take care of the Club Janeiro tonight... Right. I'll stick here all day— anytime I go out, I won't be gone more than three or four minutes... Yeah, I can count on Moocher. He was O.K. the time we got the lay on Spider Carew. He passed the word to me quick that time."

Socks Mallory hung up the receiver. He leaned back in the chair, and grinned as he lighted a cigarette. This was the call he had been awaiting— word from The Red Blot—the mastermind whose identity Socks Mallory knew.

All set for tonight. That had been the message. Much might happen between now and then, yet Socks felt no alarm. Success had been the watchword for The Red Blot's crimes; once only, during the raid on the East Side Bank, had the schemes of the supercrook been offset.

There was only one person who could have been responsible for that partial failure—The Shadow. Since then, however, there had been no further intervention. At last—Socks Mallory relished the thought—crime had been devised that was too much for even The Shadow to fathom!

Moocher Gleetz, a squad of wanted men, all able criminals—they were The Red Blot's mob. Under the direction of Socks, they had proven themselves a scourge. Dynamite Hoskins was joining them tonight, as another of Socks Mallory's subordinates.

Socks enjoyed a laugh as he thought of how little these mobsmen knew. To them, Socks Mallory was the leader, although they understood that an unknown chief—The Red Blot—stood above.

Socks Mallory—The Red Blot's right arm! But The Red Blot was not one-handed in his strokes against the law. He had a left arm also—another aide, whose identity was not even suspected.

Socks relished that thought, also. While he delivered the open blows, the man who served as left hand was used for secret thrusts. Therein lay The Red Blot's might!

Right and left—they had worked together. They would do so again, tonight. Should an emergency arise before them, those aides of The Red Blot would cooperate whenever their services were required.

Socks Mallory was wearing an air of gloating triumph when he left the little office and headed for the door at the right of the corridor. Satisfaction dominated his malicious mind. He was thinking again of the only menace whom the underworld feared—yet one who had failed to thwart The Red Blot.

Socks Mallory was thinking of The Shadow.

CHAPTER XVI
THE SHADOW PREPARES

AT the very time that Socks Mallory was thinking of such important personages as Ralph Weston and The Shadow, a visitor was being ushered into the office of the New York Police Commissioner. Weston, seated behind the huge glass-topped desk in his downtown office, was looking up to meet the keen eyes of Lamont Cranston. The millionaire was an unexpected caller.

"Hello, Cranston," greeted Weston briskly. "You caught me at a very busy time. What can I do for you?"

"Nothing, since you are busy," returned the millionaire, with a quiet smile. "I merely dropped in to learn if you could lunch with me at the Cobalt Club. I have not forgotten"—Cranston's voice had a reflective monotone—"the interesting events of our last meeting."

"At the Club Janeiro," responded Weston. "Quite a difference between that place and the Cobalt Club. If you crave the unusual, Cranston, I should advise you to choose a more likely spot than an exclusive meeting place such as the Cobalt Club."

"The Hotel Gigantic, for instance?" queried Cranston.

Weston smiled grimly. Cranston had given a keen refutation to the commissioner's suggestion. The reputation of the Hotel Gigantic allied it more closely with the Cobalt Club than with the Club Janeiro.

From a man other than Lamont Cranston, Weston might have resented the inference. The police commissioner, however, had a respect for Cranston; and also recalled the aid which the millionaire had given him only two nights ago.

"You have me this time," admitted Weston. "Frankly, Cranston, this matter of The Red Blot is one which may crop out anywhere. Nevertheless—"

Weston paused. He was on the point of discussing affairs with Cranston. The police commissioner had just returned from a visit to the offices of the Amalgamated Builders' Association. He had warned all concerned to preserve absolute secrecy regarding tonight's arrangements.

Lamont Cranston was lighting a cigarette. His keen eyes, peering past the illuminated lighter in his hand, were reading a penciled notation that lay upon the commissioner's desk. A clever ruse, this. With the flame between himself and Cranston's face, the commissioner could not detect the direction of the millionaire's gaze.

"We may be getting somewhere," remarked Weston, in a noncommittal tone. "Doubtless, you have read of the latest outrage perpetrated by The Red Blot. This time, we are awaiting a definite follow-up on the part of the criminal."

"Collection of the five-million-dollar ransom?"

"Exactly. That in itself, will be another crime— if The Red Blot attempts it. Until then—whenever it may be—I am too tied up to arrange luncheon engagements. Thanks for the invitation, Cranston—"

"Don't mention it," interposed the millionaire, rising and extending his hand. "The invitation remains open, Weston. Let us set it for the day after The Red Blot has been brought to justice— and let us hope that the day will be soon."

LAMONT CRANSTON betrayed no smile when he descended in the elevator. The brain behind that impassive, masklike face was considering the very definite facts which this casual visit had revealed.

To an ordinary person, the notations on Commissioner Weston's pad might have meant nothing. To The Shadow—guised as Lamont Cranston—they had supplied all missing information needed in this case.

Abbreviated references to "conference room," "Amalgamated Building," a time notation of nine thirty, the names of Hembroke and Cardona— these were clews to the very matter which The Shadow wished to learn at this time.

Taking a cab, Lamont Cranston rode to the vicinity of the Amalgamated Building. This was the skyscraper which housed the offices of the Amalgamated Builders' Association. Of recent construction, the building was modernistic in design. Its mighty mass pyramided from the street, in tapering, setback fashion, which was capped by a towerlike succession of topmost floors.

Leaving the cab, the millionaire entered the building and rode up to the fifth floor. He entered the anteroom of the Amalgamated Builders' Association. He inquired for Dobson Pringle. The girl informed him that the president had gone out to lunch. It was now twelve fifteen, and he had gone out at noon.

The observant eyes of Lamont Cranston were busy as the girl spoke. Peering through the glass partition that separated the anteroom from the office itself, Cranston noted the simple arrangements.

There were many desks upon the floor, and the farther end of the room was divided into smaller offices, which served for the chief officials of the organization. In the corner directly opposite the anteroom was the solid wall of a room which cut a square chunk from the floor space. There was a single door to this apartment. Upon it were the words:

Conference Room.

Lamont Cranston idled toward the elevators after remarking that he would call to see Dobson Pringle at some other time. He rode down to the street and strolled along for half a block, before he turned to study the pyramided structure from this distance.

He noted the exact location of the office which he had left. A thin, wan smile rested upon his lips. Lamont Cranston suddenly joined the throng of people who were passing. From then on, his course was untraceable.

SOMETIME afterward, a light clicked and darkness was dispelled from a solemn, hushed abode. Blue rays flickered upon a polished table-top. White hands appeared beneath the focused glare. The brilliance of the sparkling girasol threw off constant color-changing flashes.

The Shadow was in his sanctum. The clock was not upon the table this afternoon. There was time for deliberation. Envelopes opened; clippings and reports fell beneath The Shadow's hands.

Most of the latest data dealt with the mystery that had occurred in the Hotel Gigantic. The Shadow laid these clippings aside. They told the same story—an amazing abduction; a demand for five million dollars. They cried out the name of The Red Blot, and shouted for the capture of the supercrook.

But not one report carried the essential information regarding tonight's meeting at the Amalgamated Building. That had been suppressed by Commissioner Weston.

The Shadow laughed. His hand began to inscribe words in bluish ink upon a blank sheet of paper. These notations were a summary of his conclusions.

The Red Blot will send his emissary to collect the ransom. Nine thirty tonight, in the conference room of the Amalgamated Building Association. Police will be there to seize the agent. They will not succeed. The Red Blot has planned too well. The emissary will leave—with or without the five million. In either case, no injury will be done. To thwart that arrangement would prove futile. The Red Blot will not appear in person.

To the police will go the task of following that

emissary. Their work will be unsuccessful. The only way to reach The Red Blot is to find his headquarters secretly. There, his arrival must be awaited. His plans must be foiled at their inception.

The words remained in view for a short while; then, like fleeting thoughts, they began to disappear. One by one, in the order of their writing, the words vanished and left the pure blank sheet. Again, the whispered laugh of The Shadow sounded ominously in that black-walled room.

The hand inscribed a new paragraph:

The Red Blot has many henchmen. Their ways are hidden. There are avenues of escape which they can follow. These must be discovered. Lives are at stake; villains are at large. The innocent must be protected; the guilty must pay the penalty.

The words vanished as The Shadow again indulged in a burst of sinister mockery that came back in vague echoes from the weird hangings of the walls.

Another envelope was opened by the hands. It contained a report sheet, written in coded words. The Shadow read the message as quickly as if it had been in ordinary writing. The blue-inked inscription disappeared.

That was the way with The Shadow's messages. By use of a special fluid, the ink, after drying, vanished from contact with the air. This was a note from Harry Vincent, one of The Shadow's agents.

OLD clippings were handy with the message. They referred to one event: the strange disappearance of Hubert Craft, prominent architect, whose upset boat had been discovered in Long Island Sound some weeks ago.

Harry Vincent, investigating, had learned nothing. Craft frequently went to his Long Island boathouse and set forth upon the Sound. One night the boat had gone out. It had not returned. Craft had been in New York during the evening. He had not been seen since that time.

What had become of Hubert Craft?

The Shadow answered the question in enigmatic fashion. His hand appeared with a pen, and the fingers, with a quick shake, sent a blob of crimson ink upon a blank sheet of paper. The ominous fluid spread in grotesque form, and shone amid the light from above.

The Red Blot!

The disappearance of Hubert Craft had preceded the appearance of that insidious symbol. The discovery of The Red Blot, himself, would answer the other question. Hubert Craft and The Red Blot! There was an indelible link between them! What did The Shadow intend to do?

Mystery had thickened; five million dollars was at stake. Two men had been abducted: Selfridge Woodstock and his secretary, Crozer. This meeting at the conference room of the Amalgamated Builders might hold the secret of the riddle. Would The Shadow be there?

The hand wrote with the blue-inked pen. But the thoughts which it inscribed were in direct opposition to what might well have been expected. There was no mention of the meeting to be held tonight. The duty of watching that event could rest with the police.

Instead, The Shadow announced his secret intention of investigating a spot where he had been before; of going back upon a trail which the law had now abandoned. In carefully shaped characters, the hand inscribed this decision:

Tonight. The Club Janeiro.

The writing remained while silence persisted. The inked lines faded. The girasol sparkled as the left hand alone remained upon the table. The bluish light clicked out.

Amid the thick gloom of heavy darkness came a long, eerie laugh. The Shadow's mockery sounded with its note of sinister understanding. It was a token of the unexpected; the cry of one who prepared a thrust into the weakest sector of the enemy's lines.

Grim echoes caught up the awesome mirth and lisped the sound in sobbing whispers that persisted long. When the last touch of merriment had died, deep, solemn silence reigned undisturbed.

The Shadow, man of the night, had gone. From the depths of this mysterious abode—his unknown sanctum—he had set forth upon a new adventure.

While others chose to meet the menace of The Red Blot face to face, The Shadow planned a different course. Where The Red Blot least expected serious difficulty, there would The Shadow be!

Ominous had been the Shadow's laugh. The tomblike stillness of the deserted sanctum carried a touch as sinister. A weird lull lay within this room. The weird presence of The Shadow had left its mystic spell.

CHAPTER XVII
THE PRELUDE

IT was after two o'clock when Dobson Pringle returned to the offices of the Amalgamated Builders' Association. The girl in the anteroom informed him that a man had called, and left without giving his name; but that bit of news was not regarded as important by Pringle. The girl made another announcement, that was much more vital; namely that Felix Cushman and a friend were waiting Pringle's return in the president's office.

Hurrying across the floor, Pringle reached his own room, and found Cushman there. The man with the chief director was one whom Pringle immediately recognized—Detective Merton Hembroke, from headquarters.

As soon as Pringle had closed the door, Cushman motioned him to his desk and began to speak in a tense tone.

"I have brought Hembroke here," he announced, "by arrangement with Commissioner Weston. Hembroke is the principal detective on this case; and he suggested that it would be well to make an inside inspection of these premises prior to tonight's meeting."

"An excellent idea," agreed Pringle. "You mean that Hembroke will remain here after the office is empty?"

"For a short while," returned Cushman cannily. "Everyone will be gone by six o'clock. Hembroke can stay for an hour longer. But I would not deem it advisable for him to remain after seven o'clock."

"Why not?"

"Because we must adhere closely to the terms of the demand. I am convinced, Pringle, that an emissary is coming from The Red Blot. As the hour for the meeting approaches, everything must be clear."

"I can see no harm in Hembroke staying," declared Pringle, in opposition to the director's statement. "Nevertheless, my opinions seem to be considered of little weight."

"The funds are arriving at half past eight," resumed Cushman, summarily ignoring Pringle's objection. "We must all be here by then—you and I and the directors. Right there is where we have scored against this criminal with whom we are dealing. If his spies are watching outside of this building, we shall be able to completely delude them."

"How?" questioned Pringle.

"Commissioner Weston figured it out," broke in Hembroke. "He has a great idea, Mr. Pringle—"

"Which is partly your suggestion, Hembroke," interrupted Cushman in a commending tone.

"Credit belongs to the commissioner," declared Hembroke. "I was there to talk it over with him— that's all. Figure it this way, Mr. Pringle. How would anyone transport five million dollars?"

"Under police guard, of course."

"That's it. Well, the cash is coming up—in an armored bank truck. There'll be police all around the place. As soon as the dough is in—away they'll go. That will leave nearly one hour before the scheduled time."

"But we aren't all going, see? There'll be me and Joe Cardona and a dozen other detectives all around this floor. That's why I want to look over the layout. So I can arrange the posts."

"Do you understand, Pringle?" questioned Cushman. "Our directors' meeting will be in the conference room. No police in there at all. Everything in accordance with The Red Blot's terms. But unless we get Selfridge Woodstock— there will be no negotiations completed. The agent will walk into a trap. The money will be bait. All will look fair; but we will be ready to snare him."

"Well planned, Cushman," stated Pringle. "Nevertheless, I still persist in my final decision of last night. Mark my words, Cushman; and I call you, Detective Hembroke, to be witness. We are placing five million dollars in jeopardy. We may lose all, and gain nothing."

"We are chancing it," said Cushman shortly, "and the odds are all in our favor. That's final, Pringle."

"It is a very good plan," nodded the president. "It is quite natural that the money should be brought up under strong guard. Nevertheless, we might use blank paper, instead of real money. However—"

Pringle broke off and shrugged his shoulders as he saw an antagonistic glare in Cushman's eyes. The chairman of the directors arose and conducted Merton Hembroke through a door at the side of Pringle's office. This was a connection with a room which the directors used as an office.

The door closed behind Cushman and Hembroke. Pringle rang a bell for a stenographer.

IT was half past the hour before Dobson Pringle had finished with a mass of detail work. Pringle knew that by this time Cushman must have left, with Hembroke remaining in the adjacent office.

While resting in his large swivel chair, Pringle heard a rap at the outer door. He spoke; the door opened, and Carlton Carmody entered.

The white-haired architect closed the door behind him and sat down in a chair by the desk. He looked at the president with troubled eyes.

"What's the matter, Carmody?" asked Pringle, in a kindly tone.

"I'm thinking of your worries, Mr. Pringle," declared Carmody. "Last night troubled me a great deal. It wasn't fair, the way you were overruled by Felix Cushman."

"That's part of my job, Carmody," smiled Pringle.

"Things aren't right, sir," protested Carmody. "It impressed me that your opinions should at least have been given more consideration."

"Cushman holds the whip hand, Carmody."

"I know that, Mr. Pringle. Just the same, this situation has been bothering me all day. Of course, I can't say anything—I was only at the meeting in case Mr. Woodstock had wanted to put questions that I could answer. But I feel that you have been treated unjustly."

"Forget it, Carmody."

"I'll try to, Mr. Pringle. I've been working on those half-completed plans for the Soudervale Building—maybe they'll take my mind from all this trouble. But it seems as though I can't think of anything now but The Red Blot."

"Don't read the newspapers," commented Pringle dryly. "Rather a hardship, Carmody, but advisable under the circumstances. Perhaps this trouble will be settled effectively tonight."

"I hope so, Mr. Pringle."

After Carmody had gone from the office, Pringle prepared to leave for the day. The president could not forget the architect's solicitude. A good worker, Carmody; one who could scarcely hope to be the equal of Hubert Craft; nevertheless, Carmody's close attention to detail made him a valuable man to carry on the work of one whose labors had been unfinished.

Dobson Pringle's departure before five o'clock was a signal for early leave on the part of the employees. Usually the genial president set an example by staying until five thirty. A gradual emptying of offices began immediately after five; within half an hour, the place was deserted.

THE door of the directors' office opened cautiously; into the floor space now illuminated only by emergency lights stepped Detective Merton Hembroke. The sleuth strolled about the large central office, making a rather cursory inspection.

A closed door caught his eye. A light glimmered from beneath it. The door bore the title:

Chief Architect.

Carlton Carmody was still at work. Hembroke remembered the fellow from last night. A rather eccentric-looking character, Carmody. Hembroke decided to wait until the man was gone.

Instead of going back to the office where he had stayed in wait, the detective sought the seclusion of the anteroom and watched through the glass partition.

In his office, Carmody was trying to concentrate upon the plans for the new Soudervale Building. Studying the ground floor, in a space intended for a banking office, he noted a peculiar alcove arrangement, which was unmarked. Carmody wondered why that extension was in the plans.

Could it be a special vault space? Such was unlikely. No banking institution had arranged to take the ground floor of the proposed building. This alcove was not conventional; why had Hubert Craft designed it?

Thoughtfully, Carmody dipped a pen into the red ink with which he was accustomed to mark these plans. The pen sank deeper than the architect noticed. When he held the lettering instrument above the plans, a drop of ink fell free and splattered upon the very space that had caused Carmody's perplexity.

The Red Blot!

The splotch of ink resembled the strange signature that Carmody had seen upon the ransom note! The peculiar coincidence caused a strain of fleeting thoughts in the architect's bewildered mind.

An unexplained alcove in a ground-floor plan; a feature which Carmody, methodical to the extreme, had been going over with mechanical precision—and now, upon it, appeared the sign of The Red Blot.

Details impressed Carlton Carmody more than important matters. That had been the chief reason for the architect's slow rise to prominence. Yet Carmody had hidden qualities of imagination; and this stimulus caused him to picture the menace of The Red Blot in mammoth proportions.

He recalled last night's episode in the Hotel Gigantic; with sudden impulse, he went to a filing cabinet and produced the plans of that huge building which Hubert Craft had designed.

Going through the floor plans, Carmody noticed an unmarked spot that made him pause. He dropped the Gigantic plans upon those of the Soudervale Building.

The Red Blot! Carmody's mind went back to the reports that he had read of Tony Loretti's murder—the deed that had brought The Red Blot into such tremendous prominence. Loretti had been killed in the Club Janeiro. The nightclub was located in the Stellar Theater Building—an edifice which the Amalgamated Builders had also erected!

Back at the filing cabinet, Carmody discovered the floor plans of the Stellar Theater Building, and began to study the diagrams of the first floor. A new impulse seizing him, he laid this plan beside that of the Hotel Gigantic. With his red-dipped pen he shook one blot upon each diagram. Grinning wildly, he stepped back to survey his work.

Then, with the eagerness of a madman, Carmody went through the files, until he produced the plans of the building in which he now stood. He studied the fifth floor of the Amalgamated Building, and placed his finger tip upon the conference room, where tonight's meeting was to be held. With a gleeful chuckle, Carmody spotted the plan with another crimson blot!

A CLOCK on the windowsill showed half past six. Gathering the plans which he had marked, Carmody clutched them close to his body, and went from the little office. He crept across the large floor until he reached the door of the conference room. It was unlocked. Carmody entered and switched on the light.

The room had a peculiar entrance—a sort of an anteroom of its own—a space much narrower than the conference room itself. The entrance was at the outer corner of the inset square. At the left of the anteroom was a paneled wall.

Carmody went through to the large conference room. It spread to the left, where the windows were located. The architect laid his plans upon the large table in the center of the room, and began to spread them out.

He stopped, looked up, and quickly shoved the plans into a compact pile. A man had entered after him; Carmody now recognized the face of Detective Merton Hembroke. The sleuth had evidently not intended to disturb the architect. Now that Carmody was aware of his presence, Hembroke put a prompt question.

"What's the idea?" he quizzed. "No one is supposed to be in this room. What are you doing here?"

"I—I—I have discovered something," stammered Carmody. "Something very important. Yes—it may be very important."

"What is it?"

Carmody hesitated. He did not care to discuss this matter with the detective alone. He preferred to talk to Dobson Pringle.

There was a peculiar challenge in Hembroke's gaze; and Carmody suddenly repented of his action in dabbing these plans with red blotches. What would a police detective know about building diagrams? Carmody became suddenly reliant.

"I must talk to Mr. Pringle," he asserted. "It is very important that I should do so."

"Mr. Pringle has gone home," returned Hembroke. "I was just looking around here to see that the place was empty. I saw you come into this room."

"I can call Mr. Pringle," pleaded Carmody. "Really—I must discuss a most important matter with him. Very important."

"I'll call him," said Hembroke shortly.

The detective picked up a telephone. He found that it was not connected.

"I'll have to go out to the switchboard," he decided. "Come along. I'll call Pringle."

Clutching his precious plans, Carmody preceded the suspicious detective. As he saw Hembroke pick up the telephone, the architect supplied him with Pringle's number.

"It's unlisted," he explained. "Call Mr. Pringle right away. It's very important."

Hembroke put in the call. Within a few minutes, he was talking with the president of the Amalgamated Builders.

"This is Detective Hembroke," explained the sleuth. "I'm in the office in the Amalgamated Building... Just ready to leave... One of your men here—Carmody, the architect... I found him in the conference room... Wants to talk with you about some plans..."

"Tell him I must see him before the meeting!" exclaimed Carmody, in a tense voice. "I want to see him in the conference room!"

"Wants to see you personally," resumed Hembroke. "Says he wants to see you in the conference room—before tonight's meeting... No, he hasn't told me what it's about. He's all excited, and he's got a whole stack of diagrams with him... Say—maybe I ought to take this bird down to headquarters... What's that? No... Yes, I understand... All right, Mr. Pringle..."

Hembroke hung up the telephone and turned toward Carmody with a disgruntled air.

"This is a poor time to start acting loony," observed the detective, "but your boss gives you an O.K. Says he knows you're all right. He's coming down here as soon as he finishes dinner. Says for you to wait for him in the conference room."

"Good!" exclaimed Carmody, in a breathless tone.

"I'm leaving here," observed Hembroke. "I'm supposed to be out by seven. I don't like the idea of you staying—but it's on Pringle's say-so. Come on."

Hembroke conducted the architect back to the conference room. He pointed to a chair by the table. Carmody seated himself; Hembroke stalked about the room, and stared suspiciously at every corner. Satisfied that all was well, he went out and closed the door of the little anteroom behind him.

The detective paused to listen for a few minutes; then shrugged his shoulders and continued on his way. He left the offices of the Amalgamated Builders' Association, and took an elevator to the ground floor.

In the conference room, Carlton Carmody waited until he was sure that the detective was really gone. Then, with an eager smile, the architect spread the plans on the table before him. His eyes were agog as he surveyed those charts—each of which now bore a crimson spot.

Minutes dragged by. Carlton Carmody was like a man in a trance as he noted the features of the plans. He was unconscious of the passage of time, concentrated solely upon the diagrams before him. Forty minutes passed. It was nearly half past seven, and he was still immersed in his work.

Suddenly, the lights of the conference room went out. After that event, Carlton Carmody knew no more.

This was the prelude to crime that was to follow, elsewhere as well as in this very room.

CHAPTER XVIII
ANOTHER DISAPPEARANCE

IT was precisely nine o'clock when Lamont Cranston appeared within the portals of the Club Janeiro. There was something mysterious about the millionaire's arrival. The headwaiter, watching the usual entrances, did not see him until after he was seated at a table far from the screened archway that led to the offices.

There was a reason for this phenomenon. Cranston had come in by one of the side corridors—a route which the police had searched in the belief that Socks Mallory had escaped by such an exit on the eventful evening when Tony Loretti had been slain.

In fact, Cranston had done more than simply enter. He had paid a brief visit to the center of the three offices; there, he had deposited a bundle in an inconspicuous spot beneath a desk.

The millionaire had not lingered long, however. The voice of Juanita Pasquales, speaking over the telephone in an adjacent office, had caused him to stroll away before the call was completed.

When he noted Cranston, the headwater immediately started toward the screened archway. He must have met Senorita Pasquales before he reached the office, for the man returned quite promptly; and the proprietress of the Club Janeiro appeared a few minutes later.

Five minutes went by; then the events of a slowly unfolding drama began their occurrence. The headwaiter, stopping at a table where four men were seated, passed a card to one of them. This fellow, a heavy, full-faced man, who looked like an old-line political boss, nodded his head. He spoke in a low tone to his three companions.

Lamont Cranston, calmly puffing at a cigarette, observed the happening with an eagle gaze. Impassive, betraying no interest whatever, the hawk-visaged millionaire understood what was transpiring as clearly as if he had been one of the distant group.

The bluff-faced man was Dynamite Hoskins, a former denizen of New York's underworld, whose persistent use of fuse and bomb had caused him to depart for places unknown. Back in Manhattan, Dynamite was making his first reappearance at the Club Janeiro.

At the end of the interval which followed the headwaiter's message, Dynamite Hoskins arose and strolled past the fringe of tables that surrounded the dance floor of the nightclub. The spotlight was on the floor; couples were dancing there; and the passage of this one man was unnoticed—with one exception.

Lamont Cranston, his keen eye watching through the semi-gloom, saw Dynamite pass behind the screen that led to the office archway. A few moments later, Juanita Pasquales left in the same direction.

More minutes passed; then Cranston himself arose. Quietly, he strolled to the edge of the screen, paused, and stepped out of sight.

THE action brought an immediate response from the three men whom Dynamite Hoskins had left. They arose together, slunk toward the side of the big room, and sneaked in file toward the spot where they had last seen the departing millionaire.

Short, crouching forms; tight, tough fists that gripped stub-nosed revolvers; these were the three that took up Cranston's trail. Smooth and shaven faces had given a very flimsy gloss to these thugs. A stalking trio, they were now displaying themselves as hardened gorillas—paid assassins of the badlands.

Meanwhile, Lamont Cranston had passed the crossing of the corridors. In fact, he had paused there a moment. Eyes from one hallway had seen his standing form. As Cranston went on toward the central office, Juanita Pasquales slipped into an empty dressing room and pushed back a cloak that hung in a corner of the wall.

Hesitating—almost fearful of the deed she was now to perform—the woman pressed the button and let the cloak fall back in place. Hastening to the door of the dressing room, Juanita was just in time to see the three stalking gorillas pass the crossing of the corridors.

Lamont Cranston had gone straight into the center office. The three men were on his trail. Juanita stole to the crossing; she noted the stooped forms waiting at the door down the hall. With trembling step, the woman hurried toward the archway, back to the nightclub where the entertainment was scheduled to begin.

A gorilla's hand was on the door that led into the suite of offices. The barrier moved inward as the man turned the knob. Peering cautiously into the lighted room, yet seeing no one, the first of the assassins beckoned to his fellows. With guns ready, they sidled through the opening.

The leader of the trio had opened the door with his left hand. Peering past the edge, he had looked toward the office which had once been Tony

Loretti's, while the others had headed toward the little office on the right.

As the first man stepped just beyond the edge of the door the barrier was swung shut by the quick thrust of a figure that had stood behind it. The slam caused the three gorillas to swing in that direction.

Between them and the door was the sinister figure of a black-clad being that had appeared as suddenly as a ghost. A long cloak hung from hidden shoulders; an upturned collar obscured the lower portion of the face above it.

Topped by a black slouch hat, the upper portion of the countenance was concealed by the broad, turned-down brim. Two blazing eyes—optics that burned with a glaring sparkle—were the only visible features of that unseen countenance.

Blazing eyes! Threatening eyes! But they were not the only menace which the startled gunmen faced. Black-gloved hands projected from the folds of the cloak; each fist grasped a huge automatic, and the muzzles of the .45s were covering the trio who had come to slay an unsuspecting victim.

"The Shadow!"

The gasp came from three husky throats; and the echo of those words was a whispered, mocking laugh that issued from beneath the brim of the slouch hat. By a ruse as simple as it was daring, the terror of the underworld had gained the drop on the three armed desperadoes!

THE taunt of The Shadow's mirth was a command. The gesture of those looming automatics brooked no opposition. Sullenly, the gangsters backed across the room, their arms rising.

The Shadow's back was against the door; his enemies were at his mercy. One second more—his opponents would have been totally helpless.

But in that fleeting instant, The Shadow's keen eyes caught a sign that came as a strange satire to his own mighty presence. Across the center of the room, The Shadow's silhouette lay in ominous blackness. Now, from the doorway of the dimly lighted office on the right, The Shadow saw a shadow!

Someone was creeping to the edge of that door; someone lying in wait until the three assassins had acted. The Shadow had no choice. Another moment spent upon the three men before him would mean a menacing attack from the other room.

The Shadow was prepared. In that split second, he performed the unexpected. His position against the door was one of clever design. The elbow of a right arm moved beneath the folds of the enveloping cloak. It pressed the light switch at the right of the door.

Darkness. With it, two men sprang forward from the other room. As quick fingers pressed revolver triggers, the blackened form of The Shadow dropped into total darkness. That fadeaway came just before the shots were fired.

Guns roared, and leaden slugs shattered the woodwork at the spot where The Shadow had been standing. In response came fierce tongues of flame, and terrific thunder blasts, as The Shadow's right-hand automatic cannonaded its reply.

As one man hurried forward into the darkness of the center room, the other seemed to crumple in his tracks. Going down, he tried to rattle off further shots. His trigger finger faltered after the first wild bullet was discharged.

To the three gorillas in the darkened center office, these amazing events had happened with whirlwind rapidity. Accustomed to critical situations, they managed to respond after a momentary loss of action.

A rescue had been launched and thwarted—all in the space of one long, momentous second. The Shadow, he who counted time in delayed throbs, had proven his uncanny skill.

Now, revolvers about to slip from yielding fingers were caught with a new grip. Stabs of flame shot through the darkness as the three gorillas, dropping to the floor, aimed for the spot where The Shadow had been.

A master of strategy, The Shadow had expected this step. Knowing that his enemies would fire quickly, hoping to down him by spreading shots, he had not given his location by a left-hand fire against a trio of revolvers.

Instead, his lithe form had whirled across the room toward the door at the left. Three revolver shots—four—five—six—had come from gangsters' weapons before The Shadow's automatics barked their grim return.

With two guns, not with one, The Shadow aimed for those telltale jets of flashing light. Burning bullets rocketed through blackness. A scream told that one man had received a leaden messenger; an oath came as a gorilla dropped his gun and gripped his shattered right hand with his left.

Quick seconds in which more than a dozen round-nosed slugs had seared their way through that gloomy atmosphere. Burning powder bore silent evidence of the conflict. Four men were down; each a victim of The Shadow's marksmanship; yet the phantom fighter remained unscathed.

Not only in the perfection of his aim had The Shadow succeeded. The timeliness of his shots was the factor that had climaxed his success. His speed, his swiftness in shifting to a new position, had enabled him to foil his adversaries.

Well did The Shadow know the futility of trying to outdo a bullet's speed; just as certainly did he

**. . . From the doorway of the office on
the right, The Shadow saw a shadow!**

understand that the aiming of a revolver was no
more than a human action.

In the space that others had leveled their guns
at the spot where they believed the blackened
target to be, The Shadow had left blankness for
the bullets that were to follow.

SHATTERING echoes of the shots died in
quick reverberations. Well did The Shadow know
that one among his foemen was still active—one
who was crouching in the darkness waiting for
The Shadow to reveal himself.

There was one way to meet that hidden enemy.
The Shadow's hidden form stalked silently until it
stood three paces from the door of the office on
the left.

With his left hand, The Shadow fired a single shot into the room. A burst of flame; hidden behind its sudden light, The Shadow's form made another fadeaway. Not to the left, as the waiting gorilla would expect; but toward the right—away from the security of the inner office—out in the direction of the door that led to the nightclub.

The ruse was doubly effective. Not only did the lurking gunman suppose that The Shadow would dive back toward the inner office; he had also accepted the gun burst as a right-hand shot.

This last enemy was a desperate marksman. Three times his revolver coughed forth its message, directing well-sprayed shots toward the corner opening, following the course which The Shadow should logically have taken.

The answer came from the main door—the spot from which The Shadow had begun his original attack. An automatic thundered the single shot that brought quietus to the last of the three assassins.

Three jabs of flame had given The Shadow his target. A whimpering gasp announced the accuracy of his final delivery against the now defeated trio.

The way to escape was open. The Shadow did not take it. Instead, he aimed an automatic toward the office on the right—the only spot from which a new attack might come.

Splintering shots crashed into desk and chairs. A lull; the door of the center office opened and closed with a resounding slam. Silence was the condition that followed.

A long moment elapsed. Then, from that light on the right, came the figure of a man. Moocher Gleetz stood outlined in the door frame, above the bodies of his fallen gunmen. He was a safecracker, not a gunman. From the inner office he has ordered his pair of subordinates to attack from ambush.

Moocher Gleetz scowled. He shoved a body aside with his foot, and moved in long strides to the outer office. He did not turn on the light of the central office; hence he never saw the tall shape that loomed in the darkness a scant six feet away. Moocher softly opened the exit door—the opening which he believed the victor had taken.

The sound of bedlam was coming down the corridor. Moocher's cautious eye saw figures huddled by the screen. People were coming here; the quarry had escaped. Now was no time to linger. With long leaps, Moocher bounded back into the lighted office.

The Shadow moved. A long arm stretched to the closed door that led to the corridor. A firm hand silently turned the key; then softly withdrew it. Stooping, The Shadow slid the key out along the corridor.

It would be found there—apparently dropped by one who had escaped and fled, locking the door on the outside as he left!

With an automatic in his left hand, The Shadow swept boldly into the lighted office on the right, striding over the bodies of the men who lay before him. This was the way that Moocher Gleetz had taken; now, the room was empty!

The Shadow's laugh was a low, barely audible whisper. Like a creature from another world, the black-garbed phantom stalked across the room and reached the farther corner. There, against the wall, was the cabinet with its shelves. His automatic dropped beneath his cloak, The Shadow sought for the combination to this solid-set article of furniture.

PANDEMONIUM was coming from outside the door of the center office. People, in the corridor, were trying to break down the heavy barrier.

The Shadow's hands reached within the cabinet and joggled the uppermost shelf. It shifted downward. Pressing firmly, The Shadow pushed the shelf steadily. It descended, taking the next shelf with it. Small stacks of magazines and papers were compressed between.

The series of shelves, jammed down together, left a large space above them. Upon this, The Shadow rested.

A lull was apparent from the corridor. A shouting voice replaced the confused babble of excited tongues:

"Here's the key! Here's the key! We don't have to break through! Give me room—stand back!"

A black-gloved hand had gripped the back of the cabinet behind the shelves. With a quick sweep, The Shadow slid this barrier to the side. An opening was revealed in the wall.

The black form scaled into total darkness. The back of the cabinet slid shut; the shelves came up automatically, now that pressure was released.

Men were in the suite of offices. They were surveying the forms of sprawled gangsters. Two—those who had come with Moocher—were dead. To meet their desperate attack, The Shadow had fired for their hearts as they loomed from the sphere of light.

The other three were wounded. They were the ones who could tell nothing. Crippled, they had known nothing but confusion after they had fallen. They were aides of Dynamite Hoskins. Their leader had gone; their enemy had gone also.

Police were coming in to learn the details of this new gang feud. The key that had been found upon the floor of the corridor seemed proof that someone had made a getaway by that route.

Senorita Juanita Pasquales, nervous and approaching hysteria, could tell nothing. She had been on the nightclub floor when the shooting had occurred.

But in her heart the woman knew that another

man had disappeared tonight. Lamont Cranston, millionaire, had passed from view. Had he escaped? Even though she had signaled for those in ambush to arrange his certain doom, Juanita hoped that Cranston was the one who had left in safety.

The menace of The Red Blot—fear of it had made the nightclub proprietress obey the bidding of Socks Mallory. She knew the secret of that inner office; but she had stood the test of silence.

Police would come as they had come before. Nothing would be learned. Yet tonight, another man had disappeared. Lamont Cranston had left the Club Janeiro. If he had not escaped, he must be dead by now; slain by those in ambush, and carried through the secret way.

Dead or alive, he had given an amazing accounting for himself. Yet Juanita Pasquales felt positive that Cranston must either be a victim of murderers or a fleeing man who knew nothing of the mystery which enshrouded the Club Janeiro.

Senorita Pasquales did not know that Lamont Cranston had become The Shadow. Not for one moment did she suspect that he, as an invisible master of darkness, was now upon the trail that would lead to the heart of crime!

The disappearance of Lamont Cranston was of The Shadow's making. The master of detection had not only won a mighty fight. Silent and unseen, he was on his way to the lair of The Red Blot!

CHAPTER XIX
FIVE MILLION DOLLARS

IT was nearly half past nine. Far from the area where The Shadow's automatics had roared their deadly retorts to the revolvers of those who had sought to slay him, the directors of the Amalgamated Builders' Association were assembled for their crucial test.

They were gathered about the large table of the conference room. Five stories above the street, in a secluded corner of a mammoth building, they were uneasy despite the security which reason told them was theirs.

The room was lighted. Upon the center of the table lay a long box; beneath its cover was the wealth which had been brought here by Felix Cushman's order. Like a grim guardian, the black-haired man sat scowling at one end of the table.

Dobson Pringle, his gray hair giving an aged look to his peaked face, sat at the opposite end of the table. During this final lull when all were tense, he put a question which he had propounded previously.

"Where can Carlton Carmody be?" he asked.

"Will you stop asking that question?" queried Felix Cushman. "What has Carmody to do with this meeting? He is not a director—nor an officer of this association."

"He was to be here," responded Pringle.

"By whose order?" demanded Cushman.

"Mine," asserted Pringle.

"You had no right to tell him to be here," came Cushman's angry retort.

"Let me explain," persisted Pringle. "Carmody stayed late this evening. The detective—Hembroke—found him in the office. Carmody insisted that he must see me—here in the conference room—regarding plans for buildings. I told him to remain until we came—"

"Plans for buildings!" snorted Cushman, in contempt. "A fine time for such trivialities. Carmody must be crazy!"

"From what Hembroke said," declared Pringle, "the matter must have been urgent. It might have had a bearing—"

"On tonight? Nonsense. Let us discuss more serious matters. Gentlemen"—Cushman glanced at his watch and turned to the directors—"it is nearly half past nine. The outer door of this conference room—through the little entrance there—is closed. Any emissary of The Red Blot must open it to appear here."

"Detectives are planted outside. In the offices at the end of the large central room are three men. Detective Hembroke is one. Others, headed by Detective Cardona, are outside in the long corridor by the elevators and the stairway.

"They slipped in when the money was delivered. Commissioner Weston himself is with them. They are spread out—peering from side offices. They are allowing every opportunity for a man to enter—none for a man to escape.

"We must be calm"—all attention was now upon Cushman—"and we must treat with The Red Blot's emissary. I shall be the spokesman. We have the money here; we can rightfully demand the release of Selfridge Woodstock and—"

Cushman paused to stare at Dobson Pringle. The president of the association was staring beyond Cushman's shoulder, his face aghast. Other directors saw his look; they swung in the same direction—toward the entrance from the anteroom. An evil laugh greeted them.

FOUR men, each holding a heavy revolver, had entered the conference room! The leader, who stood a pace ahead of the others, was a pudgy-nosed, ugly-jawed individual, whose roughened cheeks made his appearance more formidable.

"Stick 'em up!" came the man's growl.

A thrust of the revolver caused all hands to rise. Gasps came from trembling directors; another growl silenced these audible expressions.

"No noise, get me?" said the rough-faced man. "If there's going to be noise, I'll make it, with this gat! I'm the guy you're expecting. Socks Mallory—working for The Red Blot. Shove over that kale!"

Before any of the astounded men could respond, Socks acted for himself. He stepped forward and upset the box; his big paw spread out treasury certificates of thousand-dollar denominations.

"We'll count it later," laughed Socks. "If there's any short of five million, you birds will pay the difference. You'll pay hard, too."

He beckoned to his men; as they approached, Socks replaced the stacks of bills that he had disturbed. He pocketed his revolver, closed the box, and hoisted it under his arm. With an ugly leer, Socks sidled away from the table, carrying his burden of wealth.

"If you stick where you are," warned Socks, "nobody's going to get hurt. We've got the dough—that's all we want. But we're going to blast our way out of here—and we don't want trouble from the inside. Get me?"

Socks reached the little anteroom. His men, retreating as a protecting cordon, followed. The light switch was at the door of the conference room. A growl came from Socks. One of the mobsters extinguished the lights.

Then came shots.

Bullets ricocheted against the walls. The outer door was opened. Heavy fire was breaking loose. Of the directors, Felix Cushman was the only one who kept his nerve, while the others dived for the shelter of the table. In the darkness, Cushman leaped to his feet, pulled out a revolver, and blazed away blindly through the darkness, hoping to hit any of the robbers who might be forced to retreat.

Cushman reached the door of the anteroom. Beyond, he could hear the shots of the detectives as they took up the fire.

Lights came on in the outer office. Cushman saw them as he opened the door. Out at the entrance to the corridor, Detective Morton Hembroke was firing his revolver. Answering shots reechoed from the distance.

"Come on, men!" shouted Hembroke. "They've got to double back this way! We'll hold it here!"

The other detectives joined Hembroke. Cushman stood grim, while Pringle and the directors came crowding up in back of him as their protector. Shots outside; then came the swarthy face of Joe Cardona, in from the corridor.

"Did you get them?" came his question.

"Get them?" echoed Hembroke. "They broke through this way—"

"Up toward the other end of the corridor then!" exclaimed Cardona.

Lights were on in the corridor now; detectives came around the turn at the opposite end. They stopped in amazement as Cardona approached them on the run.

"Where did they go, Joe?" came the demand.

"Your way!" cried the ace detective.

"Not this direction!" returned a detective.

Police Commissioner Ralph Weston appeared suddenly from an office doorway. He saw the signs of confusion, and put forth an angry question.

"What is this?" he demanded. "A false alarm?"

SHOULDERING his way through the detectives, Weston reached the office of the Amalgamated Builders' Association. Hembroke was standing there; he joined the commissioner as Weston strode up to Felix Cushman.

"What started it?" he questioned. "What began all this shooting at nothing?"

"What started it?" Cushman raised his voice to a snarl. "I'll tell you what started it! Four men marched into this conference room and grabbed five million dollars! What's the matter with your crowd of flatfeet! Where's the gang that took our money?"

Weston stared incredulously. He could see by the expressions of the other directors that Felix Cushman was stating simple facts. The commissioner turned to Hembroke.

"What happened out here?" he queried.

"They came out this way," returned Hembroke. "We were way up at the end—pretty far, but the only place we could be. They must have suspected we were there. They started shooting toward us. What about it, boys?"

"Right," agreed the men who had been in the other offices.

"I hopped out," asserted Hembroke. "Dropped behind a desk—had it all picked—and fired back. The crooks fired wild, and I shouted to the boys to pile out."

"Then what?" questioned Weston.

"I figured they'd head for the corridors," resumed Hembroke. "If they doubled back into the conference room, we'd have them sure. So we came up to cut them off—expecting Cardona would be on the job outside. I saw some figures in the light from the window. I kept on firing—so did my men."

"They didn't double back!" exclaimed Cushman.

"Not a bit of it," added Hembroke. "I knew that when I saw you at the door."

"They left the conference room," asserted one of the directors. "They did not come back."

His companions nodded their absolute conviction of that statement.

Weston wheeled to Cardona.

"There was a lot of fireworks in the hall," said the commissioner coldly. "It looks as though Hembroke drove the crooks right into your hands, Cardona. What about it?"

"They didn't come my way," returned Cardona. "I had good men posted at the other end of the hallway."

"This has been a big mistake," said Commissioner Weston sadly. "Four bandits run out into a corridor. They are blocked from both directions, and they make a getaway."

"It's not the first time The Red Blot's men have pulled a slip like that," declared Cardona. "I don't know how they do it—but they have a way of sliding into nowhere—"

"Except the time when Hembroke got two of them in the pawnshop," broke in Weston furiously. "I put the wrong man on the outside; that's all. Hembroke should have had that job—not you, Cardona! Get going, men! Through the building! Search everywhere! You're in charge from now on, Hembroke. You stay here, Cardona!"

Four armed bandits. Five million dollars. The Red Blot. Such were the thoughts that flashed through Joe Cardona's brain as he dejectedly heard Commissioner Weston argue the situation with Felix Cushman.

Well did Joe Cardona know what the result of this episode would be. Once again, he had been totally tricked by the cunning of The Red Blot. This would be the end of Joe Cardona's career as a detective.

There were other times when Cardona had experienced failure. But never before had a rival such as Merton Hembroke shown superior craft. Hembroke had gained some credit tonight. He had done all that could have been expected. Cardona was the one who had failed.

The Red Blot!

Cardona felt that he was helpless before the machinations of that supermind of crime. Failure tonight. Tomorrow, his resignation from the force. It would be expected.

How could one cope with amazing mobsters who vanished within the tightness of a cordon? Cardona heard Cushman giving Weston the name of Socks Mallory. So that murderer was in again—and Cardona had failed to find a single clew to his whereabouts!

Dully, Cardona knew that he was beaten. There were times when aid had come for him from a strange source—from a personage in whom Commissioner Weston expressed disbelief, but whom Cardona knew to be real—The Shadow.

This time, there had been no such aid; could be no such help. The Red Blot was a master crook beyond all credible belief. Even The Shadow, Cardona decided, could not salvage the hopeless cause that now existed!

CHAPTER XX
FINAL PLANS

A DOOR opened at the end of a stone-walled corridor. An ugly laugh sounded as Socks Mallory, chuckling to men whom he had just left, entered and closed the heavy door behind him. The Red Blot's mob leader was back in the passage that led from door to door with the stone-walled office at the side.

Under his arm, Socks was lugging the box that contained five million dollars. He strode into the underground office, and plunked the container upon the desk. Then, pushing that article of furniture aside, he drew a steel blade from his pocket, and pressed it into a crevice of the stone flooring.

A click; Socks gripped a slab with his fingers, and raised the blocking stone. A large cavity lay beneath; into it, Socks dropped the box of wealth. The murderer chuckled as he replaced the closely fitting slab.

Something was creeping along the floor; something that Socks did not see. It was not a solid object, although it moved as though imbued with life. It was a spreading black blotch that came from the door to the stone-walled corridor.

That patch of darkness was the token of a living presence. It told that The Shadow was close by! Socks, unsuspecting, arose and pushed the desk back into its place. He sat down in the chair and indulged in an evil chuckle.

A buzzer sounded. It was the signal from the outer door. Socks arose. Before he had turned, that long stretch of blackness faded with magical speed. It withdrew not only to the corridor; it continued clear to the end.

Socks, stepping through the doorway, headed in the opposite direction. He admitted two men: Moocher Gleetz and Dynamite Hoskins. They followed him into the office.

"Everything went great, eh, Socks?" was Moocher's first question.

"Yeah," returned Socks. "It always goes great with me, Moocher. How about you?"

Moocher Gleetz hesitated. Socks eyed him narrowly. Both men were intent; so was Dynamite Hoskins, who looked on without fully understanding.

None of the trio noted the phenomenon which had occurred before; the approaching blackness of a silhouette that crept in from the doorway.

"Well," declared Moocher, "here's Dynamite Hoskins."

"I can see that," retorted Socks. "What about the guy you were supposed to finish?"

"Not so good, Socks."

"What! You didn't get him?"

"Maybe—maybe not. I couldn't wait to see—"

"Come on—quit stalling! What happened?"

"I went up to the Club Janeiro," stated Moocher. "I had two gorillas with me. Dynamite came through. I sent him on ahead. Then came the buzzer. Juanita's signal. I knew that Cranston was snooping, and that Dynamite's gorillas were on his trail. So I sent my men in.

"Somehow, that guy must have cornered Dynamite's mob. That's the only way I could figure it. First thing I knew—I was back in the corner—my two men pile through the door, and this guy Cranston shoots them down. I didn't see him do it. I just saw the lights go out—heard the old gat do its work. Saw them flop, too!

"Everything broke loose. Some guy made a getaway out through the door of that middle office. I hopped out there and started to open the door. People were coming in from the nightclub. I dived back to the corner and came through with Dynamite."

"Fine stuff," ejaculated Socks. "Five gorillas against one silk hat. Say—the way you talk, you'd think that guy Cranston was The Shadow!"

"I'm not saying he got away," retorted Moocher. "I'm just saying I don't know whether or not they got him. He bumped my two gorillas—I know that. But maybe Dynamite's crew got him. Maybe it was one of those boys that scrammed."

"Let it ride," growled Socks. "If it was Cranston who got away, he's probably still running. He'll be too scared to come back. Those boiled-shirt boys seem to fall into luck sometimes. I thought you'd bring him in here, dress suit and all. We've got a good graveyard for stiffs like him. Forget it; if he shows up again, I'll get the tip-off from Juanita."

THE matter settled, Socks Mallory turned to Dynamite Hoskins and gave the full-faced man a friendly poke in the ribs.

"What do you think of our layout, Dynamite?" grinned Socks. "Didn't expect it to be as sweet as this, did you?"

"Greatest thing I ever saw," returned Dynamite.

"You've got a lot to see yet," declared Socks. "They talk about the underworld. We've got the real underworld right here. It's the works. Pick your spot—anywhere around Manhattan. I'll tell you whether or not we can take a crack at it. Say—we've been running the bulls around in loops. I'll bet Joe Cardona will be ready to quit after tonight."

"What about this guy Hembroke?" questioned Moocher.

"Him?" Socks grinned, then changed his expression to a serious one. "Say—I'm telling you straight—he's the one guy who could make trouble for us. But he won't get the chance. Leave that to The Blot, Say—he knows his stuff, The Blot does."

After this reference to the hidden chief, Socks quickly changed the subject. He came down to definite business with Dynamite Hoskins.

"We've got you in for the big job, Dynamite," declared Socks. "Tomorrow, we'll fix up the lay. You've heard of Galladay's, haven't you?"

Socks grinned as he made his reference to a huge jewelry concern that was known throughout the world.

"Well," continued Socks, "that's the nut we're going to crack. In again—out again; and you're going to help us."

"Galladay's!" exclaimed Dynamite. "Say, Socks, have you gone cuckoo? You can't crack that joint. Since they moved into that new Fifth Avenue Building of theirs—"

"That's just it," interposed Socks. "It's our gravy—that place. It's going to take two nice socks of TNT, though—and that's where you come in."

"Two?" questioned Dynamite.

"Sure," returned Socks. "One to get into the joint; the other to cover up after we come out. This is one time we're going to make a straight getaway—and we're going to leave nothing behind us."

Socks paused to let his words sink in. Then, as an encouraging thought, he added:

"Listen, Dynamite Hoskins—you, too, Moocher. This is going to be up in the millions, this job. Galladay's have got a lot of European crown jewels in that place of theirs. Say—we can all call it quits after this haul."

"That's the way The Blot figures. He's going to be in on this job himself—working with us. You get your charges set—when The Blot is ready, we'll start. Then—well, the whole world is where we'll go!"

"What about old Million Nibs from Chicago?" questioned Moocher. "Him and the others—like that fellow Carmody you dragged in early this evening."

"There'll be a sweet fade-out for them," laughed Socks. "Don't worry about that. Come on"— Socks rose as he spoke—"we'll go out with the boys. I won't hear from The Blot for a while yet."

THE long streak of blackness faded from the

floor. Socks Mallory and his companions left the office, and went toward the door at the right of the corridor.

It was after their departure that the black blotch again manifested itself. This time it crept farther and farther inward, until it had assumed unusual proportions. Then, in the doorway, loomed the figure that had caused the creeping silhouette.

The Shadow, amazing as a specter, stood within the confines of the stonewalled room. His black cloak drawn close about him; his features hidden by the brim of the slouch hat, the master of mystery was alone.

This room had resounded with Socks Mallory's gleeful chuckles. It was due to reverberate with a more sinister sound. Weirdly, the laugh of The Shadow cast its eerie whisper among the echoing walls.

The tall figure moved toward the desk. The Shadow made no effort to push the object aside. The millions were safe. He had no need to touch them now.

His gloved hand picked up the telephone. The same hand replaced it. The desk drawer opened at The Shadow's touch. Out came the folded map of Manhattan which Socks Mallory had consulted on the previous night.

With it were other papers. The Shadow spread them before him. They were the plans which Carlton Carmody had brought into the consultation room. The Shadow noted the splotches of red drawing ink which the architect had applied to certain spots.

The plans went back into the drawer. It was the map of New York which intrigued The Shadow. His gloved forefinger traced red lines. The pointer stopped on certain spots.

The Shadow was following the very thoughts which Carlton Carmody had expressed. The Stellar Theater Building; the Hotel Gigantic; the Amalgamated Building. The Shadow kept on. His finger marked a red line that led to the new Galladay Building. Then, with final action, it pointed to a short line that terminated in a spot some distance from Times Square.

The Shadow knew that location. The Falconette Apartments—one of the most exclusive places on Park Avenue. Like the Galladay Building, the Falconette Apartments had been built by the Amalgamated Builders.

The Shadow's laugh was like a dying whisper. Its echoes clung to stone walls even after the map had been folded and replaced in the drawer. Those sounds persisted after the departure of that black-garbed phantom. They continued when the final traces of his silhouette had vanished, in creeping fashion, from the floor.

The Shadow followed the corridor to the end; not the way that Socks Mallory had gone—that offered nothing new to The Shadow—but in the opposite direction. The door opened; the black form then disappeared down the stone steps.

Minutes later, the vague swish of a cloak announced The Shadow's return. There was a passage to the right. The Shadow took it. The tall, ghostly shape was lost in the gloom.

Some time later, a man in evening clothes appeared in the quiet lobby of the Falconette Apartments. He carried what appeared to be an opera cloak upon his arm. Its folds concealed the odd shape of a slouch hat.

The lights of Park Avenue glittered in the drizzly night as Lamont Cranston hailed a passing taxicab. A soft laugh sounded as the passenger entered the vehicle.

The menace of The Red Blot was doomed.

The Shadow knew!

CHAPTER XXI
THE RED BLOT STRIKES

"CALL for you, Cardona."

It was Detective Sergeant Markham who spoke from the door of Inspector Timothy Klein's office. Cardona, standing beside Klein's desk, whirled about angrily.

"I don't care who it is," he exclaimed. "Tell them there's nobody here by that name—"

"Easy, Joe," interposed Inspector Klein. "Don't give up yet. I haven't had orders to put you on the sliding board."

"Some fellow wants to talk to you pretty bad, Joe," stated Markham. "Funny sort of voice over the wire. Kind of quiet."

"Wait a minute."

Cardona sprang from the room and entered his own office. He seized the receiver and spoke quickly in the mouthpiece.

"This is Cardona. Detective Cardona."

The voice that replied came in a strange monotone which made Cardona grip the telephone. He knew that voice! He had heard it before! The voice of The Shadow!

"Receive instructions," came the solemn words. "Follow these orders exactly."

"Go on!" exclaimed Cardona breathlessly.

"Inform Inspector Klein," came the voice, "that you plan a final raid in the underworld. Request him to have raiding squads ready for your call. Tonight."

A pause; the voice resumed:

"Take three men of your own. Ten o'clock is the zero hour. Be at the Hotel Gigantic. Occupy Elevator No. 9. Descend to the level below the basement. Enter passage. Advance one hundred paces. Await distant flare."

"Elevator No. 9"—Cardona was repeating the instructions—"Hotel Gigantic—ten o'clock—"

"Advance after you see the flare. Reach large central room. Through open doorway. First room on left. Complete instructions will await you."

A click came over the wire before Cardona could respond.

The Shadow's call was ended. But the detective knew that this was no fantastic summons. The Shadow's instructions could mean but one thing: that the master of darkness has found the way to offset the terror of The Red Blot!

WELL did Cardona know the need for secrecy. He glanced at his watch. It was five o'clock—this was the afternoon following the theft of the five million dollars from the office of the Amalgamated Builders. Five hours to prepare—then to be at the appointed place!

Assuming a poker-face expression, Cardona strolled into Timothy Klein's office. Another detective had come in during his absence—Merton Hembroke. The rising sleuth welcomed Cardona with a friendly smile. Coldly acknowledging the greeting, Cardona turned to Klein.

"Well, inspector," remarked Cardona, "I think I'll stick it through until I get the bounce. If I'm slated for the skids, I might just as well make one last effort to redeem myself. I might get a break."

"Play for one, Joe," advised Klein.

"I've been doing a lot of investigation down in the badlands," continued Joe; "Never found anything yet. Just the same, something might come of it if we swooped in on those dives and hangouts."

"So far, you've advised against the dragnet, Joe."

"That's right, inspector. I figured The Red Blot was too wise to be anywhere that we might be liable to get him. But he uses a bunch of mobsters who are hiding out. Another shooting up at the Club Janeiro last night. Talk about Dynamite Hoskins being in town. Socks Mallory is around—we're sure of that. Maybe the dragnet would make a haul."

"Go ahead, Joe."

"I'll start out with a few men. Have the raiding squads ready when I give the call. That's my suggestion."

"Approved."

Klein began to make the arrangements. Cardona stalked from the office. When he reached his own desk, the detective turned to see Merton Hembroke beside him. The younger sleuth had followed him here.

"Say, Joe"—Hembroke's tone was straightforward—"I wish you all the luck in the world tonight."

"Thanks, Mert," rejoined Cardona gruffly.

"I've been lucky," observed Hembroke. "You haven't. But if you think you're on the skids, Joe, I can tell you that I'm headed the same way. The Red Blot has got me buffaloed. If I'm up against him alone, I'm licked."

Cardona shrugged his shoulders.

"The commissioner called me in today," continued Hembroke. "Told me you were through—that I'd have to carry on. I came right back at him, Joe. I told him frankly that if I'd been on the outside last night, I'd have been the goat—not you."

"You told that to the police commissioner?"

"Sure thing. Why should I try to look big—then be made small afterward? Say, Joe, I'll bet if we'd been teamed up together from the start, we'd have got The Red Blot by now! This independent working doesn't get a man anywhere!"

"Maybe you're right, Hembroke," agreed Cardona. "I like to talk with a fellow that's on the level. Maybe we've both made a mistake—going separately to—"

"I got a break down at Baruch's hockshop," put in Hembroke, "but what did it get me? Nothing. All I can say is that I've been on the job. But I didn't land my man at the Club Janeiro—or at the Hotel Gigantic—or last night, for that matter. Say, Joe, I need a fellow like you to work with me; and maybe I could give you a slant on some of the problems that you've bumped up against."

"That's fair enough," commented Cardona. "You were up at the Gigantic pretty quick, weren't you, Hembroke? Say—what about that elevator mix-up?"

"It began on the twenty-fourth floor. Someone crowned the elevator operator. Then dropped to the eighth."

"Where do you think they took off Selfridge Woodstock?"

"Anywhere along the line. Maybe below the eighth—then up again. Maybe between the eighth and the twenty-fourth. But we went through that whole hotel, Joe."

"What was the number of the elevator?"

"No. 9. Say, Joe—what's that got to do with it? Have you got a line on something?"

"What are you doing tonight?"

"Off duty."

"Want to come along with me?"

"Sure. Where?"

"To the Hotel Gigantic. I'm going to look into that elevator business."

"Say, Joe—Hembroke's tone was eager—"if you're wise to something, let me in on it! I'll give you all the credit. That would fix it great with the commissioner."

"Tonight, then."

"Why tonight? It you're on the trail of something real—say, Joe, have you been up to the Gigantic?"

"I'm going up there tonight."

"Why not go up now—together?"

"Tonight is the time. I don't want anyone to get wise."

"I can fix that, Joe. Through Belville, the chief hotel detective. Say—I can have Elevator No. 9 off duty—waiting for us on one of the upper floors—"

CARDONA considered. Here was a chance to prove the authenticity of The Shadow's call. Cardona did not doubt The Shadow; but he did respect The Red Blot's prowess. Perhaps that supercrook knew that Cardona had received messages from The Shadow in the past. Perhaps the call had been a cleverly perpetrated hoax.

"Go ahead," ordered Cardona. "Fix it with Belville."

Detective Sergeant Markham was coming in the door. Hembroke strolled out and returned in about five minutes. He gave a sign to Cardona. The ace joined him.

"All set," whispered Hembroke, as the pair left the office together.

They reached the Hotel Gigantic, and took an elevator to the fourth floor. Here they found the door open in front of Elevator No. 9. There was no operator.

"I'll take care of it, Joe," asserted Hembroke. "I can run this buggy. Which way—down or up?"

"Down."

Hembroke clanged the door and dropped the elevator to the basement level. He turned questioningly to Cardona.

"We're at the bottom," protested Hembroke.

"Try it," asserted Cardona. Hembroke ran the elevator downward. It descended another level. The detective whistled. He opened the door and peered into blackness.

"Say, Joe!" gasped Hembroke. "How did you get wise to this? This must be the only shaft that comes down here! This is the way they took Woodstock, sure enough!"

"Go easy," ordered Cardona. "We'll only move in far enough to get the lay. Ten o'clock tonight is the time we're due to be here."

Cardona stepped into the passage. His flashlight glimmered on the stony flooring. Then, before the ace detective could emit a cry, men were upon him. Stealthy figures crouching in the blackness leaped forward and fell upon Cardona en masse.

Vainly, the sleuth tried to call for Hembroke. He realized dully that the other detective would be unable to help him. There were enough antagonists to take care of two as readily as one.

A pungent odor filled Cardona's nostrils as a chloroform-soaked rag was clapped against his face. All went black after that.

The Red Blot had struck! Joe Cardona was in the hands of the enemy.

The ace detective had failed to do The Shadow's bidding. This premature investigation had been against instructions. Joe Cardona had offset The Shadow's craft by his own stupidity!

CHAPTER XXII
ZERO HOUR

IT was nearly ten o'clock. In the light of a gloomy cavern, a horde of mobsters were slowly moving toward a passageway that cut through solid rock. The outlet which they were choosing was not the only one from this spot. Rounded holes, large enough for the accommodation of a human form, led off like burrows in other directions.

Socks Mallory was in charge of this mob. Back at the side of the cavern were two other men. As the crew of thugs disappeared into the yawning gap, this pair followed.

The Red Blot and his second lieutenant! Both were here tonight. Only their backs were visible as they followed the mob led by Socks. Those backs were seen by peering eyes that keenly searched the cavern.

A hidden watcher was looking from the crevice of a partly opened door. The Shadow was behind the barrier that blocked off the corridor to The Red Blot's office and the passages beyond. He had come through from the secret way which led to the Falconette Apartments.

Slow minutes passed. It was precisely ten o'clock. The door opened; the tall figure of The Shadow stalked across the gloomy cavern and entered a passage opposite the one which The Red Blot and his hordes had taken a few minutes before.

The Shadow followed this blackened corridor until a turn put him completely out of sight from any who might have returned to the central cabin. A tube was in The Shadow's hand. It clicked. A red flare threw a weird glow along the passage.

The signal to Joe Cardona and his men, waiting in the cavity beneath the Hotel Gigantic!

Rapidly, The Shadow retraced his course. He crossed the cavern, left the door of the corridor open, and reached the little stone-walled office. There, he produced the map of Manhattan. Upon it, he placed an unsealed envelope. Retiring, The Shadow reached the gloom of the corridor and slipped beyond the door at the farther end. His hidden lips whispered a mocking laugh.

One minute—two minutes—still The Shadow waited in darkness. His keen eyes could see through the corridor; into the cavern; across to the blackened hole that led to the Hotel Gigantic.

Three minutes.

No sign of the approaching detectives. Sufficient time had elapsed for them to be here. The Shadow's laugh came low and tense. More seconds drifted by; a flashlight clicked behind the door where The Shadow was concealed.

A disk the size of a silver dollar shone upon the topmost step of the downward flight. The Shadow had not been there tonight. He knew what was below; now, he had an inkling of a disaster which had fallen.

THE black cloak swished as The Shadow swept downward. His invisible form stopped at a heavy barrier. The light focused on a padlock; then moved up to a wicket. A gloved hand slid the little opening aside.

Light from within revealed a gloomy room. The Shadow's eyes, staring through bars, saw the forms of drowsing men resting upon cots.

The Shadow had noted that collection of prisoners before; now, his quick gaze saw a new addition. On a cot close to the door was stretched the motionless form of Detective Joe Cardona!

A steel pick worked while the flashlight glimmered on the padlock. A second click—a third—the padlock sprang open. The Shadow softly slid the door into the stony wall. His spectral figure swept into the dungeon.

Joe Cardona was the first to realize The Shadow's presence. Groggy, the detective felt himself lifted bodily from the cot. As other men raised their heads to stare at the spectral form, the figure was blotted out behind Cardona's body. The Shadow dragged the half-conscious detective from the prison, and shoved the door shut. The padlock clicked.

The Shadow had rescued Cardona alone. There were other prisoners; they were safer here at present. In blackness broken only by a silvery disk that lighted up the steps above, Joe Cardona felt himself being forced toward the upper regions.

The detective was too groggy to resist. Puffs of fresh air were reviving him; yet he kept on blindly. He knew that someone was aiding him. Dimly, he thought of The Shadow. Then came the lighted corridor, as an unseen hand opened the door at the top of the steps.

Joe Cardona wavered. Powerful hands came under his armpits. With rushing stride, The Shadow swept the detective forward—into the stone-walled office, and plopped him in the chair by the desk. The jar brought Cardona to his senses.

Then came a momentary relapse. As Cardona caught himself toppling to the desk, a black-gloved hand picked up the telephone that rested there. A whispering voice spoke in the mouthpiece.

"Burbank speaking," came the reply over the wire.

"Unavoidable delay," returned The Shadow, to his agent. "Is connection still established between this wire and the outside line?"

"Connection established with telephone in Apartment 4-C," came Burbank's response.

The Shadow hung up the receiver and produced a small vial. He placed it to Cardona's nostrils.

The detective's frame shook. His grogginess was dispelled. As he gripped the arms of the chair, Cardona fancied that he heard the sound of a fleeting laugh. He turned quickly, but saw only a fading splotch of blackness at the door.

The detective's eyes went to the map upon the table. His fingers picked up the envelope. They tore it open. With startled gaze, Cardona read blue-inked lines. He dropped the paper and began to tap the map with his forefinger.

He referred again to the note. To his amazement, the writing had vanished! The momentary surprise faded. Cardona did not need those instructions any longer. The map was sufficient!

GRIMLY, the detective seized the telephone. He clicked the hook and heard the operator's response. He called for detective headquarters. He heard the voice of Inspector Timothy Klein.

"I'm in The Red Blot's hideout!" growled Cardona. "His mob has gone to raid Galladay's jewelry store. They're after a ten-million-dollar haul!"

"Get men there—quick! Surround the place. No... No... Not from the outside... They're blowing their way up through the cellar... Dynamite Hoskins is with them... Smash in from the outside..."

Cardona paused. Over the wire he could hear Klein barking out instructions to detectives who were near at hand. Quickly, Cardona gave further news.

"There's places where you've got to block them!" he exclaimed. "Club Janeiro—in the office—an outlet there. Hotel Gigantic—Elevator No. 9... Got that? Wait... There's more... Conference room in Amalgamated Builders' office... Now get this one—most important of all—emergency exit East Side subway, one hundred yards south of Eighteenth Street station... Yes... Yes... Get those places. Hold them!"

The receiver clattered on the hook. Cardona sank exhausted. There was one spot which he had not mentioned; that was the lobby of the Falconette

Apartment. There was an answer. The Shadow's hand had obliterated that station from the map!

Minutes went by. Cardona's relapse was followed by a slow revival. Half rising, the detective heard a sound which brought him to his feet. It was a distant blast—the boom of an underground explosion.

The raid had begun! Soon The Red Blot's cohorts would be returning! Cardona had been told to bring other men with him, that they might hold this spot. Cardona realized that he was alone! He reached for his pocket, realizing as he did that his revolver must have been taken from him. To his amazement, his fingers brought forth an automatic!

On his feet, Cardona found his other coat pocket heavy. He brought out a second automatic! Doubly equipped, Cardona knew his duty. He was to defend this outlet! He was to drive the returning hordes into other passageways, where the police would be ready to stop them!

The Shadow, returned to darkness, had equipped Joe Cardona for the fray that was to come!

CHAPTER XXIII
THE END OF THE BLOT

CROUCHING mobsmen were waiting in a widened portion of an underground passage. The report of an explosion was still ringing in their ears. Smoke and fumes were dispelling up ahead, where the gleams of flashlights were focused.

"That's all."

The words came from Dynamite Hoskins. They meant that the explosion was over; the way was clear ahead. Socks Mallory gave his command.

"Come along!" he ordered. "Inside there; cover the doors while we grab off everything. It will be twenty minutes before the bulls can begin to crash in!"

The horde followed Socks. Three men remained; Dynamite Hoskins stood in darkness; behind him, the bomber knew, was The Red Blot and the other lieutenant who ranked with Socks Mallory.

Little did this waiting trio realize that already a raiding squad of police was arriving at Galladay's jewelry store! Joe Cardona's tip-off was to have startling consequences tonight.

Silence persisted for long minutes. The trio waited patiently. Then a flashlight glimmered from along the passage. A frenzied mobster came staggering forward. He fell as he reached the widening of the passage. His flashlight dropped from his grasp. The man rolled over dead.

A light glimmered from the waiting trio. It was held by the man who stood beside The Red Blot. The searching rays seemed to ask regarding this sudden return; but the man whose form that light illuminated could give no answer from his death-frozen lips!

Cries—revolver shots—into the widened space came more men. With them was Socks Mallory, and the mob leader uttered a wild shout that told The Red Blot all.

"The bulls!" cried Socks. "They busted in on us! We had to scram! They're coming along—never mind the rest of the gang—they've been bumped! Block the way—quick!"

A stern voice came from the darkness. The Red Blot gave his order to Dynamite Hoskins.

"Pull the switch."

Hoskins responded.

Less than ten minutes ago, he had released a charge to blow an upward hole at the end of the passage which curved a hundred feet ahead. Now came his second release.

An explosion thundered in the curving passage. Walls caved in, entombing luckless gangsters who had staggered, wounded, after those who had escaped.

Powerful fumes, driving dust. The Red Blot and his defeated remnants of a gang staggered away from the widened space, heading back to the central cavern. They had effectively stopped any progress on the part of the police.

SOCKS MALLORY heard commands as they hurried along. He understood The Red Blot's order. He was to lead the dozen men who remained; to conduct them through the best avenue of escape from the cavern.

"The subway," growled Socks. "We can pick up any way we want from there."

The word went to the gang. The mobsters hurried ahead, while The Red Blot and his other lieutenant followed at their leisure. Reaching the central cavity, Socks chose one of the passages and ran in that direction with his men close behind him.

The long drive ended at a barricading wall. Socks turned his flashlight on the crowd. His horde had numbered nearly twenty; of these, twelve remained. They were ready to do their leader's bidding in this getaway.

Calling another man, Socks pried at the wall. It slid to the right; the mobsmen scrambled through the opening. They were in the subway, where they crouched as a local thundered past. This opening was the back wall of a flight of steps which served as the emergency exit below Eighteenth Street.

"Come on!"

The subway was strangely silent as Socks and his men invaded it. Had service been suddenly suspended after the passage of that uptown local? The train had just had time to get to the next station.

... other men raised their heads to stare at the spectral form ...

The glares of bull's-eye lanterns swept through the gloomy depths of the subway. Shouts arose from everywhere. The mobsmen realized that they were trapped. Leaping for pillars, they began to fire at the lights.

Bullets whined from echoing revolvers.

Leaden missives ricocheted against subway walls. Scattering gangsters spread—up and down along the tracks.

Well had Inspector Klein responded to Cardona's word. The squad of police and detectives was a small one, but there had been time to lay a perfect ambush. The mobsters, clustered in a group, were spreading wildly; those who fought for the law were stationed in well-chosen spots.

Groveling gangsters cursed as they coughed out their lives. One group—four together—ran the gamut and drove on toward the Eighteenth Street station. As they approached, policemen leaned from behind pillars to greet them.

Face to face, the forces clashed. One officer went down from a bullet which ricocheted from a post. But the mobsters had no chance. One was dropped as he sprang to the safety of the wall. Another fell, pulling a trigger vainly upon emptied cartridges. A third staggered while leaping toward a pillar. Only the fourth, already wounded by a glancing shot, preserved his life by dropping his emptied gun and raising his hands in token of surrender.

So far as the dozen mobsters were concerned, it was a complete triumph for the law against these wanted men. There was a thirteenth member of the group, however. He, alone, had effected a swift escape.

THE first to open the door from the secret passage beneath the emergency steps, Socks Mallory had been the last to leave. When police shots had been loosed, the leader of the mobsmen had chosen the one way to safety—back over the route toward that hidden cavern which had served as headquarters for The Red Blot's mob.

As Socks scrambled along at top speed, he heard the sound of shots. Stopping at the entrance of the cavern, he observed the body of Dynamite Hoskins prone upon the ground.

A wisp of smoke was trickling through the crevice of the door that led to the Red Blot's office. Detective Joe Cardona had downed the first man who had attempted to come that way.

Madly, Socks Mallory answered the challenge. His revolver burst forth toward the crevice. A lucky shot! It found the opening and clipped Cardona's shoulder. Hearing a sour grunt beyond the door, Socks Mallory sprang across the cavern and yanked open the door.

It was the gang leader's last deed. Joe Cardona, wounded, still could fight. The detective had staggered away from the door; but as the barrier opened, he fired a shot with a hand that was pressed close to his body. The bullet felled Socks Mallory. The gang leader's form fell forward, and jammed between the door and the wall.

Cardona was in retreat. His left hand supporting his crippled right arm, the detective staggered back into the office.

He was just in time. Two figures leaped from passageways where they had fled. Together they invaded the corridor.

The first one stopped at the office door; then entered. Joe Cardona, slumped in the chair, his right arm useless, looked up to face Detective Merton Hembroke.

For a moment, Joe was dazed. He thought that this was a rescue; then he realized that he was mistaken. There was an evil look upon Hembroke's countenance; a look that was by no means friendly.

"Thought you'd spring one on The Red Blot, eh?" jeered Hembroke. "Well, you got away with a lot—but you didn't know I was working for him, did you? Socks Mallory and I—we were the boys who put the idea across for him!"

Hembroke held a gun, but he made no effort to cover Cardona, who was helpless. Instead, Hembroke turned to the doorway and pointed to a man who was entering—a gray-haired individual, whose eyes glared maliciously.

Joe Cardona gasped as he recognized Dobson Pringle, president of the Amalgamated Builders' Association.

"Meet The Red Blot!" grinned Hembroke.

Pringle was holding an automatic. Cardona realized that only his helpless state had prevented these two villains from taking his life immediately upon their entrance. They were now prepared to make up for that brief lapse.

Cardona's automatic was lying on the table, where it had dropped from his weakening fingers. With a determined effort to go out fighting, the detective made a mad effort. He grasped the gun with his left hand, expecting as he did so, to receive a bullet in the back.

Dobson Pringle had stepped within the doorway. He was on one side of the room, Merton Hembroke on the other. As both men raised their weapons to end Cardona's life, a strange sound from the doorway made them turn. A whispering laugh—an uncanny announcement of a sinister presence—this betokened the arrival of The Shadow.

With an automatic in each black-gloved fist, The Shadow was here to prevent the murder of Joe Cardona. His powerful guns covered Dobson Pringle—now known as The Red Blot—and Merton Hembroke, the sleuth whose double-crossing activities had aided the master plotter.

With a savage cry, Hembroke hurled himself upon the tall figure at the door, raising his revolver to fire as he leaped. Swift, vicious, and determined, the false detective hoped to end the menace who had blighted The Red Blot's schemes.

An automatic spoke, as Hembroke tried to press the trigger of his revolver. The detective's leap ended in collapse. Half rising to his knees, Hembroke again attempted to use his wavering finger. The effort was in vain. The man sprawled face down upon the floor.

NOT for one instant had The Shadow's keen gaze lost track of Dobson Pringle. As a plotter, the Red Blot had shown amazing prowess; as a man of action in this crisis, his powers were not so apparent. Pringle had halted, counting upon the success of Hembroke's onslaught. Seeing the detective fall, The Red Blot backed away, raising his automatic in desperation.

The Shadow had him covered. Tauntingly, the black-garbed master awaited Pringle's action. The gray-haired man was afraid to fire; he could not beat that looming weapon which faced him. But as he hesitated, another factor came into this conflict.

Joe Cardona, his automatic successfully gripped in his left hand, rose from his chair and leaped toward The Red Blot.

With a harsh cry, Pringle acted. He leaped to the right to gain the cover of Cardona's body. His hand, its forefinger upon the trigger, thrust outward, to put an end to Cardona's clumsy effort.

Whether Pringle or Cardona would have gained the first shot, none could ever tell. For while their fingers pressed against the triggers, The Shadow's automatic sounded in advance.

Its target was Pringle's arm. The gun fell from The Red Blot's hand. A moment later, Joe Cardona's shots roared forth. Dobson Pringle dropped to the floor and lay face upward.

A sardonic laugh awoke vague echoes. Cardona turned as he heard the creepy, chilling sound. He saw no one at the door. The Shadow had departed. The detective bent above the body of The Red Blot. Dobson Pringle's lips were moving weakly.

"I—I am dying." Pringle's gasp came wearily. "I—I am beaten. You will find—find the millions—in the floor—beneath the desk—"

Cardona could see that the man was speaking the truth. Mortally wounded by Cardona's haphazard shots, Dobson Pringle had lost his malicious expression.

Rising, Cardona thrust himself against the desk and pushed it toward the side of the room, The effort was weakening. Cardona's head began to swim. He steadied himself and stared at Pringle.

The man who had termed himself The Red Blot was propped upon an elbow. His trembling finger was pointing to the crevice in the floor. Cardona saw the indicated mark.

"There!" gasped Pringle. "Beneath—beneath that stone. You—you have won. The money—"

The exhausting effort was too much. Pringle's elbow gave way. Falling upon his side, the defeated villain watched the detective claw with his left hand at the movable stone.

"The lever," murmured Pringle. "The lever on the wall—"

Cardona noticed Pringle's attempt to point. The lever which the gray-haired man indicated was just below the spot which the top of the desk had covered. Reaching up, Cardona pulled the lever.

He heard a fiendish chuckle. He stared at Dobson Pringle.

NO longer placid and weary in expression, Pringle was glaring with malicious eyes. The evil personality of The Red Blot was in his gruesome stare. His lips, foaming, spat insidious words of hateful triumph.

"Your friends"—The Red Blot's voice was spasmodic in its insidious tone—"the prisoners—the ones you have left—are doomed. You—you have slain them—rats—drowning in a deluge—"

As the voice broke off, Cardona could hear the roaring surge of a cataract far below. He realized the malice of The Red Blot's last action. Dying, Dobson Pringle had tricked him into loosing a hidden torrent of water into the dungeon where The Shadow had left the prisoners!

Was it too late?

Cardona staggered away from the wall. He slipped to his knees, weakened by loss of blood from his wounded shoulder. He could hear The Red Blot's death rattle—a gargling sound that carried a tone of glee.

As if in answer came a whispering echo—a sinister challenge that sounded from beyond the outside corridor. It was The Shadow's triumph laugh—the symbol of the departing victor. Cardona, resting upon his left hand, waited, too weak to move.

A clatter in the corridor. The voices of men. Four persons came into the room. Cardona did not recognize them; but they knew him.

The detective had been groggy during his imprisonment in the pit beneath; these men had not. They were the prisoners, freed from the dungeon—on their way up the steps at the moment when Cardona had unwittingly released the tide intended for their doom.

Selfridge Woodstock; his secretary, Crozer; Carlton Carmody—with them was a tall, elderly man, with pale face and stooped shoulders, whose facial muscles twitched as he observed the scene in this bloody room.

They helped Cardona to his feet. Then came other rescuers; Detective Sergeant Markham and a squad which had come in from the corridor to the East Side subway. Markham recognized that these were friends.

The tall, eccentric individual spoke. His statement cleared the confusion as he named his identity.

"I can explain everything," he said. "I am Hubert Craft, chief architect of the Amalgamated Builders' Association—supposed to be dead— actually held prisoner by this fiend—"

Craft pointed toward the inert form of Dobson Pringle. Joe Cardona, still game, added the final words.

"The Red Blot," gasped the detective. "Pringle—The Red Blot—"

Dobson Pringle's form was now on its face. Markham raised the body to learn that the man was dead. Clutching the motionless corpse, Markham stared—the others followed his gaze.

Where Pringle's body had lain, the floor was stained with a pool of crimson blood. Spreading slowly, gushed forth from a wound that still oozed, that fluid formed a grotesque pattern.

In death, as in life, Dobson Pringle had left the signature which he had chosen for the key mark in his villainous campaign of crime. That pool of blood remained as the final signature of The Red Blot!

CHAPTER XXIV
THE COMMISSIONER EXPLAINS

"THE most astonishing case of criminal activity in the history of the New York police!"

This assertion regarding The Red Blot came from Police Commissioner Ralph Weston. It was uttered with emphasis as the commissioner sat with his millionaire friend, Lamont Cranston, in the grill room of the Cobalt Club.

They were keeping the luncheon engagement which Cranston had jocularly arranged a few days previous. When the newspaper had blazed forth the triumph of the law over The Red Blot, Cranston had telephoned Weston to congratulate him—and to remind him of the suggested meeting.

"I have read the newspapers with great interest," observed Cranston, after he had heard Weston's all-inclusive definition, "My own experience— observations at the Club Janeiro—made me understand the remarkable features of this case—"

"That was but the surface, Cranston," interposed Weston. "The whole affair was incredible. The motive was a relentless scheme for ill gain. A criminal intelligence masked by a most disarming exterior.

"Who could have suspected that Dobson Pringle, kindly and prosperous gentleman, was The Red Blot? Yet, once the scheme was uncovered, the machinations became as plain as day. Let me give you a summary of it, Cranston.

"Dobson Pringle was a man long experienced in building. He gained access to old city maps and records; to facts that had been forgotten. He noted that Manhattan was honeycombed with abandoned conduits; with blocked-off excavations. Below the surface of the city streets was the nucleus for a remarkable underground system of passages— not to compare with the catacombs of Rome or the sewers of Paris, yet an arrangement that could be put to definite use.

"Pringle was in a position to develop that system. He saw in it the making of a real underworld. The Amalgamated Builders' Association was erecting skyscrapers, all within a short radius of Times Square. By a tie-up with Socks Mallory, then an enterprising racketeer, Pringle peopled his catacombs with a squad of wanted men—chosen ruffians who stayed below ground gladly, and who served as the advance workers. They were The Red Blot's sappers.

"Pringle made Hubert Craft, the architect, his unwitting aid. In the plans for new buildings, he urged special arrangements for hidden outlets from the structures. He explained to Craft that these might later be used for connecting links with other buildings—subways and the like—and that they would prove of value in the future."

"Craft was easily duped," observed Cranston.

"For a while, only," returned Weston. "The first of these hidden entrances to the cavernous domain was placed in the office of the Club Janeiro—beneath the Stellar Theater Building— an Amalgamated enterprise.

"That enabled Socks Mallory to go in and out; to add replenishments to his workers. Each new building had another outlet to be tapped. In the Hotel Gigantic it was an elevator shaft that descended more deeply than supposed.

"The most artful of these secret openings was in the fifth floor of the Amalgamated Building. The structure pyramids"—Weston began making a diagram upon the back of an envelope—"and the first setback comes above the fifth floor. For five floors, there are corner rooms—like the conference room of the Amalgamated Builders, shaped thus. A narrow anteroom allowed for a hidden wall space, like a large air shaft. Pringle's hidden workers installed an elevator there; one which could be reached through a secret panel in the anteroom wall.

"Galladay's jewelry store was neatly designed so that one spot would allow access to all parts of the ground floor. That, of course, was protected by installed alarm apparatus; but Pringle had made full allowance. Craft was not suspicious even then—it was when Pringle made him put in a secret entrance to the ground floor of the Soudervale Building that the architect raised an objection. He knew that the space would give access to a banking institution."

"DID Craft speak to Pringle?" questioned Cranston.

"Yes," allowed Weston. "That was the deed that started The Red Blot into action. Mobsters abducted Craft. Pringle framed what looked like a disappearance of the architect. Then trouble broke loose.

"From the central cavern of his underground realm, The Red Blot had taken a large conduit as a course to the East Side subway. Other old underground passages, a considerable distance from Pringle's domain, were tapped from spots along the subway line. To build up a reputation, to gain funds which he needed, The Red Blot launched crime attacks in parts of Manhattan where his men could escape by hidden outlets to these underground channels. After each raid they returned to their base.

"Besides Socks Mallory, The Red Blot had another capable aide—Merton Hembroke. Where Mallory served as lieutenant of the underground forces, Hembroke was a secret agent working as a detective. That was to prove vital in The Red Blot's plans. As we have pieced it, here is what happened.

"First: Spider Carew, a henchman of Mallory, who was stationed above ground, tried to squeal. We sent detectives to cover him as he rode up on the East Side subway. Hembroke tipped off Mallory to get the man. Mallory did so and escaped in the subway.

"Then Mallory slew Tony Loretti, who was a menace to The Red Blot's schemes. Juanita Pasquales has confessed that she was forced to do Mallory's bidding. Hembroke was present at the affray in the Club Janeiro. He made it look as though the killer might have escaped outward. He effectively covered the secret of the little office."

"I see," smiled Cranston.

"Then came The Red Blot's master stroke," continued the police commissioner. "Socks Mallory slugged an elevator operator and abducted Selfridge Woodstock, Chicago financier, with the secretary, Crozer. Down to the level below the Hotel Gigantic, in an elevator. There—so we believe—Hembroke took the elevator up; left it and reached the lobby, where he was on hand to gain credit for a quick investigation.

"Dobson Pringle, as president of the Amalgamated Builders, had very little money invested in the concern. He knew the psychology of the directors. He had a fake note. Its delivery caused consternation. Pringle was ready to urge the raising of the five million dollars. When Felix Cushman proposed that radical act, Pringle wisely played a conservative part.

"Then came an unexpected event. Before the meeting, set in the Amalgamated conference room, Carlton Carmody, architect, who had succeeded Hubert Craft, discovered the faults in the plans. He was seen by Hembroke—we have Carmody's own testimony for this—and the false detective tipped off Pringle. Socks Mallory came up and seized Carmody, who was held prisoner with Craft, Woodstock, and Crozer."

"Where?" queried Lamont Cranston, lighting a cigarette in absent-minded fashion.

"THAT'S coming," smiled Weston. "Mallory raided the directors' meeting and took five million dollars. Again, Hembroke covered by making it look as though the crooks had run out. Hembroke was commended. All was set for The Red Blot to pull his final coup blowing up through Galladay's floor, the jewel robbery, and an escape along a passage which would be blocked after the marauders had passed."

"Strange," observed Cranston, "that such well-laid schemes should fail—"

"Detective Joe Cardona gets the credit," interrupted Weston, in an admiring tone. "He investigated the Hotel Gigantic. He was double-crossed by Hembroke, and was captured. He escaped. He found The Red Blot's secret office. A special passage—off behind a door that was always closed—led up to the Falconette Apartments, where Pringle lived. Cardona discovered a map; it showed all the strategic points except that one, which had been obliterated. Cardona also found a telephone that was hooked up with Pringle's apartment.

"Through some lucky freak—how, we have not yet ascertained—the wire of the secret phone was temporarily connected with an outside line. When Cardona called, he got detective headquarters. Our men interrupted the robbery of Galladay's. They covered everywhere—and the crooks were shot down by the police."

"Odd," remarked Cranston, "that The Red Blot did not escape through his own private exit—"

"Cardona stopped him!" Weston was triumphant. "Cardona shot down both Dobson Pringle and Merton Hembroke. He found the hiding spot of the stolen five million dollars, which The Red Blot had returned to get.

"Inadvertently, Cardona released a flood of water—a tapped dry pipeline which The Red Blot had arranged to sweep the dungeon where he kept his prisoners, should he deem their death necessary. Luckily, they managed to escape through the door which Cardona had previously opened."

Police Commissioner Weston glanced at his watch. He arose hastily and announced that he must be back at his office. He shook hands with Lamont Cranston and departed.

A STRANGE smile appeared upon Cranston's face as he recalled a parting invitation from Weston. The police commissioner was anxious to have Cranston pay a visit to those underground passages—to see, for himself, the remarkable catacombs which The Red Blot had fashioned.

It was after the usual luncheon hour; the gloomy grill room of the Cobalt Club was empty save for Lamont Cranston. By the light of side lamps on the wall, the millionaire's body cast a long, sinister blotch upon the floor; his chiseled profile produced a weird, elongated silhouette.

The mark of The Shadow! That uncanny stretch of darkness was the power which had obliterated The Red Blot. It betokened the master who had alone detected and conquered the hordes of the supercrook.

Cardona had been a pawn in The Shadow's game; but to the sincere detective, The Shadow, always preferring the shroud of darkness, had given the credit.

The shuddering whisper of a mocking laugh crept through the gloomy room. Its eerie reverberations continued as Lamont Cranston, moving forward with steady, even stride, left the spot. The ghostly sounds were heard by a waiter who paused and quivered as he stood at the entrance from the kitchen. The last echoes of that taunting, spectral sound were terrible to hear.

The room was empty as the waiter stared. Lamont Cranston had left, unseen. The laugh of The Shadow had broken from his impassive lips—as a recollection of the story which Commissioner Ralph Weston had told.

For The Shadow had triumphed. With that weird being who dwelt in darkness save when he appeared in unexpected guise, victory was sweet only when obtained by secret action.

The Shadow, still unrevealed, was ready for new conquests. That final laugh was his last token of triumph in the case which he had just completed.

The Shadow—with no need for other aid—had obliterated the crimson scourge of The Red Blot!

THE END

SPOTLIGHT on THE SHADOW by Anthony Tollin

The stories selected for this third Shadow volume were chosen for their historical importance in the development of The Shadow. *The Red Blot* was Walter Gibson's thirty-fifth Shadow novel, but featured the first meeting between Lamont Cranston and Commissioner Weston, who had been introduced in *Hidden Death* (September 1932). The friendship would continue throughout *The Shadow* pulp novels (except for a 1934-36 period when Wainwright Barth took over as commissioner) and played a key role in *The Shadow* radio series where the perpetually-wrong Weston would often be played for comedy relief.

Readers may be puzzled by the hooded Shadow that appears on the second page of *The Red Blot*. The earliest publicity photos of The Shadow promoting CBS' *Street & Smith Detective Story Program* featured this cowled version posed for by James LaCurto, the first actor to voice The Shadow when the character debuted July 31, 1930 as network radio's first sinister mystery narrator. These hooded images were repeated on Street & Smith's earliest house ads and covers for *The Shadow Magazine*. *The Shadow* radio series will be chronicled in a photo feature in our next volume, in which The Shadow confronts *The Murder Master,* a criminal mastermind who announces his impending killings over the radio airwaves, and the novel that explained the origins of Lamont Cranston's relationship with his "friend and companion, the lovely Margo Lane," *The Hydra.*

The Voodoo Master was voted the all-time favorite Shadow novel in 1937 by the readership of *The Shadow Magazine,* was reprinted in 1943 in the second *Shadow Annual* and was again recognized as one of the greatest Shadow novels in a 1979 poll of top pulp historians. The story introduced The Shadow's first major recurring arch-foe, Doctor Rodil Mocquino, who will return to battle the Knight of Darkness in a forthcoming volume.

James LaCurto as The Shadow

The Shadow, arch-foe of crime, meets an arch-criminal of black magic, and changes black to red as, with wits and guns, he battles

The Voodoo Master

A Complete Book-length Novel from the Private Annals of
The Shadow, as told to

Maxwell Grant

CHAPTER I
THE MAN WHO STARED

"I HAVE no name."

The words were uttered in a solemn, mechanical monotone, from lips that were expressionless. The speaker was a rigid, staring man, who stood in the center of a room that was obviously a physician's office.

"What about friends? Have you any?"

The question was put by a swarthy, stocky man who was standing beside a small group of listeners.

"I have no friends."

Again the slow, mechanical tone. The man in the

center of the room retained his rigid attitude. His eyes were motionless, looking steadily at the farther wall. The swarthy questioner shook his head; then turned to a companion, a serious-faced man who was seated at a desk. The swarthy man asked:

"What about it, Doctor Sayre?"

The serious-faced man considered.

"We must talk it over, inspector," he decided. "Perhaps it would be best for us to be alone."

The swarthy-faced man nodded. He motioned to the other listeners; they were three in number and all looked like detectives. The three arose and took hold of the staring man. They started to walk him from the room. Doctor Sayre intervened.

"Leave him here," ordered the physician. Then, to the swarthy inspector: "It might be better if he heard us talk, Cardona."

The three detectives departed in a cluster. Sayre and Cardona remained in the office together; between them stood the rigid man who stared. The trio formed an interesting contrast.

Doctor Rupert Sayre possessed the proper attitude of a consulting physician. Though youngish, he was serious in manner; and his air was one that created confidence. This was in keeping with his reputation. Sayre rated high among the practicing physicians of Manhattan.

Joe Cardona, ace detective of New York headquarters, was also a man of merit. Acknowledged as a leader in his own profession, Cardona held the position of acting inspector. His dark eyes were keen; his firm jaw marked him as a man of action.

As for the staring man, he possessed features which placed him above the common run. He was above medium height, erect in carriage and handsome of countenance. His complexion was light; his hair a medium brown. His eyes, despite their stare, were clear. Their color a bluish-gray.

"GIVE me the history of this case, Cardona," suggested Doctor Sayre, in a brisk fashion. "It is quite all right to speak while the patient is listening. Your words might produce some thought impulse that would arouse him from his present condition."

"All right," agreed Cardona. "To begin with, the fellow arrived in New York at three o'clock Sunday afternoon."

"Two days ago," mused Doctor Sayre. "He was in this condition when he arrived?"

"Yes. He came from a Jersey Central ferry, at Liberty Street. He had ridden into Jersey City on an express from Mannegat, New Jersey."

"Mannegat is between Asbury Park and Atlantic City?"

"Yes; north of Atlantic City, south of Asbury Park. You reach it by Pennsylvania Railroad from Philadelphia; by Jersey Central from New York.

Well, doctor, when this fellow reached the New York side of the Hudson River, the first thing he did was walk straight in front of a taxicab. The driver jammed the brakes; the man kept on, staring dead ahead.

"Another cab nearly bopped him. That's when a patrolman stepped in. He grabbed the chap and saw what was wrong with him. He took him to the precinct. From there, he was shipped to a hospital for observation.

"Forty-eight hours ago. No change in his condition. He slept at intervals, but stayed rigid when he did. When he closes his eyes, it looks mechanical."

The staring man must have caught an inspiration from the words. He closed his eyes a moment after Cardona spoke. There was no flicker of the eyelids. They plopped shut like clamshells and remained closed.

"Outside of a few dollars," stated Cardona, "all this fellow had on him were two railway tickets. Here they are." Joe produced the items. "One is a Jersey Central receipt for a ticket purchased at Mannegat; we know that the man boarded the train there at one o'clock, Sunday afternoon.

"The other is the return half of a Sunday excursion ticket from Philadelphia to Mannegat, via the Pennsylvania Railroad. The stamp shows that it was bought in Philadelphia at nine o'clock Sunday morning."

Sayre nodded. He was listening to Cardona and watching the rigid man at the same time. Sayre saw eyelids open. Blue-gray eyes resumed their blank stare.

"What he did," assured Cardona, "was board a Pennsy train at Philly, intending to return there. When he got to Mannegat, he must have changed his mind and taken the Jersey Central into New York, instead.

"That's all we know about him. We've sent pictures to the Philadelphia police. No results. Nobody knows the fellow. He won't say anything that helps. The doctors at the hospital can't figure it. That's why I brought him here to you."

Doctor Sayre smiled.

"Why to me?" he queried. "I can scarcely be classed as a specialist in such cases as these."

"I'm not so sure of that," returned Cardona. "You've seen some cases that others haven't. Particularly when you were the guest of a man named Eric Veldon."

Doctor Sayre made a sudden exclamation. He arose and approached the staring man, to study the patient at close range. He was trying to find a likeness between this man and others whom he had seen in the past. Sayre turned to Cardona and spoke in an awed tone.

"Veldon's automata!" he half whispered. "Living dead men, who moved about like mechanical figures! Victims of operations that had made their brains mere machines in the hands of a master criminal!"

APPROACHING the standing man, Sayre pressed fingers to the back of the patient's head. He was searching for incisions, some trace of a surgical operation. He found none. This man was a different case from those whom Cardona had mentioned.

"He may act like Veldon's machine men," declared Sayre to Cardona, "but he is not the same. Of one thing I can assure you, inspector: This man's condition is the result of a nervous shock; not of a surgical operation."

"Can you do anything to change his condition?"

"I cannot promise. I should like to keep him here a while. He is not dangerous, despite the fact that you kept three detectives as his custodians."

"I only brought them to move him along. He walks like a mechanical figure. You say you want to keep him here, doctor. You mean alone?"

"Exactly."

Cardona pondered.

"All right," he decided. "This isn't a criminal case. I can leave him here, Doctor Sayre. Of course, the responsibility will be yours."

"I am willing to accept it."

"That settles the matter. He is in your charge."

"You will hear from me by this time tomorrow."

Doctor Sayre indicated a desk clock, which showed half past five. Cardona nodded as he stepped toward the door.

"By this time tomorrow afternoon," reminded the acting inspector. "If I don't hear from you, I'll come here, doctor."

Sayre had risen. As soon as Cardona was gone, he stepped squarely in front of the staring man and met the fellow's gaze. The electric lights were on in the office. The physician could see the staring optics plainly. He knew that the man was observing him; but there was no motion or change in the patient's gaze.

A human automaton. A "machine man," as Cardona had described him. Sayre was not surprised that the ace detective had classed this patient with those victims of Eric Veldon's. A flood of thoughts swept through the physician's brain.

Sayre remembered Eric Veldon. A criminal who had called himself a "master of death." A fiend who had wanted Sayre to aid him in brain operations upon captured thugs and outlaws, that they might do Veldon's bidding in schemes of crime.

Sayre, himself, had been a prisoner of Veldon's, subject to the evil master's bidding. Into that dilemma had come a powerful fighter, greater than the insidious supercrook. The result had been Sayre's rescue. Veldon and his minions had perished. Since then, Sayre had served the rescuer who had saved him.

That rescuer was The Shadow. A hidden being, a master sleuth, a fighter *par excellence,* The Shadow was one who constantly warred against crime. He was an uncanny personage, whose ways were many, whose very presence was a shroud of mystery. No matter what the mission might be, Sayre had never known The Shadow to fail.

STEPPING toward the man who stared, Sayre placed his hands upon the patient's shoulders. He gave a turning pressure; the staring man swung about without resistance. Sayre shifted hands and urged the patient toward a door.

Regularly, with slow, automatic pace, the staring man walked forward. When they reached the barrier, Sayre's pressure stopped him. The physician stepped ahead and opened the door. He turned on a light to show a small reception room.

Coming back to the office, Sayre walked the patient forward to a chair in the reception room. Again, he turned the human machine about; then pushed him downward. The rigid arms jerked sidewise and found the chair arms. Abruptly, the man took a seated position, still staring dead ahead.

Doctor Sayre locked the outer door of the reception room and pocketed the key. He went back into the office and closed the adjoining door. He picked up the telephone and called a number. A quiet voice responded:

"Burbank speaking."

Sayre replied by giving his own name. Tensely, he stated facts concerning the strange patient whom Cardona had placed in his charge. Burbank's voice concluded:

"Report received. Await return call."

Doctor Sayre hung up the receiver. Anxiously, he opened the door to the reception room and again surveyed the patient. The staring man was exactly as Sayre had left him, seated in the big chair, his face expressionless as he looked straight toward the wall. Seven minutes passed, while Sayre remained almost as rigid as the man whom he was watching. Then the telephone bell rang.

Sayre bobbed back into the office and closed the door. He lifted the receiver and announced his name. Again, he heard Burbank's voice; this time, with brief instructions.

The call completed, Sayre hung up and smiled. He opened the door to the reception room; then

The Shadow

All the world knows of The Shadow and his astounding deeds against the menace of crookdom. Wherever crime is known; wherever justice seeks to rule, there the deeds of this master of the night, this weird creature of blackness, are common knowledge.

His source unknown to the public, nevertheless, his prowess is feared by the underworld. He works as a lone hand, yet he has able aides in Harry Vincent, a presentable young man who can make himself at home anywhere; Burbank, who serves as communications contact for all the agents; Clyde Burke, reporter on the *Classic;* Cliff Marsland, who served a term in prison for a crime he did not commit and whose innocence was known only to The Shadow. Marsland, rather than show that innocence, was willing to work for The Shadow as a branded crook, for The Shadow had rescued him from death in the past. Mann, the calm-looking broker, is another link in The Shadow's small but compact army of crime-battlers.

The Shadow himself assumes the guise of Lamont Cranston, Henry Arnaud, or "Fritz," the janitor at police headquarters, whenever necessary. As Cranston he hobnobs with the police commissioner; as Fritz, he learns what Joe Cardona is doing. And he uses this knowledge to coordinate all efforts so that crime might be punished.

Other agents are at The Shadow's call, and various means which only this dark master of the night can wield, are used by him. He battles crime with thrills and chills, and smoking automatics. Let him thrill you in these tales, gathered from his private annals. Join with The Shadow to end crime.

Twice a Month      *10 Cents a Copy*

At Your News Stand!

ON THE AIR!   **ON THE SCREEN!**

went to his desk. Thanks to the opened door, he could keep tabs on his patient, should the man make motion.

No such indications came. Minutes ticked without a stir from the staring man in the next room. Doctor Rupert Sayre, however, wore a smile of absolute confidence. His chat with Burbank had given him assurance; for Burbank was The Shadow's contact man.

Sayre's report had been relayed. A return statement had been received. While dusk settled above Manhattan, Doctor Sayre could wait without a worry. Within the next two hours, the physician would have another visitor—one whom Sayre believed would surely solve the riddle of the man who stared.

The Shadow, master delver into unaccountable pasts, was coming to take charge of this unexplainable case.

CHAPTER II
THE SHADOW EXPERIMENTS

DOCTOR SAYRE'S desk clock showed ten minutes after seven, when the physician suddenly chanced to notice it. Sayre could not have explained the impulse that forced him to drop work that he was doing, in order to consult the clock. Nor could he have told the reason for his next action.

Sayre had heard nothing; yet, after glancing at the clock, he looked directly toward the outer door of the office. Tensely expectant, he expected it to open. Slow seconds passed; then the door swung slowly inward. Silent, smiling, a tall visitor stood on the threshold.

Sayre recognized the countenance that he observed. The smile was slight, formed by thin lips. The visage, itself, was masklike, with a hawkish aspect. Steady, burning eyes gazed from the immobile face.

"Lamont Cranston!"

In his greeting, Sayre spoke the name instinctively. The physician, like others, knew that Lamont Cranston was a globe-trotting millionaire, who spent occasional periods at his estate in New Jersey. More than that, however, Sayre had for a long while identified Lamont Cranston with The Shadow.

Later, Sayre had learned that The Shadow was not Lamont Cranston. There was a real Cranston, who was seldom at home. The Shadow, when he chose, used Cranston's residence and lived there, passing himself as the millionaire. This was with the real Cranston's knowledge and approval. But of the two, the only one who would be visiting Doctor Sayre was The Shadow.

Closing the door, The Shadow advanced and shook hands with the physician. Keen eyes noted the open doorway to the reception room. The Shadow spoke in a quiet, easy tone:

"Bring the man here."

Sayre complied. He found his patient still seated in the adjoining room. He urged the man to his feet and propelled him into the office. The Shadow pointed toward the desk. Sayre swung the staring man so that he faced in that direction.

Leaning back against the desk, The Shadow motioned Sayre to join him. Together, they faced the staring eyes. The Shadow nodded to Sayre. The physician understood. He tried the stock questions on the patient.

"What is your name?"

"I have no name."

"Who are your friends?"

"I have no friends."

The Shadow was watching the expressionless eyes, as the staring man delivered the mechanical monotones. There was no sign of intelligence behind the patient's bulging gaze.

"Some other experiments," remarked Sayre to The Shadow. "Ones that they tried at the hospital; and which I repeated when Cardona brought the man here."

The physician picked up a small book and held it in front of the staring eyes. Sayre asked:

"What is this?"

"A book."

"And this?" Sayre drew a fountain pen from his pocket. He held it close to the man's eyes. "What is it?"

"A fountain pen."

Sayre pressed the book into the man's left hand. He pushed the right hand toward the volume.

"Take the book," he ordered.

The staring man obeyed.

"Open it."

The patient followed the instructions.

"Look at the pages." Sayre forced the hands upward. "Read anything that you see there."

Mechanically, the man read a few words; then stopped. Sayre shifted the book. Slow lips spoke a few words more. Sayre took the book and tossed it to the desk.

"His eyes are focused," explained the physician. "He can read only the few words that come directly in front of them. That is why it is necessary to move the book. Incidentally, the man is color-blind also."

SAYRE reached over and opened a desk drawer. He removed several pencils. He held one straight across in front of the staring man's eyes.

"What is this?"

"A pencil."

"What is its color?"

Lips moved, but made no utterance. Eyes, though they did not shift, were strained as they continued their stare. The Shadow picked up a blue pencil; he took the yellow one from Sayre. He held the two so that the man could see them.

"Which one is yellow?" queried The Shadow. "This?" He moved the blue. "Or this?" He moved the yellow.

The staring man could see both. His lips moved. Each time they delivered a slow gasp. The Shadow put down the pencils and picked up another, a green one.

"This is green," he remarked, in the slow tone of Cranston. "Remember it: green."

He turned about, mixed the pencils, then raised them one by one before the straining, staring eyes.

"Name the green pencil when you see it."

The staring man's lips moved as each pencil passed his vision. Nevertheless, no words arrived. Sayre made comment.

"As I remarked," he said, "the man is color-blind."

"I disagree," returned The Shadow, with a slight smile. He tossed the pencils to the desk. "He has simply lost his sense of color perception. It is a peculiar condition that accompanies his aphasia."

Sayre looked puzzled. The Shadow explained.

"A person who is totally color-blind," he declared, "should show one of two reactions. He will either think that he knows colors and will therefore name them incorrectly, because of the shades that he sees, or he will admit his inability to recognize colors and will show no effort.

"This man has tried to identify the colors of the pencils. He has found himself unable to do so. Apparently, he has lost his color sense. Perhaps you can explain that, Doctor Sayre."

"It is puzzling," conceded the physician. "Your theory seems to strike the facts. I attribute the man's aphasia to a shock. But this matter of colors, once recognized, but no longer—"

"What sort of a shock?"

Sayre stroked his chin.

"That opens a realm of speculation," he declared. "Sound could have produced this condition, as with the cases of shell-shocked victims. Brilliance might have done it; there have been cases of aphasia among physicians who have witnessed terrific lightning flashes."

"It was color shock, in this instance."

Sayre looked toward The Shadow, as he heard the quiet statement. The physician was stopped with amazement. The possibility had not gripped him until this moment.

"Color!" he gasped. "That could account for it! Deafness after sound; blindness after brilliance! Loss of color reception, after some strange shock involving color!"

"Yes!" The Shadow pronounced the word with a sibilant hiss. "Color! That fact is known"—his voice had become a weird whisper. "Through it, we can grasp forgotten facts that dwell within this stilled brain."

AS he spoke, The Shadow reached to the wall and pressed the light switch. Ceiling bulbs faded; the only glow that remained came from a lamp upon Sayre's desk. Reaching for it, The Shadow tilted the shade upward. A spot of light was thrown upon two faces: The Shadow's and that of the staring man who gazed blankly across the desk.

Doctor Sayre watched The Shadow's countenance move eye to eye with the face of the unknown patient. Sayre caught the glint of fire sparkling from The Shadow's optics. The glow seemed to reflect into the blue-gray eyes of the staring man.

Again, The Shadow whispered. His visage, like his voice, had altered. Sayre was transfixed, as if beholding a visitor from another world. The expression of The Shadow's face was commanding, all-impelling. He was impressing his powerful personality upon the man before him.

There was something hypnotic in The Shadow's gaze. Sayre, being a physician, knew its purpose. The Shadow was gaining the full attention of the staring man, forcing him to forget all except those eyes which glowed before him. Though the staring man gave no visible sign, it was apparent that his gaze was fixed.

"Your thoughts return to the past." The Shadow's tone was solemn. "Back to the time when memory was full. Think! Remember! The scene lies all about you!"

No response from the staring man. Only sibilant echoes from the walls, reverberations of The Shadow's hissed command.

"All about you. Color! Vivid color!"

Staring eyes bulged. Lips began to quiver, but gave no utterance. Again, The Shadow whispered:

"Color! Everywhere! You remember!"

Lips were forming words, no longer mechanical. The staring man gasped:

"Yes—yes! Color everywhere—the glow—"

"Lights!" hissed The Shadow. "Lights that glowed with color! You remember the color itself!"

"The color—yes! It—it was red—red—"

"Red! Vivid red!" The Shadow's hands, rising, reached the staring man's chin. One hand on either side, The Shadow used his fingertips to tilt the man's face slightly upward. Gazing deep into the other's eyes, The Shadow delivered final utterance:

"Glowing red! Red that gripped you, that terrorized you—"

The Shadow's tone ended abruptly. His words were like a knifethrust into the thoughts of the man whose memory he sought to jab. A wild cry ripped from gaping lips. Hands came up; the victim clutched the sides of his head.

"Red! Maddening red!" His voice was hoarse as he backed away. "Red—there! Upon the walls!"

Eyes were staring no longer. They were rolling, terrified, as though viewing a horrendous scene. The man was wheeling, pointing to one wall, then to another. His head tilted toward the floor.

"Red!" he shrieked. His head went back, his eyes rolled upward as his hand pointed to the ceiling. "Red! Terrible red! The light—the red light! Take it away! Away, before it kills me!"

The man recoiled; then drove forward with furious impulse. His face distorted, he leaped toward the desk lamp. Young, powerful, he snatched the lamp from its resting place and swung back his arm, ready to deliver a terrific hurl against the wall.

The Shadow's hand shot forward.

WITH one quick grasp, The Shadow clutched the fierce man's arm. With his other hand, he wrenched the lamp from the fellow's grasp. Eyes, no longer staring, were wild with frenzy. As The Shadow wheeled away, carrying the lamp, the maddened man straightened and spun about, clutching at his hair.

"Red—everywhere!" he screamed. "Take it away—the red—the light—"

He was focused in the glow, as The Shadow turned the light straight upon him. A frenzied scream; a thwarted, desperate stare; then, with a choking gasp, the man crumpled and rolled crazily upon the floor.

Doctor Sayre sprang beside him, as The Shadow pressed the switch at the wall.

"His frenzy has overcome him," declared the physician. "The memories that you induced have caused him to reenact the former scene."

"Results have been gained," responded The Shadow, in the calm tone of Cranston. "We must be prepared for his next awakening."

"His memory will be gone—"

"Not necessarily. Come, doctor. Help me raise him."

Together, they lifted the helpless man from the floor. One supporting each shoulder, The Shadow and Sayre moved the patient toward the door. It was The Shadow who led the course; Sayre followed, puzzled. Out through an entry, to the level of the front street. There Sayre saw a waiting limousine, a chauffeur by the opened door.

The Shadow urged Sayre toward further effort. Together, they placed the unconscious man in the car. The Shadow stepped aboard; the chauffeur closed the door, leaving Sayre on the sidewalk. The face of Lamont Cranston appeared at the window.

"Tomorrow," came the quiet tone, "I shall summon you. Be ready to join me, Doctor Sayre."

"But—but the patient!" stammered the physician. "He was in my charge. You are taking him—"

"He will be in good care. Tomorrow, you will find him recovered."

"Recovered? You mean—"

"Since I have found the cause of his condition," interposed The Shadow, quietly, "I shall be able to supply the antidote."

The chauffeur had taken the wheel; the limousine pulled away. Standing on the curb, Doctor Sayre gazed after the departing car with a dumfounded expression that almost matched the blankness of the man who had stared.

Through Sayre's mind echoed The Shadow's final words. The Shadow had learned the cause. He would find the antidote. Tomorrow, the mysterious patient would be restored to a normal condition. Then would come the opportunity to learn his story.

Doctor Sayre walked back into his office, pondering. Tonight, as in the past, he had witnessed the amazing power of The Shadow. From the moment when he had begun his deductions concerning color, The Shadow had predominated, even to the point of awakening blurred memories within the mind of a man who had forgotten.

Tomorrow, Sayre was convinced, much would be learned. The Shadow's words had been a prophecy. Sayre wondered what the future would bring. Perhaps it was well that he could not guess.

For The Shadow, tonight, had crossed an unexpected trail of crime. One that was destined to produce strange consequences, where death and evil hovered!

CHAPTER III
THE SHADOW'S ANTIDOTE

AT four o'clock the next afternoon, Doctor Rupert Sayre stepped from a local train at a small New Jersey station. An automobile was awaiting him. It was the limousine that he had seen the night before. The same chauffeur was at the wheel. Sayre stepped aboard; the car rolled from the station driveway.

Settling back in the cushions of the tonneau, Doctor Sayre felt that he had embarked upon adventure. He had come to New Jersey in response to a summons from The Shadow. That fact indicated that results had been accomplished.

The staring man must have recovered from his helpless condition. So Sayre reasoned, and with good logic. Had the patient's state remained the same, The Shadow would have returned him to New York. The fact that Sayre had been summoned here seemed proof that recuperation was the answer.

The journey from the station was not a long one. Soon the limousine had threaded its way along secondary highways, to arrive at the gate of a large estate. The big car rolled between stone gateposts. It took a curving driveway and pulled up in front of a large, well-kept mansion.

This was the home of Lamont Cranston. A servant descended the front steps to greet the visitor. Sayre was ushered into a quiet living room. The servant went away; a few minutes later, a calm voice spoke in greeting. Sayre looked up to see the tall form of Lamont Cranston. Daylight from the opened window reflected a momentary sparkle in keen eyes. Sayre knew that his host was The Shadow.

"The patient?" queried Sayre, almost in a whisper. "He has improved?"

"Immensely." Lips formed a slight smile. "Several hours of intensive treatment have proven of great benefit."

"He has spoken?"

"Not yet. It was preferable to await your arrival. A short while longer would be desirable."

THE SHADOW glanced from the window as he spoke. It was plain that he was considering the matter of daylight. Afternoon was waning; the sun was on a level with high trees that fringed the grounds about the house. The glare would be lessened, once the sun lowered beyond those treetops.

"While we are waiting," remarked The Shadow, quietly, "I shall reconstruct a few items in the history of our patient. First: how he came to the condition in which he was discovered.

"He was subjected to a strange ordeal. Some enemy placed him in a room that was entirely red. I picture deep crimson curtains upon every wall; a red carpet covering the entire floor; a glaring ceiling of the same color."

The Shadow paused. Sayre started a statement:

"You said that the patient had not talked—"

"He did not have to talk," interposed The Shadow. "His actions in your office were a clear indication of the facts that I have stated. You will recall his cry: 'Red—red, everywhere' and his manner of pointing to all the walls; also to the floor and the ceiling.

"Furthermore, the room in which he had suffered was flooded with red light. That was plain because of his final action, when he tried to seize your desk lamp to bash it against the wall. He had been unable to accomplish such a deed in the red room itself. Therefore, we know that the lights in that chamber of terror must have been high, beyond his reach."

Sayre nodded. He was impressed by The Shadow's well-constructed outline.

"This room of vivid red was located somewhere in New York. Probably in Manhattan."

The statement came quietly from The Shadow. Sayre looked puzzled; then shook his head and offered an objection.

"Impossible!" he exclaimed. "The railroad tickets disprove that theory. The victim had one from Philadelphia to Mannegat, bought on Sunday morning—"

Sayre stopped. The Shadow was producing a small sheaf of papers, with timetables among them.

"At nine o'clock Sunday morning," he declared, "a round-trip ticket was bought in Philadelphia. It read to Mannegat and return, via the Pennsylvania Railroad. I have the number of that ticket. A newspaper reporter obtained it for me, during an interview with Inspector Cardona.

"Cardona, of course, has only the return stub, which was found in the staring man's pocket. He took it for granted that the victim had boarded a train in Philadelphia. It happens that the first train which leaves from Philadelphia for Mannegat after nine o'clock, makes its departure at eleven.

"The trip requires one hour and fifty minutes. Hence the train reaches Mannegat at twelve-fifty. At Mannegat, we know, the man boarded a Jersey Central express for New York. The trip takes two hours. The man arrived at three o'clock."

Sayre nodded.

"Then he left Mannegat at once," declared the physician. "He had only ten minutes to change from one train to another."

"Exactly! Cardona estimated that he had a few hours. Cardona was wrong. Ten minutes was the full time. In that ten minutes, the man would have to travel two miles, for the railroad stations are that distance apart. After that, he required time to buy a ticket to New York, via the Jersey Central."

"Close work," agreed Sayre. "I see the answer. To order a cab; to cover the intervening distance and then buy a ticket, the man must have been in normal state. But then"—he paused, puzzled—"then his experience must have occurred upon the train. That does not fit, especially with your statement that the red room episode took place in New York."

"It fits quite well," smiled The Shadow. "It proves that the victim did not start from

Philadelphia at all. He was put aboard the Jersey Central train at Mannegat, already in his staring condition."

SAYRE found himself nodding in agreement. The Shadow was right. The man could not have been normal when he took the train at Mannegat. Conversely, he would have had to be alert to accomplish so much in the time space of ten minutes.

"As proof of these statements," added The Shadow, "I have learned two facts by long-distance calls to Philadelphia. The first is, that the eleven o'clock train to Mannegat was late last Sunday. It did not arrive at its destination until twelve fifty-eight. The second fact is that the original portion of excursion ticket number 6384 was not collected."

Sayre blinked. This was double proof. Not only had the train reached Mannegat too late for the transfer, but no one had used the staring man's ticket!

"The assumption, therefore, is this." The Shadow paused. "Someone went to Philadelphia and brought the excursion ticket at nine o'clock; then drove to Mannegat immediately. The victim was already at Mannegat, in the hands of other custodians. The return half of that ticket was placed in his pocket. He was provided with a Jersey Central ticket, purchased in Mannegat, and was put aboard the express to New York."

"Amazing!" gasped Sayre. "Yet true. What was the object of this procedure?"

"To make it appear that the man had come from Philadelphia. That would have been unnecessary, unless the victim happened to be going to some place where his captors wanted no search to be made."

The answer struck Sayre an instant later.

"I see it!" exclaimed the physician. "You have uncovered a cunning device! You are right! The red room must be in New York. The rogues were smart enough to send their victim right back to the city from where he had come."

"Correct," assured The Shadow. "The ordeal took place before Sunday; probably on Saturday night. Early Sunday, one of the captors drove to Philadelphia, bought the excursion ticket and came to Mannegat. The others had carried the victim to Mannegat. He was sent back to New York.

"We have, therefore, traced the staring man's actions during the period while he was in his remarkable trance. We cannot expect him to give us the details of that interval. He will, however, tell us what occurred beforehand. Therefore, we shall have his entire story."

A glance from the window. The Shadow saw that the sun had dropped below the high treetops. He nodded to Sayre. The physician followed him from the living room. They came to a secluded door on the ground floor.

"Since color caused the patient's lapse," remarked The Shadow, while his long hand rested on the doorknob, "I have used color to aid his recovery. You will find him in a room like the one that I described; where walls, floor, ceiling—even the lights are all alike."

Sayre gave a troubled exclamation.

"A bad mistake!" he uttered. "Since the red room, with its crimson glow, was responsible for the man's condition, a repetition of the ordeal may have driven him totally mad. You have made a mistake—"

"I ordered curtains and carpet last night," interposed The Shadow. "They arrived early this morning. The ceiling was painted during the interim. I obtained lights and installed them. Our patient has been in this room since ten o'clock."

"Again, I insist!" exclaimed Sayre. "You should have told me all this before you acted. Such treatment may have proven disastrous. Since color caused the trouble—"

"Color can therefore offset it," interjected The Shadow.

"But if red produced aphasia—"

"I said color, doctor. Not red."

With that, The Shadow opened the door.

A GLOW met Sayre's astonished gaze. Instead of the fierce crimson glare that the physician expected, his eyes were greeted with a pleasing, mellow light. One that was restful from the first moment.

In the center of the room, half reclining upon the floor, was the man who had stared. His head was leaning back upon his clasped hands. With wide-opened eyes, he was absorbing the color and the glow that pervaded the scene about him. No reddish glare disturbed this peaceful room.

Curtains, carpet, ceiling—even the lights that shone from sockets in corners of the walls—all were deep-green in color. Not another shade or tone disturbed the setting. The immediate impression was one of quiet and comfort, freed from any antagonistic hue.

The staring man's face showed delight, as if his eyes were drinking in the color that enclosed him. The bulge had gone from his optics. He turned his eyes slightly; his face showed a smile of greeting as he observed the two arrivals. Slowly, the man arose and stretched himself, like one who had enjoyed a long repose.

Doctor Rupert Sayre stood silent in admiration. Through use of the opposite color; the ravaging

**DOCTOR RODIL MOCQUINO
—the Voodoo Master**

effects had been counteracted. The red room, to the patient, was a forgotten nightmare of the past. This green room symbolized the present.

The Shadow had divined the cause of the staring man's condition. The Shadow had supplied the antidote.

CHAPTER IV
CLUES FROM THE PAST

THE SHADOW closed the door of the green room. Doctor Sayre and the other man watched him while he approached a wall and found a cord within the folds of a velvet curtain. The Shadow drew the cord; green draperies slid away to reveal a window.

The Shadow repeated the operation farther along the wall. Daylight replaced the glow of greenish lamps. The Shadow found a switch and extinguished the emerald lights. Green still predominated; but the aspect of the room was changed.

Doctor Sayre was astonished to see cushions upon the floor at the spot where the patient had been reclining. He blinked as he eyed chairs in corners, other objects that had mysteriously come into view. Cushions and chairs were green. Against curtains of the same color, dyed by greenish lights, the chairs and cushions had been blotted from sight.

The glare from the window disturbed the man who had occupied the green room. Although the sun had set; though the outside scene was restful, the man began to shade his eyes. Beyond the window he saw green grass, green trees; nevertheless, he blinked.

Sayre saw the man stare suddenly. Looking from the window, the physician caught a glimpse of a cardinal bird, as it fluttered from the branches of a small cedar. Sayre turned quickly toward the patient. He saw the man's face wince.

The Shadow, too, had observed. He approached the patient and motioned him to a chair that faced away from the window. Sayre realized that The Shadow had made a test. He had learned that the patient's sense of color perception had been restored.

As Sayre watched, The Shadow produced a pair of green-tinted spectacles and gave them to the seated man. The patient donned them eagerly; then sank back with a pleased sigh.

"My name," stated The Shadow, quietly, "is Lamont Cranston. This gentleman is Doctor Rupert Sayre. You may regard him as your physician; while I am your friend."

The patient nodded; then spoke slowly.

"My name is Stanton Wallace."

"Where do you live?" inquired The Shadow.

"In New York," replied the young man. "At the Dalmatia Apartment. I came to New York from Texas."

"You have friends?"

Lips moved, but made no utterance. Eyes showed trouble through the greenish glasses. The Shadow divined the reason.

"What you tell us," he declared, "will not be repeated. You were found in a dazed condition—"

"By the police?"

"Yes. But they have placed you in full custody of Doctor Sayre. At present, you are away from New York City."

Stanton Wallace nodded. He still seemed loath to speak, although his reticence had lessened.

"To aid you," remarked The Shadow, quietly, "we must know your full story. Specifically, the facts which concern the red room."

A gasp from the young man's lips. His eyes gazed toward The Shadow's. For a few moments, they remained fixed; then confidence gripped Stanton Wallace. He was ready to accept Lamont Cranston as a friend.

"MY story is an unbelievable one," Wallace began. "It involves incredible circumstances—"

"Which we shall recognize," interposed The Shadow, "once we have heard them."

"I could be accused of complicity in crime—"

"We shall bring no accusations."

"If I am sure that I shall be believed in my statements—"

"You will be believed."

Wallace paused. His lips twitched. Again, he sought The Shadow's gaze. Eyes assured him. The young man spoke.

"I came to New York," he stated, "to handle special correspondence for a wealthy Texan named Dunley Bligh. Among other matters, I arranged steamship passage for Bligh from New York to Europe. That completed my work. I mailed everything to Bligh, so that he might take passage immediately upon his arrival in New York."

"Bligh has reached New York?"

"Not yet. But there was another point that I must mention. Bligh is a millionaire. He made his fortune from oil. Once on the steamship, he is to receive a collection of valuable gems, which he purchased recently by proxy. He is taking the jewels to Europe, there to dispose of them in exchange for paintings which he intends to bring back to America."

Wallace paused; then added an explanation.

"The jewels," he remarked, "once belonged to wealthy Europeans, who are anxious to reclaim them. Bligh can dispose of them more readily in Europe than in America. He is also anxious to please the persons who want them."

The Shadow nodded his understanding. He sensed that these statements were merely a preliminary account. Stanton Wallace had given his reason for being in New York. His real adventures would constitute another chapter.

"A month ago," declared the young man, "I met Doctor Rodil Mocquino."

The tone was awed, as though the very mention of the name brought horror to Stanton Wallace. As the young man paused, both The Shadow and Sayre could see his hands twitch and his shoulders shudder.

"Doctor Mocquino," repeated Wallace, slowly. "The Voodoo Master from San Domingo. A man with a friendly smile, with eyes that search you. A man who commands trust, but whose words are lies. A man with a blackened heart—a fiend—"

The tone was quickening; Wallace's voice had reached a higher pitch. His eyes were darting furtively; they showed terror. The Shadow caught the man's shoulder and forced him to meet a steady gaze. Fear faded as Stanton Wallace stared into the eyes of The Shadow.

"Proceed."

The Shadow's command was a whisper, in the sibilant tone which he had used the day before. Sayre saw Wallace nod his obedience. The young man's voice was calmed, when he spoke again.

"MY meeting with Mocquino seemed a chance one," declared the patient. "We were both strangers in New York. We became friends; Mocquino spoke of his adventures. He discussed the voodoo rituals held in Haiti and San Domingo."

Sayre saw that the speaker was depending upon The Shadow's gaze. The eyes before him enabled Stanton Wallace to crowd out fears of the past. His voice had become a steady monotone. The Shadow, it seemed, was drawing forth the story.

"One evening," proceeded Wallace, "Mocquino amazed me with the statement that a voodoo cult existed in New York. He asked if I would care to attend one of the rituals. I was

STANTON WALLACE—the "staring man" whom The Shadow rescues from Mocquino's Clutches

intrigued. I went. There, I gained new astonishment. Mocquino was more than a privileged spectator. He was the leader of the cult!

"Picture it—a dozen persons, about an artificial fire that was weirdly realistic! In a room arranged to resemble a West Indian jungle, with natives beating tom-toms! I can hear the rhythm of those steady beats. Terrible—impelling—"

The Shadow's eyes were steady. Wallace hesitated; then a growing frenzy faded from his voice. Steadied, the young man proceeded:

"Before that meeting ended, I had been seized by the lure. I, too, was willing to accept Doctor Mocquino as my leader. I went to other meetings, a full-fledged member. Like the others, I recognized no one present except Doctor Mocquino. He called himself our parent.

"One night, Doctor Mocquino produced a wax effigy of a human being—a tiny figure no more than six inches tall. He named it. He said that it was Myron Rathcourt. One of our members stepped forward and claimed recognition. That member must have been a friend or relative of Myron Rathcourt.

"Doctor Mocquino took a long pin and thrust it through the heart of the wax figure. He was fiendish—and we echoed his delight. All of us, including the man who had recognized Myron Rathcourt. Three days passed." Wallace paused, his voice awed: "Then I read a newspaper account of Myron Rathcourt's death. Rathcourt was a Chicago millionaire. He died of heart failure."

A pause. Sayre's brain was drumming. He, too, had read of Myron Rathcourt's death. But no newspaper had hinted at any other cause than a natural one.

"One week later," continued Wallace, "Doctor Mocquino produced another effigy. To this one, he gave the name James Lenger. A member of the cult claimed recognition. Doctor Mocquino opened a penknife. Savagely, he severed the head of the figure from its body.

"Two days afterward"—the speaker's tone was sinking to a whisper—"just two days afterward, the New York newspapers carried a story of James Lenger's death. Lenger had made a lone trip up the Amazon River. He was slain by native headhunters. His body, alone, was discovered by an expedition. He had been decapitated; his slayers had taken his head as a trophy."

STANTON WALLACE'S face was tilting forward. The Shadow spoke a single word. Wallace's eyes came up to meet an impelling gaze. Mechanically, the young man resumed:

"Like the other members of the cult, I gloated. We were proud of Doctor Mocquino's power. I looked forward to the time of the next meeting; for I had imbibed the fiendish joy that predominated at those voodoo rites. Then came the last time. The night that broke the terrible spell of the false jungle fire and the beating tom-toms.

"Doctor Mocquino had led us in a ghoulish chant, wherein our voices joined instinctively with his. He called for silence. He produced a new effigy. He named it; and called for recognition. His eyes were toward me when he pronounced the name of Dunley Bligh.

"I advanced. I looked in horror at the effigy! It was a miniature of the man whom I was serving in New York: my employer, Dunley Bligh! My mind filled with understanding. I looked at Doctor Mocquino. His smile was the distorted gloat of a fiend. I knew Mocquino's game.

"Murder! His voodoo rites were a sham. Mocquino had urged me to talk of Bligh's affair. Mocquino knew that wealth would be in Bligh's hands. Because of the information that I had heedlessly given, my friendly employer would be doomed to die like others whose death Mocquino had ordered.

"I was dumbfounded! I watched while Mocquino thrust a long pin through the body of the wax image. A jeering chant rose from the throng about me. Angered, I seized the effigy and smashed it upon the floor! I sprang at Mocquino's throat! His servants seized me!"

Stanton Wallace was staring with fixed eyes. He was coming to his final recollection of that terrible night.

"I shall never forget what resulted," he stated, slowly. "Doctor Mocquino became a demon. His frenzied followers screamed for my blood. I expected terrible torture; but of a physical sort. Instead, I was subjected to a mental anguish. Doctor Mocquino had me carried to the red room.

"I had seen the horrible place before. Curtains—walls—ceiling—all of that blood-red color. But when I was placed, bound, within the walls of the terrible room, the ordinary lights were extinguished. Instead, crimson bulbs began to glow. Walls took on depth. I was in an abyss of redness!

"I remember Mocquino's devilish face, reddened by the glow. The gold cloth of his robe was bronzed by the glare. The red scarf that he wore about his waist was blotted from my view. He looked like a living creature in two sections. Then Mocquino left me. The red lights glared, more terrible with every passing moment! I was frenzied, screaming for death in preference to such torture! When I closed my eyes, the red light penetrated my eyelids.

"Then came oblivion. I have only a hazy recollection of walking, of encountering crowds, of persons who forced me or guided me. My thoughts regained alignment only after I found myself in this green room."

Dusk was streaking the outside lawn. Modulated light was soothing. Stanton Wallace again settled back in his chair. He seemed refreshed, since his mind was unburdened.

The Shadow spoke.

"YOU have told your story," he remarked in the quiet tone of Cranston. "Your memory is restored. Therefore, you should remember the place where Doctor Mocquino holds his meetings with the voodoo cult."

"I do," nodded Wallace. "I cannot recall the street number; but the house itself is easily located. It is an old mansion with closed shutters. The first house east of the new Europa Building. It is entered from the basement of another house—the next beyond. The meetings are held upon the second floor of the empty house."

"When will the next meeting be?"

"Not for a few days. To be exact, on the same day that Dunley Bligh sails from New York. His ship will leave in the afternoon. The cult will meet that evening."

Wallace paused; then added, suddenly:

"Bligh must be warned! He will be in danger after he leaves for Europe. There is still time to save him. The cult meets on Wednesdays and on Saturdays. We still have until Wednesday, before Dunley Bligh sails from New York on the *Doranic*—"

Doctor Sayre was staring, puzzled. Before the physician could speak, The Shadow intervened. Stanton Wallace was sitting upright; The Shadow motioned him back in his chair.

"Bligh will be protected," he assured. "I shall inform him of the danger. Meanwhile, you must rest. Remove the glasses and enjoy the twilight. Doctor Sayre will visit you before it becomes dark."

With a motion to Sayre, The Shadow opened the door. The physician followed. Together, they went to the living room. There, Sayre put an anxious question.

"What does Wallace mean by 'until Wednesday'?" he asked. "Does he think that this is an earlier day?"

"He does," replied The Shadow. "His ordeal took place last Saturday. He does not recall the time lapse. He thinks that this is Sunday."

"But today is Wednesday! And that means the *Doranic* will leave New York, with Dunley Bligh aboard—"

"The *Doranic* has already sailed."

"Then Bligh is doomed!"

"Not yet." Calmly, The Shadow picked up a telephone. He gave a number; then pressed a button on the wall. "You will remain here, Doctor Sayre. Call Cardona; tell him that you wish to keep the patient a while longer. Do not let Stanton Wallace learn that today is Wednesday."

A servant entered while The Shadow was still holding the telephone, awaiting his connection.

"Go at once, Richards," ordered The Shadow, in the methodical tone of Cranston. "Tell Stanley to have the coupe ready. I am going to the Newark airport."

Richards went out. The Shadow began to speak into the telephone. He was connected with the airport. Doctor Sayre, listening, began to understand. The Shadow was right; there was still a chance to save Dunley Bligh.

The Shadow, himself, was preparing for a race against death. He, the master who stood for right, was setting forth to balk the evil plans of Doctor Rodil Mocquino!

CHAPTER V
MILES OFF SHORE

DUSK had ended. Stars were brilliant in the clear sky above the Atlantic Ocean. The steamship *Doranic* was plowing through long swells, four hours out of New York harbor.

From atop the liner, searchlights were swinging long beams toward the sky. Passengers, assembled on the decks, were watching the process with keen interest. Those shafts of light indicated something unusual. A stocky man with black mustache made inquiry of a deck steward:

"What is the purpose of the searchlights?"

"A plane is expected, sir," replied the steward. "It is bringing a passenger from New York."

"An airplane?" queried the mustached man. "How can it expect to make a night landing on the steamer's deck?"

"It will be an autogiro, sir. Such was the radio message from New York. The passengers are anxious to see it land."

"An autogiro. Humph! Have none of the passengers ever seen one of those before?"

"Not one like this, sir. They say that this autogiro is wingless. The improved type that can take off vertically."

The mustached man walked away. He glanced upward at the searchlights; for a moment, he hesitated, as if intending to remain on deck. Then, with a shrug of his shoulders, he reverted to his original plan. He entered a doorway and followed deserted passages until he reached the purser's office. An assistant purser was on duty.

"My name is Dunley Bligh," announced the mustached man. "I have come for a package which was left for me. You will find it in the safe."

The assistant purser found the package. An envelope was with it. He drew out a folded paper and read a message within.

"You must identify yourself by a special code word, sir—"

"I understand," broke in Bligh. "The code word is 'aurora'; you will see it in the note."

The ship's officer nodded. He gave the package to Bligh, who signed the receipt and then walked away in the direction of a stairway. The purser's assistant started to resume his chair; then stopped as a steward came dashing into view. Shouts could be heard from the outer decks.

"The autogiro!" exclaimed the steward. "It has landed! Hear the passengers cheering?"

"I thought that we would hear the motor first—"

"So did we; but it fooled us. The giro came straight down from the sky. The landing was perfect!"

"What about the passenger aboard it?"

"He is coming here now, accompanied by a friend."

THE steward's words were almost a prophecy. Two persons appeared from the deck, followed by a throng of excited passengers. Stewards urged back the crowd, while the arrivals approached the purser's window. One man was slight of build, but wiry. He grinned as he nodded to the ship's officer.

"I'm your passenger," he stated. "My name is Clyde Burke. Reporter for the New York *Classic*. What cabin are you giving me?"

The purser's assistant brought out a chart.

"Could I see the passenger list?" inquired Burke.

The officer nodded and passed out the list. It was a logical request, coming from a reporter, particularly when Burke added an explanation:

"This is a news stunt. I was going abroad, anyway, to handle some foreign correspondence for the *Classic*. But that wasn't to be for a couple of weeks. I had a lucky chance to catch the *Doranic* by a trip in an autogiro, so I took it. Since I have to write a story, I'd like to know who is on board."

The assistant purser was nodding, while he still consulted the chart. At last he assigned a cabin:

"Stateroom 411-B."

As he looked up, the ship's officer noted Burke's companion. This second arrival was a tall personage, with hawklike countenance. Burke had finished with the passenger list. His friend was scanning the list of names.

"This gentleman?" inquired the assistant purser. "Is he also a passenger?"

Burke shook his head.

"This is Mr. Cranston," he explained. "Owner of the wingless autogiro. He's going back to New York. How about it, Mr. Cranston?" He turned to his friend. "Have you time to take a look at my cabin?"

"Certainly, Burke."

A steward accompanied the two arrivals to 411-B. As soon as the steward was gone, Burke yanked open a suitcase. He pulled out a deck plan of the *Doranic* and made quick comment:

"Bligh is in 316-C," stated the reporter. "There is a stairway on the right—"

A quiet whisper interrupted. Burke looked up. Already, his tall companion had drawn garments from the suitcase. Black folds of cloth were settling over shoulders, to form a covering cloak. A slouch hat was coming from the bag, along with gloves. Clyde Burke eyed a brace of automatics. The Shadow, too, had noted the number of Bligh's cabin from the purser's list; in addition, he had already been familiar with the deck plan of the *Doranic*.

CERTAIN cabins on the C deck of the liner were arranged in connecting pairs. From the main corridor of the deck were short side passages, dead ends that led to the deck wall. Entrances to the cabins were from the small side passageways. Thus one side passage had doors 314 and 315 opposite. The next had 316 and 317 as opposite doors.

Cabins 315 and 316 formed a suite, with a connecting door between the two rooms. For this voyage, the connecting cabins had been occupied as separate rooms.

In the darkness of 315, a man was listening at the connecting door. He could hear sounds of motion, which meant that Dunley Bligh was in his cabin.

Beside the listening man was another, who wore a white coat that showed in the gloom. The listener arose from the door and turned to his white-jacketed companion.

"It's Bligh, all right," he whispered, hoarsely. "Get ready, Hoke, in case we need you."

"All right, Borey," returned the man in the white coat. "Only I can't work nothin' until we hear from Hummer."

"That's Hummer now!"

A slight tap at the outer door. Hoke started to answer it. Borey pushed him aside with a growl about keeping his coat out of sight. It was Borey who opened the door to admit a third man.

"What about it, Hummer?" demanded Borey, in a harsh whisper. "Did he pick up the package?"

"Sure thing!" returned Hummer. "I was

watching from around a corner. I trailed him until I was sure he was going to 316."

"Then why did you keep us waiting?"

"There wasn't any hurry. Bligh had the package."

A grunt from Borey. Then the man spoke.

"You're right, Hummer," he said. "Listen: The whole thing is a setup, the way it stands. I planted the fixed glass in 316. When Bligh takes a drink out of it, he's done. The only thing was, we didn't want him to plop until after he'd gotten the jewels from the purser.

"That's why I had you here, Hoke. In case Bligh didn't bring the sparklers, it was your job to get him out of the cabin before he used the glass. That's why you're wearing the steward's rig—so you could give him a phony message, or an excuse to get him back on deck.

"But since he's brought the package, all we've

DUNLEY BLIGH—whose jewels are saved in mid-ocean from Mocquino's henchmen

got to do is wait. When he keels over, we barge in and grab the sparklers. Nobody's going to suspect us, on account of the regular medicine that Bligh takes."

"But suppose he don't take it?" queried Hoke. "What'll we do about it then?"

"We'll gang him, in a pinch. Make him swallow it. Listen: Dill is in 317, across the passage from Bligh's cabin. You go in there, Hoke, faking that you're a steward, in case Bligh's door is open. With two of us here in 315 and two in 317, Bligh won't have a chance to go out."

"Do we leave the door open, Dill and I?"

"Not a chance. Keep it closed, like this one. We don't want no snoopers. You'll hear Bligh if he comes out."

Hoke departed. He followed the short passage, rounded the pair of cabins and entered another passage that brought him to the door of 316. It was closed. Hoke turned to the door opposite—317—and knocked softly. The door opened. Hoke joined Dill. The door closed.

Back in 315, Borey, listening, spoke to Hummer.

"Just heard a gurgle," whispered the listener. He arose and stepped back from the connecting door. "Bligh has poured water out of the bottle! It's curtains for him, quick!"

IN Cabin 316, Dunley Bligh was standing beside a table. He had opened his package. From it, he had brought glimmering gems to form an array upon the table. Rubies, sapphires and emeralds formed a galaxy of sparkling possessions. Bligh's face showed pleasure.

He had finished his preliminary survey. He had taken a drinking glass and a water bottle from a shelf above the washstand. He had poured a glassful of water—the gurgle that Borey had heard—and he was placing the glass upon the table.

Bligh corked the water bottle. As he did, he fancied that he heard a slight click. He turned toward the outer door; then smiled at his own qualms. He had locked that door and left the key on the inside. No one could possibly enter.

So Bligh thought. He did not note that the key was turning, as if clipped by thin pliers, thrust through the outer keyhole.

Bligh went to a suitcase. He brought out a small pillbox and carried it to the table. He opened the box and extracted two tiny pills. He put the box beside the glass of water, where the table lamp shone upon it. The box lid bore a pharmacist's formula; beneath it, the warning: "Two pills only!"

The pills that Bligh held were grayish. He placed them on the tip of his tongue and swallowed them with a gulp. He reached for the glass of water. His eyes were still upon the gems; he did not notice a change that had occurred in the liquid. Bligh had let the water stand. A grayish scum was forming on its surface.

As his right hand fondled a brilliant emerald, Bligh raised the glass of water with his left. The tumbler came toward his lips; but Bligh never quaffed the liquid. A hand shot forward into the glare of the table lamp. A black-gloved fist gripped Bligh's wrist. Water bobbled, but did not spill.

Bligh wheeled; a gasp froze on his lips.

Standing before him was a shape in black, a being that could have been a spirit conjured from the sea. Silent, unseen, this visitant had entered the cabin. He was cloaked in black; his eyes burned from beneath the brim of a slouch hat. His gloved hand furnished a viselike clutch.

Bligh, his own lips wavering, was conscious of a whispered tone that spoke from the folds of an upturned cloak collar. The words—the eyes—both commanded silence. Though fearful, Dunley Bligh nodded. Somehow, he understood that this weird arrival was a friend.

The Shadow had arrived in time. Silently, he had entered Bligh's cabin almost through the midst of watchful foemen. Instantly, he had discovered the death that threatened.

The Shadow had prevented doom!

CHAPTER VI
BACK TO LAND

"WHO—who are you?"

Dunley Bligh gasped the words; his voice was scarcely articulate. Heeding The Shadow's warning, he could not even whisper his question.

"A friend." The Shadow's tone was a low whisper. "One who has uncovered a plot upon your life. These pills"—with his free hand, The Shadow raised the rounded box—"are poison!"

"So I understand." Bligh managed a smile. "They were prescribed for me by a specialist. They are safe, so long as I take no more than two at a single dosage."

"You have already taken two."

"Yes. But I intended to swallow no more."

"Look at the glass which you hold."

The Shadow's hand released its grip. Bligh lowered the tumbler. His eyes opened wider as he saw the grayish scum, which the jogging of the glass had stirred further. Eyeing still closer, Bligh noted that the floating substance was formed of tiny flakes.

"Powder!" he gasped. "Pulverized from— from—"

"From pills of the sort that you have taken," interposed The Shadow. "Powder placed in the glass, which you later filled with water. Enough to triple your usual dosage."

"Enough to kill me!"

"And make your death appear an accident—or suicide."

Shakily, Bligh lowered the tumbler toward the table. The Shadow plucked the glass from the man's hand. Stepping toward the opened porthole, he tossed the tumbler and its liquid contents out into the ocean. Bligh turned to face The Shadow, as he returned into the light.

"You are a friend," acknowledged Bligh. "Tell me—how did you learn of my danger?"

"Through Stanton Wallace," returned The Shadow. "He experienced an accident. Otherwise, he could have warned you. Some enemies learned that you intended to receive jewels aboard this ship."

"Those enemies"—Bligh paused, troubled— "perhaps they are close at hand?"

"They are. They intend to take your jewels. A prize that would net them at least two hundred thousand dollars."

"Possibly more. I value these gems at a quarter million. That is why I took precautions about their delivery. You are right." Bligh mopped a perspiring brow. "Murder and robbery could both have been committed without a trace. And even now— even now there is danger—"

"Which can be eliminated."

Bligh looked up, his eyes wide open.

"Men of crime are lurking," informed The Shadow, in his low whisper. "They will enter. If they encounter trouble, they will have reserves. They are murderers. We must lure them to their own undoing."

THE SHADOW pointed to Bligh's suitcase, where a revolver glimmered. The man from Texas reached for the weapon. The Shadow pointed to the floor.

"Fall, and carry the table with you," he ordered. "Let the gems scatter. Keep your revolver ready beneath you. Do not move until they have taken the bait."

Bligh saw the gloved hands produce a pair of automatics. Nodding, the Texan gave his agreement. He watched The Shadow step to a darkened corner of the cabin. Then, with a sideward drop, Bligh sprawled to the floor. His gun hand was doubled inward; with his free arm, he tipped the table.

The ruse was perfect. Above the rhythmic beat of the liner's engines, Bligh's drop combined both thud and clatter. The table crackled as it fell.

A creepy laugh had shuddered to their ears. They saw the being who had uttered that whispered taunt. The Shadow!

Gems skidded across the carpeting, to lie about like glittering markers.

Ten seconds passed. Then the connecting door opened. A face appeared from the darkness of Cabin 315. A hand motioned. Borey crept into view, followed by Hummer. Both were sliding revolvers back into their pockets. Borey chuckled as he pointed to Bligh; then his voice uttered a growl:

"Dead as a block of wood," voiced Borey. "But look at the sparklers! They've gone all over the joint! Come on! Get busy! We've got to snatch 'em up in a hurry!"

Both men stooped beyond Bligh. Eager fingers reached for sparkling stones. Hands halted suddenly, as if the gems were hot coals. Borey and Hummer spun about. Their lips coughed oaths. A creepy laugh had shuddered to their ears. They saw the being who had uttered that whispered taunt.

The Shadow!

THUGS by profession, Borey and Hummer recognized the figure that had stepped deliberately into the light. They stared helplessly. Slowly, they shifted upward, raising their hands. Terror gripped their evil faces. They thought that Bligh was dead; that The Shadow had found them with a victim.

Slowly, The Shadow circled, his gun muzzles looming toward the crooks. He neared the outer door. He drew the staring faces away from Bligh's direction.

Peering along the floor, the Texan saw the move. He came up to a half-seated position, gripping his revolver.

The Shadow had left the outer door unlocked. He was approaching it, to hold his position there while he dealt with these two murderous men. He was not quite to the door when he stopped. At that moment, the door swung open. A white coated man appeared in the light. It was Hoke; behind him, another thug: the man called Dill.

The pair had also heard Bligh's fall. They had come to join Borey and Hummer. The Shadow hissed a command to Bligh. He was to pounce upon Borey and Hummer, while The Shadow dealt with this new duo.

Bligh misunderstood the order. He caught a motion of Hoke's gun. Quick on the trigger, the Texan aimed for the white-jacketed crook.

The revolver roared. Hoke staggered. The shot brought Borey and Hummer into action. Seeing Hoke fall, their only thoughts were those of battle. Yanking their guns, they sprang in different directions: Borey toward Bligh, Hummer toward The Shadow.

Bligh was caught flat-footed because of Borey's speed. Had The Shadow not performed amazingly, murder might yet have been accomplished. The Shadow, however, took in the entire scene. He handled events with complete control.

The Shadow met Hummer's leap halfway, without firing a shot at the fellow. He tossed aside his left-hand automatic and faded to the right as he caught Hummer's gunhand. With his right hand, he tugged the trigger of his automatic; but his .45 was aimed at Borey, not at Hummer.

A sizzling bullet withered Borey's gun arm. The man's hand dropped as he sought to fire at Bligh. The Texan, beaten to the shot, suddenly gained the advantage. He fired his revolver twice; both bullets found Borey. The crook sagged; then rolled to the floor.

IN this melee, Bligh had forgotten Dill, who had dropped back to the passage. Dill could easily have picked off Bligh; but The Shadow spoiled his opportunity. Grappling with Hummer, The Shadow drove his adversary straight for the outer door, fully blocking Dill's aim.

The outside crook was snarling his rage. He could not reach The Shadow with a shot, for The Shadow had twisted Hummer toward the door.

Then, as Bligh scrambled toward a point of safety, The Shadow sprang another ruse. He jolted backward, carrying Hummer with him. Dill thought that Hummer had gained an advantage. With a mad cry, the outside crook plunged into the room. He learned his mistake as he saw The Shadow's right-hand swing with a short sidewise jab. The automatic cracked the side of Hummer's skull. The Shadow hurled his human shield aside.

Like a living arrow, he dived straight for Dill. His free left hand gripped the ruffian's gun wrist. His right fist drove another sledgelike stroke that crashed down Dill's warding arm and reached the head beneath. Dill sprawled sidewise and fell helpless. The Shadow stepped over and picked up his extra automatic.

"Take credit for the victory," he ordered, as he turned to Bligh. "I fired only one bullet. It will not be noted. Call upon Clyde Burke, a reporter who has come aboard. He will declare himself to be your friend and will substantiate any statements that you make. You have no other enemies on board. Rely upon Burke for aid and advice, when you reach the end of the voyage."

Borey was dead; Hoke was gasping his last. Hummer and Dill lay stunned. The Shadow knew that excitement would soon reign aboard the *Doranic*. He had no need to remain. Cutting through Cabin 315, he reached the passage beyond. Peering from its end, he saw two excited stewards, who had heard the shots. They had listened; hearing no further fray, they were hurrying away to summon aid.

The Shadow reached a deserted companionway. In its gloom, he whisked off his cloak and placed it across his arm, stuffing the slouch hat beneath it. He gained the deck, divesting himself of gloves. His automatics were buried beneath his coat. His cloak appeared to be a light cape that he was carrying over his arm.

Quick pacing brought him to a cluster of passengers, close beside the autogiro. The plane was standing on a landing platform, its fan blades turning lazily like the arms of a giant windmill. Beside it was the pilot, anxious-faced, ready for the takeoff. The Shadow stepped up beside him.

"Sorry, Crofton," he remarked, in the casual tone of Cranston. "I did not realize that I was delaying the takeoff. I was talking with some passengers."

"We're all ready, Mr. Cranston—"

"Then let us depart."

The Shadow stepped aboard; the pilot with him. Passengers fell back as broad blades whirled to rapid spin. Faced toward the ship's bow, the autogiro started forward. Its wheels made no more than a double revolution. Aided by the headwind caused by the liner's speed, the plane rose from the landing space. It poised in air, at the same speed as the *Doranic;* then climbed upward. Searchlights showed the autogiro rising high into the night.

WITHIN the gloom of the autogiro's cabin, The Shadow delivered the echo of a whispered laugh. He had managed this mission well. Miles Crofton, his skilled pilot, had happened to be in New York, to test the new wingless autogiro. By taking the trip to the *Doranic* as a passenger, The Shadow had been able to handle Bligh's enemies and then depart.

No one could connect his brief visit with the fray on shipboard. Clyde Burke's entry as a friend of Dunley Bligh would be regarded as the natural action of a newspaper reporter. Bligh, himself, would be wise enough to follow The Shadow's instructions. Recovered crooks would be placed in irons.

Bligh, warned against future danger, would be safe, particularly with Clyde Burke as his friend.

The Shadow had chosen the first of important clues. Aid to Bligh had been imperative. The Shadow had given it. He had thwarted death that had been ordered by the evil Voodoo Master, Doctor Mocquino. The time had come to take up the second clue: the trail to the voodoo cult itself.

The Shadow placed earphones to his head. He began a wireless signal from the autogiro. He gained contact; coded messages came in return. The Shadow recognized the words. Burbank was reporting. Other agents of The Shadow had been posted in Manhattan. They were watching the headquarters of Doctor Mocquino.

Miles Crofton was heading back to Newark. Time was ample tonight. The cult would meet, undisturbed. The Shadow would have opportunity to reach New York from the airport, long before the meeting ended. He was counting upon a chance to deal with Mocquino before the voodoo master would guess that he was in the game.

Luck alone could balk The Shadow. Chance was the one element that he could not counteract. Oddly, fate was tricking him tonight. While the autogiro sped shoreward, minor events were happening over which The Shadow had no present control. One such occurrence was due to bring trouble.

The Shadow's trail to Doctor Mocquino would be a quicker one than The Shadow had originally planned. But because of haste that would soon prove necessary, the trail would become incomplete. Danger, struggles, blind search—all would be involved before The Shadow would gain his final goal.

Doctor Rodil Mocquino, the Voodoo Master, was destined to become a foe of formidable proportions. One who would fight The Shadow to the finish.

CHAPTER VII
THE LAW INTERVENES

WHILE The Shadow was engaged in the rescue of Dunley Bligh, Doctor Rupert Sayre had remained in charge of his patient, Stanton Wallace. With sunset, Sayre had turned on the emerald lights in the green room. Wallace had laughed at the procedure.

"Give me a break, doctor," he had insisted. "I'm feeling fit again. Let me sit around in a regular room. Provided, of course, that there is nothing red to disconcert me."

Sayre had approved the suggestion. He had gone to Cranston's living room and had ordered Richards to remove some red books and other small objects. Then he had taken Wallace to the new quarters. The patient had found himself quite at ease.

In Wallace's presence, Sayre made a call to Joe Cardona, telling the acting inspector that he would like to keep the patient under further observation. Sayre had mentioned nothing about Wallace's recovery. He was careful not to tell Cardona the young man's name.

Leaving the living room, Sayre had met Richards and had quietly instructed the servant to make sure that Wallace did not gain a copy of today's newspaper.

Oddly, the newspaper was the first thing for which Wallace asked, when Richards entered the room an hour later. Wallace had finished looking at some magazines. He was leaning back in a comfortable chair, smoking a cigar; and he seemed bored when he questioned:

"Isn't there a newspaper somewhere about?"

"Today's paper?" queried Richards.

"Of course," returned Wallace. "I'd like to read the news."

"Sorry, sir. There was only one newspaper here and Mr. Cranston took it with him."

"What about yesterday's newspaper?"

"We have that somewhere, sir."

"Let me see it then. I may find something in it."

A clock was chiming the half hour when Richards returned. It was half past nine. Wallace received the newspaper that the servant handed him. Richards walked out, smiling to himself. He had not mentioned this matter to Doctor Sayre, who was at present in the library. Richards thought that he had followed the required instructions.

Wallace's reading of the newspaper was brief. Certain headlines puzzled him. He glanced at the dateline and saw the word "Tuesday." For the moment, he thought that Richards had given him a journal that was several days old. Then he glanced at the date itself.

Realization struck him. With a startled cry, the young man crumpled the newspaper and threw it to the floor.

"Tuesday!" he exclaimed aloud. "Next Tuesday—and yet the flunky said that it was yesterday's newspaper! This is Wednesday, not Sunday! Wednesday—next Wednesday—"

He rose to his feet and clutched his head, half dazed. A whirlwind of thoughts overwhelmed him. This was Wednesday night; Dunley Bligh had already sailed from New York. To Stanton Wallace came bitter belief that he had been betrayed. Then resignation gripped him.

"Sayre has kept it from me," he groaned. "He knows that Bligh has met death. But he should have told me—he should have told me—"

He paused, distracted; then, pacing the room, he mumbled:

"They fear Doctor Mocquino. I must call upon someone else to aid. Someone else—I have it!"

BOUNDING to the telephone, Wallace raised the receiver. In a tense voice, he asked for a connection to New York detective headquarters. Soon a gruff voice spoke across the wire. Wallace asked for Inspector Cardona. He was informed that Cardona was out.

"Give him this message," urged Wallace. "Tell him to hunt Doctor Rodil Mocquino... Yes; Mocquino. He is in the first house east of the new Europa Building... On what charge? Murder!... Yes. Mocquino is a murderer..."

Footsteps beyond the door of the living room. Suddenly alarmed by his own action, Wallace hung up the receiver. He dropped the telephone and settled back into his chair, just as the door opened. It was Doctor Sayre.

Wallace, leaning back in the chair, began to mumble. Sayre looked worried, to find the patient talking to himself; then Wallace's smile reassured him. Sayre sat down to have a chat. He did not notice the newspaper, which lay beyond the table. Thus he failed to gain an inkling of the deed which Stanton Wallace had just performed.

AT New York police headquarters, Joe Cardona strolled into his office to find two detectives arguing over a crank call that had just been received. They passed the news to Joe. The ace detective questioned the man who had answered the telephone.

"You're sure of the name? Mocquino?"

A nod from the dick.

"And the call was cut off?"

Another nod.

"It doesn't sound phony," decided Cardona. "I've got a hunch this means something. That moniker—Mocquino—it sounds like an alias. What's more, cranks either cut off quick or they stick a long while. This fellow was interrupted. Come on; we're making up a squad. I'm going to take a look at that house."

THE Europa Building was a towering structure that fronted on an avenue and extended a half block deep. The street beside it was poorly lighted; most of the buildings in the rear portion of the block were old and dilapidated. When Cardona and four detectives reached the place that Wallace had mentioned, they found the street deserted.

Standing across the farside of the street, Cardona eyed the front of the first house. It was a four-story building with a brick front. All windows were shuttered; the front door needed paint. Joe studied it by the glow of the nearest street lamp. He saw a rental sign on the house.

"That place is supposed to be empty," he stated. "If we take it easy, we can pry the door without too much noise. Nobody's got a right in there; and we're acting on a tip that prowlers are about the premises. Two of you patrol while the rest of us work on the door."

The squad crossed the street. Immediately, a hunched figure shifted from a doorway on the side where they had been. Unnoticed, this man scudded to an alleyway, some distance along. He dived into darkness.

"Cliff!"

A voice responded to the hunched man's hoarse whisper.

"What's up, Hawkeye?"

"Cardona and a squad just showed up from headquarters! They're going to bust into Mocquino's house!"

"On a tip-off?"

"Yeah, from what Cardona said."

"Hawkeye's" words made a profound impression on the listener. Cliff Marsland, agent of The Shadow, was stationed here to watch the front of the house next door to Mocquino's; for Wallace had said that entry was made through adjoining cellars. Harry Vincent, another agent, was at the back, in the next street. The arrival of the police was a bad factor.

"Put in a call to Burbank," whispered Cliff to Hawkeye. "Then duck around and tip off Harry. Slide in here afterward."

Hawkeye scurried through the alleyway. He found a cigar store one block distant. He entered a phonebooth and called Burbank. The contact man received the report. Hawkeye knew that it would go to The Shadow. He did not guess, however, that the relay would be made by coded wireless to a wingless autogiro, at present over the ocean near New York harbor!

So far as Hawkeye knew, Cliff and Harry were on duty only to await The Shadow. No information had been given as to The Shadow's whereabouts.

Somewhat assured by Burbank's calm acceptance of his report, Hawkeye took a circuitous course that brought him to Harry's outpost. He told Harry about Cardona; then made another circuit and arrived back with Cliff. Hawkeye found Cliff peering from the alleyway.

"There goes the door," groaned Cliff. "Cardona and his bunch have wedged it open. If the chief had only arrived here!"

"It's been ten minutes since I talked to Burbank," returned Hawkeye. "Maybe The Shadow will be here soon."

"We'll stick tight. That's all we can do."

ACROSS the street, Cardona and his two companions had entered the gloomy first floor of the empty house. Flashlights showed the place to be deserted. Cardona went to the door and signaled for the other two detectives.

"Not much chance of trouble," he told his crew. "Close the door. We'll all stick inside. Five of us will be too many for any bird that's got a hideout here. Let's take a look up those stairs."

They crept up to the second floor, with flashlights blazing the trail. They reached another deserted hallway. Closed doors showed all along the line. Cardona opened the first and entered a small, deserted room. The detectives were finding other doors locked. They came to the front and joined their leader.

"Listen!"

Cardona gave the whisper for silence. A rhythmic beat was coming from beyond a doorway at the rear of the front room. There was a sinister sound to the thrum. Instinctively, the five invaders crept toward the doorway.

"Sounds like a tom-tom," said one detective, in a tense voice. "What's that doing here?"

"It don't sound human," came another comment. "Say—this house gives you the jitters—"

Cardona gave a growl for silence. His hand seemed numbed as he moved it toward the handle of his revolver. He was about to order his detectives to copy his example, when an unexpected happening occurred. A click sounded. The bare room was suddenly flooded with light. The glare arrived from sockets in the ceiling.

"Cover the hall door!" barked Cardona.

Two detectives wheeled. They stopped short. A pair of dark-faced men had bobbed in from that direction. Each was holding a revolver. They had the detectives covered. Cardona was facing the inner door at the back of the room, expecting it to open. Instead, a *click* came from another corner. A panel opened. Cardona and the other two detectives swung; then stopped.

They, too, were covered by a pair of revolvers. One was held by a dark-faced servant, who looked like the ones at the other door. The second man was obviously the leader of the outfit. He was of medium height, dark-faced and smiling. His visage was friendly; yet there was a dangerous sparkle in his blackish eyes.

MOST remarkable was the man's attire. Though his servants were clad in old, rough clothes, the leader was splendid of garb. He wore a robe that looked like burnished gold. His waist was girded by a sash of deep, yet vivid, crimson. Thrum of tom-toms came more strongly, drumming through the thoughts of the astonished headquarters men.

The robed stranger cried a word in a strange tongue. The drumbeats ceased.

As a background to the opened panel, Cardona and the others could see a flicker that looked like the reflection of a blaze. They heard the robed man give another cry. The flicker ended. Scuffling footsteps sounded in the room beyond. Cardona realized that there were others beside the four who had trapped himself and the detectives.

"Why have you come here?"

The inquiry was musical. It came from the smiling lips of the robed man by the panel. Cardona saw fit to answer.

"We heard that there were prowlers in this house," he stated. "We entered to make a search."

"Who gave you that information? The owners?"

"No. We received an anonymous call at headquarters."

The robed man laughed. His dark-faced retainers grinned.

"You have spoken the truth," declared the robed man, suavely. "That was wise of you. Since

I am the owner of this building, you could not have received a bona fide complaint."

"You are Doctor Rodil Mocquino?"

Cardona regretted the question, the moment that he put it. A change came over the smiling face. Evil eyes glared. Lips snarled vicious words.

"You have learned my name! That changes everything! Fools! To intrude upon me in my own abode! You shall regret this action! Stand as you are! One move means death!"

Before Cardona or his men could offer response, Mocquino and the man beside him had stepped back into the next room. The panel clicked shut. As the headquarters squad looked toward the hallway door, the two men there sprang from sight. The door slammed. A bolt clicked.

Detectives ejaculated triumphant cries. Cardona alone called for caution. The others, staring, saw the reason. Loopholes had opened in the walls—three from the side toward the inner rooms; three from the wall to the hallway. Revolver muzzles were sliding into view.

The detectives stood rooted, expecting instant death from foemen against whom they could not fight. The guns, however, did not blaze. Cardona suddenly understood why. He could hear scraping sounds from beyond the rear wall. Grimly, Joe held his own counsel.

He knew Mocquino for a villain—one who deserved the brand of murderer. But the fiend had a reason for delaying slaughter. He was moving out of the room beyond. He was giving up this abode. Not until his paraphernalia was on its way would Mocquino give the command for massacre.

The best plan was to wait. Perhaps, if flight proved easy, Mocquino might decide to let the prisoners go. A slight hope, at best. More logically, Cardona realized, Mocquino simply preferred to withhold the clatter of guns. Nevertheless, there might be some intervention. Nothing could be gained by present action. Nothing could be lost by waiting.

OUTSIDE, Cliff Marsland was still watching from the entrance to the alleyway. He was alarmed concerning Cardona and the detectives. If their search had been barren, they should have returned. If they had captured someone, or met with opposition, at least one detective should have appeared to summon police or call headquarters.

Cliff sensed the truth. Though he had been deputed merely to watch here, he had learned through Burbank that Doctor Mocquino might prove dangerous. Cliff was troubled. He feared to call the police; Mocquino might well be prepared for such invaders. Cliff could see only one hope: The Shadow.

Hawkeye was straining. He started to speak. Cliff stopped him. From high above, Cliff had caught an unexpected sound. One that purred from the sky; then ended suddenly.

Looking up, Cliff saw a whirling motion, faint in the reflected glow of city lights. Grabbing Hawkeye, Cliff started from the alleyway.

They dashed across the street. Cliff yanked open the basement door of the house next to Mocquino's. He sent Hawkeye scudding through, with the quick command:

"Get Vincent!"

Glimmering a flashlight, Cliff searched along the wall toward the next house. He spied a closet door. He yanked it open and ripped away a hanging mass of clothes. A yawning cavity gaped in the glare of his flashlight. It was a passage through to the supposedly empty house. Tensely, Cliff waited for Hawkeye to arrive with Harry.

ABOVE Mocquino's house, a spinning object had taken shape. With swift descent, a toylike plane enlarged. Downward, almost skimming the granite wall of the fifty-story Europa Building came The Shadow's wingless autogiro. Its objective was the roof of Mocquino's four-story house. The Shadow, contacted by a wireless report from Burbank, had ordered Crofton to New York instead of Newark.

The Shadow had taken the helm for this descent. His close scrape of towering walls was a stroke of perfect piloting. He had allowed for air currents; his calculations were correct. With its windmill blades spinning furiously, the autogiro edged away from the Europa Building and settled squarely upon the flat roof of Mocquino's house.

A blackened form dropped from the giro. With blades still whirling, the machine rolled forward. The motor roared with sudden speed. At the edge of the roof, the autogiro took off and gained a vertical ascent, to clear the houses across the street.

Crofton had taken the controls. He was whirling off to Newark. This brief descent amid Manhattan's towers would never be suspected.

With the Europa Building as a sure landmark, The Shadow had arrived ahead of schedule. A cloaked shape on the roof, he was ripping open the customary trapdoor that he found there. While his ready agents were invading from below, The Shadow was crashing through from above!

The law had intervened. Cardona and four others had been trapped. But rescue was coming from two unexpected quarters. The Shadow was here with aid!

CHAPTER VIII
THE ESCAPE

WITHIN the barren front room, five men still retained their rigid attitude. Detectives were copying Cardona in his lack of action. They were relying upon their leader to pull them from this trap. Joe knew it; and the thought harassed him.

Scraping sounds had ceased. He guessed that rapid packing had been completed. Minutes alone remained until the stroke of doom. Those gun muzzles from the wall meant marksmen, stationed in the room beyond. Cardona looked toward the other wall. He pictured gunners in the outer hall.

Joe had seen that hall; hence his visualization was accurate. But had he viewed the hall itself, he would have found reason for new hope. There, three dark-faced servitors were peering above the muzzles at the loopholes. A single ceiling light had been turned on; it showed their figures plainly.

The glow revealed something else. Blackness on the stairway to the floors above, where all rooms were deserted. Blackness that moved, took shape. Blackness that formed a living figure as it crept downward. The Shadow stood looming above the vassals of Doctor Mocquino.

Hidden lips delivered a whispered laugh. The weird sound was spectral in that gloomy hall. It caused heads to turn. Glaring faces met blazing eyes. A shout came from one of the marksmen, as The Shadow's laugh rose to a taunting crescendo.

Madly, Mocquino's henchman yanked his revolver from the loophole and fired a wild shot at The Shadow. The others followed suit.

As they fired, The Shadow's automatics answered. From his post, The Shadow had pictured the situation. Doomed men in a trap. One way to save them. That was by drawing away the entire trio of sharpshooters.

These minions of Mocquino were savage. But their very frenzy ruined that. Quick shots sizzled wide; but The Shadow's did not fail. Spurts from the automatics sent the henchmen sprawling.

One managed a dive that carried him beyond the stairs. He pounded at a door which The Shadow could not cover. The barrier opened. The man rolled through. The others lay where they were. The Shadow swung into the hall. Seeing no opposition from the rear, he sprang to the bolted door.

BEFORE he acted, The Shadow had pictured the arrangement of the room where Cardona and the detectives were trapped. He had done this by a simple deduction, based on the room's position in the house. He had seen the marksmen in the hall. He had known that others would be aiming through another wall. But through one wall only,

for the room was at the front corner of the house.

By eliminating the sharpshooters in the hallway, The Shadow had given Cardona and his fellow prisoners a perfect chance for safety. He was relying upon Cardona to take it; and The Shadow's faith in the acting inspector proved justified. Cardona had been thinking things over during the wait for death.

The moment that shots had sounded from the hallway, Joe had noticed the disappearance of the guns on the hall side. The departure of those muzzles meant that the fire could come from but one line: the wall of the rear room. That wall, itself, offered safety. Cardona had shouted to his companions to follow him.

With a dive, Joe reached the wall between the outpoked revolvers. The muzzles began to blast; but detectives were already on the jump. One dick staggered, wounded. Joe yanked him to safety. Gun muzzles swung viciously; they could not make the angle. Cardona and his men were safe. The guns were jerked from view.

Evidently, Doctor Mocquino had not anticipated a happening like this. A two-walled trap had seemed sufficient. It had proven otherwise. Joe Cardona voiced a grim chuckle; then snapped a command to his men.

"Cover the panel! In the far corner! That's where they'll come from!"

A *click*. A harsh, venomous voice. Cardona wheeled. He saw his mistake. Mocquino had crossed them. For this time, it was the rear-room doorway that had opened. Again Cardona and the detectives were caught unaware. First they had covered the door to the rear room, not knowing of the panel. This time, they had covered the panel, forgetful of the door.

Two ugly, leering servitors were with Mocquino. Loopholes had dropped shut everywhere, impelled by a switch that Mocquino had pressed. The Voodoo Master wanted them no longer. Slaughter in cold blood, face to face— such was his present plan.

"One move!" snarled the Voodoo Master, still resplendent in his golden robe—"one move and we fire—"

His leer told that bullets were his intention, no matter what Cardona and the others did. His delay was merely a bluff, a part of Mocquino's gloating, baiting game. This time, he had underestimated the situation. Mocquino had not seen the power of the opposition that had stricken down his henchmen in the hall.

The door from the hallway swung open. Mocquino snarled; two reserve henchmen aimed point-blank in that direction. But their murderous efforts were too late. They expected a foeman who would stop. Instead, a mass of living blackness hurtled clear to the center of the room.

Revolvers spoke in vain. Automatics tongued flame as The Shadow wheeled. One man sprawled; the other dived back. Mocquino and his closer servitors scrambled to the doorway, firing.

The Shadow faded back toward the outer door. Detectives jumped out into the center of the room. Guns roared in unison.

Despite his valiant effort, The Shadow was faced by desperate odds. Mocquino and his men had swung back too quickly for Cardona and the detectives to aid. Only a skillful, unexpected fling saved The Shadow in that moment. Slugs whistled through the folds of his black cloak. One bullet slashed The Shadow's left forearm. His hand dropped momentarily.

Then came shots from the inner room. Mocquino hurled his henchmen back from the door. The Shadow blasted two bullets toward the Voodoo Master. An intervening servitor saved Mocquino without intention. As the howling man spun about, Mocquino slammed the door. The sagging henchman was hurtled headforemost to the floor.

THREE men had come into the inner room: Cliff, Harry and Hawkeye. The valiant trio had found a secret stairway up through the center of the house directly into the middle room. They had smashed open an unguarded door at the head of the stairway, in time to begin fire upon Mocquino and his clustered men.

This middle room, like the front one, was barren; but its furnishings had been only recently removed. Mocquino must have possessed a dozen servants; for he still had ruffians about him. The Shadow's aides had dropped a pair before Mocquino turned. But before they could give further battle, a new door opened into the middle room. The new door was from another room, the third farther back. Through it piled half a dozen wild-eyed men. Unarmed, they flung themselves upon The Shadow's agents. These unexpected attackers were members of Mocquino's cult, come to aid their master when his servants failed.

Cliff and Harry sprawled to the floor. Guns were wrested from their fists. Hawkeye, twisting, managed to retain his feet. He saw blows descending toward the heads of his companions. Wildly, he delivered counterstrokes. He floundered instantly beneath an overwhelming crew.

A shout from Mocquino. It saved the would-be victims. Not because Mocquino held mercy, his lips would have snarled denial of such a thought. Self-preservation was Mocquino's motive. Already the door from the front room was crashing under the drive of Cardona and his detectives.

The cult members heard Mocquino's order. They sprang for the secret stairway up which The Shadow's aides had come. Behind them came Mocquino and his men. The Voodoo Master stopped as his henchmen took to the stairs. The Shadow's agents were rising unsteadily from the floor, gunless. Mocquino prepared to slaughter them.

The door from the front room ripped clear of its hinges. Cardona and a pair of detectives surged through. Even then, Mocquino would not have given up his vicious purpose had he not seen a black-clad figure hard behind the invaders. The Shadow's .45 was looming. With a maddened roar of final venom, Mocquino chose the door to the rear room.

Two barriers slammed: one from the secret stairway; the other from the rear room. Detectives sprang to pound at both. Half groggy, The Shadow's agents joined them in the effort. The stairway door was first to give. Cardona and the sleuths surged downward, abandoning the other portal. The Shadow, alone in the center of the room, hissed a command. His agents completed the work at the rear door.

They sprang into a lighted room beyond; this also was barren. The Shadow, however, knew the former arrangement. The middle room had been the meeting place of the cult. The rear apartment had been the red room. Across it was another door. The Shadow knew that it must lead to a rear exit. He watched his aides rip at the barrier. It came open, showing a short passage to an old fire escape.

This was the way through which the furnishings had gone. It explained why The Shadow's agents had not encountered the bearers on the way up.

The Shadow ripped open the window and leaped to the fire escape. Shouts, wild gunfire came from below.

Two trucks were speeding away from an alley behind the house. These had arrived during battle. The police, coming on the scene at sounds of battle in the house, were too late to stop them. So was The Shadow. His automatic blazed final bullets; but the range was too long to clip the tires, as the light trucks shot out to the street beyond.

The police took up pursuit.

Doctor Mocquino had lost his prisoners. Doomed men had escaped, thanks to The Shadow. But Mocquino, in turn, had managed his own escape, with the remnants of his henchmen and the members of his voodoo cult. Sprawled men lay upon the floor of the front room. Those that lived would be prisoners of the police. As for Mocquino, the law could more easily trap him tonight than could The Shadow.

The cloaked fighter gave an order to his agents. They followed him hurriedly down the fire escape, knowing that they would have time to depart from the vicinity. The law was off to a chase. Whining sirens told that patrol cars were joining in the quest.

Perhaps the law would trap Doctor Mocquino. If so, The Shadow would be satisfied with the result. If not, the quest would again become The Shadow's. There was a chance that Mocquino's flight would end in freedom. The Shadow already had a plan, if such was the outcome.

For The Shadow still held another clue that Stanton Wallace had provided. The Shadow had met Doctor Mocquino and had driven him to flight. He could find a new route to reach the insidious Voodoo Master.

CHAPTER IX
THE CONFERENCE

AT three o'clock the next afternoon, Doctor Rupert Sayre was seated in Lamont Cranston's library, perusing a rare book that dealt with voodoo rituals. A streak of blackness hovered above the page. Sayre looked up quickly; then smiled as he saw the tall figure of Cranston.

Again, Sayre knew that this was The Shadow; and with good reason. The Shadow's left arm was bandaged and in a sling. Doctor Sayre himself had bandaged it, last night. The Shadow had come back to New Jersey after the flight of Doctor Mocquino.

"How is Stanton Wallace?"

The Shadow made the query in the quiet fashion of Cranston. Sayre placed his book to one side.

"When you left for New York this morning," stated the physician, "Wallace was still asleep. He awoke shortly before noon. He seems quite normal; but he is not talkative."

"You tested his color perceptions?"

"Yes. Red no longer annoys him. So I have allowed him to stroll outside. At present, he is in the living room."

Richards entered as The Shadow ceased speaking. The servant had come to announce a visitor.

"Mr. Vincent is here, sir."

"Good," spoke The Shadow. "Conduct him to the living room, Richards. Doctor Sayre and I will be there. After that, you may dismantle the green room. Pack the draperies and put the lights with them."

THE SHADOW went to the living room, accompanied by Doctor Sayre. Just as they entered, Harry Vincent arrived. The Shadow greeted him; then introduced him to Stanton Wallace, who had risen from his chair.

The Shadow eyed Wallace when the latter studied Harry. He saw that the patient was impressed by the newcomer. That was as The Shadow had expected. Harry Vincent was a clean-cut chap, whose frank friendliness immediately commanded respect.

The group seated themselves. The Shadow turned to Stanton Wallace. Quietly, he announced:

"Today is Thursday."

The unexpected statement brought an instant response. Wallace began to speak; then became confused. His face flushed. He stammered:

"I—I thought—that is, I guessed—well, today should be Monday. Perhaps, though, I was mistaken—"

He paused, his words a giveaway. Doctor Sayre realized at once that Wallace had somehow learned the actual day of the week. The physician was both startled and perplexed. The Shadow calmly pressed the button to summon Richards. He ordered the servant to produce the day's newspaper.

Richards went out and returned with a Thursday morning sheet. Eagerness replaced Stanton Wallace's pretense. His eyes were avid, as he seized the newspaper and scanned the headlines. His lips phrased an ejaculation.

"Dunley Bligh is safe!" he exclaimed, gladly. "He defended himself aboard the *Doranic!* This is certainly wonderful news—"

"Read the third column to the right," suggested The Shadow.

More blurted words from Wallace.

"Doctor Mocquino in flight!" cried the young man. "Sought by the police! For attempted murder! Mocquino and all those with him!"

There was another paragraph on the front page, that The Shadow did not mention. It referred to a successful trip by a wingless autogiro, to and from the liner *Doranic.* Apparently, it bore no connection with the other stories. Nor, for that matter, did Bligh's battle and Mocquino's flight appear to be related.

"You wanted Bligh," declared Wallace, seriously, as he placed the newspaper aside. "I suppose that you also planned to deal with Mocquino."

"I did," responded The Shadow, quietly.

"Then I am to blame," confessed Wallace. "I learned by accident that yesterday was Wednesday. I called New York police headquarters. I was the person who tipped off the law. I imagine that injured your plans."

"You did." The Shadow's slight smile showed that he had already divined the source of the tip-off. "Nevertheless, you are not to be blamed for the mistake. You can make amends by answering certain questions."

"Gladly!" agreed Wallace.

"First," queried The Shadow, "tell me if you gave your name to the police when you called last night?"

"I did not," replied Wallace. "I lacked suffi-cient time."

"Did you state that you were the man whom they placed in custody of Doctor Sayre?"

"No."

"Did you tell where you were?"

"No."

"Did you talk to Inspector Cardona in person?"

"No. He was not in his office. I left the message for him."

"Why did you end the call so abruptly?"

"I heard Doctor Sayre at the door. I was afraid that he would disapprove of my action."

A PAUSE. The Shadow knew that Stanton Wallace had answered truthfully. Since the law had no clue to the patient's recovery, all was well with The Shadow's future plans.

"Doctor Sayre is returning to New York." The Shadow's tone carried the semblance of a command. "You will remain here, Wallace, while he requests further time to study your case. Vincent will remain here also. Meanwhile, I shall search for Doctor Mocquino.

"The Voodoo Master has proven slippery. Despite the swiftness of the police, he has eluded them. Through quick action, the law covered every bridge, tunnel and ferry that offered departure from Manhattan. All trucks were stopped. Mocquino's were not among them.

"All garages have been questioned. Every parking lot has been searched. No trace has been gained. Mocquino has gained some remarkable hideout, apparently in Manhattan itself."

The Shadow ceased his quiet speech. Stanton Wallace blurted a question:

"Then how do you expect to trace him?"

In reply, The Shadow produced a sheaf of papers. He flipped them open with his right hand and spread them upon the table. He pointed to one sheet.

"This concerns James Lenger," he stated. "The information was not difficult to obtain from back files of newspapers. James Lenger was slain on the Amazon, presumably by headhunters. That was not astonishing, in itself. But when one studies the reasons for Lenger's trip to the Amazon country, an answer begins to develop.

"Lenger had been to the Amazon a year ago. Old clippings state that he went to locate a cache of gold that had been left somewhere along the river, years ago, by Portuguese explorers. On his recent trip, Lenger made no statement of any purpose."

"He had learned something!" exclaimed Wallace.

"Probably," remarked The Shadow. "He may have actually located the gold on his first trip and left it where it was. Assuming such to be the case, it is likely that only a few of his closest friends would have known that his last trip was to reclaim the gold."

"And one friend was a member of Mocquino's cult!"

"Yes. Someone who talked about Lenger as you spoke concerning Bligh. Mocquino sent his own agents to reclaim the gold. They finished that work by murdering Lenger. Headhunters were not involved."

"And by tracing James Lenger's friends—"

"Unfortunately, that is almost impossible. Lenger was something of a mystery man. He presumably kept all his business to himself. Hundreds of persons were acquainted with him. Which ones had his confidence is a difficult matter to learn."

WALLACE sank back in his chair, his face troubled. The Shadow referred to another document.

"The case of Myron Rathcourt," he remarked. "The Chicago millionaire who died of heart failure. In all probability, his death was cleverly arranged by Mocquino, who profited thereby."

"But how—"

"All of Myron Rathcourt's estate was left to his nephew, Elridge Rathcourt. The latter lives in New York."

Wallace started to speak. He paused; The Shadow was pronouncing his very thoughts.

"Doctor Mocquino could profit only through Elridge Rathcourt," declared the calm-voiced speaker. "Therefore, we may believe that Elridge Rathcourt is a member of the cult. He was the man who showed glee when Mocquino thrust a pin through his uncle's effigy.

"Controlled by Mocquino, Elridge is furnish-ing funds to the Voodoo Master. He has come into a large fortune. Mocquino will eventually acquire all of it. Elridge Rathcourt is his complete dupe. Similarly, Elridge Rathcourt is the man through whom we may find a new trail to Mocquino."

The Shadow removed one paper from the sheaf. Harry Vincent, close to the table, noted a telegram addressed to Rutledge Mann. The latter was an investment broker, who served The Shadow as an agent. Mann had made moves in tracing Elridge Rathcourt.

"It proved possible," stated The Shadow, "to trace Elridge Rathcourt through an investment house in Chicago. Through such a process,

ELRIDGE RATHCOURT—
who comes under the spell of
the Voodoo Master

I learned that young Rathcourt is living in New York. His residence is the penthouse of a small hotel called the Delbar.

"Elridge Rathcourt once purchased securities through a concern called Voder & Co. That brokerage house is now defunct. But Rathcourt would not be surprised if a former representative of the concern should call upon him. Today, a telephone message went to the Hotel Delbar, stating that James Rettigue, formerly of Voder & Co., would like an interview with Elridge Rathcourt."

A pause. Harry Vincent guessed that the supposed James Rettigue had been The Shadow.

"Elridge Rathcourt is out of town," resumed The Shadow. "He will not return until tomorrow night. Presumably, he is in Atlantic City. His valet took the message. Hence Rathcourt will not be surprised when he receives James Rettigue as a caller tomorrow night.

"Until that time, the police are welcome to proceed with their futile search for Doctor Mocquino. Real results will be accomplished when Elridge Rathcourt is interviewed by James Rettigue."

THE SHADOW arose. He turned to Doctor Sayre and asked if the physician was ready to return to New York. Sayre nodded his affirmative. It was apparent that The Shadow was also going to the metropolis. But before departure, he turned again to Stanton Wallace.

"You have spoken frankly," approved The Shadow. "In return, I have given you a full outline of immediate plans. Doctor Mocquino is still at large. You are in no danger while he does not know your whereabouts, nor has knowledge of your improved condition.

"Therefore, you must remain here and hold no outside contact. Vincent will stay here also, for your own protection. You will find him an agreeable companion. I know that you and he will become friends. This arrangement should prove satisfactory."

"It is," declared Wallace, seriously. "I owe you thanks, Mr. Cranston. Also an apology for my folly—"

"That is forgotten."

Turning, The Shadow left with Sayre. Stanton Wallace remained with Harry Vincent. He looked toward his new friend and gained further confidence. Harry's air of self-assurance marked him as a man who would prove reliant in an emergency.

Stanton Wallace smiled in relief. His outlook on the world had changed. He realized that results had already been accomplished. For the first time, he understood that he had given three potent clues concerning Doctor Mocquino. Two had already been followed. The Shadow had saved Dunley Bligh. He had later delivered a thrust at the headquarters of Doctor Mocquino.

Though progress was temporarily halted, The Shadow would soon begin a new endeavor. He had developed his third clue, through an investigation of Elridge Rathcourt, who must certainly be a member of the voodoo cult. The future looked bright to Stanton Wallace. He could see trouble for Doctor Rodil Mocquino.

But in his survey of the future, Stanton Wallace made few allowances. That, perhaps, was because his present security caused him to minimize the craftiness of Doctor Mocquino. Careful consideration would have brought realization that Mocquino's schemes were not yet beaten.

The Shadow, alone, could have predicted the grim obstacles that still might rise along the trail to the evil Voodoo Master.

CHAPTER X
CARDONA GAINS SUSPICIONS

AT half past six the next afternoon, Joe Cardona was absent from his office. The acting inspector had gone out to dinner, leaving

Detective Sergeant Markham in charge. Markham, a capable routine man, was pondering over a large map of Manhattan that lay on Cardona's desk.

The map was marked with pencil lines and dotted with circles that had been inscribed in colored crayon. It represented Cardona's efforts of Wednesday night, when the ace had attempted to box the elusive Doctor Mocquino. The dots were located at important ferry slips, at bridges, and at the entrance to the Holland Tunnel. There were others at the stations of the Hudson and Manhattan Tubes.

Markham was growling as he talked to a detective who was standing near the desk. While speaking, he fingered a pile of report sheets. Those referred to the search of Manhattan garages.

"This business don't click with me" was Markham's opinion. "There's too much chance for a leak. How can we figure on catching Mocquino this way?"

"Everything's covered," put in the detective.

"Yeah?" queried Markham. He pointed to the map. "Look at all these subway routes to Brooklyn and Long Island. What's to prevent Mocquino and his bunch from going in and out by those lines? Answer that one, Cassidy."

"You can't load a couple of trucks on board the subway," returned Cassidy, promptly. "That's what the inspector was saying just before you came in, Markham."

"Humph! Maybe not. We had a good description of those trucks, too. Well, it beats me, Cassidy. Look. Here's all the schedules of every regular ferry service. Men watching every slip. They've stopped cars going and coming at the bridges and the Holland Tunnel. There's only one answer: Mocquino is still in New York."

Cassidy grunted his agreement; then looked at his watch. He had completed his hours on duty. The detective went out, leaving Markham alone in the office.

SEVERAL minutes passed. Markham heard a footfall. He looked up to see a slender, stoop-shouldered man at the door. The fellow's face was darkish; he looked like a Cuban. His head craned forward from his neck, and Markham noted a beady, ratlike glimmer in his eyes.

The arrival was smoking a cigarette. Nonchalantly, he flicked ashes to the floor; then took another puff. Markham scented the aroma of heavy cigar tobacco. The man eyed him more directly; then spoke in an inquisitive purr:

"Inspector Cardona—is he here?"

"Out to dinner," returned Markham. "What can I do for you?"

"Ah! Too bad." The man clucked. "It was Inspector Cardona that I wished to see."

"About what?"

The darkish man paused; then approached the desk.

"I am from Philadelphia," he stated. "I read the newspapers of that city. I learned of a man who had come here to New York. His eyes were staring straight ahead." The darkish man paused and tapped his forehead. "His mind—it was like a blank."

"You know the fellow?" demanded Markham.

"I am not quite sure," came the reply. "The picture of him was very poor. Unfortunately, I could not give his name, even if he should be the man I think."

"How's that?"

"I am a Mexican," explained the darkish man. "My name is Jose Arilla. I once operated a roulette wheel in Tia Juana. It was there that I saw this man first. Months ago, I came to Philadelphia. I saw him there, twice again, in a gambling room."

"What good would it do if you saw him again?"

"Ah! There are names that I could mention. Persons who might be his friends. Perhaps, though, the unfortunate man has already recovered?"

"I don't think so. Here—sit down."

Markham picked up the telephone and dialed a number. There was no response. He hung up the receiver.

"Can you stay in town a while?" he questioned.

"If you wish," replied the darkish man. "If I could be sure—"

"Of seeing this bird that stares? I think you can, Mr. Arilla. We placed him in charge of a doctor named Sayre. That's who I just called. Sayre isn't in his office."

"You will call him again?"

"Yes. Inside half an hour."

Arilla glanced at a wristwatch. Again, his rattish eyes gleamed. But his suave voice offset the expression of his face.

"I, too, must have my dinner," he laughed. "I shall call back here, sir. In one hour."

With that, Arilla departed. Markham methodically made a notation to call Doctor Sayre at seven o'clock. As an afterthought, the detective sergeant checked Sayre's number by the telephone book and found that he had it correctly. Markham resumed his study of the map.

SEVEN o'clock. Markham had accidentally guessed the hour of Sayre's return to his office. It was precisely seven when Rupert Sayre stopped at the street door and unlocked it. The physician went into his office; there he stopped and sniffed.

There was an aroma of tobacco in the room; not surprising, since Sayre himself smoked frequently. But the doctor's preference was for cigarettes. This odor was that of a heavy cigar tobacco.

Sayre looked at the ash stand. There he saw nothing but cigarettes. He did not notice that one stump was thicker and rounder than the others, that flakes of dark tobacco projected from it.

Sayre went to open the window. It was locked; but the catch turned loosely in his hand. As he opened the window, Sayre decided that the catch would have to be repaired. The possibility that it might have been forced loose did not occur to him at that moment. The sudden ringing of the telephone bell brought Sayre from the window.

"Hello, hello..." Sayre paused. "What's that? Detective headquarters?... Oh, yes. Sergeant Markham... About the patient? I see... Yes, I can produce him if necessary... His condition? Somewhat improved... Better have Inspector Cardona call me later..."

Sayre hung up. He paced the office. Previous thoughts were forgotten. A breeze from the window had cleared the darkish odor of the room. The physician paused, musing. He did not notice that the door to the little reception room was ajar. Had he turned, he might have seen a shrewd, ratlike face peering from that opening.

Instead, Sayre picked up the telephone. Tensely, he put in a call to New Jersey. He pronounced the number clearly. When a voice came across the wire, Sayre questioned:

"Is this the residence of Mr. Lamont Cranston?... Good... Ah, yes. Richards, of course... Yes, this is Doctor Sayre. I should like to talk with Mr. Vincent..."

A pause. Harry's hello came over the wire.

"Vincent!" Again Sayre was tense. "I have heard from detective headquarters... Yes... About Stanton Wallace... I shall have to tell Cardona where he is... I can explain it satisfactorily... But perhaps Cardona will want to see him...

"Yes... Agree to any request that comes from detective headquarters... Certainly... Bring Wallace there if they want him... That is the idea. Tell him to act as if he were still dazed. Yes. It will conform with my story of his partial improvement..."

Sayre sat down at the desk. The door from the reception room closed. Sayre had begun to drum with his fingers. Otherwise, he would have heard the slight *thump* from the door. Suddenly, the physician arose and went to the reception room. He opened the door and turned on the light.

The room was empty; but had Sayre looked at the window on the other side, he would have noted that it was open an inch from the bottom.

Someone had scrambled from that window and had not fully lowered the sash. The lurker had reached a small courtyard that offered exit, by a passage to the front street.

THERE was a *clang* from the doorbell. Sayre went back through the office and answered the summons. He blinked in surprise as Joe Cardona shouldered in through the door. Cardona motioned Sayre into the office. The ace looked about; then appeared to be satisfied.

"I talked with headquarters," explained Joe, "right after Markham had called you. I was near here, so I hurried over. Markham is coming up. He's on his way."

"What about?" queried Sayre.

"Markham pulled a boner," returned Joe. "A guy came into my office and asked about that stiff-eyed patient of yours. Markham did too much talking. That's why I asked him what the inquirer looked like. He said the fellow was a Mex."

"What was the man's name?"

"Jose Arilla. Do you know what I think, doc? My hunch is that Mocquino sent Arilla to talk to me. This chatter about the staring man was Arilla's bluff. Markham said that Arilla looked like a rat.

"I know what you're going to say: Why would Mocquino send a bird that looked suspicious? I'll tell you why. He probably didn't have anyone else who was smart enough to send. Arilla had a good story. Good enough to bluff Markham, until I got busy with some questions.

"Markham mentioned your name. There's a chance that Arilla might come snooping up this way. Maybe there's some connection we don't know about—between your patient and Doctor Mocquino. Let's look around."

Cardona strode into the reception room. His inspection was brief. He wanted to satisfy himself on one point only: that no one was at present on the premises. Not knowing of Sayre's call to New Jersey, Joe did not consider the possibility that Arilla might have already come and gone.

Nor did Sayre enlighten him. The physician was in a quandary. He wanted to say as little as possible until he had opportunity to communicate with The Shadow. Unfortunately, Sayre had seldom served The Shadow as a regular agent. Most of the physician's aid had been concerned with medical matters. Hence Sayre, troubled by events, did not connect possibilities.

Quick rings sounded from the doorbell, as Cardona and Sayre came back into the office. Someone was jabbing the button hastily. Cardona answered. It was Markham. The detective sergeant had made a speedy trip from headquarters. He was highly excited.

"I came in a cab," reported Markham. "Just as we swung in here, I saw a guy doing a quick sneak for the corner! I spotted him. It was Jose Arilla! He grabbed a cab of his own. I dropped off and flashed my badge to another hackie who was standing there. He'd heard the address that Arilla gave. Arilla has headed for Red Mike's!"

"To the new joint?" queried Cardona. "Over in Hell's Kitchen?"

Markham nodded.

"That's where we'll travel," decided Cardona. "It's a cinch that Arilla sneaked up here. He saw you come in, doc. He was watching for his chance to enter when he saw me show up. He beat it the first moment he could; but Markham was lucky enough to spot him."

Sayre saw the logic of Cardona's theory. It destroyed all other inklings. The physician's chance to reconstruct the recent past was gone. Sayre, himself, would have been amazed and unbelieving had he been told that Arilla had been listening to the call that Sayre had telephoned to New Jersey.

IT was nearing eight o'clock when a sedan stopped near a corner not far from West Twenty-third Street and close to the Hudson River. Three men were in the back seat: Cardona, Markham and Sayre. They looked toward a cheap restaurant on the other side of the street. Lights showed through lowered blinds on the floor above.

"That's Red Mike's," growled Cardona. "The hash house is the blind for his joint. He used to run a basement dive. He's gone up in the world. Using a second floor now."

A car rolled by and turned the corner. Hardly had its lights passed before a grimy-faced man sneaked up to the sedan. Cardona spoke to the fellow through the window. The man shuffled away. The observers saw him cross the street and enter the beanery.

"That was Tyke Lugan," explained Cardona in an undertone, to Sayre. "He's a stoolie. A smart guy for a pigeon. He's gone in to see if Arilla is there. The car that went by is going around the block to another street. It has three headquarters men in it.

"Cassidy is in charge. We were lucky enough to get hold of him when I called headquarters just before we started over here. Cassidy saw Arilla in the hall when the guy was on his way in. There's only two ways out of Red Mike's. Markham is here in front; Cassidy watching in back."

"And we both know Arilla," put in Markham.

A few minutes passed. A sneaky form came from the hash house. Tyke Lugan crossed the street. Sidling to the sedan, he whispered a quick story.

"De guy's in dere," he informed. "A dead ringer for de mug you told me to look for. He's waitin' for a phone call. Sittin' right by de little room where de phone is."

"Let him get his call," decided Cardona. "Keep on going, Tyke. We don't want you mixed in it."

Then, as the stoolie made eager departure, Cardona added:

"Wherever Arilla goes, we'll trail him. See ahead there?" He pointed to a corner where a man was lounging against a wall. "That's Dowley, from headquarters. Knows how to play the part of a bum. Parker is down at the next corner, sitting in a parked cab. Nothing suspicious about it; over here, the hackies work on eighteen-hour shifts. That's why they call them 'coolies,' and they're liable to stay in one spot for half the night."

Cardona paused to chuckle.

"If Jose Arilla comes out the front door," he said, "Markham identifies him and we signal Dowley. If he comes out the back, Cassidy spots him and flashes the tip-off to Parker. Either way, we have two cars starting out to trail him. We'll let him go where he wants."

Again a pause; then, with a tone of conviction, the ace sleuth added:

"Wherever Arilla leads us, that's where we'll find Doctor Mocquino!"

CHAPTER XI
WHEN TOM-TOMS BEAT

WHILE Joe Cardona was watching at Red Mike's, events were beginning in another section of Manhattan. Near Times Square, a tall stroller was walking along a crosstown street where occasional twenty-story buildings loomed like mushrooms among smaller, antiquated structures.

The stroller was The Shadow. He paused to study one of the taller buildings. The light above the marquee flashed a name: "Hotel Delbar."

Keen eyes followed upward. Constructed in limited space, the Hotel Delbar was straight-walled almost to the top. At one side only did it show a pyramid formation. The inward setbacks were slight and narrow, scarcely more than ledges, except for the nineteenth floor. That offered a wider margin.

The twentieth floor was the penthouse, and it had its own veranda. The penthouse walls were sheer, except at that one end. There, the nineteenth floor was decorated with a row of clumpy trees. They looked like potted cedars, along the low bulwark of the nineteenth floor.

The Shadow was considering the possibilities of scaling the penthouse wall. His survey ended, he approached the hotel from across the street. He paused to light a cigarette when he neared the lighted area beneath the marquee.

The Shadow was clad in street clothes. His attire was drab; his face, too, lacked impressiveness. It was less hawklike than the countenance of Lamont Cranston. His features were long and dreary; his eyelids droopy. No chance observer would have picked him for The Shadow. He was playing the part of a mythical personality: James Rettigue.

With a peculiar flick, The Shadow tossed his match away. The motion was performed with his right hand. His left remained motionless. Though his arm was no longer in the sling, it was heavily bandaged from wrist to elbow.

A watcher saw the flip of the match. He shuffled forward from beside the wall, an ill-clad, huddled man. It was Hawkeye; as he approached the standing figure of The Shadow, the little spotter looked like a typical bum seen on a side street near Times Square.

With a panhandler's whine, Hawkeye asked for a dime. This was for the benefit of passersby. They shied away, figuring that they would be touched if the bum failed to receive money. They saw a sour look on the features of James Rettigue. Hawkeye was grinning, while The Shadow fumbled for a coin. With a wary dart of his eyes, Hawkeye saw a chance to speak.

"Rathcourt is in," he whispered. "Cliff spotted him in the lobby. Slipped the news to me when I was touching him for two bits."

The Shadow passed coins to Hawkeye.

"Got in at eight," he added. "No messages for him. Nobody's been about. Cliff is gone."

"Off duty."

As he heard The Shadow's whisper, Hawkeye mumbled thanks for the money. Jingling the coins, the spotter slouched away, looking back and forth as if fearful that some policeman had seen him make the touch.

THE SHADOW strolled into the lobby of the Delbar. He approached the desk, announced himself as James Rettigue and asked for Elridge Rathcourt. The clerk put in a call to the penthouse, then nodded. It was all right for the visitor to go up.

While ascending in the elevator, The Shadow's lips formed a sour smile that well-fitted the rather cynical character of James Rettigue. His expression, however, had a significance that escaped others in the elevator. The Shadow was deliberating upon the simplicity of this expedition. He had chosen a direct measure as a start.

The Shadow knew that Elridge Rathcourt was a man controlled by Doctor Mocquino. Because of that, The Shadow had considered the plan of making a cloaked entry, coming from outside the penthouse. Such a system would certainly have proven a mental jolt to Rathcourt. He would have found himself faced by a being fully as terrible as the Voodoo Master.

Contrarily, The Shadow had pictured Rathcourt's present mental condition. The Shadow was sure that members of the voodoo cult must be having qualms because Mocquino was, at present, a hunted villain. A worried man would be apt to seek confidence in anyone who came to him as a friend. As James Rettigue, The Shadow might play such a part with Elridge Rathcourt. Hence The Shadow had finally decided to utilize the mythical personality.

ARRIVING at the penthouse, The Shadow stepped into a small reception room to find a stocky, solemn-faced menial awaiting him. This was Rathcourt's valet, the fellow with whom The Shadow had talked by telephone.

While the elevator door was clanging shut, The Shadow inquired for Mr. Rathcourt. Before the valet could reply, a strained voice sounded from an inner room.

"Who is it, Manuel?" came the query. "Mr. Rettigue?"

The valet turned.

"Yes, sir," he responded. "Shall I usher him in?"

"At once!"

The Shadow entered a living room to be met by a long-limbed, peak-faced man whose eyes blinked nervously. Elridge Rathcourt was chinless, his handshake flabby. With a shaky gesture, he urged his visitor to an inner room, which was larger than the first. Beyond it were curtained French windows that led to the penthouse veranda.

Rathcourt closed the door of this private living room. Still shaky, he produced a box of imported cigars.

"Have a corona, Mr. Rettigue. Then we can talk business. About bonds. You used to be with Voder & Co.?"

The Shadow nodded.

"We never had direct transactions, though? You and I?"

"No," admitted The Shadow. "I simply obtained your name from Voder's list."

"I see, I see." Rathcourt was biting at the end of his cigar. A match went out as he tried to light it. "You must excuse me, Mr. Rettigue. My nerves are bad. I need a rest. That's why I went to Atlantic City."

"Yesterday morning?"

"Yes. No, no—it was the day before. I wanted to stay there a while. But I had to come back. I rode in on the *Blue Comet* late this afternoon."

Though his own attitude was listless, The Shadow could easily separate truth from falsehood as he listened. He knew that Rathcourt had actually gone to Atlantic City yesterday; not the day before. Fear that he might be connected with the voodoo cult had caused the man's change of statement.

As for the time of his return, that was accurate. Rathcourt had shown relief when he spoke truth. The time element was also proof. The Shadow knew that the *Blue Comet,* crack flyer of the Jersey Central, arrived at the Jersey City station at about half past seven.

"I had dinner on the train," continued Rathcourt. "I came here from Liberty Street. Manuel told me of your message. Of course I wanted to see you. But tell me one thing, Mr. Rettigue"—he paused, eyeing The Shadow quickly—"tell me just one thing. Your business concerns nothing other than investments?"

"Hardly," replied The Shadow, with a sour smile. "Since I sell securities and you buy them, I could scarcely have another reason for coming here."

"Of course!"

Rathcourt smiled in relief. The Shadow flicked cigar ashes into a tray.

"I felt privileged to visit you," he stated in a precise tone, "because I previously had negotiations with your deceased uncle."

Rathcourt suppressed a gasp of alarm.

"Your uncle's death was most unfortunate," added The Shadow. "It was heart failure, I believe?"

"Yes." Rathcourt was fidgety. "Heart failure. Of course."

"Many persons die of heart failure. That is, supposedly of heart failure. It is a fact, however, that many cases are not heart failure at all. Since a man's heart naturally fails when he dies, it is easy to attribute a death to heart failure, even when other causes may have been contributory."

"But my uncle's heart was weak! Very weak! He was ordered not to exert himself—"

"Indeed!" The Shadow's tone changed suddenly. "Then perhaps his death was actually due to overexertion."

"It was. No, no—it wasn't! That's—well, he should have remained in his bed. He was not well. A paroxysm must have seized him. Of course, you understand I was not in Chicago at the time—"

THE SHADOW'S eyes had lost their droop. Steadily, keenly, they were staring at Elridge Rathcourt. The young man's weak lips were quavering. He was caught by the glow of the optics before him. The Shadow's eyes were like orbs of fire that burned deep into Rathcourt's thoughts.

"There were servants," protested Rathcourt. "They—they found my uncle. If he—if he—"

"If he had been dragged from his bed—"

"No, no! That couldn't have happened. Yes, it could have happened!" Wildly wavering his head Rathcourt was denying his own statements. "I thought of that at the time. But there was another reason—"

"Another reason why your uncle died before his time?"

The Shadow had risen. His eyes were coming closer. His voice, though lowered, still carried a semblance of Rettigue's tone. But it also held a sinister touch that drilled deep into Rathcourt's brain.

"Another reason?" repeated The Shadow.

"Yes!" Rathcourt gasped the word. "It could have been—have been the spell—the voodoo spell! I saw—I saw the effigy—"

He broke off; then sinking back, delivered a hopeless cry. As The Shadow, advancing, stood above him, Rathcourt stared straight upward into the burning eyes. The Shadow's right hand clamped the young man's shoulder. To Rathcourt, it felt like the grip of threatening death.

"It began when I met Doctor Mocquino." Rathcourt spoke mechanically. The Shadow's burning gaze, no longer tempered, was drawing forth the man's true story. "Doctor Rodil Mocquino—the Voodoo Master. He took me to the meetings of his cult. I came beneath his sway.

"My thoughts—my ambitions—my very life—all seemed to tune with the rhythm of the chants I heard. The glow of the fire—the beat of the tom-tom—they made me obey. I gloried in evil! I rejoiced when I saw Doctor Mocquino thrust the pinpoint through the heart of my uncle's image!"

A pause. Rathcourt breathed in short, quick fashion, as though his statements had cost him great exertion.

"My uncle died. I believed that Mocquino's charm had caused his death. Away from the voodoo meetings, I wondered. Servants—paid murderers of Mocquino's—could have dragged my uncle from his bed. He could have died in fighting them off.

"But when I returned to the meetings, my doubts faded. I believed again in Mocquino's power—until two nights ago. It was then that Mocquino fled. He carried all of us with him. Later, he sent us on our separate ways. I went to Atlantic City; then returned here."

PANTING, Rathcourt showed terror. His hands came up and clutched The Shadow's arm.

"Mocquino does not know!" gasped Rathcourt.

"He does not know that I doubt him! But he does know that I would fear to talk to anyone—except—except to someone like yourself. He has bled me of nearly all my inheritance! Though I learned, two nights ago, that Mocquino's strength could fail; still, I cannot disobey his last command!

"Tomorrow night! Then the cult will meet again, at the new place that Mocquino has chosen. I must go, to calm Mocquino's suspicions. Once I am there, I shall fear him as I did before! When tom-toms beat—"

Rathcourt was wild-eyed; his chin was shaking. He was chewing at his lips, trying to avoid repetition of the words that he had last uttered.

"When—when tom-toms beat—"

The Shadow's grip tightened. His eyes came closer. His lips spoke whispered words:

"Speak! Name the place where Mocquino now has his headquarters!"

Elridge Rathcourt started to reply. Words failed to reach his lips. His clutch became clawish upon The Shadow's arms. When he found speech, Rathcourt reiterated his former statement; but this time, his voice was a whispered gasp.

"The tom-toms! I hear them! Drumming—drumming—beat—beat! Like the rhythm of the savage jungle! Drums that beat for me!"

For an instant, The Shadow believed that the man was the victim of his own imagination. Then, suddenly, came a different answer. Rathcourt, in his strained, wild state had heard a sound before The Shadow caught it.

The beat of tom-toms—from the walls of this very room! From walls that were undraped. A rising thrum, like the beat—beat—beat that Cardona had heard two nights before. It came from all about—from the ceiling, as well as the walls. Steady in its beat, but quickened in its loudness, the pound of the tom-toms reached a threatening cadence.

THE doors from the roof veranda trembled. The Shadow saw them; yet he wheeled instinctively, to face the door of the outer room. It was opening. The Shadow swung his right hand toward his coat, to draw a gun.

At that instant, Elridge Rathcourt emitted a terrorized scream. With terrific frenzy, he doubled his arms, to clutch The Shadow's right arm with a death grip.

The pull was a maddened one. The Shadow could not wrench his arm free.

Nor was there time to hurl Rathcourt aside. Instead, The Shadow sped his left hand toward a hidden gun. Instinctive in action, he forgot his wounded forearm. A stabbing pain jabbed above his wrist. The Shadow's fingers numbed. They faltered as they reached the edge of his coat.

Then action was too late. The outer door had swung wide. Upon the threshold stood Doctor Rodil Mocquino. Arms folded, he was backed by two dark-visaged henchmen who held leveled revolvers. At the same moment, the doors from the porch ripped open. Another pair of grinning servitors aimed with ready guns.

Thrum—thrum—the drumming continued from all about. Mocquino, though clad in tuxedo instead of his golden robe, was as evil in appearance as when The Shadow last had seen him. Gloating, the Voodoo Master gazed upon the rigid figure of The Shadow and the cowering, clutching form of Elridge Rathcourt.

Doctor Mocquino had gained a triumph, while the hidden tom-tom beaters drummed their fiendish cadence of conquest!

CHAPTER XII
MOCQUINO DECREES

DOCTOR Mocquino stood in full control.

Wisely, The Shadow had stopped all effort to defy the Voodoo Master. The moment for battle had passed. The Shadow had lost the vital opportunity that he always required in such emergencies as this.

Luck had tricked The Shadow. Elridge Rathcourt's sudden, frenzied clutch had stayed his right hand. An unexpected twinge had halted his left. Covered by four weapons, The Shadow was too late to offer immediate resistance.

Rathcourt had dropped away. Seeing The Shadow's dilemma, the cringing man had lost faith in his protector. As Rathcourt sagged moaning into a chair, The Shadow's right hand was loose; but he made no attempt to draw an automatic. Instead, he slowly raised both hands. Wearily, he faced Mocquino.

An ugly chuckle came from the Voodoo Master. Surveying The Shadow, Mocquino saw the soured features, the droopy, tired eyelids of James Rettigue. He knew that this was The Shadow. But Mocquino believed that the superman had yielded.

After a contemptuous leer toward Rathcourt, Mocquino advanced. Reaching The Shadow, the Voodoo Master thrust his hand beneath the latter's coat. He found two automatics. He brought them forth and tossed them to the floor.

All the while, tom-toms pounded in their torturing rhythm like beats of doom upon throbbing ears. Mocquino uttered a sharp command. The throbs ceased. The silence of the room was charged with menace. Then Mocquino spoke.

"One fool," he sneered, "has lured another. Both unwittingly. You, Rathcourt—you were the first fool! I knew that you would talk, once you gained the opportunity."

"He—he made me talk!" panted Rathcourt, pointing toward The Shadow. "*He* is the one to blame! Take *his* life, Mocquino—not *mine!*"

"Silence!" hissed the Voodoo Master. Then, his tone becoming suave: "You were the bait, Rathcourt. Good bait—only because you did not know my plans. I sent you to Atlantic City yesterday. Why? So that I could turn this penthouse into a snare."

The Voodoo Master clapped his hands. His four henchmen moved in closer from their opposite doorways. Then two others appeared: one was Manuel, the valet; the other, a rogue who might have been the fellow's brother. Both were carrying tom-toms.

"Manuel and Fernando," chortled Mocquino. "They prepared this trap. They admitted my servants and myself. All was ready hours ago. Look!"

MOCQUINO went to the wall and pulled away a forward-tilted picture. Behind it was a disk: a loudspeaker. The Voodoo Master wrenched the device from its socket. He strode to a corner and whisked the cloth covering from a small table. He produced another amplifier. From a bookcase, Mocquino yanked two massive volumes. A cord came with them. The books fell apart, to show a third loudspeaker.

Manuel and Fernando had laid aside their tom-toms. They had pocketed The Shadow's guns. They gathered the amplifiers and Mocquino added a fourth that he brought from behind a radiator. He pointed to a telephone that stood on a table in the corner. The instrument had a wire that terminated in a wall socket.

"Some time ago," purred Mocquino, "you had special wiring placed in this penthouse, Rathcourt. You were pleased by the idea of a telephone that could be detached and plugged in elsewhere. Quite a convenience."

Picking up the telephone, Mocquino removed its cord from the wall. He carried the instrument to a table in the center of the room and plugged the wire into a floor socket.

"While the place was torn out for the wiring," remarked Mocquino, "Manuel and Fernando added sockets of their own. Those were the hidden plugs for the amplifiers. I knew that someday I might need to terrify you, Rathcourt, with tom-tom beats from everywhere. Tonight was the time. Manuel and Fernando drummed their tom-toms from another room. A microphone picked up the sounds and brought them here."

Mocquino had raised the cradle-type telephone. He was dialing a number. A voice came over the wire. Mocquino showed a suave smile as he spoke:

"Ah, Jose! I knew that you would answer... You are ready?... What?... Yes, there is time to tell me... Ah, you went there? Good! And afterward?... Ah! Even better! *Bueno,* Jose! That means another task for us tonight...

"You have already called Cordez? Good! That was right... He is to be ready with the automobiles... Yes, I am at Rathcourt's. I want you here, Jose... When you have joined us, we shall be ready for departure..."

Mocquino laid the telephone on its stand. He looked toward The Shadow, who was standing close by.

"Sit down!" snarled Mocquino. "We have fifteen minutes yet. I wish to talk with you."

The Shadow complied in a fashion that befitted his character of Rettigue. Once in a large armchair, he relaxed and let his hands rest upon the arms. Doctor Mocquino stepped back from the center table.

"YOU are The Shadow," sneered the Voodoo Master. "I saw you two nights ago. I listened through an amplifier while you questioned Rathcourt tonight. You do not believe me? Look!"

He opened the front of a humidor stand and revealed a microphone. The instrument had picked up sounds through holes bored in the door of the square stand. Mocquino chuckled, as he detached the mike.

"I ordered the tom-toms," he purred, "before Rathcourt could say too much. You were asking him where I have my new headquarters. I shall tell you. In a place that you will never guess or find.

"By that I mean a place that you never *could* find; because you will have no further opportunity to search for it. Death will be my decree tonight. Death for The Shadow!"

Hideous gloats showed on the faces of Mocquino's henchmen. Rathcourt gasped pleading words.

"Kill him, Mocquino! But spare me—"

"You will not die." Mocquino wheeled to Rathcourt. Then, as the weakling raised his hands in gratitude, the Voodoo Master issued new words: "You will live. You will become a zombi!"

"No, no!" cried Rathcourt. "That would be like death! I saw—I saw—"

"You saw a zombi once," gloated Mocquino. "A man who stared. One who lived no longer, except as a walking corpse! I made that man a zombi"—Mocquino's tone was fierce—"because he was ready to betray me! You were betraying me tonight, Rathcourt. *You* will become a zombi!"

Hopeless terror dominated Rathcourt's chinless face. The man's gawky form was hunched. He gibbered inarticulate words, while his teeth chattered their fear.

Mocquino looked toward The Shadow, whose features had retained their listlessness. Apparently, the Voodoo Master thought that he could make The Shadow register emotion.

"In Hispaniola," purred Mocquino, his tone insidious, "the masters of voodoo control beings whom they term 'zombie.' A zombi is a living dead man, whose body has been disinterred from its grave, then imbued with life at the command of the voodoo worker.

"The zombie are slaves, vitalized corpses that behave like mechanical figures. But I hold spells and incantations more powerful than those of ordinary voodoo workers! I can transform a living man into a zombi! It is too bad"—he paused, an evil twist upon his lips—"too bad that you cannot live to witness the fate of Elridge Rathcourt."

The Shadow made no comment. Mocquino thrust his leering face closer.

"The same fate," he hissed, "that overtook Stanton Wallace!"

MOCQUINO hoped to learn whether or not The Shadow would recognize the name. He was disappointed. The Shadow's face retained its dreariness. Mocquino's lips fumed; his jaws tightened.

"Enough!" he gritted. "Jose will be here soon. Then you will die—and we shall depart! Come, Manuel! Fernando!" The Voodoo Master wheeled. "Carry away those amplifiers and the other apparatus. Pack them; then come back for Rathcourt. He will be in your custody."

Manuel and Fernando complied. Rathcourt, hunched against the wall, was wild-eyed as he watched their departure. Then, half shrieking, the future zombi crept forward. He managed to mouth words as he approached Mocquino.

"Spare me," he wailed. "You have one victim! Kill him—make him a zombie—do what you will! But let me serve you as I did before, as a member of the cult—"

"I have declared your fate," rasped Mocquino. "My decisions never change; nor do my purposes fail!"

"You failed with Dunley Bligh!"

Rathcourt fairly shrieked the words. He had read the newspaper accounts of the fray aboard the *Doranic*. That memory awoke him to sudden argument.

"Bligh still lives!" Rathcourt was persistent. "Let me live also!"

Savagely, Mocquino thrust his face toward Rathcourt's. His tone became a disdainful snarl, as he issued his command:

"Stand back! I have decreed your fate! You are to be a zombi!"

As Mocquino hissed the word "zombi," all reason left Elridge Rathcourt. Stark fear accomplished more than if the man had gained a new-found courage. With a frenzied bound, Rathcourt sprang forward. His clawing hands drove for Mocquino's throat.

The Voodoo Master had baited his dupe too long. A maddened man had turned upon his persecutor. Mocquino staggered back, writhing to free himself of the attacker.

The Shadow watched.

CHAPTER XIII
DEATH IN THE PENTHOUSE

SCATTERED thoughts had suddenly gathered within Elridge Rathcourt's brain. The dupe had realized that Doctor Mocquino was not infallible. In addition, he had found an answer to a problem which had terrified him.

Though Rathcourt had pleaded for life, he had gained the belief that death itself would be preferable to the fate of a zombi. Rathcourt had seen Stanton Wallace, after the latter had visited Mocquino's red room.

Death! In a sense, Rathcourt wanted it, and he had tried a way to force it. If he could not kill Mocquino, he would at least compel the guards to slay him, Rathcourt, instead. Yet none were moving forward—and The Shadow knew the reason.

Those four thought that Mocquino would overpower Rathcourt. They awaited their master's call before they acted. Even should it come, they would not try to kill Rathcourt. Mocquino wanted him for a zombi. His henchmen had heard the decree.

The struggle was fierce between Rathcourt and the Voodoo Master. Out of the midst of the scuffle came an articulate gurgle. It was the only cry that Mocquino could utter: a call for aid. Rathcourt, strong in frenzy, was choking the Voodoo Master.

The two guards from the outer porch sprang forward. The pair at the inner door hesitated; they were covering The Shadow. Both could not give up that vigil. One man grunted to the other, then sprang in to give new aid to Mocquino.

Elridge Rathcourt was a madman, wrenching away from the three guards who seized him. A lone gun was covering The Shadow; above the revolver, the scowling face of the darkish man who held it. A quick move by The Shadow would have brought prompt bullets.

The Shadow waited, as listless as before.

The Shadow sledged the scowling rogue with the finish of the driving swing. When the telephone met the dark guard's skull, the fellow's body crumpled to the floor.

The lone guard leered contemptuously. He heard a shriek from Rathcourt, as the maddened prisoner went down beneath a sudden surge. At the cry, the single guard darted a quick glance toward the melee, where Mocquino had come free, puffing as he rubbed his throat. The guard looked back toward The Shadow. He was an instant late.

The Shadow had sprung to his feet. His right hand had swung to the table. Quick fingers were clamping the telephone, swinging it from the table, yanking the wire from the plug beneath. As Mocquino's henchman dropped back to gain new aim, The Shadow drove the telephone downward with a long, swift stroke.

THE guard's revolver barked. The bullet sizzled just beneath The Shadow's swinging arm. That was the only shot. The Shadow sledged the scowling rogue with the finish of the driving swing. When the telephone met the dark guard's skull, the fellow's body crumpled to the floor.

The guard's revolver clattered. The Shadow made a feint to gain it; then twisted amazingly in the opposite direction. The move was masterful. Mocquino's other henchmen had suppressed Rathcourt. They were turning hurriedly. They fired in the direction of The Shadow's feint. Their whistling bullets thudded the wall.

The Shadow was whirling away in an amazing spring toward the penthouse roof. One guard alone was close enough to dive across his path. The others aimed, expecting The Shadow to clear the blocker. Instead, The Shadow made a sharp stop by the outer door. His right fist jabbed upward and caught the blocker's chin, just as the man swung downward with his gun.

The guard's head went back; but his revolver sped on, through the French windows, to clatter on the porch. As the guard sagged, The Shadow made a sidewise dive to the outer porch itself, pounced on the gun.

Mocquino's two remaining henchmen fired, just too late. For a moment, they hesitated; then Manuel and Fernando dashed in to join them. Four in all, Mocquino's minions sprang forth to the chase.

The Shadow had sped to the side rail of the roof. He jabbed two quick shots as he turned about. One pursuer gave a cry and dropped his gun arm. The others spread. Their revolvers were barking; but The Shadow was away, zigzagging toward the far rail.

Seeing the move, the three converged, piling in to trap The Shadow from different directions. Diving straight into the throng, The Shadow met the middle man, Fernando. With a slash of his revolver, he disarmed the rogue; grappling one-handed—he forced himself to use his injured left arm—he dragged Fernando back toward the outer rail. At the same time, he jabbed quick shots that sent the other two killers diving for cover.

The Shadow had numbed Fernando's hand with the heavy blow. He was grappling with his right; Fernando with his left. But the rogue's hand recovered. His right fist shot to his belt; it came up wielding a long-bladed knife.

The Shadow twisted away; he hoisted himself half across the rail, in order to avoid the coming slash.

Fernando made a balk; then changed direction. His arm stabbed downward. The Shadow's gun tongued up. With the flash, Fernando jolted. His arm swung wide; his knife clattered from the railing. His body sagged forward on The Shadow.

A fierce roar from the penthouse doorway. Poised on the rail, his right arm down, The Shadow saw Doctor Mocquino. The Voodoo Master had recovered. He was ready with leveled revolver, finger upon trigger. The Shadow gave a roll. Mocquino fired.

Timed with the shot, The Shadow sprawled beyond the rail. Mocquino's revolver blasted at vacancy. He ceased his fire; his lips phrased a triumphant cry that was echoed by his last two henchmen. Mocquino pictured The Shadow on a final, headlong plunge to the ground two hundred feet beneath.

MOTIONING to his henchmen, Mocquino started back into the penthouse. There he encountered an excited arrival. It was Jose Arilla. The rat-faced man gripped the voodoo doctor's arm.

"The police!" he ejaculated. "They trailed me here! I could have slipped them; but they heard the shots, just as my cab was stopping outside! I beat them to the elevator—"

"Come!"

Mocquino started toward the front portion of the penthouse. He would have forgotten Elridge Rathcourt; but the rescued man came bounding suddenly from behind a chair, brandishing a revolver.

Mocquino snarled. He pumped four shots into Rathcourt's body. As Rathcourt slumped, Mocquino fled.

He and his followers gained a stairway just as an elevator arrived at the penthouse level. Joe Cardona and a squad of detectives began a hurried chase. Downstairs, floor after floor, through an echoing fire tower, where wild revolvers barked.

The Voodoo Master and his men gained the rear street. Cardona and the squad arrived too late to stop them, as they dived aboard two waiting automobiles and sped away.

When Joe Cardona returned to the penthouse, he found Doctor Rupert Sayre upon the roof. Cardona growled the news of the escape; then added:

"We ought to nab them, though. The radio patrol is on the job. The bridges and the ferries are still covered. They can't get through the Holland Tunnel."

WHILE Cardona was ordering the removal of bodies, Sayre stopped by the farther rail. He had seen detectives carry away the body of Fernando. A thought had struck Doctor Sayre. Casually, the physician looked over the rail. He saw two cedar trees tilted outward from the ledge of the nineteenth floor. He noted something sprawled beside them.

Doctor Sayre strolled through the penthouse. He took the stairs down to the floor below. He found a window at the end of a corridor. He stepped out to the ledge. There, he found The Shadow. The cedars had partly broken the lone fighter's dive; but the crash had been sufficient to stun The Shadow.

Sayre propped The Shadow against the inner wall. He began measures to revive the injured fighter; but he worked slowly, for he wanted to keep The Shadow here until the law had gone. Mocquino had gained another start. Sayre could see no immediate duty for The Shadow.

In that decision, Sayre made another error. The minutes that he let slip past were precious. The physician was listening as he watched The Shadow's pale, disguised face; he was hoping that soon there would be no sounds from the penthouse porch above. Then, he felt, he could revive The Shadow fully. For Sayre had already dodged explanations to Joe Cardona; and he wanted to avoid another complication. He preferred that the acting inspector should not know of this discovery on the nineteenth-story ledge. But while Sayre was keeping up a bluff with Cardona, he was also making trouble for The Shadow.

Doctor Mocquino, in flight, could prove as dangerous as in battle. With the Voodoo Master, even a retreat could be a forward move. The Shadow had guessed that Mocquino would find a new objective. That was why he had chanced the plunge to the cedars that he had noticed beneath the penthouse wall.

Unfortunately, the fall had brought temporary oblivion to The Shadow. Had Sayre revived him hurriedly, The Shadow could have told the physician what to do. Sayre, in delaying, had become the unwitting aide of Doctor Mocquino.

Again, The Shadow would be forced to seek the Voodoo Master; this time, without a clue. Elridge Rathcourt had died; with him had perished the last thread that The Shadow needed.

Moreover, when The Shadow once more began his search, the tracing of Doctor Mocquino would be doubly imperative. It would involve the lives of men who had served The Shadow! For Harry Vincent was still at Lamont Cranston's estate in New Jersey, unknowing of the fray in the penthouse.

CHAPTER XIV
FLIGHT BRINGS RESULTS

"A GRAY sedan bearing New York license. Number—"

Harry Vincent clicked off the radio in Lamont Cranston's living room. It was a shortwave set; Harry had been using it to listen in on New Jersey police calls. There was a reason why Harry cut off the call before he heard the license number of the gray sedan. Stanton Wallace had just entered the living room.

"What is it, Harry?" questioned Wallace, anxiously. "Something about Mocquino?"

"Yes," replied Harry, quietly. "But don't let it worry you, Stan. The police are after him again."

"Where? In New York?"

Harry nodded.

"It is murder, this time," he stated. "Not merely armed resistance of the law. Mocquino has killed Elridge Rathcourt."

Wallace did not speak. He sat down; his face troubled.

"He entered Rathcourt's penthouse," resumed Harry. His tone was reassuring. "The police trailed him there; but he made a getaway. I caught snatches of the story, tuning in by shortwave. They were starting to describe two automobiles. One was a gray sedan.

"They've boxed Mocquino in Manhattan. This time, he shouldn't have a chance. The outlets are already watched. I don't see how he can leave the Island. Nevertheless, the New Jersey State police are watching this side of the river."

"Mocquino made a getaway with the trucks, two nights ago," mused Wallace. "Bridges and ferries were watched then. He didn't have time to make the Holland Tunnel."

"I know. But he may have been lucky, Stan. This time, the police are already covering. Mocquino is more likely to head for Long Island. Still he'll be blocked at any of the East River bridges."

"Probably he'll stay in Manhattan, Harry."

"I think so, Stan."

Strolling over, Harry thwacked his new friend's shoulder.

"Buck up, old man," he said. "Forget Mocquino. We've got something else to think about. Remember that call that came at seven o'clock? From Doctor Sayre?"

Stanton Wallace nodded.

"It's after nine, right now," observed Harry, glancing at the clock. "From the way Sayre spoke, we're liable to hear from Joe Cardona at any time. If he shows up, you know what you're to do."

"I'll act dumb," assured Wallace. "I'll keep staring and pretend that I'm dazed—"

A knock from the door interrupted. Harry called to enter. Richards appeared.

"A car has just arrived, Mr. Vincent," said the servant. "I thought it was Stanley, so I went out to the driveway. A man spoke to me. He said he was a detective."

"From where?" queried Harry.

"From New York," answered Richards. "He said that Inspector Cardona sent him. He wants to see Doctor Sayre's patient, to take him back to New York with him."

"Did you ask him to come in?"

"He said he would wait outside. Inspector Cardona prefers the visit to be kept a secret."

"Of course."

HARRY turned to Stanton. He gave a nod which the other understood. Mechanically, Stanton arose from his chair. Richards looked puzzled as Harry guided him to the door. Still wondering, the servant followed through the hall.

"Shall I turn on the porch light, Mr. Vincent?"

Harry shook his head in response to the inquiry from Richards. He opened the door and guided Wallace out into the darkness. Harry spoke in a whisper.

"The bluff will be easier in the darkness," he remarked. "I'll introduce myself and go along. I'm your attendant. Sayre will back it."

A car was standing in the driveway. In the gloom of night, the automobile was no more than a long, colorless shape. Dimmed headlights; red sparkles at the rear. Those were the only distinguishing marks. The motor was idling in rhythmic fashion.

A man was barely discernible beside the car. He stepped forward as Harry and Stanton approached. He put a gruff question:

"Is this Doctor Sayre's patient?"

"I am bringing him," replied Harry. "My name is Vincent. Doctor Sayre left me in charge of the man. You are from New York headquarters?"

"Yes. I'm Detective Sergeant Berrani. Inspector Cardona sent me. I've got a squad with me. On account of trouble across the river. Here, let me help you get this fellow into the car."

The door of the car was open. Harry and the other man helped Stanton aboard. They pushed him to the rear seat, past another man who was hunched on a folding seat. Harry climbed in beside Stanton. Berrani took the other folding seat. He closed the door; the car started out the driveway.

Harry noted two men in front; the driver and the man beside him. The presence of four detectives gave him confidence. Harry gained a feeling of greater security as they swung to the roadway outside the drive. This came when Berrani turned in his seat, to give a nudge toward the rear window.

"Another car is coming with us," informed the gruff speaker. "Look back and you'll see it. I had it waiting outside."

Harry looked back. He saw the headlights of a second automobile. The two cars were driving eastward.

"We're keeping off the main roads," continued Berrani. "The inspector wants us to come into town quietlike. There's too much excitement on the other side. They've got a new trail on this murderer, Mocquino."

"What has he done?" queried Harry, feigning anxiety. "I thought the fellow had disappeared."

"He bobbed up again. Bumped a guy named Rathcourt at the Hotel Delbar. They're hunting all over Manhattan for him—"

Berrani paused to stare ahead. They had pulled away from the car in back and had come to a well-paved highway. Up ahead, a man was standing in the center of the road, signaling for the car to stop. Harry recognized the uniform of a New Jersey State policeman.

The big car halted. The trooper stepped in from the glare of the headlights. Berrani leaned from his window and flashed a badge. He spoke in his gruff, slightly accented tone.

"We're from New York headquarters—"

A second trooper interrupted. He had stepped up in back of the car. His fist came up from a holster, carrying a gun.

"Yeah?" he queried. "What are you doing in this gray sedan, with the license number we're after? Where did you pick it up?"

"A few miles west of here—"

"Without notifying the local authorities? That doesn't listen good to me. Come on, all of you! Pile out while we talk this over!"

A fierce hiss came from the man seated beside the driver. Like a whip, the big car snapped forward. The low gear whined as the machine whisked away from the astonished State policeman. A revolver spoke too late. The trooper was slow with the trigger.

A gasp had come from Stanton Wallace. Forgetting his pretended daze, Stanton was declaring his recognition of the snarled voice that had come from the front seat:

"Doctor Mocquino!"

HARRY heard the gasp. He lashed forward to strike down Berrani. A revolver muzzle jabbed Harry's ribs. At the same instant, the man in the other folding seat leaned back to cover Stanton. Berrani spoke harshly. By the glare of an approaching car, Harry saw the supposed dick's face. It was ratlike.

"No tough stuff!" came the order. "If you try it, we'll rub you out and dump you!"

"Very good, Jose," purred the man from the front seat. He had turned; Harry saw Mocquino's gloating visage. "Ah! We have two prizes! I have seen your face before." He leaned over the seat to eye Harry. "Yes. You were one of those who fought against me the other night."

The flash of light had passed. Mocquino's purr continued while gun muzzles held Harry and Stanton at bay.

"So you came along with Wallace," chortled Mocquino. "And Wallace is a zombi no longer. More of The Shadow's doings. The Shadow! Bah! He will trouble me no longer. He is dead! At least, he should be dead. He fell twenty stories to the ground.

"He tried to balk Mocquino. He failed. Yes, failed!—like all who believe that they can offset my power. I possess strength that no one can defeat!"

Shots were popping from behind the fleeing car. The troopers were pursuing in a sidecar motor cycle. Mocquino delivered a sharp command. Brakes crunched; the big sedan veered sharply and skidded to a side road. It began to slacken speed.

A siren whined. The motorcycle wheeled to complete the chase. From the side window, Harry saw a car that Mocquino had spotted before he gave the order to turn off. It was a police car, coming up the main road. It swung in behind the motorcycle.

The gray sedan was stopping. Harry wondered why. He could not picture Mocquino in the act of sudden surrender. The State police had ceased their fire. Harry saw Mocquino's hand extending a white handkerchief from the window. Despite that signal, the officers were wary.

They dropped from sidecar and automobile. Half a dozen strong, they started to deploy. They intended to surround the gray sedan, to approach it from all angles. Suddenly, Mocquino rasped another order. The sedan shot forward.

Revolvers spoke. The police car started forward; Harry could see its headlights in the mirror. Two officers had remained in their automobile. A machine gun began its drill, as others leaped to the running board. In a minute, the gray sedan would have been crippled and overhauled. But Mocquino had allowed for that.

JUST as the police barrage began, headlights blazed from the entrance to the side road. Mocquino's second sedan had arrived. His rear guard was taking up the battle. Submachine guns rattled, as the reserve crooks bore down upon the law.

The gray sedan was swinging another turn. Again from the side window, Harry saw developments. The police had quickly ceased their fire. A brilliant searchlight from Mocquino's second car enabled Harry to witness how the officers escaped death.

The driver of the police car ditched his machine. Troopers dived from doorways and rolled beneath the rails of a fence. Those who had deployed were quick to drop for cover. Riddling bullets from machine guns found only the motor cycle and the abandoned police car.

Mocquino's reserves roared onward, to follow the gray sedan. Troopers sprang up from cover, to blaze with their revolvers. The gray sedan was well out of range. The second car was speeding rapidly enough to escape the hurried shots. Pursuit was ended; for the motorcycle and the ditched police car had been rendered useless.

Mocquino and his double crew had run the gauntlet. Lost in Manhattan, they had reappeared in New Jersey. Again, they were headed toward New York.

To Harry, the sequence was amazing; but it aroused him to a fit of fury. Catching a sudden opportunity, he snatched at Jose Arilla's gun. He wrenched away the pretended detective's weapon.

Stanton Wallace saw the move. He jabbed a punch to the jaw of the man who had him covered.

Wildly, Jose hoisted Harry upward. Doctor Mocquino, snarling, dived over the back of the front seat. His fierce hands caught Harry's throat. Choking, The Shadow's agent subsided. At the same moment, Stanton's adversary managed a return punch. It was a squarer, harder stroke than the one that Stanton had given. With a groan, Stanton Wallace slumped back.

A few seconds later, the prisoners were suppressed. Doctor Mocquino had gained a bottle from the front seat. The odor of chloroform filled the car. Flapping cloths were pressed to the faces of the prisoners. Struggling weakly, Harry and Stanton sank into oblivion.

A gloating chuckle came from Doctor Rodil Mocquino. The Voodoo Master had suppressed all opposition. His prisoners were helpless; his car was speeding on to safety. Mocquino's flight had brought him new success!

But in Manhattan was The Shadow, winged temporarily, under the care of a physician, but gaining new strength to take to the trail of the Voodoo Master.

CHAPTER XV
SAYRE RECEIVES VISITORS

SATURDAY morning was a busy one for Doctor Rupert Sayre. He had postponed appointments from earlier in the week. The result was a flood of patients. It was after two o'clock when he stepped into his reception room to find a lone patient waiting. This was a chubby-faced man, whose expression was serious. Sayre invited him into the office.

"You had an appointment?" inquired the physician. "I do not recall your name—"

"I am Rutledge Mann."

Sayre showed a relieved smile. He had expected a visit from this gentleman, ever since his last call to Burbank. Over the telephone, the quiet-voiced contact man had stated that Sayre would soon have a chance for conference. Like Burbank, Mann was one of The Shadow's passive agents. But where Burbank made contact by telephone alone, Mann carried on such negotiations in person.

"How is your patient?"

Mann's slow, deliberate query roused Sayre. The physician arose and conducted his visitor through a short passage. He opened a door and showed a darkened room. A figure was stretched upon a cot. Steady breathing could be heard.

"He is asleep," whispered Sayre. "It would not be wise to awaken him. He has a slight concussion."

"Will it be gone when he awakes?"

"I believe so. He struck his head when he fell to the tiles beside the cedar trees. The blow was not severe, but it left him dazed. I just about managed to get him out of the Hotel Delbar."

SAYRE and Mann returned to the office. The physician felt that he could rely thoroughly upon this solemn-faced investment broker. Burbank had assured him that he could speak in detail. Mann's appearance gave Sayre added confidence.

"Cardona knows nothing of this," informed Sayre. "He called me an hour ago and stated that he was very busy tracing Mocquino."

"He has had results?"

"None. Mocquino's appearance in New Jersey, an hour after the fight at the Delbar, has left Cardona baffled."

"What else did he say?"

"Merely that he could not spare time to examine the staring man. He wants me to keep Stanton Wallace for further treatment. Cardona, of course, does not know Wallace's name. Nor does he definitely connect the episode of the staring man with Mocquino's machinations—"

"One moment, doctor. You say that Cardona has not seen Wallace recently?"

"Of course not."

Mann looked troubled.

"I have just come from New Jersey," he stated. "I went there as Mr. Cranston's investment broker. I talked with Richards."

"Did you see Vincent? Or Wallace?"

"No, because they had gone. Richards said they left last night."

"Where did they go?"

"Men came for them. Detectives from New York headquarters. They said Cardona wanted to see Wallace. Vincent went along."

"But Cardona could not have sent for him! Cardona was hot on the trail of Mocquino—"

Sayre broke off speaking. He sank back in his chair. The answer had dawned.

"It was Mocquino!" gasped the physician. "He trapped Vincent and Wallace! That is why he was in New Jersey!"

"So it appears."

SAYRE sat drumming the desk. Mann retained his calmness. When the contact man spoke, his words were definite. "Every emergency offers a solution," declared Mann. "Fortunately, Burbank and I are well supplied with details. We can face the facts. Vincent and Wallace are prisoners. The Shadow is unable to aid them."

"He will be, soon."

"Before tonight?"

"I am sure of it."

"Good! That brings us to another fact. Tonight, Mocquino meets with his voodoo cult."

"Where? Do you know?"

"I have no idea. Nevertheless, The Shadow may learn, once he has recuperated. If Vincent and Wallace are as yet unharmed, it is unlikely that they will suffer prior to the meeting."

Sayre nodded. The statement was convincing. He knew Mocquino's flare for the theatrical, the way in which the Voodoo Master handled his dupes.

"Of course," agreed Sayre. "Mocquino must impress the members of his cult. Whatever he does to Vincent and Wallace will be in the presence of the circle. I think I know what it will be. I delved deeply into the study of voodoo practices.

"Mocquino unquestionably used Wallace as an example. He thrust him into the red room and made him a temporary automaton. In that state, Wallace would have passed for a zombi—a living dead man. Voodoo doctors claim the power of obtaining such results.

"Moreover"—Sayre paused and stared toward the room where The Shadow rested—"last night, coming here from the Hotel Delbar, The Sha— that is, my present patient—repeated that one word: 'zombi,' time and again."

"Then all depends upon his prompt recovery," announced Mann, rising. "If he can locate Mocquino's present headquarters, he will be able to strike at once. He ordered certain equipment for such an expedition."

"Equipment?" queried Sayre.

"Yes," replied Mann. "It is at present in my office at the Badger Building. That is where I shall remain until I receive further word. You will give this information to The—to your patient, as soon as he awakes.

"Meanwhile, I shall arrange for your protection. Since it is possible that Mocquino has connected you with Wallace, we must make provision. It would be unwise for you to appeal to Cardona. So I shall notify Burbank to post watchers outside. They should arrive here presently."

Sayre shook hands with his visitor. Mann departed. Returning to his desk, Sayre methodically made a notation on a memo pad: "Equipment ready at Mann's office." That done, Sayre began to ponder upon circumstances.

He realized that The Shadow possessed an organization of efficient workers; that Burbank and Mann could supply orders for active agents to follow, even while The Shadow was incapacitated. Routine performance, however, could not prove sufficient to cope with Doctor Mocquino.

Where was the missing voodoo doctor? His name was emblazoned in headlines. His description was known to a T. After his escape from Manhattan, he had reappeared in New Jersey; but there he had been hounded eastward. His only refuge seemed to be New York, where the hunt still persisted. Did the Voodoo Master actually possess some witchcraft? Sayre actually paused to consider that outlandish theory.

Trucks—automobiles—henchmen—these were gone with Mocquino. As for his cult members, none were known. They were probably all persons of supposed repute, like Elridge Rathcourt. But they would not speak; and there was no new trail to any of them.

A CREEPING sound halted Sayre's reverie. The physician looked up from his desk. Alarm seized him as he observed a man who had entered the office. The fellow was darkish, his features ratlike. Sayre pushed his right hand toward a desk drawer. A warning came from the intruder's lips. A revolver glimmered in the man's hand.

"Good afternoon, doctor."

The rat-faced visitor pocketed his gun as he spoke. He had no further need of it. Two others had appeared at the doorway of the office. Both were armed.

"Allow me to introduce myself." The darkish intruder smiled in ugly fashion. "I am Jose Arilla. You have heard my name, eh?"

"Yes," admitted Sayre, "I heard it mentioned."

"By Inspector Cardona, I suppose?"

Arilla paused to extract a cigarette from his pocket. He lighted the cigarette and puffed. Sayre scented the aroma of heavy tobacco. He recalled the odor from yesterday. He had noted that same smoke here in this office. For the first time, Sayre realized that Arilla had been here, listening to that call to New Jersey.

"I come from Doctor Mocquino," announced Arilla, smoothly. "He is very clever, Doctor Mocquino. He told me that I would find no police here. He was right. He said that you had not told Cardona of Wallace's recovery; on that account the police would be absent."

A pause. Arilla delivered a polite bow.

"Doctor Mocquino extends his respects," he added. "Since you found some way to restore his zombi, he would like to know the details. He regards you as a man worth meeting. He would like you to be his guest."

"Suppose that I decline?" demanded Sayre. "What then?"

"Ah! You cannot refuse. Doctor Mocquino would not hear of it. You see, he intends to make Wallace a zombi once again, along with another man who is also a prisoner. A man named Vincent. You must come, Doctor Sayre, to witness the experiment.

"You must also be prepared to stay a while. Doctor Mocquino does not care to have his zombis restored to regular life. Since you have found some method of changing a zombi's condition, you belong with Doctor Mocquino. Come! You must accompany us."

ARILLA motioned toward the door. The others aimed their revolvers. Sayre had no choice. Slowly, he walked forward. He realized two points: first, that he might treat with Doctor Mocquino when he met the Voodoo Master; second, that The Shadow must be kept free. Otherwise, all hope would be ended.

By prompt submission, Sayre fancied that he would draw his captors from these premises without further search. His hopes sank, however, after he had allowed himself to be conducted to the street.

There, he was urged into a taxi manned by a dark-faced driver: another of Mocquino's West Indian servitors. One of Arilla's aides stepped in beside him. Arilla turned to the other.

"Come, Manuel. We will look about the doctor's office."

The two departed. Sayre realized that Arilla's companion was Rathcourt's former servant. Would they find The Shadow? Sayre could only wait, tense as he hoped that their search would not cover the entire place. He feared to start a battle, lest Arilla would guess the reason.

Sayre was counting, too, upon the protectors

promised by Mann. If those aides would only come! The future, it seemed, was hinging upon the next few minutes.

Mocquino's men of murder were at large. The Shadow, helpless, might become their prey!

CHAPTER XVI
DARK BRINGS THE SHADOW

JOSE ARILLA chuckled when he returned to Doctor Sayre's office. He glanced at the desk clock; then toward the window. He turned and spoke to Manuel:

"Nearly three o'clock. *Bueno!* That is a time when this office should be shut, on Saturday. It is well that we waited until the last patient had left. This place should look as if closed. Draw the curtains, Manuel."

Manuel complied. The room became gloomy when the shades were drawn. Arilla opened the door to the reception room. He pointed to another window.

"That shade also, Manuel. This is the room where I listened, yesterday."

Manuel entered the reception room and darkened it. Arilla indicated the doorway to the passage.

"Look through there, Manuel. Tell me about any other rooms you find. *Pronto!*"

Arilla went to Sayre's desk. He opened a drawer, found a revolver and dropped it in his pocket. He tapped his own gun with his right hand, Sayre's with his left. He turned about, to see Manuel returning. There was just enough light for Arilla to discern the other's face. Manuel closed the door of the passage.

"I looked into a darkened room," stated Manuel. "There I saw a cot. I thought that I heard breathing, as of a man asleep—"

"Who was there?"

"I do not know. Since the shades were drawn, I thought that the room was as you wanted it."

"You fool!" spat Arilla. "Go back! Find what is there! Wait! I am going with you."

Manuel was opening the door. As Arilla stepped to join him, the fellow dropped back. In the gloom, Arilla saw a figure, a tall shape that leaned against the door frame. Manuel, closer than Arilla, recognized a face. He cried a name:

"The Shadow!"

RATHCOURT'S servant had seen the features of James Rettigue. The Shadow, weary of countenance, looked weakened. He was clad in slippers, dark trousers and white shirt, open at the collar. His face was pale; but his eyes, fully opened, held a glimmer.

Manuel's trip to the darkened room had awakened The Shadow. He had heard the intruder leave. Though weaponless, he had come to investigate. As Sayre had hoped, The Shadow's brain had cleared. Weakness was his only handicap.

Arilla spun toward the outer door, whipping out his revolver. Manuel, rooted, yanked forth his own gun, which he had previously pocketed. His hand came snapping upward, straight for The Shadow's body.

A strange laugh escaped paled lips. With that peal of mockery, The Shadow drove his right arm downward, while his left shoulder hooked the door frame. His clutching hand met the upswing of Manuel's revolver. Fingers clamped the gun barrel; The Shadow's sweeping hand wrenched the weapon from Manuel's grasp.

The action was a crosswise sweep that carried The Shadow almost clear of the door frame. He was off balance. Manuel, his gun gone, made a dart for The Shadow's throat. With a twist, The Shadow came up, his long arm swinging in a backhand stroke. The handle of the revolver thudded the side of Manuel's jaw.

Manuel sprawled. Rolling over, he dived past Arilla, anxious to gain the outer door. Arilla, snarling, aimed for the motionless, half-turned figure of The Shadow. He pressed the trigger of his revolver. His action was deliberate, too much so for his evil purpose.

The Shadow wrenched backward, just as Arilla fired. The revolver bullet pinged the wall beside the doorway. This time, The Shadow's left hand, though still stiff from the bullet wound, had not failed him. A quick grip, a jerk of his shoulders— he had swung clear just before Arilla's shot.

The Shadow's right hand was not idle. As his body rolled, that hand performed a maneuver. Fingers flipped the revolver in the air; instantly, the waiting hand caught the weapon. The Shadow's forefinger found the trigger. Arilla saw the gleam of the gun. He fired as he dived through the outer door, following Manuel. Arilla's shot zoomed wide, just as The Shadow fired.

A bullet whistled past Arilla's neck. The Shadow, too, had missed; but only because he had fired the first shot while the revolver was still settling in his hand.

Seeing Arilla's flight, The Shadow bounded forward. His foot caught the telephone cord beside the desk. With a long sprawl, The Shadow flattened upon the floor, still gripping Manuel's revolver.

OUTSIDE, listeners had heard the shots. An instant later, they saw Manuel and Arilla come bounding across the sidewalk. Doctor Sayre was already covered by a revolver. He could not budge. Manuel and Arilla piled aboard. The fake taxi driver had the cab in motion the instant that they arrived.

Doctor Sayre managed to glance through the rear window as they rounded the corner. He saw no sign of a pursuer. Arilla was growling to Manuel in Spanish. Sayre could not tell whether they had fled to avoid a challenger; or because they had committed murder. He feared that it was for the latter reason. For Sayre's last backward gaze was proof that no one was upon the trail.

The physician set his lips to suppress a groan. Three guns were jabbing him. There was no chance to return. The shots from the office had been muffled. No passerby had been present to hear them. Sayre could picture The Shadow lying upon the floor, mortally wounded.

THE first portion of Sayre's picture was correct. The Shadow still was prone; but he lay unwounded. The jolt of his fall had weakened him. Dizzy, he preferred not to rise. There was still a chance that invaders would return. From this position, with gun thrust forward, The Shadow could meet them most effectively.

Minutes passed, while The Shadow waited. Slowly, his upraised hand began to lower. Even this effort was wearisome. The Shadow let the revolver clatter to the floor. Rising up on both hands, he found the edge of the desk. He reached for the telephone, still intact from The Shadow's tripping on the cord. His hands missed it. Head swimming, The Shadow sagged back to the floor and lay there, motionless.

The desk clock ticked slowly, steadily. It was sounding the passage of precious minutes. The Shadow had lapsed into oblivion. Sayre was a prisoner; he would not return to aid his weakened patient. But others were due.

At the end of thirty minutes, footsteps sounded softly from the outer passage that led in from the street. Whispered voices followed.

"Wait here, Hawkeye—"

"Look, Cliff! On the floor!"

A few moments later, Cliff and Hawkeye were stooping above The Shadow's prone form. Together they lifted their chief and carried him to the inner room. They placed him on the cot. Cliff produced a glass of water. He forced the liquid past The Shadow's lips. Eyes opened wearily.

Hawkeye was about to raise the window shade. Cliff stopped him. The Shadow spoke in a tired tone. He pointed to a coat and vest that were hanging on a chair.

"The vial. In the lower pocket of the vest—"

Cliff found a tiny bottle and uncorked it. He brought it to The Shadow, who took it and carried it to his lips. A purplish liquid showed in the gloomy light. The Shadow swallowed the entire potion. Slowly, he began to strengthen.

"I must rest," he decided. "A short while only. After that—food. Bring it—while I rest—"

The Shadow's head settled back upon the pillows. Cliff left Hawkeye in charge and went outside. He stepped aboard a waiting taxi, driven by Moe Shrevnitz, another of The Shadow's aides. Cliff went to a restaurant. He returned with a large container filled with soup.

The Shadow stirred when Cliff arrived. He managed to prop himself against the pillows; then he began to partake of nourishment. Cliff and Hawkeye sat by in the increasing darkness. It was after four o'clock, heavy clouds were bringing early dusk. Very little light reached this secluded room.

THE SHADOW rested after he had eaten. Minutes ticked past, while his agents waited. At last The Shadow spoke. His voice was steady.

"Tell me all the details," he ordered, "beginning with last night."

"Rathcourt was murdered by Mocquino," stated Cliff. "Doctor Sayre found you on the nineteenth floor of the Hotel Delbar. He brought you here. You were dazed."

"I remember portions of the trip."

"Cardona pursued Mocquino. The Voodoo Master slipped him. Every outlet was covered; but he got away to New Jersey."

"To New Jersey—"

"Yes; an hour later. He fought a battle with the State police. They forced him toward New York. Once more, Mocquino disappeared. Today, we learned that he had—"

Cliff paused. The Shadow spoke quietly:

"Mocquino captured Vincent and Wallace?"

"Yes!" exclaimed Cliff. "But how do you—"

"How do I know? Their capture would have been the only reason for his appearance in New Jersey. Tell me: what traces has the law gained?"

"They had none," replied Cliff, "until a few hours ago. On our way here, I bought an extra. Mocquino's two trucks, used to escape from the house next to the Europa Building, have been found abandoned in New Jersey. The two cars he used last night are—"

"Here in Manhattan."

Again Cliff was amazed. The Shadow had stated the exact case. The police had found the sedans in a New York garage. They were baffled by the situation; yet The Shadow had divined it.

"New York and New Jersey," declared The Shadow. "Stanton Wallace was taken from New York to New Jersey; then sent back to New York. Elridge Rathcourt was in New York with

Mocquino. He was sent to Atlantic City. He returned to New York.

"Last night, Mocquino left New York. He arrived in New Jersey. He has not been seen since. Perhaps it is because he believes that I am dead. That is something that Doctor Sayre could answer. But Sayre is no longer here. He, too, was taken."

"By Mocquino?" gasped Cliff. "We were afraid that he—"

"By those who served Mocquino. They, too, move fast. From your account, they must have gone to New Jersey last night, along with the Voodoo Master. Mocquino has played his trump too often!"

THE SHADOW'S voice had taken on a sinister tone. His eyes were no longer wearied. Cliff could see them gleaming in the gloom.

"Once—twice—that would have been enough!" pronounced The Shadow. "Mocquino was prepared for flight from which he could strike when occasion called. But he has counted too much upon his unique situation.

"He has baffled the law; but I can name his method. Simply because it allows but one solution. All that I need is information. I can use whatever the law has gained. Go, Marsland, telephone to detective headquarters. Ask for Cardona."

"And when he answers?" queried Cliff, anxiously.

"Tell him that you are speaking for Doctor Sayre," replied The Shadow. "Mention that Sayre has been called from the city. State that Sayre may return. Ask when Cardona can see him."

"And if Cardona is not there?"

"Learn when he will be. It is best to call from here, instead of through Burbank. Then you can answer directly, if there is a return call."

Cliff went from the darkened room. He returned a few minutes later.

"I talked to Markham," he explained. "He says that Cardona is in conference with Commissioner Weston. He will be back at headquarters by seven o'clock."

The Shadow made no response. Cliff added a comment:

"I found a notation on a memo pad on Sayre's desk. It says that the equipment is ready in Mann's office."

"What time is it at present?" inquired The Shadow.

"It was quarter of five," replied Cliff, "when I looked at Sayre's desk clock."

A pause. Then came the Shadow's whisper.

"Instructions!" The sibilant tone carried command. "Send Shrevnitz for the equipment. Bring it here. Arrange for the light truck to be ready at the New Era Garage. After that—"

A pause, The Shadow's tone had changed. He was quiet in speech as he leaned back upon his pillows:

"After that, remain here. Call me at half past six."

The Shadow's eyelids closed. His breath came with a deep sigh. A few minutes later, he was sleeping, while Cliff and Hawkeye stood silent and dumbfounded.

Worriment, too, wrinkled their features, for in the minds of both was the question whether The Shadow was physically equal to attempt rescue of Vincent, Sayre, and Wallace.

CHAPTER XVII
MOCQUINO ENTERTAINS

"GET up!"

Harry Vincent responded to the growled order. He blinked as he arose from the floor. He was in a square room with plain walls; a single light was dazzling his eyes. Coming to his feet, he stared at two of Doctor Mocquino's servants.

"Get up!"

The repeated growl was not for Harry. It was addressed to Stanton Wallace, who was also coming to life. Harry saw his friend rise drowsily. He was not surprised. He felt dopey; he knew that he and Stanton had been drugged.

Harry could remember intervals in the past. All had been hazy moments of blackness. He realized that he and Stanton had been kept in this windowless room, without light. Harry could not guess how long.

"Come!"

One of Mocquino's men opened a door and led the prisoners through a narrow passage. Harry noted a smooth wall on the right; other doors on the left. The smooth wall was slightly curved. At last it ended; but the passage still continued. The smooth, curved wall had been replaced by a straight, rough one.

At last they came to a door. A servitor opened it. Harry and Stanton stepped into a widened room, that was large in size but odd in shape. It had three doors, all in one long, straight wall. Harry and Stanton entered by a door near one end of the straight wall.

The remaining walls were curved and paneled. In a sense, they formed a single wall, like a semicircle. The woodwork on the curving wall appeared like a barrier that was hiding something beyond. Another oddity existed at the end of the room, toward the center of the long curve.

There, Harry saw two upright posts, several feet apart. Beyond them was a larger support, much thicker than an ordinary post. It was at least four feet in diameter. It made the nearer posts look flimsy.

A man was seated in a chair placed between the two thin posts, his back toward the huge pillar. It was Doctor Rodil Mocquino, attired in golden robe and crimson sash. In front of the Voodoo Master was a table, set for four. The servants ushered Harry to one end of the table; Stanton to the other. The prisoners sat down.

"Dinner will be informal," purred Mocquino, glancing at his unshaven visitors and noting their rumpled attire. "Another guest will join us very shortly. It is time that you dined."

Stanton was silent; but Harry boldly put a question:

"What time is it?"

"Exactly six o'clock," replied Mocquino, "and this is Saturday evening. You have—shall we say slept?—since last night. You must be hungry."

"I am," admitted Harry.

"And you, Wallace?" queried Mocquino, focusing his eyes upon the other prisoner. "Come! Speak up!"

"Saturday," mumbled Stanton. "The night that the voodoo cult meets—"

"Of course," chuckled Mocquino. "Yes, Wallace, you will again hear the tom-toms. But forget them for the present. Our last guest is arriving."

STANTON WALLACE pulled himself together with a shudder. Harry saw it, and experienced an odd sensation. He would have sworn that the room shivered with Stanton's action. Then, muffled, Harry heard a beat. He could not guess the source of the slow thrum. It was not the stroke of a tom-tom. But it seemed to add force to Mocquino's prediction.

Dopily, Harry began to sway in his chair. He caught himself and steadied; but he could not overcome the impression that he was being carried off through space, together with this room. He saw a leering smile on Mocquino's face. Then a door opened at one end of the straight wall.

Harry stared when he saw Doctor Rupert Sayre.

The physician was calm as he approached the table. He smiled encouragingly to Stanton; then nodded to Harry. At Mocquino's suggestion, Sayre took the chair opposite the Voodoo Master. Mocquino clapped his hands. Two servants arrived, bringing food. Mocquino and his enforced guests began their repast.

Harry realized that his mind was in confusion. He heard sounds that he could not identify. He ceased to try; but still the sounds continued. The *thrum-thrum*, in its monotone. Odd rumbles that seemed from afar. All the while, he felt himself swimming; nevertheless, he ate, confident that food would restore his senses. Stanton copied Harry's example.

Mocquino was smiling wisely, talking to Doctor Sayre.

"Our companions," observed the Voodoo Master, "do not know their present whereabouts. It would be unwise to inform them, doctor. I see no need of doing so."

"Nor do I," returned Sayre, finishing a plate of soup. "Where they are will not help them."

"Wisely spoken." Mocquino's chuckle was malicious. "Their status is quite different from yours. But we can discuss that later. By the way, doctor, may I ask what mode of treatment you used to restore Wallace to his normal condition?"

"I chose a method opposite to yours."

"Ah! You guessed my method? The way in which I change a man into a zombi?"

Stanton Wallace gulped. He was losing interest in food. Harry, too, was showing a troubled expression. Sayre eyed Mocquino. He thought it best to talk bluntly with the Voodoo Master.

"By your method," said the physician, "I supposed you mean the red room. Am I correct?"

Mocquino nodded.

"My antidote," resumed Sayre, "was a green room. With green lights. I installed it in New Jersey, simply to have Wallace close to the green surroundings of the countryside."

"Very interesting. A device quite worthy of The Shadow."

"I am not The Shadow."

"Of course not. But you must have acted upon his advice. Too bad about The Shadow. I should have liked to have him here tonight. But since he is dead—"

MOCQUINO broke off. He looked beyond the table. He saw Jose Arilla standing by the door. The rat-faced man was making gestures.

"What is it, Jose?" inquired Mocquino.

"I must speak to you," returned Arilla. "Privately, master."

"Come! Speak at once! It will not matter if these persons hear."

"But it is about The Shadow—"

"All the more reason why you should speak promptly."

Arilla nodded; then bared his teeth.

"The Shadow!" he snarled. "The Shadow is not dead!"

"What?" Mocquino glared as he came up from his chair. "The Shadow still lives? After that twenty-story fall?"

"He was at Doctor Sayre's—"

Mocquino stared at Sayre, expecting an explanation. The physician stopped eating and gave a cryptic explanation.

"The Shadow did not fall twenty stories," he said. "He fell a considerable distance, though.

Enough, perhaps, to have killed any ordinary man. But The Shadow is not an ordinary man."

"You found him?" scowled Mocquino. "You took The Shadow to your office?"

"Yes. He was not seriously hurt. He was quite improved when your servants came for me."

"That is true, master!" cried out Arilla. "He came upon us like a ghost! He snatched away Manuel's gun! He fired at me—"

"And you ran from him?"

Mocquino was threatening. Arilla looked about. Manuel had entered and was close beside him. With supporting testimony, Arilla was inspired to resist Mocquino's challenge.

"The Shadow is not human!" he gasped. "He is what I say—a ghost! Bullets pass through him like a vapor! We do not doubt your power, master. But The Shadow, too, has power—"

Manuel was nodding. Arilla kept on:

"At the old house!" he panted. "I have talked with those who fought there. No bullets could harm The Shadow! He advanced in the face of guns! At Rathcourt's—I have talked with Manuel—let him speak—"

"I saw The Shadow at Rathcourt's," put in Manuel, promptly. "I saw guns pointed toward his heart. I saw those weapons fired. One would have thought that the cartridges were blank—"

"And today," added Arilla, "I fired point-blank. My aim was perfect! My bullet did not even stop The Shadow's laugh!"

Mocquino was glowering. Sayre, turning, saw the fearful expressions on the faces of the Voodoo Master's minions. Harry and Stanton were looking on, elated. Sayre saw a chance for a conclusive statement.

"They are right, Mocquino," expressed the physician. "Scientifically and from a medical standpoint, The Shadow is superhuman. When he fell four stories from the penthouse roof, last night—"

SAYRE'S bluff hit home. He knew that Mocquino had no knowledge of the fact that The Shadow had dropped but one floor. Sayre specified four floors, as just enough to make Mocquino ponder. Had he said more, the Voodoo Master would not have believed him.

As it was, Sayre had added one too many. Had he said three, Mocquino would have been convinced. The mention of four made the Voodoo Master believe for a few moments. Then Mocquino's face showed doubt.

The full effect, however, was impressed upon Arilla and Manuel. They believed, and with good judgment. They had accepted Mocquino as a master who possessed occult powers. They served him because they feared him. The Shadow, too,

had inspired their dread. Sayre's statement fulfilled their capacity for belief.

"The Shadow is a voodoo also!" cried Arilla. "You must believe it, master! We know the truth. Your spells can overpower ordinary persons; but not The Shadow!"

"The Shadow is not your equal, master," added Manuel, anxious to temper Arilla's words. "But he has power of his own. He cast a spell upon Elridge Rathcourt! That was why Rathcourt failed you."

"Yes!" exclaimed Arilla. "And there will be others like Rathcourt here tonight. When the cult meets, master, they may be thinking of The Shadow."

"Silence!" rasped Mocquino. "I shall tell them that The Shadow is dead!"

Sayre, watching, saw pained expressions show upon the faces of Arilla and Manuel. Doctor Mocquino had made a bad slip. His promise of a false statement made his henchmen waver. Their confidence had ended. Sayre looked toward Harry.

Here was opportunity. A mad attack upon Mocquino! There was a chance that his two henchmen would desert; that they would cry out their master's lie to others who might enter. But before Sayre could move, Mocquino, too, had realized the mistake. The Voodoo Master smiled cunningly.

"I shall tell them that The Shadow is dead!" he repeated. "Dead, because he is a spirit. He is a ghost, who has taken on a human form. Look!" He pointed to Stanton Wallace. "This man was a zombi once! Who but a living ghost could have restored him?"

Arilla and Manuel were babbling. Mocquino was pretending to accept their belief. Through that, he had regained their temporary confidence. His leer gleamed. It was meant for Sayre.

"Ghosts are not real," sneered Mocquino. "I have dealt with them before. Both of you"—he was facing his two henchmen—"you know the way that ghosts are slain."

"By the silver bullet!"

The exclamation came from Jose Arilla. Mocquino nodded wisely.

"Tonight," he promised, "I shall state the facts about The Shadow. I shall prepare the silver bullet and load it in the ghost gun. Should The Shadow come, I shall destroy him!"

SAYRE'S hopes faded. Mocquino had clinched the argument. In his reading of voodoo lore, Sayre had noted the potent claims attached to silver bullets. Those who followed voodoo rituals believed that such a charm could never fail.

Sayre saw Arilla and Manuel serenely fold their arms. They were in the know. First of all Mocquino's followers, they had heard the news of Mocquino's forthcoming plan.

The Voodoo Master settled back into his chair. Quietly, he asked:

"What else, Jose?"

"Nothing, master," replied Arilla. "I delayed coming here only because I feared the place was watched. That is why we kept Doctor Sayre in the taxicab until nearly six o'clock. We stayed in the old garage, which the police searched earlier today."

"The summons has gone to the members of the cult?"

"Yes. They will arrive at eight."

"Good! They will not be suspected, even if they are observed. The meeting will begin soon afterward."

Harry and Stanton had resumed eating. They had gained enough encouragement to continue. Arilla and Manuel stood by with folded arms. Mocquino clapped for service; other henchmen entered and cleared the table, to bring on the last course.

The meal ended shortly afterward. Mocquino ordered Arilla and Manuel to return the prisoners to their little room. The Voodoo Master kept Sayre as a guest. As soon as they were alone, Mocquino smiled.

"My congratulations, doctor," he purred. "You are clever. You would prove useful as a member of my cult. No?" He laughed gloatingly, as he saw contempt in Sayre's expression. "Ah! You must wait until you hear the beat of the tom-tom—"

"And the other bunk?" interposed Sayre. "Like your silver bullet?"

"The silver bullet?" Mocquino raised his eyebrows. "Ah! A silver bullet can prove quite as deadly as any other. Provided that it comes from a gun held by a steady hand. Such a hand as this."

Mocquino extended his fist. It looked like the talon of an ugly, mammoth bird.

"You shall choose your own fate, Sayre," decided the Voodoo Master. "I can use your knowledge; therefore, I shall treat you well— provided that you pretend to believe in my powers, even though you may not actually imbibe the beliefs of my cult.

"Or you may die, if you wish. Pleasantly, of course, since I bear you no malice. And if you pre- fer"—the last words were accompanied by an insidious chuckle—"you may become a zombi. But my zombis will no longer wander at large— not while The Shadow still lives to find them.

"He will die, The Shadow! Whether he comes to find me, or whether I am forced to seek him.

That, however, is a matter to be considered later. Let me show you something that will interest you more. The place where I put those who incur my wrath. The red room."

ADVANCING from the table, Mocquino crossed the room and opened the center door in the straight wall. Sayre saw a room that he expected: one with walls, floor and ceiling entirely of red. The background was plain, for the room was lighted with ordinary bulbs. Mocquino pressed a hidden switch. The glow changed. Fierce, crimson light pervaded the room.

Background deepened. The room became a setting for a nightmare. From high up, at unreachable spots, blood-red incandescents streamed their flood of horror.

Mocquino stepped across the threshold. His face became the ruddy countenance of a demon. Only his golden robe showed in the light. His red sash vanished with the background. As Stanton Wallace had once described it, Mocquino looked like a man without a middle.

The Voodoo Master stepped from the chamber of horror. He let the red light burn and closed the door. Once more of natural appearance, Mocquino turned to Sayre. The Voodoo Master spoke:

"Within that room, all but red vanishes. With it goes all reason. Red dominates. Red maddens. You shall see—tonight."

Grim dread gripped Doctor Rupert Sayre as he thought of the fate reserved for Harry Vincent and Stanton Wallace. All chance seemed feeble when confronted by the machinations of Doctor Rodil Mocquino.

Cardona and his men were undoubtedly still on the lookout, but they had no trail to follow.

Sayre could rely on but one remaining hope.

The Shadow.

CHAPTER XVIII
CARDONA FINDS A CLUE

IT was quarter past seven when Joe Cardona arrived back at headquarters. The ace was dis- gruntled when he entered his office. Detective Sergeant Markham was seated there. Joe growled in disgruntled fashion, while Markham listened sympathetically.

"You can talk all night to the commissioner," declared Cardona, "but sometimes he won't listen. I didn't get any further at the finish than at the start. It all comes back to the same argument: Why haven't we grabbed Mocquino?"

Joe opened a small briefcase. He drew out envelopes, pulled back the flaps and let an assortment of small articles slide to the desk.

"Look at this junk," he remarked. "Stuff that we found up at Rathcourt's. Voodoo charms, or whatnot. Here's a gold-ink talisman, inscribed on parchment. Lamp the three-headed dame looking in different directions."

"What's it for?" queried Markham.

"Supposed to protect those who have secret enemies," returned Cardona. "Rathcourt must have thought the thing would keep him safe. Some of the superstition that Mocquino foisted on the guy.

"Look at this medal, with a five-pointed star on one side and a zigzag on the other." Cardona clanged a gold pocket piece, the size of a half dollar. "That's a double luck talisman. A pentagram and a swastika. Supposed to protect all who carry it.

"Here's another dandy." Joe unrolled a huge sheet of parchment that was inscribed with a mass of cabalistic signs. "A Hindu scroll, for invoking the aid of hidden spirits. Rathcourt must have thought that he had chances of becoming a voodoo doctor on his own."

"How'd you learn what this junk was for?"

"From these books." Cardona produced three thin volumes, bound in red leather. "They're loaded with occult hokum. A guy would go screwy reading these. But Commissioner Weston thinks they're important. He dug the dope out of them, while I sat by saying nothing."

"And then what?"

"I showed him the city map and explained how we were covering everywhere. But he didn't spend much time looking at it. He kept on beefing about these charms and talismans. He calls them clues. I don't see how he figures it. This junk doesn't tell us a thing we didn't know before.

"It proves that Mocquino has buffaloed a bunch of saps; and that Rathcourt was one of the dumbest. Reading up on this business would make any guy believe that Mocquino was a big shot in the voodoo line. Say—if I called these things clues, I'd start to believe that Mocquino had disappeared into a cloud of smoke!"

A pause. Sourly, Cardona added:

"It wouldn't be a tough job to believe it, either." He produced the big map of Manhattan and spread it on the desk. "Because there's not a loophole that we haven't covered. How did those trucks get over to New Jersey? How did the sedans get back here? How did Mocquino go where he wanted?"

Markham shrugged his shoulders.

"And where's his hideout? It's not in New York; it's not in New Jersey. But he's got one. He's got to have one. He needs it to hold that outfit of his together. Someplace—somewhere— for that cult of his to meet. But as far as I can

guess, the joint may be in one of those spirit planes that these goofy books tell about."

BLACKNESS appeared upon the desk. Cardona looked up; he grinned when he saw the cause. A tall, pasty-faced janitor had entered the office. Stoop-shouldered, he was approaching the desk. Cardona looked at the fellow; then asked in puzzled tone:

"Thought you'd gone home long ago, Fritz."

"Yah."

With that comment, the janitor unlimbered mop and bucket. He tightened the straps of his overalls and began to mop the floor. Markham put a query.

"What's the idea, Fritz?" asked the detective sergeant. "You cleaned this place at noon."

"Not goot."

Fritz shook his head sadly.

"Not a good job?" bantered Cardona. "What do you mean?"

"People." Fritz paused and leaned listlessly on the mop handle. "Too much people. Job no goot."

"I get it," laughed Joe. "Too many of us coming in and out. The place needs cleaning again. Well, that's not your fault, Fritz. Maybe you'd better have a helper. I'll see about that. Anyway, forget it for today. Go along home."

"I go home."

Fritz made the statement in dull fashion; but he did not budge from his position.

"All right," put in Markham. "Go along home. Why don't you get started? What are you standing around for?"

"I go home."

"You mean you went home?" demanded Cardona, suddenly interpreting the janitor's remark. "You went home and came back?"

"Yah."

"And you'd rather be back here?"

"Yah. Goot here."

"Domestic troubles at home?"

Fritz made no reply. Markham saw a chance for more comedy.

"Say, Fritz," suggested the detective sergeant, "where do you live, anyway? Tell us about the place."

"I show you."

FRITZ placed the mop in the corner. He came to the desk and began to study Cardona's map. He was muttering to himself, apparently puzzled. Cardona and Markham exchanged grins. Suddenly Fritz extended a long finger and placed it on the map.

"Don't tell us that's where you live," guffawed Markham. "That's a ferry slip, Fritz."

Fritz was looking up, his dull eyes puzzled.

"He doesn't mean he lives there," put in Cardona. "He's wondering what the green pencil mark is about."

"Yah—"

Fritz nodded. His finger was touching a green circle. Cardona winked at Markham.

"I'll explain it, Fritz," volunteered Joe. "First off, we're after a crook named Mocquino. Have you heard about him?"

"Him goot?"

"Mocquino good? I'll say he's good!" Joe's tone was sarcastic. "He's good enough to keep us guessing. He's good, all right; but he's no good. No good. Get it?"

"No goot."

"That's drilled through your bean. All right, Fritz. That brings us to the circles. We're trying to trap Mocquino. So we've got men stationed everywhere. See these red circles, up at the top of the map?"

"Yah."

"Those are bridges out of Manhattan. Keep following, along down the East River. More red circles. More bridges. Queensborough—Williamsburg—Manhattan—Brooklyn—all bridges. Over here, crossing the Hudson is the George Washington Bridge.

"See those blue circles? Those are tunnels. The main one is the Holland Tunnel, because that's the only one for vehicles. But we've been watching the Hudson and Manhattan Tubes, just the same. So they're marked blue.

"That brings us to the green circles. They mean ferries. West Shore, Lackawanna, Erie, Pennsylvania, Jersey Central—mostly railroads own them. But there's some others beside. One over here on the East River, at Thirty-fourth Street, where there's no bridge near. It's being watched, too.

"Then there's the Bay ferries, to Staten Island and Brooklyn. No use going into a list of the lot. They're all marked in green—"

"Nein!"

Fritz had put his finger upon a black circle. Markham looked; then guffawed.

"He got you there, Joe!" laughed the detective sergeant. "All green, you said, but Fritz slipped one past you. He found a black circle."

"Sure," acknowledged Joe. "There's a bunch of them. But take a look at them. The one Fritz is pointing to, for instance. Look where it runs to. Up the East River, from Twenty-third Street to Welfare Island. Can you picture Mocquino getting anywhere on that boat?"

"That would be a pip," agreed Markham. "Mocquino going to Welfare Island. That's where we want him to be."

"Yah?"

Fritz had moved his finger to another black circle. Cardona shook his head. He was enjoying the game.

"Take another guess, Fritz. That ferry has been abandoned. The black circles are the ones that don't need watching. Savvy?"

"Yah?"

ANOTHER black circle, on the East River. With his other hand, Fritz tapped a final black circle, located on the Hudson.

"That's funny," remarked Cardona. He turned to Markham. "Fritz picks what's left and he gets two that are connected."

"What do you mean?" demanded Markham. "Don't tell me there's a ferry that runs around the island, from one side to the other. What would be the idea?"

"It's two lines," returned Cardona, "but one boat does for both."

Markham looked blank. Cardona pushed Fritz aside. He wanted to explain it to the detective sergeant.

"One line starts here on the East River," he explained. "It runs around lower Manhattan, past the Battery; then up the Hudson, clear to Weehawken. Takes it pretty near an hour to make the trip."

"What does it carry?"

"A few trucks, under sort of a contract arrangement. That boat is an old Hudson ferry, a two-decker; but the whole upstairs part has been boarded shut. It doesn't take passengers."

"It runs on a schedule?"

"No. It's irregular. Contractors bring their trucks down to the East River pier. So do a few vegetable truckers. When there's any trucks to go, the old ferry takes them. From the East River, down around Manhattan, up to Weehawken on the Jersey side. Then back again."

Markham nodded his understanding. Then a question popped into his mind. He pointed to the ferry slip on the Hudson side of Manhattan.

"Where does this line come in?" he queried. "You said there were two in one."

"There's an old ferry company," explained Cardona, "called the Mid-Hudson. It's got a franchise and wants to keep it. The company has to run at least one ferry a day. It had an old tub and a crew; but the boat got junky and the crew cost too much.

"So the Mid-Hudson made a deal with Captain Juggers. He's the old guy who runs the boat from the East River up Weehawken. They pay him a regular sum every month. Once a day—whenever it suits him—he stops off while he's on his way between the East River and Weehawken.

"He pulls his tub into this Hudson River slip; then goes across the river and stops at a junky old pier on the New Jersey side, at Hoboken. After that, he comes across the Hudson again. He makes another stop; then returns to his usual route."

Markham laughed.

"I get it," nodded the detective sergeant. "He goes through the motions, just to keep the franchise alive. Say—I didn't know there was such a line as the Mid-Hudson."

"Neither did I," stated Cardona, "until I talked with old Cap Juggers. When I found out the kind of business he does between the East River and Weehawken, I figured there was no use detailing a man to watch his boat. Juggers knows all his customers. If any strange trucks or cars came aboard, he'd simply stay hitched to the pier. Then he'd come ashore and call us here at headquarters. That's the arrangement I made with him.

"As for this Mid-Hudson trip that Juggers takes when it pleases him, he doesn't pick up any loads. The franchise specifies that the boat must run; that's all. Juggers keeps a log for the owners. He doesn't want to be bothered by any cars or passengers coming aboard."

"He must be a card, this Juggers."

"He is. He's an old duck with side-whiskers and his boat is called the *Cantrilla*. He told me he used to handle another franchise job across the East River; but the owners of the franchise called it off. Juggers said they got tired waiting for the Manhattan Bridge to fall down."

Cardona folded the map.

"That's all there is to it," he stated. "There's a chance, though, that Mocquino has managed to slip across an East River bridge and reach Long Island. I'm having the Long Island Sound ferries watched, in case he leaves College Point or some other place along the Sound. Mocquino might head up into Connecticut."

"If he's on Long Island, he might."

"And that's where he may be. Trucks abandoned in New Jersey; cars left in Manhattan. My hunch is that Mocquino is somewhere else."

FRITZ had gone back to his halfhearted mopping. Seeing Cardona look in his direction, the janitor apparently remembered Joe's suggestion to stop work. Fritz picked up mop and bucket. He shuffled from the office. From that moment on, Cardona put the fellow from his mind.

Out in the corridor, Fritz shambled to an obscure locker. He drew out folded cloth. Blackness enveloped him as a cloak slipped over his shoulders. A slouch hat settled on Fritz's head. A whispered laugh escaped hidden lips as the shrouded form glided through the corridor.

A half block from headquarters, The Shadow paused beside a parked taxi. It was Moe Shrevnitz's cab. The Shadow whispered an order. Hawkeye scrambled from the taxi and headed for a cigar store, to put in a telephone call to Cliff Marsland. The Shadow stepped aboard the cab.

Moe, the shrewd-faced driver, was quick to hear another order. The taxi pulled away. The Shadow picked up an oblong package that lay upon the floor. This contained the equipment that Moe had brought from Mann's office. Its contents had been prepared for the time when The Shadow would deal with Doctor Mocquino, in the latter's own bailiwick.

That time was coming soon. The Shadow had guessed the Voodoo Master's mode of action. As Fritz, The Shadow had gone to headquarters, to see if the law had learned anything of import. The Shadow's trip had been successful. Information had been at hand.

In The Shadow's own presence, Joe Cardona had found a clue. But the ace sleuth had unwittingly dropped his find. The Shadow, instead of Joe, had snatched up the thread.

The Shadow was banking all upon Cardona's clue.

CHAPTER XIX
THE VOODOO CULT MEETS

SHORTLY before eight, the ferryboat *Cantrilla* jogged into its East River slip. The ferry had left there at six, for a trip to Weehawken. It had consumed nearly an hour in each direction. Ordinarily, this trip would have been its last.

But tonight, the *Cantrilla* was receiving passengers. A dozen persons were waiting upon the almost-forgotten pier. They crowded into the long passenger compartment on the left side of the ferry. Oddly, that lengthwise space was darkened.

Hence crew members caught but momentary glimpses of the passengers. Most of them were men; but there were a few women among the dozen. All were well-attired. Apparently, they were a fashionable party on a lark.

Once inside the long, darkened cabin, the passengers whispered among themselves. Then came footsteps, shuffling up a stairway. After that, the closing of a barricade. Then silence.

A clumsy truck rumbled over the cracked boards of the ferry dock. A rough-faced driver leaned out and shouted to a member of the crew.

"Makin' another trip to Weehawken?"

The crew member nodded; then asked:

"Who are you from?"

"Benny Tuppen, the poultry man. He told me about this boat—"

"Wait'll I see Captain Juggers. Maybe he ain't goin' to make a trip, after all."

While the big truck waited, a light truck drew up behind it. The driver alighted. He was Cliff Marsland. The Shadow's agent approached the truck ahead.

"This tub going to Weehawken?" queried Cliff. The truck driver nodded.

"Guess so," he said. "But they're kind o' particular on this packet. Looks like you gotta have credentials. They asked who it was that sent me down here."

"Who was it?"

"Benny Tuppen, the poultry man. Know him?"

"Sure thing." Cliff chuckled. "Say, it was Benny told me to come here. He must have an interest in this line. When I was talking to Benny Tuppen, he said that—"

Cliff broke off. A whiskered man had arrived. He was wearing rough overalls; but his weather-beaten cap bore the frayed gilt statement: "Captain." It was Juggers. The skipper had heard Cliff's words.

"You're from Benny Tuppen?" queried Juggers.

Cliff nodded, pointing back to his own truck. Then he indicated the driver of the big truck.

"So is this fellow."

"All right," decided Juggers, gruffly. "Haul aboard. Reckon I can make another trip, seein' as there's two of you. We do contract business on this boat. That's why we don't take strangers. But Tuppen is one of our regular customers. It's all right if you're from him."

THE big truck rolled aboard the *Cantrilla* and took the vehicle passage on the right. Cliff returned to his truck, drove onto the ferry and ran through the left passage. The two trucks parked side by side, forward. Captain Juggers had gone to the pilot house. Chains clanked. The ferry glided from its slip.

Hawkeye was seated beside Cliff, huddled and inconspicuous. Both heard a whispered order from within a truck. Then a figure dropped to the vehicle passage. Creeping through darkness, The Shadow made for the back of the ferryboat. Beneath his cloak, he carried the oblong package.

Trucks had stopped their motors. The driver of the big truck leaned out and spoke to Cliff.

"Hear that?" he queried.

"What?" asked Cliff. "The engine?"

"No. That funny beat—like drums."

Cliff listened. He recognized the muffled drum of tom-toms. He grunted.

"It's nothing," he decided. "Just something cuckoo with the machinery. This scow is lucky it hasn't sunk. Must have been the first two-decker that they ever built."

The truck driver was satisfied with the explanation. But Cliff and Hawkeye sat tense.

THE *Cantrilla,* being a conventional ferryboat, was double ended. Most of the crew were at the end which at present served as front. None were about to witness happenings at the back. There, a blackened figure had stepped upon the rail of the open deck at the end. Arms stretched; gloved hands wedged a package beneath the rail of the upper deck.

The cloaked figure followed. The Shadow hoisted himself across the rail and reached the upper deck that completely circled the boat. He studied the windows of the huge, oval-shaped cabin as he made a circuit of the deck. All were tightly boarded.

Back at his starting point on the left side of the ship, The Shadow picked up the oblong package. He went to a steep, outer stairway and ascended to the roof of the upper deck. He was close beside a vacant pilot house, used only when the *Cantrilla* was making its return trips.

Captain Juggers was in the pilot house at the other end. The tall, smoking funnel lay between, softly chugging forth volumes of black smoke. The Shadow recognized that both pilot houses would be identical. He decided to investigate the vacant one first.

The *Cantrilla* was rounding the Battery. The bulky skyscrapers of lower Manhattan showed spotted gleams from offices where night workers were on duty. Beyond those buildings was the glow of the uptown district. Manhattan was on the right; to the left were the lights of Governor's Island. The lights of other boats showed from blackening waters, through wisps of gathering fog. Above the mist, Liberty's torch shone as a distant beacon.

After a brief notation of the present location, The Shadow entered the vacant pilot house. A tiny flashlight glimmered below the windows. Its beam settled on the floor. It showed the outline of a small trapdoor. The Shadow's whispered laugh filled the confined space.

The Shadow had counted upon such a discovery, with definite reason. He knew that the *Cantrilla* must be Mocquino's boat; that Captain Juggers was in the game. The usual route in descending from a pilot house was by way of the outer stairs to the upper deck; then through the upper cabin and down the inner stairs.

But with this boat, the upper cabin was completely boarded, its doors blocked along with its windows. The Shadow had learned that on his tour of inspection. There was only one way for the captain to reach a pilot house. That would be a direct inside route from the upper cabin.

The trapdoor furnished such passage; but the trap was bolted from below. The Shadow placed his package to one side. He produced a portable jimmy and set to work. Boards resisted; then yielded. The bolt loosened. The Shadow raised the trapdoor.

His flashlight showed a narrow, circular stairway—a metal spiral within a sheet-iron cylinder. The Shadow descended. The stairway ended at the back of the cylinder. The Shadow found a sliding sheet of metal. He tugged it upward, slowly. He listened.

From faraway, he heard the muffled beat of tom-toms. The Shadow edged out through the opening and pulled the sliding section downward.

THE SHADOW had reached the room wherein Doctor Mocquino had dined. He had come from the big pillar near the end. Originally a support for the pilot house above, that pillar had been made into a tubular shell for the insertion of the spiral stairway.

Like most ferryboats, the upper section of the *Cantrilla* consisted of three ovals, one within another. The outer was the deck; the middle one the cabin; the innermost the engine space, extending up between the vehicle passages, forming a funnel passage to the top of the boat.

Doctor Mocquino had altered the interior arrangements of his squatty ship. He had cut it into various rooms, with partitions between. This dining hall, with its hollow pillar and tiny posts, took up but half the cabin's end. Looking toward the front, The Shadow saw the straight, blockading wall with its three doorways.

Those at the sides must lead past the inner, solid-walled oval. The Shadow knew their purposes. The central door indicated the existence of a special room between the passages, since a portion of the cabin's end had been cut off for it. The Shadow opened the center door.

The red glow met The Shadow's gaze. He eyed the crimson depths of the walls, which seemed to lead to limitless space. The Shadow entered the red room and looked for the lamps that Mocquino had left burning. The Shadow was carrying the oblong package. He laid it upon the floor as he looked about.

The menace of the red room was apparent. Flooding lights produced heat; the atmosphere was stifling. The Shadow formed a figure of deep maroon, his garments dyed by the reddish glow. He was plainly visible in the terrible light.

Minutes passed while The Shadow surveyed his surroundings. He knew that this room was prepared for victims. He sensed that they could not stand a prolonged ordeal.

OUTSIDE, all was quiet in Mocquino's wide dining hall, except for the distant thrum of tom-toms. The Shadow had closed the door of the red room. At last, he opened it again and stepped forth, carrying the crumpled wrapping of the package. He had left his equipment within the red room.

Closing the door The Shadow went to the hollow pillar and stowed away the wrapping. He could feel the motion of the ferry, as he returned and opened one of the doors at the side of the long wall. The Shadow entered a longitudinal passage, where light was dim.

A deep-throated blast came muffled from the ship's whistle. The *Cantrilla* had reached the channel of the Hudson and was pushing northward through the river traffic. The Shadow paid no attention to the blare from above. He was studying the makeup of the passage.

On the right, he had come to a smooth surface that curved. It was the central, oval wall of the ferry. On the left were doorways, set in partitions. These represented small rooms which Mocquino had fashioned as living quarters for himself and his servants. One space of wall, wide between two doors, was indication of the barricaded steps that led below.

The Shadow paused, opened a doorway and found a blocking door to the steps. He unbolted the barrier; then turned to the passage and continued forward. The beat of tom-toms sounded closer. The Shadow reached a door at the end of the passage. It slid sidewise. The Shadow peered through curtains.

The tom-toms sounded loudly. The flicker of artificial firelight flared like flames from a volcano's mouth. A chant was beginning, sung by voices in unison. Inch by inch, The Shadow spread the curtains; then became motionless. He had reached his goal.

The Shadow had become an unseen witness to the ritual of Doctor Mocquino's voodoo cult.

CHAPTER XX
THE HALTED ORDEAL

THE room into which The Shadow gazed was large, for it occupied the entire front of the ferryboat's cabin. Like the other end of the boat, it had a huge pillar to support a pilot house; and on the near side of the pillar were the same slender posts. Between these was Doctor Mocquino, seated upon thronelike cushions.

Clad in his golden, red-sashed robe, the Voodoo Master formed a contrast to his surroundings. The room was fitted to resemble a jungle. Palm trees sprouted from clumps of artificial grass. All about were masses of dense foliage. Scenery hung from

With a loud cry, Mocquino dipped his hand deep into the cauldron.

He swished it back and forth, while his evil face gleamed triumphant.

the walls; half obscured by the palm trees, the painted backdrops looked like jungle depths.

Brawny, bare-armed servitors were at either side of Mocquino, beating tom-toms. One grinning, dark-faced fellow toyed with snakes that coiled about his arms. The Shadow recognized one reptile as a fer-de-lance, most dreaded of all poisonous snakes in Haiti.

Before Mocquino, seated in a semicircle, were the members of the cult. They had changed their attire to West Indian costumes. This accounted for their departure along with Mocquino, the night when Cardona had attacked the cult's headquarters. The cult members had been carried to the ferry-boat, there to resume their American attire.

Well had The Shadow reconstructed Mocquino's past. The Voodoo Master had first used this ferry to convey Stanton Wallace to New Jersey, along with automobiles. On the night of Cardona's raids, he had brought loaded trucks aboard, with all the cult members.

Some—Elridge Rathcourt, in particular—had been dropped on the Jersey side. The trucks had been driven off and abandoned, far from the Weehawken landing. Last night, Mocquino had ordered the *Cantrilla* to remain at the New Jersey side of the Mid-Hudson Ferry. He had driven there with his two sedans. Juggers had kept the boat waiting for him, during the expedition to capture Harry and Stanton.

Returning, Mocquino had brought the cars aboard. They had later been driven off on the Manhattan shore. All the while, Mocquino had kept a perfect hideout, a headquarters aboard the *Cantrilla* itself!

Joe Cardona had unwittingly described the game, when he had said that Mocquino could be in neither New Jersey nor New York. But Cardona had not suspected that the Voodoo Master could be between both shores. Only The Shadow had seen that answer.

MOCQUINO'S jungle set was portable. The Shadow noted that fact as he watched the voodoo doctor's followers sway to the rhythm of the tom-toms. Like theatrical equipment, the scenery could be packed in a hurry. That accounted for Mocquino's quick departure on Wednesday night. But The Shadow did not speculate long upon such matters.

His eyes were focused upon the center of the semicircle, directly opposite Mocquino. There sat Harry Vincent and Stanton Wallace, bound hand and foot. Doctor Rupert Sayre was with them. The physician was free, but helpless against great numbers.

Counting Arilla and Manuel, Mocquino possessed a full dozen henchmen. His original crew must have numbered more than a score. The ranks had been thinned in battle; therefore, Mocquino had none left for outside guards. He could probably have spared a few of the present quota; but obviously the Voodoo Master relied upon the security of his position aboard the ferry.

The chant was rising. Cultists were on their feet, swaying while the tom-toms beat with added fervor. Imbued with frenzy, faces were leering. A mad dance was beginning. Arms were beating; hands were clawing. Mocquino, his face demonish, was keeping time to the wild ritual. The scene matched all descriptions of a voodoo tribe in action.

An artificial fire formed the center of the circle, but its glare was realistic. Long streaks of blazing light were increased by crackles like those of flaring logs. The ceremony had become a Haitian nightmare, transplanted to the neighborhood of Manhattan. Only the faint quiver of the ferry's engines remained as a reminder that this was taking place upon the broad channel of the Hudson River.

Doctor Mocquino clapped his hands. The effect was magical. Chanting ceased. Tom-toms died. Frenzied dancers halted.

"My followers," spoke Mocquino, amid silence, "I have brought you here with purpose to-night. Listen while I speak. Listen, for you are my children!"

Cultists and servants alike were attentive. The Shadow knew of the primitive voodoo belief, in which the worshippers regarded their leader as a "papa." Originally brought from Africa, the voodooism of the West Indies had retained much of its simple lore.

"I have much to tell you," purred Mocquino. "Questions have come to your minds. Some of you have wondered why death did not befall a certain man whose effigy I stabbed. I refer to Dunley Bligh."

Slight buzzes from the throng. Mocquino silenced them with a handclap.

"Bligh did not die," explained Mocquino, "because his effigy was broken. There you see the man who destroyed the image. You will remember; for it was in your presence."

He pointed to Stanton Wallace. Harsh cries came from many throats. Again, Mocquino clapped for silence.

"I punished Wallace," rasped the Voodoo Master. "I made him a zombi! I paraded him, staring, here before the fire! He does not remember; but you who saw remember. I sent him helpless out into the world!

"My spell was offset by an enemy who found him. That enemy is called The Shadow! He is one against whom my servants battled. Their bullets failed. Therefore, they fear The Shadow!"

BUZZES of consternation. Mocquino drew an old-fashioned pistol from beneath a cushion. He brandished the weapon. His face developed a fierce grin.

"I do not fear The Shadow!" stormed Mocquino. "My bullet will not fail! No human hand can thwart me when I meet The Shadow! Nor can he remain immune to the shot that I shall fire! This gun contains a silver bullet!"

Wild yells of exultation. Mocquino glowered for silence.

"My power is vast," he croaked. "Look! Here is an image of The Shadow." He brought a blackened effigy from beside him. He stabbed a long pin through the waxen statuette. "Through the heart! The Shadow's heart! That is the course my silver bullet will take!"

A pause. Mocquino placed gun and effigy aside. He eyed the group; then spoke coldly.

"Perhaps some still doubt my power. Watch! I shall perform a test. Bring the cauldron."

Two servants advanced, bearing a large glass globe filled with water. Another approached with a tripod. The bowl was placed upon the stand. Mocquino ignited a burner beneath. Gas hissed, while the voodoo cultists watched.

Mocquino droned a chant. The Shadow, peering from the curtains, remained motionless. Though he was armed, he saw the danger of attack. Mocquino commanded the loyalty of a dozen ferocious servants, who were fully convinced of their master's power. With their native costumes, all were carrying revolvers or knives. They would intervene to block an attack upon Mocquino. The Shadow wanted to reach the Voodoo Master first, if possible.

Moreover, Harry and Stanton were powerless, in the very center of the floor. Cultists, frenzied, would seize them if a fight began. The Shadow had other, better, plans, which offered later opportunity.

He waited.

The water in the cauldron began to boil. Mocquino extinguished the burner. Still the water bubbled. The Voodoo Master plucked a palm leaf and thrust it into the liquid. Waterdrops sizzled as he flicked them to the floor. Again he thrust the palm leaf into the bowl and stirred the water. Then he cast the leaf aside.

With a loud cry, Mocquino dipped his hand deep into the cauldron. He swished it back and forth, while his evil face gleamed triumphant. He stilled his hand and grinned; then slowly drew his arm upward. He let the water trickle from his hand. The boiling liquid had shown no effects.

The staring followers gaped; then shouted their acclaim.

"Proof!" spoke Mocquino. "Proof that no physical pain can annoy the Voodoo Master! My life, like my hand, is protected by a potent charm!"

THE SHADOW knew the trick which had amazed the gullible onlookers. Hot water had risen; it had boiled at the top while the bottom liquid still was cold. Mocquino's stirring with the palm leaf had mixed the liquid. His hand-thrust had completed the job. Stirred together hot and cold had produced a temperature that was more than warm, yet far below the boiling point.

Yet the believers had accepted Mocquino's miracle. They were ready to serve this savage master. The voodoo doctor could depend upon his deluded band. The Shadow could see a troubled, hopeless expression upon the face of Doctor Sayre.

"I have withstood an ordeal!" grated Mocquino. He pointed to Harry and Stanton. "Can these men do the same? I say 'No!'—and I shall prove my statement. They will be placed where they can undergo a test. Within the room where every wall is red!

"There they will lose all knowledge of time, all sense of space! They will become men who walk, but who no longer live. Each a zombi! One who was a zombi before; the other a man to whom the experience will be new. But zombis both! Their very actions will be proof of my power!"

Mocquino was rising. His handclaps brought servants. Others arose, Sayre silent among them, while two of Mocquino's henchmen dragged Harry and Stanton to their feet.

Mocquino was pointing to the very curtain from which The Shadow watched. He was holding his pistol in his other hand; it was apparent that the Voodoo Master intended to carry the gun, hopeful of an encounter with The Shadow.

Before men could advance to the passage, The Shadow glided quickly away. In the dim light of the corridor, he was peeling off his black cloak, his gloves and his slouch hat. He opened the last door on the right and hurled the garments into a darkened room. He hurried into Mocquino's dining hall and closed the door behind him, just before the procession arrived at the far end of the passage.

Lacking his cloak, The Shadow appeared long and lithe. He was clad in dark, tight-fitting clothes, which had previously been covered by Fritz's overalls. He had dropped the janitor's garb when he had donned his black cloak. At present, he looked like a gymnast. Rubber-soled shoes made his quick tread silent, as he sprang toward the central door in the straight wall of this empty room.

THE SHADOW was gone when Mocquino and the others arrived. The Voodoo Master ordered the cult members to form a semicircle, facing the door of the red room. Clutching Sayre's arm in a clawlike grasp, Mocquino held the physician beside him; then commanded servants to carry Harry and Stanton into the room of horror.

The door was opened by Arilla. Four bearers hoisted the prisoners into the midst of the red room and sprawled them, still bound and helpless, upon the floor. The glow made the captives look pitiful. They were like puppets, balanced in the center of crimson depths.

Mocquino clapped his hands. The servants emerged. Arilla closed the door. Cushions were placed for the Voodoo Master; he drew Sayre to the floor beside him. With croaking gloat, Mocquino awaited developments.

"A dozen minutes" was his prophecy. "Then they will begin to weaken. After that, we can open the door and watch their final throes. They will be too far gone to gain relief by staring toward us. This will interest you, Doctor Sayre. Perhaps—"

A man came bounding in from the passage. It was Manuel. His face was wild; in his hands he carried garments of black, which he flourished before Mocquino's eyes.

"This cloak!" cried Manuel. "I found it in one of the dressing rooms! It—it is The Shadow's. He is here—among us—"

Mocquino snarled. He came to his feet, clutching the pistol that held the silver bullet. Fiercely, he studied every face in the throng. He recognized all as followers and servants, with the exception of Sayre. A vicious hiss formed the finish of the Voodoo Master's snarl.

"Open that door!" Mocquino pointed to the entrance of the red room. "At once! Be ready with your guns! Shoot down the prisoners if you find them free. The Shadow may have aided them."

Arilla leaped to the door, prepared to open it. Sayre tightened his fists as he watched the move to halt the ordeal. The torture of the red room might be ended for Harry and Stanton; but its finish would be death.

Again, Sayre could find but one possible form of hope. The Shadow had come at last. Perhaps the master fighter would appear, in an effort to ward off doom!

CHAPTER XXI
OUT OF THE VOID

THE door of the red room swung open. Jose Arilla stood staring into the chamber. Beside Arilla was Manuel; behind the pair, a cluster of Mocquino's crouching henchmen. The Voodoo Master himself was stalking forward to join the throng.

A cry came from Arilla. The fellow pointed. Others saw Harry and Stanton. The prisoners were no longer prone. Halfway to their feet, they were struggling to release themselves from bonds which had somehow become loosened. Arilla remembered Mocquino's order. He spat one word:

"Kill!"

As gun hands came up, a fierce laugh burst from within the red room. It seemed to come from the vast spaces of that weird chamber, where Harry and Stanton were the only visible persons. The room itself was mocking.

Crimson depths were hurling a challenge to Mocquino's startled crew.

"Kill!"

Arilla panted the word, in defiance of the laugh. Revolvers turned toward Harry and Stanton, who were several feet apart. Mocquino's marksmen were divided in their aim; but they were prepared to deliver death, despite their terror. Again the fierce laugh echoed from the void.

Then, in the very center of the red room, two guns appeared as if by magic. Those weapons were automatics; they were conjured in midair, at a spot where none of Mocquino's henchmen were aiming. Before a single finger could pull a revolver trigger, the suspended automatics blazed.

Each .45 was withering. The aim of those weapons was incredible. They must have been held by living hands, even though such fists were invisible, for bullets found the bodies of Mocquino's henchmen. Arilla sprawled; Manuel fell beside him.

Others, driving forward, forgot the prisoners and aimed for the floating guns instead. The automatics had the bulge. Like living creatures handling themselves, they pointed, fired, then recoiled.

The doorway cluttered with Mocquino's henchmen. Half a dozen were flattened before the others dived away for cover. That open door meant death.

Mocquino knew it, and his hiss was venomous. The voodoo doctor had also leaped aside. But he had reached the wall outside the red room. His fingers clicked a switch.

THE lights of the red room were controlled from either side of the wall. Mocquino's action changed the glare. Ruddy bulbs faded, ordinary light replaced them. The red room was a void no longer. It had become a crimson-walled compartment.

Sayre, the only one in position to see within, was astonished by the sight before him.

A figure stood in the very center of the room—
a cloaked shape, with collar upward. A shape that
wore a downturned slouch hat, with gloved hands
that gripped those dreaded automatics. It was the
figure of The Shadow; but changed. The Shadow
was not clad in black.

Hat, cloak and gloves were crimson! A red
Shadow! One whose whole attire matched the

**The physician leaped forward as the Voodoo Master turned. Wildly,
Sayer clutched Mocquino's arm just as the villain fired.**

walls of the crimson torture cell. This garb had been the "equipment" in The Shadow's package. He had left his outfit in the red room. That was why he had thrown aside his customary garments of black.

The Shadow had remembered Stanton Wallace's detailed description. He had listened to the account of how Mocquino's crimson sash had vanished, its color absorbed by the glow of the red incandescents, against the blood-hued background. Sayre himself had seen the same phenomenon. Hence he could understand The Shadow's ruse.

The Shadow had prepared for a meeting with Mocquino. In hope of finding the Voodoo Master's lair, he had ordered these garments of red. A garb that he was wont to wear; but of a different color.

The Shadow's strategy had worked. Reaching the red room, he had donned his deceptive garments. The lights and the curtains had rendered him invisible!

Mocquino had regarded the red room as his greatest weapon. It had become a boomerang. The horror chamber had served The Shadow. He had been releasing the prisoners, but had been forced to desist when Arilla opened the door. A few minutes more and The Shadow could have sallied forth with Harry and Stanton behind him.

Instead, The Shadow had been forced to fight alone; but the consequences had been even worse for Mocquino's band. Mocquino had lost half his crew. He had saved the balance only by altering the lights. Mocquino saw Sayre's amazed gaze. The Voodoo Master guessed the rest.

WITH a wild bound, Mocquino leaped straight in front of the red room door, twisting about as he sprang. Clicking his heels as he stopped, the Voodoo Master had his pistol leveled. His frenzy had given him a lucky opportunity. He aimed at The Shadow.

Doctor Sayre had seen Mocquino coming. The physician leaped forward as the Voodoo Master turned. Wildly, Sayre clutched Mocquino's arm just as the villain fired. Whether that jog disturbed Mocquino's aim, or whether the Voodoo Master's own wildness overruled, Sayre could never guess. Whichever the cause, the silver bullet failed.

Timed almost with Mocquino's shot was a blast from The Shadow's right-hand gun. Again, a laugh came from lips above the red collar. It was a taunt that spelled the end of villainy. The Shadow's red form never wavered; but Mocquino, fuming, sagged in Sayre's grasp.

Crimson splotched the front of Mocquino's golden robe, as the Voodoo Master stretched upon the floor. Red—the color that Mocquino had chosen for his own; but this red was blood! A waxen effigy clattered from Mocquino's red sash and broke asunder when it struck the floor. It was the blackened image of The Shadow, that Mocquino had so lately pierced.

The Voodoo Master's prophecy had been reversed. His silver bullet had never reached The Shadow. Instead, a leaden slug had found its home in Mocquino's breast.

WITH long stride, The Shadow sprang from the red room, leaping over sprawled bodies. Screaming, the members of the voodoo cult dived to the walls and threw up their arms in surrender. But Mocquino's remaining servitors were maddened by their master's death. A trio aimed with revolvers; the rest flashed long-bladed knives and leaped forward.

The Shadow was firing when Sayre grabbed up a revolver. Then came other shots, just as Sayre joined in. Harry and Stanton were free. They had followed The Shadow. Gaining revolvers from the floor, they had entered the fray.

Snarling foemen pitched to the floor. Revolvers fell; knives clattered. Mocquino's last henchmen were routed.

Two of Mocquino's servitors rallied to a strange task. Leaping away from their sprawling companions, they snatched up Mocquino's flattened form and dragged the Voodoo Master to the pillar. Shoving the cylindrical panel upward, they gained its interior before The Shadow could fire to halt them.

To them, Mocquino was a fetish. They had obeyed the Voodoo Master in life; though his body had the rigid, motionless attitude of death, they wanted to carry it from the scene of fray. They were unwilling that even Mocquino's corpse should be captured by The Shadow.

The escape of those two murderous henchmen was something that The Shadow would not allow. He reached the panel as it fell. Wedging it up, he gained the spiral steps. Clatter told that Mocquino's carriers had arrived at the empty pilot house. The Shadow followed.

Madly, Mocquino's men had made fast progress. When The Shadow reached the deserted pilot house, he saw them. They were on the roof of the upper deck, with Mocquino's stretched form at the edge, ready to leap into the river. The searchlight of an approaching boat outlined the henchmen as they dropped their burden and aimed revolvers toward the pilot house.

The Shadow fired simultaneously with his automatics. He clipped his foemen; their revolver shots were wide. Bullets shattered glass windows of the pilot house; but The Shadow stood unscathed.

One enemy plunged headlong to the river. The other rolled; convulsively, he grasped at Mocquino's form, dragged it with him; then lost his hold. The henchman rolled off the edge of the roof.

Mocquino's robed form was a grotesque sight. Its golden garb glistened in the yellow light; the crimson splotch showed a larger blotch of life-blood. Balanced on the edge of the deck roof, the Voodoo Master's form swayed mechanically; jarred by some motion of the ferryboat, Mocquino's body teetered and slithered over the brink.

A dull splash sounded from below. The Voodoo Master had joined his dead henchmen in the river.

THE SHADOW had seen no need to gain Mocquino's body as a prize. Already, he was dashing down the spiral, to rejoin his own men. When he reached the room below, he found matters as he had left them. Harry and the others were in full control. Stepping into the room, The Shadow closed the sliding door of the pillar.

Shots sounded from below. Harry heard them; he was dashing for the stairs at the moment of The Shadow's return; leaving Sayre and Stanton in charge of the prisoners.

The members of the voodoo cult were cowed. Calmly, The Shadow picked up his garments of black. Sayre saw him stalk in the direction that Harry had taken.

The shots had been fired by Cliff and Hawkeye. It had been their task to come up from below. The Shadow had unbarred the stairs for that purpose. Cliff had heard the muffled shots; but when he and Hawkeye had started, members of the ferryboat's crew had tried to stop them.

The Shadow had sized the situation. Cliff and Hawkeye could take care of themselves, for they were competent fighters. He wanted them to keep the battle below. Harry, dashing down the stairs, found his fellow agents in the cabin on the left, firing at crew members who were trying to duck in from the front deck.

When Harry arrived, the trio made a sortie. Crew members scattered, throwing up their hands. The *Cantrilla* had stopped in the center of the Hudson. The ferry was drifting, while shrill whistles announced that police boats were on hand. Closer, Harry heard the rhythm of a powerboat.

Shots from high above. Captain Juggers had spied The Shadow's agents. He was firing from the front pilot house. Cliff and Harry dived for cover; Hawkeye was already out of danger. The crew members rallied; then, in this desperate moment, a gun spoke from the front darkness.

The Shadow had arrived. Again in black, he had dispatched a single bullet to the pilot house. The shot had clipped the skipper. Captain Juggers was sagging, wounded. The Shadow turned. He fired other shots. Crew members went scudding through the vehicle passages.

The agents started to the chase. The Shadow's hissed order stopped them. Shouts were sounding from the rear of the ferry, which had stopped in midstream and was pointing toward New Jersey. The police boat had reached the other end of the *Cantrilla*. Officers were boarding the old ferry.

The Shadow pointed forward. His agents saw the long, trim shape of the speedboat that Harry had heard. Following The Shadow, the agents clambered aboard. Miles Crofton was at the helm. The motor roared as the trim craft shot away from the *Cantrilla*. The police had invaded the inner stairway of the ferry. They would take over the prisoners. Explanations would rest with Doctor Sayre and Stanton Wallace.

A parting laugh came from The Shadow. Harry Vincent heard it, as he had often in the past. Triumphant mirth that sounded like a knell. A mockery that told of right triumphant. Men of evil had recognized that laugh in the past. It had marked their doom, as it had told of death tonight.

But of all who had failed before the might of The Shadow, none had been more venomous than the villain of tonight. Doctor Mocquino had deserved to die.

The Voodoo Master's evil career was halted. Doctor Mocquino had met The Shadow in red!

But one thing still remained. The Shadow looked over the water to see if Doctor Mocquino's body was recovered. It was not in sight. Possibly the police had already picked it up.

Possibly, though, they had not. The Shadow could not pause longer, but later he was to learn that this was not the end of Doctor Mocquino. The weird Voodoo Master was to return again to menace The Shadow, and civilization, to furnish another thrilling adventure in the annals of The Shadow!

THE END

Coming soon: THE SHADOW - Volume 4: "The Murder Master" and "The Hydra"
DOC SAVAGE - Volume 3: "Death in Silver" and "The Golden Peril"
For ordering information, visit www.nostalgiaventures.com or email sanctumotr@earthlink.net

Walter Brown Gibson (1897-1985) loved to mystify people. From an early age, he delighted in telling scary stories. One day he came running from his bedroom, terrified. The eight-year old tearfully explained that he'd been writing a mystery story and somehow managed to frighten himself!

This carried over into his days as a camp counselor when Gibson would tell campfire tales—starring Dracula! When Bela Lugosi first starred in the stage play version of Bram Stoker's novel in 1927, Walter Gibson saw it firsthand, thanks to a magician friend who was supervising special effects for the Broadway production. Gibson sat in on rehearsals. He was particularly impressed by the black-cloaked Dracula's spooky entrances and trapdoor vanishes.

"The Shadow as a character had people guessing right from the start," Gibson later related. "Now the pattern which inspired me was *Dracula* by Bram Stoker. I was very fond of *Dracula,* and things of that sort. So Dracula as the villainous character crept in and got more weirder and weirder as the thing went on. And it all sounded very real. Well, I was confronted with something like that with The Shadow. I felt I had to take this nebulous character and make him believable. He was sort of like a benign Dracula, you might say."

Or a cross between Count Dracula and Sherlock Holmes!

Gibson's fascination with the uncanny included real-life tales of the occult. Back in the 1920s, before The Shadow overtook his life, Gibson edited *Tales of Magic and Mystery* (purchasing one of H. P. Lovecraft's early stories, "Cool Air") and *True Strange Stories.* He also wrote for *Ghost Stories.* In later years, he became an expert on ESP and psychic phenomena, and as "famous author, lecturer and expert on strange and weird events" narrated ABC's spooky 1955 radio series *Strange.*

Walter B. Gibson in 1937

In his earliest Shadow novels, Gibson imbued the Master of Darkness with hypnotic powers and pitted him against spectral foes like the Ghost Makers and the Master of Death, who specialized in creating living dead men. Gibson painted his cloaked avenger in near-supernatural colors, often describing him as "a monstrous batlike form ... like a huge vampire."

But Street & Smith wanted The Shadow kept firmly in the mystery-suspense thriller genre, so Gibson had to be content to hint at rather than develop his ultimate eerie potential.

It was necessary in writing stories like *The Voodoo Master* to find ways to exploit mystic lore without delving into the true depths of the occult.

To bring Dr. Mocquino and his mindless zombies to life, Gibson dipped into his dark bag of magician's tricks, creating the *illusion* of the supernatural. The climax of *The Voodoo Master,* for example, was inspired by the famous Red Room, a bizarre chamber in which walls, floor, doors and ceiling, as well as every stick of furniture, was dyed same sinister shade of scarlet. (It was rumored to be so unnerving that if one stayed too long, one went mad.) For, contrary to the radio incarnation of The Shadow, whose powers of invisibility were an occult skill, Walter Gibson's Master of Darkness, half-magician, half-Ninja, utilized a practical form of invisibility. It was based on the Black Art Illusion wherein a conjuror, garbed all in black, could disappear into a black velvet environment. Here, like the word wizard that he was, Walter Gibson gave this true-life trick an astounding twist for one of his finest Shadow denouments.

The Voodoo Master and similar stories may have been the inspiration for many of *The Shadow* radio episodes that came later. As scriptwriter Eric Arthur once related, stories about zombies and various forms of the Living Dead quickly became a Shadow broadcasting staple. "Walter Gibson left us sharply drawn characters and well developed story patterns to follow," he observed. "As long as we held to his formula, the plot for each episode was left to our imaginations. With those guidelines, we pitted Lamont Cranston and Margo Lane against a galaxy of vampires, zombies ('walking dead') and other antisocial creatures."

It quickly became too much of a good thing.

"On one occasion," Arthur added, "the main sponsor of the program, the Blue Coal Company, ordered us to lay off the zombie bit for a while. Mothers all across the country had complained that we were scaring their children with too many scripts about 'the walking dead.'"

Walter Gibson would have relished that.

—Will Murray